BOOK TWO

AN ECHO IN TIME

ATLANTIS

First published in 1997 by Voyager Australia

ISBN 9781922598394 (print)
ISBN 9781922598684 (ebook)

Published in Australia and New Zealand by:

Brio Books, an imprint of Booktopia Group Ltd
Unit E1, 3-29 Birnie Avenue,
Lidcombe, NSW 2141, Australia

Printed and bound in Australia by SOS Print + Media Group

MIX
Paper from responsible sources
FSC® C011217
FSC
www.fsc.org

The paper in this book is FSC® certified. FSC® promotes environmentally responsible, socially beneficial and economically viable management of the world's forests.

Proudly Printed
in Australia

booktopia.com.au

AN
ECHO
IN TIME
ATLANTIS

TRACI
HARDING

b **brio**
BOOKS

Contents

CHARACTERS OF THE DARK AGE

Queen of Gwynedd	Tory Alexander
King of Gwynedd	Maelgwn
High Merlin	Taliesin Pen Beirdd
Prince of Gwynedd:	Rhun
King of Powys:	Calin Brockwell
Queen of Powys:	Katren
King of Dumnonia:	Catulus
Ruler of Dyfed:	Vortipor
Ruler of Dalriada:	Fergus MacErc
Ruler of Alban:	Cailtram
Ruler of Mercia:	Ossa
Eldest Son of Ossa:	Ongen
Youngest Son of Ossa:	Eormenric
Daughter of Ossa:	Aella
Maelgwn's Champion:	Tiernan
Tory's Champion:	Ione
Maelgwn's Keeper of Rec:	Rhys
Maelgwn's Rep. Aberffraw:	Angus
Court Bard:	Selwyn
Maelgwn's Squire:	Tadgh
Brockwell's Sons:	Bryce, Blain, Owen, Cai
Rhys' Son:	Gawain
Tiernan's Son:	Gareth
Rhys' Wife:	Jenovefa
Vortipor's Daughter:	Bridgit
Sir Angus' Daughter:	Javotte
Sir Angus' Wife:	Alma
Ossa's Crone:	Mahaud
Mahaud's Pupil:	Vanora

Britain 539 AD

Dalriada
The Scots

↑Alban
The Picts

Cumbria

Northumbria

Mon

Gwynedd

Mercia
The Saxons

Powys

Dyfed

The
Kings Men
Stones

Gwent
is Coed

Exter

Dumnonia

Britain 559 A.D.

PART ONE

LIFE

PART ONE

LIFE

1

OSSA AND THE ELDER TREE

The night was dark and the storm was fierce. Onward they rode at the mercy of the howling winds. The open plain offered little shelter for Ossa and his band, but they pressed on in the hope of finding a refuge nearby.

The whole of Saxony had been ravaged by storms for months. Unharvested crops lay rotting in the fields from Northumbria to Kent, whilst the menfolk struggled to divert the worst floods in their settlement's history. Meanwhile, the rain just seemed to avoid the lands belonging to King Maelgwn and his allies; the western kingdoms had reaped enough produce to sustain them the length of ten seasons.

Why was the Goddess compelling him to make war on her native people? If this rain persisted, Ossa's winter stores would not see his army and kin through the Fall. Perhaps the Great Lady sought to test his oath, but if there was not some sign of relief soon, Ossa felt he'd be forced to go back on his word to her. Every day the Saxons grew weaker, whilst the neighbouring Britons grew strong.

The time-worn Saxon warlord was not so old that he'd forgotten the battle at Arwystli. How could he forget when he'd lived in the shadow of defeat every day since?

The moment any Saxon, Angle or Jute makes war on my native people, thou shalt all be driven from this land.

Twenty years had come and gone, and still the prophecy of the Goddess remained chiselled in his memory.

If thou cannot live here in peace with us . . . . thou shall not live here at all.

Ha! Ossa scoffed at the echo of her words; flooding his lands and starving his people was not his idea of living together in peace.

The promise of the Goddess' wrath had subdued his advancement into the

3

west because he still feared her might. However, his youngest son, Eormenric, believed the sorcerer of King Maelgwn of Gwynedd was to blame, the one they called Taliesin. Eormenric felt that the Merlin was as responsible for Ossa's tribe being tricked into defeat at Arwystli twenty years ago, as he was for the sad predicament of their lands this day. It was known that Taliesin had used wizardry in the past to enchant the very elements to war. Ossa had seen this first-hand, as had Octa, his father, before him, thus Ossa felt there could be some merit in Eormenric's theory. Octa had waited his entire reign for the aging wizard to die, as had Ossa, but it would seem the Merlin had found a way to cheat even death.

I shall be seeking a way to cheat death myself if I don't get out of this blasted rain, Ossa considered, as the gale force winds threatened to blow him from his mount.

'My Lord.' One of the soldiers directed Ossa's attention to a white light up ahead.

As they neared it, the light turned a deep red and the band of Saxons slowed their horses to a halt.

'What dost thou thinkest, Lord . . . sorcery?' The young soldier was wide-eyed with amazement.

'Perhaps.' Ossa was intrigued. 'Wait here.' He dug his heels in and went to investigate.

Eormenric, feeling he was the only man present who could get away with disobeying the order, took off after his father.

Ossa stopped and dismounted, still some way from the light's source. When Eormenric rode up to join him the Warlord became most disgruntled. 'Go back to the men. Who shall take charge if something should happen to me?'

'No harm shall befall thee.' Eormenric decided to push his luck and sprang from his mount. '*I* am here,' he explained in a cocky manner, which Ossa couldn't help but admire.

'Oh alright . . . but stay alert.'

Lightning lit the sky above, awarding them a better view of the area. 'This place be marked as sacred.' Ossa noted the large stones that encompassed the seething spring of misty red.

'I think thou art too easily spooked,' Eormenric whispered in jest as they crept closer to the circle, seeking cover behind a tree that grew just outside it.

Ossa's brow raised at his son's blatant scepticism. 'Had thou ever seen true sorcery at work, thou would be of a different mind.'

Eormenric looked to the blackened sky and held out his hand, which was instantly filled to overflowing by the teeming rain. 'I have seen it.'

Indeed. A malign whisper echoed past them. *And what defense dost thou have against it?*

Eormenric, startled at first, became irked when he couldn't spy their voyeur. 'Show thyself,' he demanded.

Ossa clasped a hand over Eormenric's mouth, recognising the evil accent. He knew the voice belonged to the wicked old crone named Mahaud. At one time, she had been ally and sorceress to a fallen compatriot of his, Chiglas. But they had all parted company when the treacherous king's capital city in Powys, Arwystli, was taken by Maelgwn Gwynedd and those now known as the Twelve Masters of the Goddess.

'This witch can set a man ablaze by the very thought of it,' Ossa hissed quietly. 'So hold thy tongue, lest we both end up naught but flaming corpses.'

If I had wanted to kill thee, Ossa, I would have done so twenty years ago.

Ossa and his son jumped away from the tree they huddled behind, as the voice seemed to be coming from within it. 'Really . . . then why did thou not finish Maelgwn Gwynedd, instead of allowing him to destroy the king and kingdom that thy magic wast supposedly safeguarding?'

The Goddess be too powerful to assault directly. But I believe she can be overthrown . . . indirectly.

'How?' Eormenric could not contain his curiosity.

'Ask nothing of the foul hag.' Ossa belted his son for his ignorance and led him away.

I can wait, Warlord. Come back and see me when thy kingdom hast turned to a lake. Her dry, confident tone filled Ossa with great loathing. She could feel his hatred brewing. How attractive this emotion was to her; it was the ticket to her release.

'Thou cannot help me, witch. One so evil cannot be of help to any man.' Ossa turned back and roared, ensuring that he was heard.

Be that so?

The teeming rain eased to a light drizzle and the winds just died away. Ossa and Eormenric were stunned to a standstill.

'Perhaps we art being a bit rash, Father. Be this . . . Taliesin any different?'

'Taliesin doth not disappear when the odds art against him,' Ossa snarled at the elder tree, none to eager to admit that the witch might be of use to him.

Self preservation, she explained. I told Chiglas it was suicide to withhold the payment he had promised thee. And kidnapping the Queen of Gwynedd was not my idea of a brilliant move, either! I was not about to hang around and suffer the repercussions of Chiglas' feeble-minded decision making.

'Well, if thou could not defeat the Goddess at Arwystli, what makes thee think that thou could defeat her now?' Eormenric received a pat on the shoulder from his father for having asked a valid question.

I just calmed a storm of her making, did I not?

'Aye,' Eormenric acknowledged, cocking an eye. 'So thou did.'

She hadn't, as the storm had been of her making in the first place; the witch had a real knack for twisting the truth to her advantage in this manner. There were certain creatures from the deva kingdoms between the earthly plane and lower realms — where Mahaud was currently biding her time — and, just because *she* was banned from functioning within a first plane reality, some of her fellow archfiends did not mind whipping up a storm at her request. They enjoyed nothing better than wreaking havoc for havoc's sake.

The Dragon can be destroyed from within . . . I have foreseen this.

The dragon was the guardian spirit of Britain; thus she referred to Maelgwn, King of Gwynedd.

'Then why not just do it, and put us all out of our misery,' Ossa smirked.

That would give me the greatest of pleasure. The crone was growing impatient with him. But as I have been banished from the earth plane, I am finding it a bit difficult!

'Oh! . . . I see.' Ossa delighted in her problem. 'And what guarantee do I have that thou shall not turn thy sorcerous ways on me, should I free thee?'

Without a patron to serve, I am without purpose . . . I have no direction, no cause for being. I desire the downfall of Maelgwn Gwynedd more than the entire populace of Saxony combined . . . including thyself, Ossa.

The malice Mahaud bore for the High King of the Britons was made plain in her harsh inflection. Although Ossa was curious to learn her reasons, he hadn't ruled out the possibility of trickery. 'Why dost thou despise the Dragon so? Because of Chiglas?'

She laughed hysterically, then stopped abruptly, her mood becoming altogether more sinister.

I think not. Maelgwn Gwynedd, his whore of a Queen, King Brockwell of Powys and Myrddin were the ones who had me exiled to the lower etheric world. But I have been watching them from my timeless prison cell and they all possess certain flaws in their nature that, with just a tiny bit of encouragement from me, could cause divisions in the Dragon's kingdom and restore the perfect little world of the Britons to the chaos of yesteryear. There shall be fine plunder and spoils for whomever releases me to spin my web of retribution. With me to enchant, no one will even suspect foul play until their defeat is complete. I shall make Maelgwn Gwynedd look so wretched in the eyes of his people that he shall be remembered thus for all time. The ways of the Goddess will be cast aside once more, and my Lord will be the hero in history's eyes.

Ossa and Eormenric were mesmerised by her ploy, but it still sounded too good to be true. 'And what shall become of thy compatriot after the Dragon's defeat?'

What kingdom dost thou fancy, Warlord? The possibilities art endless.

The voice of the enchantress was so inviting; she made it sound so easy.

This was the ally Ossa had been waiting for, his key to the greater mysteries of this land. 'If I agree, what must I do in order to release thee?'

Dig under this tree and there ye shall find a cauldron buried with a map. Do not open the cauldron, but take it directly to the house marked on the map. A woman lives there who was my prize student until Taliesin stole her away and brainwashed her with all his positive nonsense.

'Vanora,' Ossa surmised. 'The daughter of Chiglas.'

Aye, she confirmed in encouragement, pleased that he was seriously considering her proposal. Now, although she may appear as pure as the virgin snow, all ye must do to bring her to her senses be to lift the lid from the cauldron and persuade her to look inside. Vanora will know what is required for my release and will devise a means.

2

LUGHNASA –
THE GATHERING

The month-long festival of Lughnasa had always been celebrated by the native Britons to honour the harvesting of their yearly crop. But for the past twenty years, the feast of the God of the Sun also commemorated the signing of the pact that now bonded each British kingdom to the other. Every year these great kings and leaders met to discuss their progress and the problems facing their alliance. This gathering was held at Arwystli, in Powys, for it was the most central point of allied Britain.

In addition to the normal festivities that such an occasion would suggest, Arwystli was also celebrating the twenty years of prosperity it had seen since Powys had been freed from the tyrannous reign of King Chiglas. Powys had then entered into an alliance with neighbouring kingdoms, under the guidance of Chiglas' successor and its current ruler, King Brockwell.

Brockwell was the great-grandson of the famous warrior, Cunedda, as his predecessor Chiglas had been, and although Brockwell was originally a son of Gwynedd, the people of Powys adored him. For this king was of good heart and possessed a fearless disposition. Nominated by the Goddess to lead Powys out of darkness, lead them out of darkness he did. The kingdom's fields overflowed with the bounty of the Goddess and peace had prevailed in the wake of the eons of turmoil their forefathers had known.

Brockwell's Queen, Katren, was the epitome of a rags to riches story. Born the daughter of a simple farmer, she had elevated herself in society through her acts of bravery for king and country. The first female warrior to be initiated into the 'circle of twelve', known as the Warriors of the Goddess, she had won her social standing and the heart of Brockwell during the debacle of Chiglas. As tiny and petite as she was beautiful and chaste, Katren had blessed the kingdom with three fine, strapping sons to succeed the king.

Her eldest son, Blain, aged eight years and ten, was heir to the throne of Powys. Owen, her second-born, was five years and ten, and Cai, her youngest, was two years and ten. The eldest son of King Brockwell was Bryce, aged five years and twenty. Bryce was the adopted half brother of the other three, who, due to a confusing set of circumstances early in life, also carried the title Earl of Penmon (his father's estate in Gwynedd). Bryce would have been the heir to Brockwell's throne in Powys had he not been illegitimate. But as it was, his three younger legitimate brothers all had the right to claim the crown before him.

Though the Queen had not borne Bryce of her own loins, she loved him dearly. So much so that she found herself favouring him over the others at times — for how could she help but feel responsible for doing him out of his inheritance.

Tory had a lot on her mind as she followed the maid to the High King's chamber at Arwystli. She'd been mindful of the sad state of the lands that lay in the east, and an updated report had her worried.

For it seemed somewhat suspicious to her that the farmland of their foe could be so badly ravaged, when the allied kingdoms under her husband's rule had reported a greater yield than ever before. Undoubtedly, the Saxons had figured a way to pin the blame for their misfortune on allied Britain. *They'll be blaming it on sorcery, most likely.* But whatever the cause truly was, this imbalance had to be rectified or it would plunge Britain into war.

I shall put this forward at the meeting. For if we do not attempt to aid these people, they will surely set about to take what they need to survive the cold seasons.

Tory's word was second only to the High Merlin of the Druids during these annual meetings of the alliance, and she was the only woman permitted to attend. For she was the chosen representative of the Goddess, through which the divine mother spoke in council to guide the leaders of Britain.

'Thy room, Majesty.' The head maidservant announced, as she entered and stood aside for the High Queen to enter. 'I have prepared a hot bath, just as it pleases thee.'

'Many thanks, Ganivra. This place seems like a second home these days.' Tory breezed into the room, placing aside her hand luggage and making herself at home on the lounge.

'We aim to keep it that way, Majesty. King Brockwell does look forward to thy visits.'

'As do I,' Tory assured her.

'Majesty!'

Tory turned in her seat to find Katren poised in the doorway, the skirt and sleeves of her gown still caught up in the vacuum of her hasty entry.

'Why did thou not send a messenger ahead?' Just for a second, Katren appeared disappointed. 'I wanted to greet thee upon thy arrival.'

Tory stood as Katren approached with her arms outstretched. 'Oh Katren, thou art well aware of how I detest formality.'

The Queen of Powys beamed with excitement as she embraced the High Queen. 'And thou art well aware of how I adore it.'

'I much prefer to be welcomed in this way.' She held Katren at arm's length to look at her.

'It feels like an eternity since last I saw thee.' Katren was so overjoyed that she burst into tears. 'I do miss thee so . . . and the Masters.'

'Well, here I am.' Tory smiled. 'And please, stop calling me Majesty.'

'But, Majesty! Thou art the High Queen of Britain now.'

'Katren!' Tory found it hard to believe that anyone could be such a stickler for ceremony. 'Okay . . . I forbid thee to call me anything but my given name.' She grinned, satisfied that she'd now get her own way.

'If that be thy will.' Katren gave in gladly.

Tory resumed her seat, half expecting her friend to settle beside her. 'How fares all with thy kin?'

'Well, actually, my boys are awaiting an audience just outside.' Katren waved a finger over her shoulder. 'Should I summon them in?'

Again Tory was surprised at her. 'Why, of course!'

Ganivra left them at Katren's word, and the next moment all four brothers came striding through the door. Bryce approached Tory first, as he was best acquainted with the High Queen.

'Sensei, welcome.' He bowed deeply before her, his hands clenched in front of his solar plexus as they did in Mastery.

Bryce had replaced his mother in the 'circle of twelve' at the age of five years and ten, making him the youngest initiate to date. Ten years down the track, he was one of the finest warriors Tory had ever trained.

Tory returned the gesture in a not-so-formal fashion and then hugged him. 'Dear Bryce, I do swear thou art the spitting image of thy father at times.'

I have need to speak with thee. Bryce bethought her, knowing his sensei would hear him if he willed it hard enough. He then stepped aside for Blain and smiled, as if he'd thought nothing of the like.

A feeling of urgency accompanied his message, but Tory inquired no further; she would know the all of it soon enough.

'Majesty.' Blain came forward and bowed in the regular fashion. 'I have need to speak with thee — '

'Wait!' Tory held out her hand. 'Let me guess. Thou hast heard that there will soon be a position within my circle of twelve, and it be thy wish to compete for the seat.' Tory raised her eyebrows as Owen and Cai confirmed her guess with a 'Gosh!'

Blain staggered back, grinning from ear to ear. 'Majesty, thou art a wonder to me . . . those were the exact words I would have chosen.'

'Indeed.'

'So what be thy answer?' His piercing blue eyes compelled her to speak.

These eyes were one of the more distinguishing features of the Brockwell clan — all the sons had inherited them. Although Bryce and Blain had their father's long dark curls, Owen's hair had shimmers of his mother's coppery colour, and Cai was as fair as they come. Bryce had grown taller than his father, who only stood around one hundred and sixty centimetres, and, although his brothers had yet to reach their father's height, they would all maintain the same stocky build when fully grown. The only other unmistakable feature Calin Brockwell had passed down to his sons was that of the dimple on his chin, though Bryce and Cai were the only recipients.

Tory teased Blain with her pondering. 'Maybe. I shall think about it.'

'But Majesty, I am heir to the throne of Powys, and Rhun be one of the twelve . . .'

'Give Rhun his due, Blain. He started his training before thou wast even born.'

Rhun was Tory's only child and sole heir to the throne of Gwynedd. Her lack of offspring had been quite purposeful in that she wanted none to contest Rhun's right to the throne in his father's wake. This way, there would be no needless blood-feuds that might throw Gwynedd back into turmoil during his reign. As soon as Rhun could walk, Tory started training him in the skills of self-defense. He was three years older than Blain, and although they were fast friends they were also fiercely competitive.

'But Rhun had the good fortune to be trained by thyself, Majesty. Will thee not at least give me that same chance?'

'Bryce be one of the finest trainers I have, Blain. Thou should be proud to have him as thy sensei. However, as I said, I shall think about it.'

The High Queen looked to Owen, who'd been patiently awaiting her address.

'Of course.' Blain backed off, feeling rather put in his place. They all favoured Bryce. Why had he thought that the High Queen would be any different.

Owen bowed and wore a cheeky grin on his face as he politely took up Tory's hand and kissed it. 'It be a pleasure to see thee, Majesty. Thou art as radiant as ever.'

Tory glanced at Katren, who rolled her eyes. 'My, but thou hast a good serve of thy father in thee, too. What dost thou want of me?'

'Nothing at all, Majesty. I am perfectly content,' Owen seemed rather pleased to admit.

'Then tell me, Owen, what be happening in thy world?' Tory hadn't encountered these two younger boys very often.

'I thought thee could tell me.' He commented in a playful manner.

'Well Owen, I could . . . if that be thy wish,' Tory offered, very much doubting that he would want his brothers and mother to know of the young housemaid that was driving him to distraction.

'Nay, Majesty, 'twas a joke.' He blushed, wondering if she knew; legend had it that she knew everything about everyone.

'Tell us, Majesty,' Blain teased Owen, taking hold of him in a headlock.

'Not now, Blain,' his mother scolded, urging her youngest son to come forward.'

'By the Goddess!' Tory was taken aback. 'This could not be little Cai!'

Cai bowed astutely and Tory hoped she'd not embarrassed him.

'Aye, Majesty.' His eyes wavered between her face and the floor.

Cai was shyer than the others and spent most of his time with his head in a book: 'How go thy studies, Cai?'

A smile swept over his face. *She remembers!* 'Very well, Majesty. Very well, indeed.'

'He hast become rather proficient on the harp, also,' Katren added with pride, as if she and the High Queen had never discussed his talents before.

'So art thou ready for Selwyn yet?' Tory questioned, completely stunning the boy.

Selwyn was Chief Bard in the court of the High King, but he was also a Merlin amongst Druids. He'd studied under Taliesin a good part of his life, and was regarded as one of the wisest men in the whole of Britain.

'Dost thou not expect me to be a warrior like my brothers and father before me?' Cai was beaming now, scarcely able to believe that she knew of his aspirations.

'We do need scholars, too, Cai.'

'Hey!'

Everyone present turned to behold Rhun leaning in the doorway with a goblet of mead in his hand.

'What shall a lad do for amusement around here?' The young Prince of Gwynedd did not enter, but rather waited for everyone to come to him — all of the boys did, bar Bryce.

'How did thou manage to sneak in?' Owen was clearly overjoyed to see him.

'An excellent surprise!' Blain stepped up after Owen to give Rhun a high five; it would appear a little something still remained of Tory's twentieth century childhood. 'Who be holding the fort if thou art here?'

'Sir Tiernan stayed behind in Rhun's stead this year,' Tory explained with delight.

She was proud of him; Rhun was a handsome piece of work, just like his father. He'd inherited her art of truthsaying, and as he knew everybody's thoughts, he knew exactly how to keep everyone happy. It was common knowledge that no maiden was safe from him, and Tory knew this was no exaggeration.

'Aye, I hope ye all appreciate that I had to beg to get here.' Rhun grinned, though he tried to sound put out.

'Thou begged to come see us?' Bryce had to laugh. 'I think not! I think thou hast heard that Vortipor finally got up the courage to bring his daughter, and thou hast come to see her.'

Rhun looked to Bryce and gave him a wink. 'And so I say, lead me to her.' He spurred his three young companions off on a quest.

'Duty calls.' Katren made after them. 'I am not entirely sure Bridgit can handle all four of them at once.'

'I shall be down shortly.' Tory looked to Bryce. 'Well, sir, I pray thee speak. I am listening.'

Bryce seemed hesitant to voice his mind at once. 'Come on, Bryce, out with it.' Tory closed the door.

He was still pondering how best to put forward his dilemma as he raised his big blue eyes to look at her. 'Dost thou think Blain shall get the seat in thy circle, sensei?'

'Well, there are other candidates, but Blain stands a fair chance.' Tory was straight with him. She had known there would be brotherly friction between Bryce and Blain. It had just been a matter of when. 'He be thy pupil, Bryce. Surely thou wants him to succeed?'

'Aye, sensei, I do. Then he would become a trainer, as I am, and could instruct here in Powys in my stead.'

Tory returned to the lounge and sat down. 'Why, where art thou off to?' she questioned with a laugh in her voice.

Bryce made haste to sit beside her. 'I wish to return to Gwynedd, Majesty. After all, I wast born there. Ione shall be resigning as thy champion before long . . . I wish to compete for her title and serve under thee all the time.'

'But thy father needs thee here, Bryce. Hast thou discussed this with him?'

'Nay. But if Blain becomes one of thy Masters, he shall not need me as much.' He looked a little sad to concede this.

'Blain be very young, and hardly a worthy replacement for one with thy experience,' Tory assured him honestly.

'Blain shall be king, not I. Surely . . .'

'Be that the real problem, Bryce?' It was not like him to be jealous.

'In a way.' He was disinclined to admit it. 'But, as it no longer be my fate to be king, I feel I must follow my own destiny. And I wish, more than anything, to be a champion of Gwynedd like my father once was. It be all I have ever desired, sensei, and thou knows I would serve thee well.'

Tory could not disagree with his reasoning. It was true that he had always aspired to hold the position his father once had. Yet she could not see Brockwell wanting to release Bryce from his role as trainer to his armies here in Powys. For Brockwell, as a king, had little time to spend instructing his soldiers and he would not entrust the responsibility to one as young as Blain. 'In a few years perhaps — '

'Nay, sensei, please! Thou dost not understand the full extent of it.' Bryce stood, driven by his belief. 'Father will never entrust Blain with any responsibility whilst I am still here. Already Blain feels the king favours me, as doth our mother most of the time.'

'I see.' Tory motioned him to be seated and calm himself. She should have known Bryce could never be impelled by selfish cause. 'Thou dost feel thou art treading on his toes.'

'I know it, sensei.' Bryce sat as instructed. 'And Blain be more than capable of succeeding me . . . just wait until thou sees him in action, he shall make a fine master.'

'Well, as I said, Blain be not the only candidate I have.' Tory took up his hand and patted it. 'I shall see what I can do.' Her mind boggled at the chore. 'But only the Otherworld knows how we shall get around thy father.'

As Rhun entered the huge banquet hall with the rest of his entourage in tow, he spied Gawain and Gareth already approaching to acquaint him with the situation.

Sir Gawain was the latest initiate to the 'circle of twelve' and son of one of the High King's most trusted advisers, Sir Rhys. Although Gawain was a year older than Rhun they were of similar build, both reasonably tall, lean and broad-shouldered. They were often mistaken for brothers. They both had the same straight, dark hair, yet where Gawain's eyes were steely blue, Rhun's were dark brown. Sir Gareth, on the other hand, was a year younger than the prince. A good height and size for his age, Gareth's hair was the colour of honey, and his eyes were a pale, icy blue. His father, Sir Tiernan, had charge of the High King's armies at Aberffraw, where Gareth, Gawain and Rhun had grown up.

This was the first time in ages that all the sons of the 'circle of twelve' had been brought together in the one place. These lads were the brightest stars in Britain's future and it was clear to all in the banquet hall that they knew it, too. For theirs was a very noisy reunion — that is, until Queen Katren entered, whereupon they all simmered down to polite conversation.

'Damned shame thy father had to stay home this year.' Blain nudged Gareth with his shoulder.

'Aye, damned shame,' Gareth considered with a smile on his face.

Sir Tiernan, in addition to his responsibility for training, was still the High King's champion at the age of eight years and fifty. He was feared by these boys, and thus did a fair job of keeping them all in line. But it was Ione, Gareth's mother, that his friends feared more. She trained the female warriors of Gwynedd and was the champion of the High Queen, which was the greatest honour any fighter within the alliance could have.

'Mother stayed at Aberffraw, too,' added Gareth.

'Phew . . .' Owen voiced the general view. 'The Goddess be truly smiling on us this year.'

Rhun was still watching Queen Katren, who'd crossed the room to speak with a group of maidens. One of the girls turned to look in their direction.

'That must be her,' Rhun announced discreetly to the others. 'Queen Katren hast gone to forewarn the maiden.' He raised his eyebrows as he took a seat at the closest bench to begin feasting.

'Art thou not going to speak with her, then?' Owen wondered.

'Nay. I shall wait for the lady to seek me out.'

Gawain laughed. 'She will never come over here whilst there art so many of us.'

'Well, then?' Rhun grinned, raising his eyebrows as Gawain and the others stared back at him blankly.

'Shall we leave then?' Blain suggested, making his offer sound more like a dare.

'Would thee? How kind.' Rhun thanked them as they parted company. 'Cai can stay, though, if he chooses.'

Cai, pleased to have been chosen, sat where Rhun motioned him and joined the feast.

'So tell me, Cai, what are the maidens doing now?' Rhun continued selecting food at random from the platters before him and popping it into his mouth.

Cai observed a moment before reporting. 'I think they art being introduced to Gareth, Gawain and my brothers.'

'What!' Rhun had to look for himself. 'Oh dear.' He shrugged off his defeat with a sigh. 'We shall just have to get drunk on our own then.' The prince raised his goblet to Cai's and clinked it.

'Wait a moment.' Cai froze, his eyes still fixed on the cluster of women. 'One of the maidens be coming this way, but not the one who wast observing us before.'

'Interesting.' Rhun refilled his goblet. 'In a word, how would thou describe her?'

'Ah . . . stunning,' Cai concluded without hesitation.

Rhun became more interested. *Stunning, ay?*

'Majesty.' She requested his attention, having reached them.

When Rhun turned to view the maiden he was more than pleasantly surprised, for here was a face that caught the eye. It gave host to features that were almost angelic, and skin that glowed as soft and fair as a child's. Long, thick masses of auburn-brown curls had been rolled, and pinned off to each side of her face. But the bulk of her hair sat in long clusters that fell about her shoulders and down her back. Despite the rest of the maiden's slender, yet shapely, form Rhun's eyes did not waver from her face. *Exquisite would have been my description.* 'Can I help thee, Lady?'

'Nay,' she giggled. 'I am the maid of Lady Bridgit, who — '

'How unfortunate.' He took hold of her hand and coaxed her into taking a seat beside him. 'Do have a drink . . . what did thou say thy name was?'

'Ah . . .' She was hesitant to answer right away; his forward, though charming, manner had her in a bit of a fluster. 'Lucinda, Majesty. But my La — '

'Well, do have a drink, Lucinda.'

The prince was so amiable that she nearly succumbed to his kind offer. 'Nay, Majesty, really. I am just here to deliver a message.' She rose, observing the expression on his face, so soft and open for one of his ilk. The prince had suddenly become so intent upon hearing her message she almost forgot it. 'The Lady Bridgit . . .'

'Thy mistress,' Rhun interjected, to confirm he was following her tale.

'Indeed.' The maid found herself frowning and grinning at once; how peculiar he was. 'She be wondering if thou would grant her an audience?'

Rhun laughed, seemingly delighted by the notion. 'After such a becoming invitation, how could I possibly refuse?'

The maid bowed graciously, sporting a half grin on her face, when Rhun stood to block her escape. 'I am pleased to make thy acquaintance, Lady Bridgit. Please sit down and have a drink with us.'

Her eyes, the colour of amber jewels, were wide at his words. 'Majesty, why dost thou insist I am who I have already told thee I am not?'

Rhun looked to Cai who was following the conversation with decided interest. 'Dost thou think she could possibly see fit to test me further?'

Cai nodded with a shrug. 'I guess she doth not know then?'

'Know what?' she inquired.

Rhun turned back to the maid to enlighten her. 'How I detest being tested?'

She was taken aback by his tone, and so resolved to be open with him. 'My game be up then?' she asked Rhun.

Cai and Rhun nodded in sympathy with her predicament.

'They said thou could not be fooled . . . though I have led the others a merry dance.' She sounded pleased to have accomplished that much. 'They art still making eyes at my maid.'

The three looked to the parties to which she referred, spurring the two princes to laughter.

'It be a pity really . . . that thou found me out so soon.' She cast her sights to Rhun, who stood right beside her. 'It could have been fun.' She smiled with a pout, and wandered away.

'Whoa there.' Rhun went after her. 'Nobody said we had to tell anyone.' He turned Bridgit around and led her back. 'Cai can keep a secret . . . and, after all, if I say thou art the maid, I doubt even thine own father would disbelieve it.'

Everything she'd heard about Prince Rhun was true. Bridgit's smile broadened; she liked him already.

3

THE CAULDRON-BORN

On the map, which Ossa and his men had dug up from under the elder tree, X marked a spot right in the heart of allied Britain. It appeared that the Princess Vanora now resided on the outermost tip of the Isle of Mon, which was territory owned and frequented by the Dragon himself. The Gwynedd stronghold was situated on the mainland at Degannwy, but King Maelgwn's home and training ground were at Aberffraw, on Mon. Thus, the Saxons expected the island would be well guarded.

Along with the map, the witch had left a spell with them. She claimed the incantation would shield whomever bore her cauldron from the eyes of the Otherworld, so they could pass through the land that the Goddess safe-guarded without fear of detection. However, it would only cloak the party from Otherworldly eyes — Ossa still had to deal with those of a physical nature.

Eormenric mapped a course that would take them round all of Gwynedd's major strongholds, yet they still had to devise a means to cart the weighty cauldron across the Menai. The easy way, in his mind, was to take the barge across the strait as the locals did.

'Thou dost already speak the local dialect, thanks to thy dealings with Chiglas,' Eormenric put forward. 'We could enter Gwynedd in the guise of peasants . . . shave and dress as the Britons do.'

'I would rather fight the whole of Britain than shave this beard.' Ossa motioned to the growth on his chin that fell in two long braids down the length of his body.

'Father, even I would not recognise thy clean-shaven face.' Eormenric knew his father was going to be difficult about this. 'Once we free Mahaud, I am sure she will restore thy beard.'

'Thou art assuming an awful lot,' Ossa snarled. But the aging warlord knew he would not see too many more adventures of this magnitude in his lifetime. Thus he was finally persuaded.

They cast the witch's spell over their party under the conditions that she had outlined.

Only those who would make the journey were present — Ossa, Eormenric, and their two finest warriors. The midnight hour approached as they stood in a clearing of the forest that bordered the Dragon's realm. It was a still night with no moon.

To recite the incantation, Ossa and his men stood in a circle that was marked by four lit torches to their north, south, east and west respectively. The words of the incantation meant nothing to the men, as they were in a foreign dialect that was neither Anglo-Saxon nor the native tongue. Ossa was unsure as to whether they were even pronouncing the chant correctly, until the atmosphere surrounding them became unsettled.

Tiny whirlwinds rose out of the forest floor, stirring up the dead foliage that lay about the ground. The breeze built steadily to a gale that howled up and down through the trees, routing the wildlife, who fled the area.

At the end of the third, and final incantation, the wind ripped around the clearing, extinguishing all four torches in turn.

An eerie silence hung over the place in the wake of the disturbance and the air, now stagnate, felt deathly cold. The presence of the dark force they'd invoked to protect themselves was making itself at home.

The conference was going splendidly. These leaders very much enjoyed their annual reunion, revelling in the company of those who could truly understand their aspirations, responsibilities and woes. Thankfully, their woes had been few of late; the various kingdoms within the alliance boasted of their harvests and of the progress their cities and industries had made during the relative peace of the past year. It wasn't until Tory suggested giving aid to the lands in the east that the leaders seemed to lose their high spirits. Still, old King Catulus of Dumnonia had to laugh.

'One doth not aid thine enemy when he hast been substantially weakened, Majesty. Now would seem a better time than any to drive them out.'

'I agree.' The other representatives backed his view, all bar Maelgwn; he'd learnt to hear Tory out before trying to win an argument against her.

'I beg to differ, gentlemen.' Tory's voice rose over the din. 'I have learnt from my own experience that war begets war, peace begets peace.'

King Brockwell, though he loved Tory dearly, felt he must strongly protest. 'Nonsense! If the situation wast reversed, dost thou think for a moment that they would do the same for us?'

'Nay, I do not.' Tory was short with him. 'That be all the more reason why we should do it for them. I am not asking this council to supply them with weapons, just food enough to see them through the snowfall. For if we do not, starvation shall surely push them to plunder to sustain themselves.'

'If the Saxons make war on us, we shall cast them out of this land as the Goddess forewarned.' Vortipor, the Protector of Dyfed, took a stand on the issue. 'I shall not feed their children so they can live to take the lands of my descendants.'

'Here, here!' Fergus MacErc of the Scotti agreed wholeheartedly.

Tory shook her head, disappointed that the council could not see the opportunity for lasting good relations with their neighbours. 'Thou shalt all have to lose thy fear sometime.'

'She speaks wisely, gentlemen.' Taliesin, who'd been keeping a low profile during the proceedings, finally came forward to voice his view. 'Our mother-land be experiencing a major imbalance. Though one half of her lives in the sunshine and prospers, the other half lives in dark despair. Now what hast been the cause of this dis-ease I cannot say, but it will surely spread into our lands if not addressed soon.' The Merlin looked to Brockwell. 'So ask not if they would do the same for thee, but rather, how would thee have them treat us in the same circumstance.'

'I already know how they would treat us.' Brockwell was getting edgy.

'Be that so? Think about it?' Tory strengthened the argument. 'Thirty years ago, who would have thought that thy good selves would prosper within this association? We have brought about peace and co-operation between half the kingdoms in this land. Why should it end there?'

'What makes thee think they would accept our help?' Maelgwn grinned at his lovely wife; she was doing a fine job, as always.

'Do we have to call it charity? Call it a peace offering, a token of friend-ship, or goodwill.'

'Well . . .' King Catulus decided to give the High Queen's notion some consideration; she'd never steered them wrong before. 'We could send some poor, suicidal knight to Londinium with a letter of our intent . . . see what kind of response we get?'

'All in favour?' Maelgwn raised his hand, followed by Catulus and the others. Only Brockwell remained opposed to the notion.

'Not the Saxons!' Brockwell pleaded, collapsing onto the conference table as if he would cry.

'Come on, Brockwell . . .' Tory nudged a little harder. 'Just let go of thy fear.'

He finally gave in, raising his arm in the air.

'So be it.' The council declared.

It was decided before the meeting adjourned that one of the 'circle of twelve' should deliver the message. Sir Tiernan, Ione, Sir Angus, Lady Alma and Sir Rhys were not present, as they'd stayed in Gwynedd to look after its affairs whilst Tory and Maelgwn attended the conference. Brockwell and

Vortipor, as heads of state, could not be sent. Thus, only Bryce, Gawain and Rhun remained as possibilities. After some discussion it was decided that Bryce, as the eldest and most experienced, should go. Only one soldier would accompany him, as they did not want to alarm their foe by sending a whole battalion to deliver a message.

Naturally, his father was not completely thrilled by the idea, but Bryce was the obvious choice.

Maelgwn and Tory returned to their chamber after the long day in court to find their son sprawled across one of their lounges, engrossed in a book.

'How went thy meeting?' Rhun rested his reading matter on his chest as they entered.

'Thy mother stirred up a hornets' nest.' The king didn't sound too worried about it. He took hold of his son's feet to twist him around, and then let them drop to the floor. 'Why art thou not out playing with that maid, whatever her name wast?' Maelgwn took a seat beside Rhun.

'So many people, for too long, make me dizzy . . . all those minds thinking at once.' Rhun pulled himself back up to a seated position. 'And her name be Lucinda.'

Tory laughed. 'Bridgit, more like.'

Rhun's head shot up, as did his father's.

Tory laughed again. 'The pair of thee have not still got everybody fooled, surely?'

Rhun grinned. Even though he'd scarce seen his mother since they arrived, he should have known she would find out. 'A fine performance by anyone's standards. None had guessed till now.'

'Thou art not fooling around with Vortipor's daughter?' Maelgwn sounded perturbed. 'He hast been looking for an excuse to challenge me to a sword fight for the past twenty years.'

'Fear not,' Rhun assured. 'She be safer with me than anyone.'

Maelgwn split his sides laughing. 'Her father doth not agree. He arranged a guard for her as soon as I mentioned I brought thee.'

'I know,' Rhun informed him. 'They art fooled, too. They have been guarding her maid these two days past. It be a good thing Vortipor sent Bridgit away to Brittany for so long . . . no one seems to know what she looks like. Except her father, of course, and he's been too tied up to expose us.'

Tory couldn't help but be amused, though Maelgwn was looking a little pale. 'So long as thou art treating her as a lady of royal blood.' She came to sit between them, taking hold of Rhun's hand.

'Mother, thee would know if I did not,' her son said emphatically. Then, perceiving his mother's mind, his expression became more disturbed. 'Why art thou sending Bryce to Londinium?'

'The council hast decided to see if we can aid the Saxons in their time of need,' Maelgwn put forward in an impartial fashion, interested to see how his son would respond.

Rhun stood, taking a few paces away then turning back. 'I see the sense of it . . . but, let me go. Bryce doth not have the same talents for reading people that I do.' As his parents both moved to contest him, Rhun added quickly, 'And do not try and tell me heirs to the throne cannot risk this kind of quest — look at what Father accomplished on his own before he assumed his position.'

The young warrior, having been raised in peacetime, hadn't seen much action, and a royal errand into the centre of enemy territory sounded terribly inviting.

'That was part of Maelgwn's inauguration, a challenge thee, too, will face in time. Bryce, most likely, shall never face that kind of initiation. Thus, I feel this quest be the chance for him to prove to himself his own worth.'

Rhun was aware of what Bryce had been going through these past few years, with Blain out to establish himself as a suitable heir. 'Could I not accompany him then? Together we will be invincible.'

Tory and Maelgwn looked to each other; it was hard enough risking Bryce on the errand, but their own son?

'I speak the language better than he does. I am much more diplomatic, not to mention charming.'

'Enough!' Tory knew he was right. What's more, Rhun knew she knew it, and he smiled broadly in spite of being interrupted. Maelgwn had won wars at Rhun's age, and with far less training than his son.

He didn't wait to hear his mother's verbal response; Rhun felt her let go of her dread. 'Many thanks for the vote of confidence, Mother. I shall make ready.' He was out the door before his father had the chance to comment.

'Tory!' Maelgwn looked to his wife, who was almost in tears.

'That was the hardest thing I shall ever have to do.' Tory's wise and strong state of being departed as she realised what she'd done. 'Due to a notion I had a few days ago, two of my master's must risk their lives. I very much despise my position at times.'

Their expedition had been a misery, and it seemed like one of the longest Ossa had undertaken in his life.

One cart and two horses to carry four men and a cauldron may have been fine on the eastern plains, but through the mountains of Gwynedd it was a nightmare.

The freezing cold presence their hex had conjured hung over them like a curse. On the second night of their travels they'd been robbed of their weapons and food as they slept. They'd been bogged, lost and now they were hungry, too. All four men were suffering from the extreme cold and running a fever, hence the entire party was short on patience; no matter how hard they tried, they could not cooperate or agree with each other.

The sight of Bangor (a small fishing community on the banks of the Menai Strait) raised their spirits considerably. The party found the local people very helpful. They believed Ossa's 'poor farmer and his three sons seeking better fortune in Aberffraw' story and provided accommodation, a hot meal, and instructions as to where and when they could catch the barge.

Gullible fools, the Britons, Ossa thought in retrospect, as he made the final leg of their trek across the more obliging terrain of the island. If not for the Goddess, I would have possessed this land long ago.

Yet Eormenric's thoughts were of a different nature. These folk were not at all like he'd expected. How generous they were to have given all four of them shelter and food, when they'd nothing to give in return. Even the ride across the Menai had been rendered free of charge. The ferrymen had laughed when his father informed him they had no money to pay.

'We art in the service of the crown, Sir,' the ferryman had explained. 'None of the High King's subjects art expected to pay to cross the strait . . . where would our industries be?'

Where indeed, Eormenric thought. We could learn a thing or two from these people. What a fine race they seemed, too — so happy, healthy, and full of praise for their king. They also acclaimed his Queen, though the locals referred to her as the Goddess.

'Why do they call Maelgwn's queen the Goddess?' Eormenric had to ask.

His father, who sat beside him driving the cart, was distracted by the question. 'I do not believe the wild tales the Britons spin.'

'What tales?' Eormenric prompted.

Though Ossa wasn't thrilled about his son's chosen subject matter, the pace of their journey was slow and some conversation seemed better than none. 'Well . . . the story goes that she wast brought from the future by the Old Ones.' He shrugged to imply that he didn't know who the 'Old Ones' were. 'They say it was she who formed and trained the circle of twelve. For she brought with her the knowledge of an advanced fighting skill, which I glimpsed only once at Arwystli. A warrior who had trained under the Goddess, the one they call Ione, disarmed me in single combat. I was so stunned by her bold fighting technique and her beauty, that I offered to swap our mutual enemy, Chiglas, in exchange for her. Maelgwn Gwynedd refused.'

'Hast thou met the Goddess?' Eormenric wondered if Maelgwn's queen was the one his father had lived in fear of all these years?

'Aye.' Ossa went silent.

The memory of her angelic presence and the divine authority of her voice brought a tear to the warlord's eye. But Ossa repressed his guilt quickly; the Goddess had caused his people pain, and now her people would suffer.

The errand Bryce and Rhun were embarking upon was known only to the immediate members of the alliance and the messengers themselves; not even their destination had been disclosed. It was decided by the council that their intent should remain a secret until such time as they'd received an answer. They'd allowed six days for the princes to return, or send word. If any dispatch they sent was not signed by the both of them, the council would presume the worst and take action.

'Camp tonight this side of Powys' border,' Maelgwn advised his son in a whisper. 'Then ride until thou hast reached Ossa.'

'I promise,' Rhun assured, breaking into a smile. 'Father, stop worrying. I shall be fine.'

The young Prince of Gwynedd looked to his mother. He felt the conflict eating away at her, just as she felt the excitement welling within him.

'Thy decision be a sound one,' Rhun told her. 'Dost thou think for a moment I would go along with it, if it wast not?'

'Make me proud.' Tory smiled, despite the tear that escaped her eye.

'That goes without saying.'

Bridgit waited patiently for Rhun to finish speaking with his mother. The High Queen smiled as she addressed him, giving all the impression that her son was heading off on no more than a picnic. But when she held him close in parting, a brief flash of sorrow swept her face. This led Bridgit to believe that perhaps Rhun's mission was indeed as dangerous as he'd boasted the night before.

Why did I not submit when I had the chance? she scolded herself. *All he'd wanted was a kiss. What if he gets killed? I may never see him again.*

Rhun turned and made for his mount when a hand touched his shoulder to delay him. He knew it was Bridgit before he'd even turned. 'My Lady of Dyfed.'

'Majesty.' She curtsied quickly, all in a fluster. 'I wanted to say how sorry I am about last night. I should have believed thee.'

Rhun laughed, for he'd had quite a bit of mead at last night's feast. 'Nay, thou acted wisely. Truth be known, thou probably saved my life.'

'Well, in any case . . .' Bridgit persevered to speak her mind, pulling Rhun's knife from its sheath at his waist, 'I wanted thee to have this.' She cut off one of the many tiny braids that were bound with ribbon and laced through her curls. 'For good luck.' She explained as she placed it in his hand. Then in front of the entire gathering, she kissed him.

'Looks like he accepts favours from the hired help, too,' Gawain commented, fetching a chuckle from his peers.

'Get him away from my daughter!' Vortipor roared, striding towards the couple to reclaim his kin.

'What?' Blain, Gareth, Gawain and Owen all exclaimed at once.

Cai began to chuckle. 'It seems thou art the ones who art chasing the affections of the hired help.'

'Damn it.' Blain conceded defeat. 'He did it again!'

Rhun glanced around, and it appeared that everyone had seen them. 'Thou art a crafty woman, my lady. They shall be expecting me to marry thee now.'

The smile he wore made it difficult for Bridgit to tell exactly how he felt; he'd certainly cooled since last night. *He enjoys confusing me.* 'Surely, thou art not serious, Highness?' She smiled as Vortipor took hold of her. 'Father would never allow it.'

'Keep thy claws off my daughter, little dragon, or I shall be forced to squash thee.'

Bridgit raised her eyebrows and shrugged as Vortipor led her away, thus it was Rhun who was left wondering.

The braid in his hand would have much to tell when he had the time to sit down and concentrate on it. Right now, however, as Bryce was already mounted and obviously eager to get on the move, Rhun made haste to his horse.

By nightfall, Ossa's party had found the cottage they sought. It was a small yet cosy dwelling, and if all was as it seemed Vanora lived alone.

A tall, slender maiden opened the door. This was the daughter of Chiglas, Ossa was quite sure about it; she didn't appear to have aged a day. Her black, curly hair, longer now, was neatly tied off her face. Her facial expression had lost the sternness Ossa remembered, though her eyes, black as night, were a steadfast reminder of the wild child she'd been when last they'd met.

'Can I help ye, sirs?' she inquired, politely.

'Aye.' Ossa grinned; she did not recognise him. 'Art thou the maiden, Vanora?'

'I am.'

'I have been bade by the High King to dispatch this crate to thee.' Ossa motioned to the back of his cart.

Vanora looked puzzled, though delighted, by the announcement. 'What hast the High King sent me?'

'I do not know, Lady.' Ossa humbled himself. 'He said only that it was something that once belonged to thee.'

Vanora was intrigued. 'Then, if ye would be so kind as to bring it inside, I shall fetch some water and food for ye all. It be quite a hike to get to these parts, ye must be exhausted.'

Eormenric was completely dazed by her sweet smile; she was nothing like what he'd expected. She looked hardly a day older than himself, yet by his father's reckoning she was aged eight years and thirty. She was a vision, as Mahaud had foretold, but he could scarce believe her to be the wretched woman his father had described.

'Heartless and cruel,' he'd said. 'She bewitches many and loves none. Men died for her and yet I never saw her shed a single tear.'

Ossa was busy supervising their soldiers to move the crate when Eormenric spied Vanora battling to raise a loaded bucket from the well.

'Ah!' She gave a laugh as he took the load from her. 'The Goddess always provides.' She wiped her hands of the chore.

Eormenric smiled; although he hadn't understood much of what she said, she seemed thankful for his aid. She wandered away from him a little and stopped on the hill's incline, looking down through the trees to the ocean beyond.

How dost thou survive in this remote place all alone? Eormenric wanted to ask, although the maiden appeared quite joyous and content. He wasn't so sure about exposing her to this witch any more, for Mahaud certainly hadn't done them any favours. Their whole party wore several layers of clothing, yet still they felt the cold of the cursed presence looming over them.

What if Mahaud lied? Eormenric considered. *What if the spell was a curse to insure that we delivered the cauldron to Vanora? For until we persuade her to look into it and recall her sorcerous ways, we shall never learn how to lift the icy shield we've cast.*

Nobody outside their party seemed to notice the lack of warmth, life, moisture or breeze, though the folk at Bangor had commented that none of their party appeared at all well.

I cannot let him do it. I must warn her. Eormenric decided, lifting the bucket from the well. *But how?* They didn't even speak the same language.

A hand clamped down hard on Eormenric's shoulder and startled him.

'Get that inside.' His father grumbled softly, before looking to Vanora and stating in a manner more becoming. 'Thy crate be in thy house, my lady.'

The three of them entered the cottage to find that the soldiers had removed the wooden packaging from their load.

'Why it be a cauldron.' Vanora seemed stunned. 'I do not recall ever owning such an item. There must be a mistake.'

Vanora moved to fetch a jug and goblets, appearing not the slightest bit interested in investigating it further. Eormenric smiled at this, though his father was appearing a mite frustrated.

'The cauldron might be just the container, Lady. Perhaps the item to which the king referred be inside,' Ossa suggested, one side of his mouth curving to a smile.

'Perhaps thou art right.' Vanora placed the jug of water aside and approached the huge iron pot.

'No!' Eormenric cried, and although it was Anglo-Saxon he spoke, his intonation was clear enough to deter her.

'Silence.' Ossa was outraged and lashed at his son with a backhander to the face. Eormenric hit the floor before having a chance to say more.

'What art thou doing?' Vanora rushed over to see if the young man was alright.

'So sorry, Lady, but he knows better than to speak out of turn.' Ossa looked down on his son, spread-eagled on the ground before him.

'Well, why wast he so alarmed?' She held his face gently to look it over.

'Do not look into the cauldron. It be a trap,' Eormenric mumbled, bleary-eyed.

Vanora was bemused. 'I cannot understand him.'

Ossa went down on one knee by his son. 'He said not to bother thyself, Lady. He doth not wish to keep thee from thy business.'

'Oh.' Vanora leant back on her haunches.

Eormenric was frustrated; what was his father telling her? 'No, I think he lies!'

With an explanation already brewing in his mind, Ossa thumped Eormenric out cold. 'Take him outside,' he instructed the other men.

'I do not understand.' Vanora backed up, fearful and suspicious. 'What did he do to warrant such cruelty? What did he say?'

'Do not concern thyself, Lady. He be nothing but a Saxon and a traitor. We art in the process of reforming him, but I dare say he needs a few more years in prison before he can truly be of any use to our community. I would rather not repeat what he said to thee . . . it would be better if thou did not know.'

'Oh.' Vanora felt rather rattled after the scene. His explanation seemed as though it could be truthful. 'I do apologise to thee. I misunderstood.'

'It be I who should apologise to thee for any unpleasantness taking place in thy home.' Ossa smiled sweetly.

Vanora turned her attention to the large obstruction in the middle of her room and circled it once before reaching for the handle. 'What dost thou think might be inside?' she questioned playfully, raising the lid to peek underneath.

'Some old memories perhaps?' Ossa grinned with satisfaction as a tremendous rumble resounded deep in the belly of the pot.

The lid suddenly shot from Vanora's hand and was cast across the room. From within the seething misty haze of the cauldron sprang long, spindly arms that were transparent and red in colour.

'Release me,' demanded a voice of beastly strain.

The maid was stunned speechless, until the gangly hands reached out and took hold of her head. As they pulled her toward the pot's churning red centre, Vanora screamed in terror and resisted with all her might.

'Remember me!' the feral voice from within the cauldron taunted.

'Help me, please!' Vanora looked to Ossa in a final plea. 'Just replace the lid.'

But the warlord looked away, blocking out her screams for assistance.

He allowed the beast to draw her in.

4

RUINATION

Bryce and Rhun reached the border earlier than expected, so they hunted up a couple of pheasant for dinner and made camp before sunset.

They discussed their plans for the next day whilst they ate, and placed bets as to how long it would take to reach the said destination — Rhun's estimation being the more optimistic of the two.

Afterwards, with their bellies and minds filled to overflowing, they lay next to the small campfire in relative silence. It was nice laying out under the stars for a change; they hadn't done so in years. Still, tonight it was altogether more exhilarating, as this time they really were on a mission.

Bryce emerged from his contemplation and glanced across to Rhun, whose sight was entranced by the firelight as he held the braid of the Lady Bridgit in his hand. His friend's expression wasn't that of a man reflecting on a fair maiden; he was, for some unknown reason, deeply grieved and concerned. 'Bad news?'

'Sorry?' Rhun snapped out of his daze.

'The maiden.' Bryce motioned to the lock of hair in Rhun's hand. 'Be something amiss with her?'

'Nay,' Rhun smiled, his thoughts wandering again. 'I cannot seem to concentrate . . . my mind keeps being distracted by something else.'

'What?'

'I do not know, I cannot see it . . . it be a little hard to explain.' Rhun brought his attention to the fore to try and clarify. 'These abilities I have extend from the Otherworld, but they also extend into it . . . that be how I am granted the information I seek.'

Bryce gave a nod to acknowledge he was following.

'Yet sometimes I perceive information I have not asked for and, as I do not know anything about it, I must ask the right questions before I can draw any meaning from it.' Rhun looked perplexed.

'So what hast thou seen that disturbs thee so?'

'In this case it was felt, and again, it be rather difficult to verbalise.' He didn't want to unduly alarm his companion, but Bryce motioned him on. 'I feel a great unease within the Otherworld, and when I asked what wast causing this . . .' Rhun shrugged, 'all I felt was an icy chill. All I saw was a great darkness.'

'That doth not sound very promising,' Bryce conceded. 'And nothing on the girl?'

'Nay.' Rhun tucked the braid gently back into his shirt. 'It be difficult to access answers when the spirits art so disgruntled.'

Bryce exhausted his powers of reason trying to figure out what it could mean, but as he was not very knowledgeable about such matters he lay back against the base of the tree behind him to rest. 'Well, let me know if anything comes to thee.'

'I shall,' Rhun assured him with a smile, before his eyes were drawn back to the lapping flames.

Eormenric was seeing stars when he woke, thousands and thousands of stars. One side of his face ached with a vengeance, and, as he managed to raise himself to his elbows, he realised he was in the back of a cart.

It took a moment to recall exactly where he was as he didn't recognise anything at first glance , but as he spied the cottage upon its peaceful aspect overlooking the ocean he remembered the maiden and the sum of her woes.

What hast happened! He leapt from the cart, his ailing head catching up with the rest of his body when his feet hit the ground. Even though all appeared calm and well, Eormenric ran to the doorway and burst into the room.

'Do not argue with me. I must go alone,' Vanora told his father in Eormenric's own tongue as he stumbled through the door. She glanced to the intruder, not really paying him much mind. 'Half of Gwynedd knowing of thy involvement be the last thing we need.'

The maiden's demeanour seemed to have changed somewhat. Suddenly it was not so hard to believe the stories Ossa had told about her. *What have we done?*

'But I want to be there to see it,' Ossa grumbled, obviously disappointed.

'Believe me . . .' she smiled in a cold, calculating fashion, 'thou shalt be able to see it from quite a distance.'

'See what?' Eormenric demanded.

Ossa turned in his seat to acknowledge his son's presence. 'So. Thou hast finally come to thy senses. I still pack a fair punch, ay?'

Surprisingly, his father seemed rather cheery. Eormenric had felt sure Ossa would have him hung as a traitor for what he'd done.

Ossa grunted. 'Well, I hope I knocked some sense into thee.'

Vanora rose and slowly approached Eormenric, seeming so amiable that she near took his breath away. 'So this be the one who tried to save me.' She giggled, amused by the notion. 'What be wrong, Eormenric?' She circled him, running a hand across his broad shoulders. 'Dost thou not like me this way?'

The chilly atmosphere of the curse that was upon him suddenly became cooler and he shuddered. Vanora's fingers felt like ice against his skin and as beautiful as she was, her face had lost all its lustre. She smiled, yet her huge, dark eyes were devoid of all emotion, as if she'd died inside. 'Dost thou like thyself this way?' he said, finally.

'Of course I do. Dost thou think I enjoyed living in the isolation of this place? I have been a prisoner here for twenty years!' she informed him, as if he were some kind of idiot. 'I wast brainwashed and robbed of my kingdom.'

'Forgive me, I had not considered . . .'

'Indeed.' She brushed off his apology. 'So, from now on, do not try and do me any favours.'

She looked away before Eormenric could respond. *The poor woman dost not even control her own will anymore.* Much to his horror, Vanora cast a cool glare back in his direction.

'Oh aye, I do. And tomorrow eve, thou shalt see for thyself just how much control and willpower I have.'

Come dawn, Bryce and Rhun ate the leftovers from the night before and then rode as hard as they could through the land of their foe — stopping only twice to answer nature's call.

The errand had taken on a whole new meaning for the young Britons, for they could hardly believe the devastation that surrounded them; the farmland looked more like marshland. The Goddess had been right in saying these people needed help.

Rhun set a deadly pace over the precarious terrain, but they didn't enter the outskirts of Londinium till just after dark. Bryce considered that they must have set some sort of record. Needless to say, Rhun won their bet, as they reached their destination before midnight.

At the gate to Ossa's fortress, the pair were removed from their horses and searched. As they bore a dispatch and were unarmed, bar a bow and knife for hunting, they were permitted entry. A guard of ten soldiers led them to Ossa's council chambers, where they were left with four guards both in and outside the door.

'Well, we art still alive.' Rhun gave Bryce a slap on the shoulder to lighten the sombre atmosphere that hung in the room.

Bryce looked to his companion, rather dumbfounded by his jovial mood. 'Only because they have yet to think of a good reason to kill us.'

Rhun laughed out loud. 'Then we shall not give them one.'

They turned as the door opened. Much to their surprise and delight it was not Ossa who entered, nor one of his sons, but a beautiful young maiden who was still half asleep.

She looked at the guards. 'Where be Ongen?' she questioned one of them.

'We art still searching for him, lady. Hopefully, he will not be long.'

The maid seemed a mite perturbed by the absence of her associate, but maintained a good mood as she addressed the messengers. 'I am Aella, daughter of Ossa. My brother, Ongen, shall join us presently.' She motioned politely for them to be seated. 'What can we do for ye, gentlemen?'

Rhun bowed as a messenger would to a lady of Aella's stature. 'We bear thee a cable from the council of united kingdoms of Britain.' Rhun looked to Bryce to produce the dispatch, but his friend's attention seemed somewhat preoccupied with their hostess.

After a nudge, Bryce realised that he'd missed his cue. He stepped forward, to present the scroll bearing the Dragon's seal to her, bowing as he did so.

She couldn't help but smile at their antics, as she graciously accepted the dispatch. Were these men a typical example of her supposed foe?

Though Bryce didn't want to appear rude, he couldn't take his eyes off the girl. How could such a fragile little angel be Ossa's daughter?

'Be this some kind of joke?' Aella didn't sound angry, but rather, stunned, and a smile swept her face.

'Nay, lady.' Rhun smiled warmly. 'I swear to thee. The united kingdoms want nothing more than to see the whole of this land prosper in peace. Thus, we cannot sit by and watch half of it forced into penury by the cursed weather.'

She very much liked how relaxed and confident these men were and tended to believe their intent was of a completely innocent nature. Nevertheless, she was fairly sure her brother would not take the same view. 'Thou art very fluent in our language, sir.'

Rhun bowed his head to accept her compliment. 'It be my job to possess such skills.'

'I wish I could return the consideration and thank ye in thine own tongue, but I have scarce seen any of the native people, let alone spoken with them.' She smiled at Bryce, who still appeared rather overawed by her presence.

'Then I hope thy first impression of the Britons be a pleasant surprise, lady.'

'Aye,' she confirmed, before her attention skipped back to Rhun and the cable in her hand. 'But thou must realise this; thy kind offer be so timely and well needed, it seems almost too good to be true. I dare say my brother shall not be so willing to believe the sincerity of it.' As she heard a group of men approaching, she added quickly, 'Please have patience, he shall see reason in the end.'

Bryce, Rhun, and Aella looked to the door as Ongen entered. He was the oldest son of Ossa, and thus it was he who had charge of the affairs of state in his father's absence.

Ongen, tall and top-heavy, as his father had been in his younger days, stopped just inside the door and looked to the messengers of the council. 'Arrest them,' he ordered without blinking an eye.

Bryce looked to Rhun, hoping he hadn't understood Ongen correctly.

'Now we art in trouble.' Rhun confirmed his friend's fears.

'Nay! Warn him of Britain's intent if the council do not hear from us,' Bryce implored Rhun as the soldiers took hold of them.

Aella spoke up. 'Ongen, they have brought a peace offering. The Britons wish to supply us with food enough for the winter.'

'Aella, thou art so gullible!' Ongen scolded. 'Can thou not see it be naught but a trick?'

'Look, I hate to interrupt . . .' Rhun sounded awfully calm as he was escorted past Ongen, 'but the council will retaliate if we do not return.'

Ongen smacked Rhun fair in the jaw. 'Let them.'

Bryce broke free of his captors to catch his friend before he hit the floor.

'Ouch!' Rhun mumbled, as Bryce set him back on his feet and threw an arm around his back to walk Rhun out of the room. 'Perhaps we should not have mentioned it.'

'Just let them return home,' Aella pleaded. 'We cannot afford to go to war!'

'Quiet!' Ongen thrust her to the floor, just a little too roughly for Bryce's liking. Bryce left Rhun to his own devices and barged through the guard toward the lady's assailant.

When Ongen turned back to view the disturbance, all he saw was the bottom of Bryce's boot as it encountered his face.

As the Saxon leader hit the floor, blood streaming from his nose, Bryce held a hand down to help Aella to her feet.

Her large blue eyes gazed up at him in awe; such gallantry expended on a female was unknown to her. 'I am indebted to thee, sir.' She smiled and held out her hand to place it in his, but her brother's soldiers dragged him away.

The tower of Ossa's fortification in Londinium, if nothing else, did afford a splendid view of the city below. Even at this time of night, fires and torches were blazing for as far as the eye could see.

'Londinium be bigger than I imagined.' Bryce peered through one of the many long, slender slits in the wall.

These windows were designed to be wide enough to shoot an arrow from, yet too narrow for even a young child to squeeze through.

'I wonder if all their women art as fair as Aella?'

Rhun's thoughts were back in Ossa's room of court also, only with Ongen. '*Let them.*' Rhun mused over the warrior's final words to him. 'He sounded pretty confident, considering their state of affairs. I dare say, I would not be inviting a war in the same circumstance.' Rhun looked to Bryce, who was not listening to him.

'Did thou see her hair? Straight and fair, just like thy mother's. It near touched the floor.'

Rhun couldn't believe it. Bryce was seldom preoccupied with those of the fairer sex — bar the High Queen, of course. What a time for Bryce to go soft on him. 'Forget the girl. Show me thy boot.'

'What?'

'The one thee struck Ongen with.' Rhun beckoned with his fingers for Bryce to comply.

Bryce rested his foot on the bench by Rhun, appearing puzzled.

'Ah-huh!'

'What?'

Rhun wiped his fingers across the leather and held them up triumphant. 'Blood. Ongen's blood.' He smiled.

'Aye.' Bryce grinned. 'I got him good.'

This was not what Rhun had meant, however. He considered that even though Ongen had asked for the belting, it was not the most diplomatic course of action to have taken — but, hopefully, it would serve them now. 'Go back to thy vision, friend. I have need to concentrate.'

'Dost thou think thou may be able to learn something of Ongen?'

Rhun rubbed the tips of his fingers against each other, getting a feel of the individual from whose body the blood had flowed. 'Perhaps.' He closed his eyes to focus. 'Let me be awhile.'

Bryce moved away to the windows, though his eyes remained glued on his friend. Rhun was peaceful a few moments, then he began to quiver violently. 'Goddess preserve us!' His eyes shot open. 'They art going to release Mahaud.' He rushed to a puddle of water on the stone floor by the windows to scrub the blood from his hands.

'Holy mother! We must stop them.' Bryce raced for the stairs.

'Hold on.' Rhun recommended a little restraint. 'I have an idea, but I need total silence. So please, just sit.'

Rhun walked into the centre of the round room and took a seat, assuming the lotus position. It was a long time since he'd tried to bethink his mother thus, and never had he attempted it from such a distance. But still, as Taliesin said, it be only a matter of will; time and space art an illusion.

Vanora entered the inner bailey courtyard at Aberffraw sometime around noon. So many maids wandered in and out in the course of a day, going about the duties of the house, that the guards let them pass without questioning every one as to her errand. As Vanora appeared well kept and was alone, she passed right though the guards without either one batting an eyelid.

She awaited the midnight hour by the sundial, which was located amongst the extensive gardens in the huge courtyard of the High King's manor. When the waxing moon was high in the sky, marking a time of new beginnings, Vanora emerged from her hiding place. The silvery light from above shed scatterings of light upon the area she approached. This sundial marked the sacred site through which Mahaud had been banished, hence it was from here that she must be released.

Vanora set down the utensils for summoning the evil spirit of her mentor in their respective places around the sundial. Mahaud's crooked old wand was laid in a southerly position to summon the element of fire. A smaller cauldron, used by the old witch for such purposes as this, was placed to the west to invoke the element of water. A large hunk of crystal, black as night in colour, sat to the north to summon the element of earth. Vanora placed the sword of Vortigern, arch-traitor of Britain, in the easterly position. The sword of Vortigern was a memento of one of Mahaud's past encounters: she had been known to advise the warlord on occasion, and, ever since his death, the witch had found his weapon most effective for conjuring up the more mischievous elementals in the air.

When all was placed as it should be, Vanora stood just outside the circle and directed her energies into the centre. She focused herself a moment, the better to concentrate on her summons.

Vanora chanted her verse three times over, in accordance with the law of three requests:

'O fire of demons, water of drought,
I call on thee to draw her out.
The one who hast served thee
and granted thee power,
release from her prison
in this midnight hour.
Air of suffocation, darkest side of mother earth,
Thy combined force can give her birth.
The one who wast banished here
and cast from this plane,
grant her the means
to be born again.'

Upon her first utterance, the ground within the centre of the circle began to glow red with a throbbing motion.

Upon her second recitation, the ground beneath the sundial began to rumble and break up.

As Vanora neared the end of her third and final rendition, guards began to flood the grounds, but they were too late.

The sundial crumbled into the earth as the ground beneath it split apart. A thick stream of glowing red and black gas shot into the air, forming one glowing mass of energy that covered the sky as it extended itself over the manor.

The witch's advocate screeched with exultant laughter as an electrical storm erupted, the like of which none had ever witnessed before. It appeared as if the sky was on fire and red bolts of lightning tore through the rumbling clouds. All of Mahaud's sacred implements were sucked into the raging torrent of energy, whereby Vanora calmly turned and walked toward the closed inner bailey portcullis.

Guards pursued her, only to be struck down in flames by the lightning from above. The large, iron portcullis, deeply inset into the stone walls of the house, was blasted from its foundations. The guards could do naught but watch as the culprit walked out through the gaping hole left in the wake of the explosion.

The High Queen had barely slept since her son's departure. Not that she really needed much rest. Immortality did have its advantages — or drawbacks, as these past two nights had seemed endless to her.

Tory remained motionless and silent in the darkened room, her thoughts roaming the Otherworld in search of some news of her Masters. The strange thing was, the spirits seemed deathly silent. All she was able to perceive was a great expanse of blackness that accompanied an eerie chill.

Please Goddess, help me, she pleaded, feeling a sudden sense of urgency. *A glimpse of them is all I ask.*

From within the blackness behind her eyes, the image of her boy took form.

Mother. Hear me, please.

I hear thee, Rhun, she assured, relieved beyond all belief. *Where art thou? How fares thy mission?* She was proud that he'd attempted to make contact with her thus. She would have had great difficulty finding him otherwise.

Never mind about that, we have far greater problems.

Rhun was fairly confident he could get Bryce and himself safely out of their predicament on his own, so he mustered the most positive sense-of-being that he could, to prevent his mother being distracted from the more important task.

Ossa intends to release Mahaud, and she hast given him the means to do it. He left near a week ago with the witch's cauldron, of the mind to seek out Vanora.

That explains the great blackness. Tory considered the possibilities. *He must*

36

have cast a shielding spell over their party, or we surely would have known of this sooner.

Indeed, Rhun confirmed.

But what of thee? A huge disturbance, formed of a red flare of light, engulfed her vision of Rhun. When it passed, he was gone. Rhun. Rhun! But there was no response. Her etheric sight perceived naught but the dark, cold silence.

Damn it. Tory sat back in her chair, pausing to think a moment. I need to speak with Taliesin at once.

No sooner had she decided this than Taliesin passed right through the wall of her room to speak with her.

'Majesty. I fear something loathsome hast happened. Did thou feel it?'

'Aye I did,' she was sorry to admit. 'And, unfortunately, Rhun had just got through informing me that Ossa planned to release Mahaud. Hence, I suspect he hast succeeded.'

Taliesin's solemn expression became even more so. 'Then it be worse than we thought.'

'How so?' Maelgwn inquired, as he approached them. He was belting on his trousers, having just woken from a deep sleep.

'Ossa can only release the witch from the place she was banished.'

Tory and Maelgwn looked to each other, horrified. 'Aberffraw!'

5

BETRAYAL

The royal house at Aberffraw shook furiously and the walls had begun to crumble by the time Sir Tiernan and Ione reached the doorway to the courtyard. They were scarce able to believe the apocalyptic scene that awaited them there.

Ione drew her sword, her anger mounting with every rumble of the earth and every flash of deadly lightning. She was more than ready to challenge those responsible, though amid the chaos of the disaster who could tell friend from foe.

'Nay!' Tiernan urged her over the din. 'We cannot fight this. We must get everybody out.'

Ione nodded in confirmation, replacing her sword in its scabbard as she quickly made for the maidens' quarters.

Javotte, daughter of Sir Angus and Lady Alma, had already started directing the younger noblewomen out one of the windows that led to the courtyard when Ione flung the door open.

'Javotte, get out quickly!' She urged the young warrioress to follow the others out the window. 'The building be about to fold.'

'Nay.' Javotte ran in Ione's direction. 'I must find my parents.'

The ceiling of the room collapsed behind her and Javotte barely made it into the hallway where Ione awaited her.

'I shall make thee pay for that,' Ione told her with a smile.

Javotte was her prize student and had as much gall as the best of the male warriors. She was rumoured to become the next to be initiated into the circle of twelve.

'Let us go, *now*.' Ione sprinted toward the west tower. She held little hope of them making it out through the house to the main door, thus they would have to risk the secret passage. At low tide, the tunnel from the west tower granted one an escape onto the beach via the cliff face — if, of course, the passage hadn't collapsed.

Sir Angus and his wife, Alma, raced out of the house and through the courtyard, the ground between them beginning to break up.

'Angus!' Alma fell to her knees to prevent herself diving into the gaping cavern that had erupted before her.

'Goddess be merciful!' Angus neared the ever-expanding edge of the chasm between himself and his wife. 'Jump, I shall catch thee.'

The ground to the other side of her began to fall away. In a few moments, she would find herself on an island of flimsy soil that would simply crumble beneath her. Alma, as virile as she was, knew she could not make the jump her husband was asking her to attempt. 'I love thee, Angus,' she vowed, as the earth rumbled again.

'Damn thee, Alma!' The tears rolled down his cheeks as he, too, realised that the jump would surely kill her. 'There must be a way. Thou must try.'

They'd just about reached the west tower, when Javotte stopped to approach one of the large windows that afforded a view of the courtyard. From here, she witnessed her parent's sad circumstance.

Her father was on his knees, his arms outstretched towards her mother, when the tiny piece of earth on which Alma sat crumbled into the abyss that separated them.

'Mother!' Javotte cried, smashing her fists against the window.

As the glass shattered, Ione grabbed Javotte around the waist and hauled her into the tower. Somehow, she managed to avoid the falling debris from above, for even the stone towers were starting to collapse. Ione set the girl on her feet and pushed her down through the trapdoor. 'Run!'

Ione closed the door behind them and scampered down the ladder after Javotte. The heavy stone from the tower walls crashed down onto the trapdoor overhead, which threatened to collapse on top of them at any moment. As Ione's feet hit the ground she dived for the entrance of the tunnel that led to the beach, taking Javotte with her. The wooden floor above finally gave way and a mound of rubble showered down to block their place of entry.

Ione rose, brushing the dust from her face. 'Well, we art not getting out that way.' She turned her sights to the darkened cavern on her other side.

Javotte raised herself to a seated position, and then burst into tears.

Lady Alma had been a close friend of Ione's for many years and she would grieve her loss, but this was neither the time, nor place, to lament. The tremors were intensifying. Ione dragged Javotte to her feet. 'Cry on thy own time, soldier.' She thrust Javotte off in the right direction.

Yet the girl stopped abruptly, still stricken with grief. 'Thou hast no heart,' she sobbed.

'And thou hast no sense.' Ione grabbed her by the wrist and took off down the tunnel, dragging her reluctant student along behind her.

Although Maelgwn had never gone so far as to learn how to teleport his physical body from one place to another (although he had mastered the art with his etheric form), between Tory and Taliesin they managed to transfer all three of them to Aberffraw without too much delay.

The storm and tremors had passed by the time they materialised on the beach facing the house. Only now, there was no house; every last one of its foundations had been engulfed by the earth.

'This be Mahaud's work alright!' Maelgwn's rage and hatred consumed him; this house had belonged to his family for hundreds of years.

That explains what happened to the mythical city of Aberffraw, Tory concluded with regret. Back home, in the twentieth century, they were still trying to decide whether or not it had ever existed, and looking at the demolition job the witch had done on the place it wasn't hard to see why.

'Why did we not foresee this?' The High King directed his query at Taliesin, but didn't wait for an answer. He'd caught sight of Ione running up the beach toward them and strode down to meet her halfway.

'Majesty, praise the Goddess thou art here.' Ione reached him puffing and panting from her lengthy sprint across the sand. Javotte was not far behind her.

'What happened, Ione?'

'The house starting shaking, Majesty, and the sky turned blood red.' She paused for a breath. 'Fire shot like lightning from the —'

'Did thee see any Saxon troops?'

Ione's eyes opened wide as she realised she had no idea who their foe had been. 'Nay, Majesty, nor any other.' She hung her head in shame.

'Well, with all hell breaking loose I suppose it was a bit difficult to assess the enemy.'

Sir Angus came up to them, and the king calmed himself as he witnessed Javotte collapse into her father's arms, both of them in tears. 'How many have been injured, Ione?'

Ione looked to Angus and Javotte. 'Alma wast killed. How many others I do not know.'

'I see.' Maelgwn withheld his emotions.

'Will thou excuse me, Highness? I wish to seek out Tiernan's whereabouts.'

'Of course.' The king prayed his champion had not perished in the disaster. 'Send him to see me when thou hast found him,' he called after her.

Maelgwn walked back to Tory; she was so mortified by the sight of the void that had once been their home that she still hadn't moved from the spot where they'd first materialised. He approached his wife from behind, wrapping his arms about her shoulders. 'I promise not to take it badly if thee will, too.'

'Oh, Maelgwn.' She breathed a heavy sigh. 'Every memory of home I had wast in that house.' All, except one pair of jeans, her old steel-capped boots and a T-shirt that were in her luggage at Arwystli. One of her three saxophones had also been saved, as it had made the trip to the council meeting with her.

'It could have been worse.' The king accepted the loss. 'We nearly left Rhun here.'

Despite her tears, Tory let out half a laugh as she turned and kissed him. He was right; she still had her son and her husband. Anything else, she could bear.

'Majesty, thou asked to see me?' Maelgwn turned to see Tiernan's beaming face.

'Thou art safe.' Maelgwn took hold of his champion by both shoulders.

'Of course I am.' He shrugged off the experience light-heartedly, before his manner became more serious. 'Believe it or not our casualties art fewer than one would expect.'

'But?' The king released him; Tiernan always told him the good news before he delivered the sting.

'I have been unable to locate either Sir Rhys or Jenovefa. Their wing was the first to go, Majesty. I sincerely hope I am wrong . . .'

The king placed a hand on Tiernan's shoulder and patted it, though his eyes looked to the ocean. 'I hope so, too.'

Late on the second night of their imprisonment, Rhun and Bryce were honoured by a visit from Aella. She entered and ascended the stairs of the tower so quietly that neither of the men were aware of her presence. It was only the light of her candle that gave her away.

'Aella.' Bryce stood and bowed, feeling himself go weak in the knees, but it was Rhun that approached to speak with her.

'My lady, what art thou doing here?'

'Shh,' she whispered. 'We have no time to waste. Follow me.'

After checking that the corridor was devoid of life, she led the pair out of the tower and escorted them into Ossa's library across the hall.

Rhun was turning circles at the enormous expanse of literature. 'Just imprison me here for the next twenty years.'

Bryce was hot on Aella's heels; he didn't care if she was leading them to death's door, he was happy to follow her anywhere. She approached the back wall of the huge room and called to Rhun, who'd stopped in front of a book lying open on a bench. 'Please, we must hurry.'

Aella pushed one of the thousands of knots that ran down both sides of the large bookcase, which rotated to reveal a passageway.

'What a woman,' Bryce commented as Rhun caught them up. 'Ask her why the tower wast unguarded.'

Rhun did this and she explained as they descended the long, stone staircase.

'I gave them leave to go up to the roof to witness my father's homecoming. My brother hast gone to meet him at the gates of the city, which be the cause of our haste . . . ye must leave before he arrives.'

Rhun conveyed her response to his friend.

'Art thou aware of what his mission hast been?' Bryce pulled her to a stop when they reached the bottom, and Rhun again translated for her.

'Just a few silly rumours, really.' She seemed to shy away from the question.

'If these tales have been of an evil, all-powerful witch, they art not false. Her name be Mahaud and she be travelling with thy father as we speak. Hence thou art in grave danger, lady.' He nodded to Rhun to tell her.

'Please, sir,' she urged Rhun. 'Tell thy friend that his safety be a far greater concern at present. We must keep moving.' She strode off ahead before Rhun could relay the message.

When they emerged from the tunnel into the open air, the moon shed its light over a large expanse of land; Aella had obviously led them all the way to the Common. Their horses grazed before them and were suited up and ready to ride.

'Excellent.'

Rhun mounted his steed, but Bryce was not prepared to leave the maiden to Mahaud's discretion.

'Come with us,' Bryce pleaded. 'Rhun, tell her it be not safe for her to stay here now.'

'Bryce, we cannot take her. Ossa shall think we have abducted her.'

'And what shall he do when he discovers she hast let us go? Please tell her.' Rhun was growing impatient, but gave in to his friend's wish so they might depart before sunrise. 'Lady, Bryce asks that thou come with us.'

'Nay, I could not!' She looked to Bryce, thankful for his concern. 'If this witch be as evil as ye say, I must stay and try to prevent any harm befalling my family.'

Rhun rubbed his forehead. 'Thou doth not understand. If thy kin have come into contact with the crone already, there will be nothing thou can do to save them. Mahaud changes people, so much so that thine own father would betray thee before he crosses her. At least if my lady comes with us, the Goddess may be able to offer thee some protection.'

Aella shook her head. 'Again, many thanks for thy warning, sir . . .' She raised herself on her toes and kissed Bryce on his cheek, 'but my place be here.' She darted back into the darkened tunnel and was gone.

'Bryce,' Rhun cautioned him in regard to going after her. 'We have her answer, now let us make ourselves absent.' He dug his heels in and took off across the field.

Bryce was torn only a second. Then he was on his horse and in hot pursuit of Rhun; his first duty was always to the Goddess.

A few hours later Ossa and his party entered his room of court, weary from their travels, yet exalted by their victory. A feast had been prepared in advance and only the warlord's two sons and Vanora were permitted to stay.

Eormenric was relieved to find his health and appetite restored, for Vanora had excused the icy presence that shielded their party as soon as they'd cleared allied Britain.

Demons disperse into the air
and spread thy dis-ease elsewhere.
Converge upon the Dragon and his kin,
and lead them into darkest sin.

This simple verse had seemed to work and, he wondered, as he watched Vanora across the table, if there was a rhyme that would release her from her bewitchment as easily.

She raised her dark sights to glare at him and he feared for a moment that she would voice his mind to his father, but she did not.

'So where be Mahaud?' Ossa raised his glass to Vanora. 'I wish to thank her for the wondrous spectacle we have witnessed.'

'I am right here, Warlord.'

Ossa turned in his seat to find a hooded figure that had yet to assume a full physical form. She floated just above the ground behind him, the bottom of her robe tapering off into nothingness. The crone's eyes glowed red within the dark hood, yet her face was well shadowed and could not be seen.

'Thou hast served us well, Mahaud.'

She laughed. 'That! . . . 'Twas nothing. The fun hast only just begun.'

'Thou speaks as if thou hast already a scheme in mind . . . do share,' he urged.

'Next shall be a simultaneous attack on Powys and Gwynedd that we shall not even have to leave Londinium to execute.' She suddenly became distracted by something far more interesting. 'King Brockwell's eldest son and the son of the Dragon have been in this room just recently.'

All eyes looked to Ongen, who near choked on his mead at the news. 'The council of the Goddess did send two messengers, who claimed they were here to offer us support.'

'Support!' As outrageous as it sounded, after meeting some of the Britons Eormenric didn't entirely doubt the possibility.

'Aye,' Ongen laughed. 'They maintained they wished to supply us with enough food to survive the cold seasons.'

Ossa burst into laughter.

If the Goddess and her kin were responsible for the sad state of our lands, why then offer us assistance? Eormenric wondered.

'A trick,' Mahaud explained to him, causing Eormenric to shrink in his seat. 'Where art they now?' The crone turned her evil eyes to Ongen.

'I had them locked in the tower, of course.'

'Good.' There was a smile in her voice. 'Bring them before me at once.'

They'd reached the outskirts of the city when Rhun, who often went into a trance state when he rode, brought his horse to a stop.

'What be wrong?' Bryce pulled up alongside him.

'Damn it!' Rhun hesitated. For although he felt obliged to inform his friend of what he'd foreseen, it went against his better judgement. 'Mahaud hast informed Ossa and his sons of our true identity. Thus, when they find us missing, it shall not take the witch very long to disclose who it was that aided our escape.'

'I must help her.' Bryce begged Rhun's leave.

'And I must return to Gwynedd.' Rhun let Bryce know that he would be on his own. 'For I believe there be evil afoot and I must help defend against it, if I can.'

'I understand. I shan't be far behind thee.'

'I wish thee luck then.' Rhun clasped hold of his friend's hand. 'May the Goddess guide and protect thee, Bryce.'

'And thee.' Bryce slapped his shoulder. 'Till next we meet.'

The two parted company to go their separate ways — one to face the witch and the other her wrath.

Upon discovery of the prince's escape, Ongen had his sister dragged before their father for questioning at Mahaud's request. The girl had no need to confess the part she'd played in the affair, for Mahaud confirmed her deceit as soon as she laid eyes on her.

'Kill her, Warlord. She be the one who hast betrayed us,' the witch announced with confidence.

'Father, have mercy,' Aella sobbed, terrified of the foul-smelling apparition that was advising her father. 'I wast not to know who they were. The Britons planned to attack us if their messengers did not return. I believed I wast sparing us from a war.'

Ossa was considering her plea until the crone crushed it. 'She lies. She holds feelings for the son of Brockwell. This be why she set him free and for no other reason.'

'Aye, Father,' Ongen confirmed. 'This gash on my face wast incurred when one of the Britons came to Aella's defense.'

Ossa was outraged by the news; no daughter of his would give her heart to one of his enemy. 'This be treason, girl! How could thou betray me in such a fashion?'

'Thou art the one who hast betrayed thy people.' Aella knew her fate was sealed; thus she found the courage to speak her mind. 'We could have had peace and plenty, but now thee and thy witch shall plunge us into war.'

'Silence!' Ossa roared. 'Thy every utterance tightens the noose around thy neck.'

'Hanging be too good for her, Warlord,' Mahaud commented. 'What I have in mind shall be far more befitting, and shall help our cause at the same time.'

Eormenric could hardly believe his ears. Aella had always been his father's pride and joy — nothing was too good for her. Yet now, he was considering handing her over to this foul beast to do with as she saw fit.

'Hold on one moment.' Eormenric could not keep silent. 'She be but a child, Father . . . and if Brockwell's son be as charming as his father wast said to be, be it not likely he hast just drawn her in to suit his own purposes?'

Ossa looked to Mahaud for her opinion. 'Nay, she betrayed thee of her own free will, as I believe her defender will, given time.'

Ossa looked to Eormenric. 'Be this true?'

'Nay, Father, I would never betray thee. But, the witch I do not trust and she knows it. Already she would have thee kill one who loves thee dearly.' Eormenric motioned to his sister. 'Doth thou plan to do away with us all thus?' he put to the witch.

'It was not I who released the hostages, Eormenric.' Mahaud was not too worried about the boy; he fancied Vanora, and could be seduced. But this girl, Aella, had the purest of souls. It would be easier to do away with her than to waste the time it would take to break her spirit. 'I have, however, done all I said I would do for thee. What further proof of my loyalty dost thou need?'

Eormenric hung his head; no matter what he said, the witch would have a comeback.

As his son had seemingly given up on Aella's defense, Ossa's stern sights returned to her. 'Dost thou have anything else to say for thyself, before I have thee taken to the tower?'

Aella looked to her father, unable to believe how callous he'd become. The Britons had been right about the crone; she should have listened to them. 'I love thee, Father,' she sobbed as his guards took hold of her. 'And if thou cannot see that, then I can only hope that the Goddess will prevail and bring thee to thy senses.'

Ossa stood, outraged by the very mention of that name. 'Get her out of my sight!'

Ossa turned to the crone beside him as Aella was led from the room, his eyes ablaze with fury. 'Make them pay for this . . . make them pay dearly.'

'Aye, my lord, that I shall.'

After salvaging the little they could from the remains at Aberffraw and relocating the local villagers to other estates within the kingdom, the High King, his Queen, Taliesin and their chief advisers made for Degannwy on the mainland.

Sadly, the Goddess had lost two members of her circle in the disaster, Sir Rhys and Lady Alma, and she needed to replace them as quickly as possible. The position of financial adviser to the king would be offered to Gawain, Rhys' son, who'd been groomed by his father to succeed him in office. Lady Alma's position as trainer to the children of the kingdom would be filled by her daughter, Javotte, if she proved herself worthy to become one of the 'circle of twelve'.

King Maelgwn had been coping quite well with the disaster, but an unexpected gift was about to turn his whole world upside down . . .

In the evening after everyone had eaten, they lay about the dining room at Degannwy engrossed in conversation, games, music and the like. Maelgwn had been left to his own thoughts, as Tory was across the room discussing metaphysical matters with Taliesin. It was then that a young maiden of the house approached the king.

'Majesty.' She bowed and crouched beside him so that none might notice her.

'Can I help thee, child?' He smiled; my, but she was a pretty little thing.

'I know thou hast lost much in these past few days, Highness, thus I brought thee a gift.' She held out her offering, wrapped up in silk of deepest red.

'Well, now . . .' He thought her sentiment rather sweet and so humoured her. 'What could it be?'

As Maelgwn accepted the present the atmosphere surrounding him became icy cold, so much so that it sent chills down his spine. 'Be there a draught in here?' he commented, looking around for the source.

'Nay, Majesty,' she replied, wide-eyed with anticipation.

He shrugged off the observation and unfolded the silken material to disclose what he thought was a mirror, till he discovered he could see straight through it.

'It be a looking-glass, Majesty,' she said, with excitement. 'But it be very special . . . for it shall allow thee to see things most other people cannot.'

Maelgwn held up the large, golden-framed piece of glass, and at first glance all appeared as normal. 'What kind of things?' He looked down to question her further, but the girl had vanished.

Strange. The king shrugged; perhaps he'd frightened her. He raised the looking-glass again and viewed the room from end to end, finally noting something was indeed amiss.

Across the room he viewed his wife, but she looked no older than the day he'd married her. Now this came as no great shock to Maelgwn; he'd known for some time that Taliesin had given her an immortality potion which saved her life at the battle of Arwystli. Beside her sat the Merlin, who the king had always perceived to look as old as time itself. Yet the man he viewed through the looking-glass, holding hands and consoling his beloved so intimately, appeared not much older than Rhun and just as handsome.

Be this how Tory sees him? The voice of jealousy niggled away at his peace of mind. Surely in twenty years of marriage she would have mentioned it? Tory had sworn to him when he found out about her immortality that they'd keep no more secrets from each other.

But she might have figured that I would never have permitted Taliesin to train her, if I had known he appeared thus to her, Maelgwn reasoned, angering himself further. Please Goddess, do not let it be so.

Taliesin had served his family for generations, yet, strangely enough, the notion that the Merlin was an immortal had never really occurred to Maelgwn. Perhaps it was the old age that had thrown him, as an immortal was usually construed as ever-young.

So why, when the Merlin had been saving this immortality potion for eons, did he suddenly decide to spare Tory's life with it?

At the time, Maelgwn had needed a miracle to save his love. When that miracle came about, he'd not questioned the why and wherefore. Now that he considered that Taliesin may have had ulterior motives for saving the Queen, a hidden agenda of a personal nature, Maelgwn's heart grew heavy with suspicion and loathing.

Bryce re-entered Ossa's fortification in Londinium the same way he'd left it. The long passageway was pitch dark and rather slippery, so he was forced to proceed slowly.

When he finally reached the top of the stone staircase, he realised he had no idea how to open the trapdoor from this side. He fumbled around the wall in the darkness and came across a lever.

As it was mid-afternoon, not the best time to execute a rescue, Bryce took a seat on the floor to rest and await a more suitable hour. He knew Mahaud was in the same building and, in the hope of shielding himself from her perception, he imagined himself surrounded by white light. His sensei had said this once assisted her to trick the crone when they'd banished her from the earth plane all that time ago.

In the dark silence, time did seem an illusion. He drifted in and out of sleep with no concept of how long he'd been there, though his stomach indicated it had been quite a while.

He raised himself and again found the lever, which he only lowered far enough to peek inside the library. As the room appeared free of inhabitants, he slipped through the opening and crept across the room. He came to a standstill at the door that led to the corridor and, opening it to a crack, he spied two guards at the post outside the tower.

If they have a guard on the tower and we art no longer in it, who art they guarding now? he wondered. One way to find out. He closed the door quietly then knocked on it a couple of times.

One of the guards moved from his post to investigate, and as he entered the room the door slammed closed behind him.

All was silent a few moments before the knocking was repeated.

The second guard drew his sword and approached the door, swinging it wide open in front of him. As he saw no one, including his comrade, he entered. The soldier slowly turned a full circle, spying a shadow of someone concealed behind the door. He quietly edged round and thrust his sword into the trickster. The door swung closed as the wounded man collapsed in a heap on the floor. To the guard's great dismay, it was his partner who lay dying before him.

'Huh?' The soldier moved to turn, aware of a presence behind him. He was not fast enough, however, and joined his comrade on the floor.

Bryce took the key to the tower and a sword before checking that the corridor was deserted.

In the tower's prison cell he found Aella huddled in the middle of the room, her head in her hands as she wept.

She believed it was her father's soldiers coming to lead her to the crone and her demise, but as she raised her tear-stained face she discovered it was the British prince who stood before her.

'Thou came back for me?'

Bryce held out his hand and helped her to her feet, whereby she fell sobbing in his arms. 'Shh.' He comforted her in a universal language. When she calmed a little, Bryce motioned her to the exit.

Aella wiped her face, nodded, and smiled . . . . 'I shan't argue this time.'

6

HISTORY'S REPRISE

The High King had Taliesin summoned to his room of court. It was not unusual for Maelgwn to work straight through till morning, as sleep had never come easily to him. As the Merlin approached the court room, he noted four guards posted outside the door, which was a rather curious thing.

There had been a time, not too far gone, when Taliesin knew of every decision quite some time before it was made manifest. Yet, as the course of British history changed for the better, the future was becoming harder to predict. Take this imbalance in their homeland, for example. Taliesin couldn't believe he'd failed to foresee it, or to guess Mahaud's involvement. He now recognised the crone as a karmic force coming round to kick him in the butt.

Tory had been absolutely correct to want to aid the Saxons and befriend them, only this resolution had come about ten years too late. How foolish he was to have thought he could concentrate so much positive energy on just one half of the country and not upset the balance. For, although bringing Tory back to the Dark Age to guide and train the native Britons had served him well, turning a blind eye to the foreigners had allowed Mahaud all the space she needed to manifest herself again. He considered Mahaud to be history's slap on the wrist for his attempt to cheat it.

The guards opened the doors for the Merlin, then left him alone in the room with the High King.

Maelgwn stood at the far end of the long table of court with his back to Taliesin, his hand resting upon one of the two dragons that were carved into the high back of his chair.

The Merlin noted how distressed his king appeared as he turned to face him. 'Hast something happened that I am not aware of? What ails thee so?'

'Oh, thou art aware of it alright.' Maelgwn would have laughed at the query, had he not been so irate. He looked away from the old man and took a deep breath to contain his brewing hatred.

Maelgwn's feeling of betrayal radiated across the room in waves, and the Merlin noted the looking-glass stuck through his king's belt. When perceived clairvoyantly, the piece was shrouded in dark shadow.

'I would ask thee, High Merlin, to assume the same form thou dost take with my wife.' The king's dark eyes returned to Taliesin to catch his reaction.

'Who gave thee the looking-glass, Majesty?'

'Never mind who gave it to me. Just do as I bid thee.'

With little choice, the Merlin bowed his head and complied.

The years began to fall away from him, until a man near half the king's age stood before him. 'Why, Taliesin?' Maelgwn shivered from the cold and agony that gripped his heart. 'Why have ye deceived me so?'

'Tory had nothing to do with it.' The Merlin noted the *ye* in the king's accusation and wanted to clear that misunderstanding up straight away. 'I chose for her to see my true form from the day we met, so she hast never seen me any different.'

This was not entirely true, for although he and Tory had met at various times in history after he'd obtained immortality, Taliesin had also known her in most of the incarnations he'd had before this.

'But she never saw fit to mention it, either!' Maelgwn's jaw was clenched. 'It hast been thy little secret all this time.'

The Merlin's brow became drawn. 'I chose for thee to see me as old, because I wanted to avoid thy father's jealous streak, which thou hast quite obviously inherited.'

'Do not lie to me anymore!' Maelgwn thumped the table with both fists and began to pace. 'Dost thou think I have not worked it out!'

'Sorry?' Taliesin was concerned. 'Exactly what twisted, dark scenario hast Mahaud implanted in thy mind, Maelgwn?'

Maelgwn stopped his pacing and slowly shook his head, unable to fathom why he'd ever believed a single word that left this man's mouth. 'I defy thee to deny thy love for Tory!'

'I love all I serve.' Taliesin remained calm.

'But it was not everyone that thou decided to give everlasting life to, Merlin. Why did thou choose my wife?'

Now even Taliesin was battling to stay civil. *It be the work of the crone that compels him. Do not allow her any pleasure. For how could he snap the king out of his bewitchment, if he didn't stay in control himself. If things turn ugly, I know what must be done.* 'Tory saved my life once. I was just repaying the favour . . . the potion wast the only means I had. If I could have spared her without cheating her of part of her spiritual evolution, I would have done so.'

'When did this take place, exactly?' Maelgwn sounded sceptical. 'That she saved thy life.'

'It wast in a past incarnation of mine, Majesty, long before I wast reborn of the Goddess Keridwen.' Taliesin tried not to sound as hesitant as he felt in broaching the subject and prayed that Maelgwn took it no further. The Merlin didn't want to lie to his patron, yet the truth would surely condemn them all.

He was hiding something more, the king could sense it. 'Alright then . . .' he challenged. 'Assume the form thou held at that time.'

'I am not sure if I . . .'

'Be that so?' Maelgwn pulled the looking-glass from his belt to view the Merlin through it.

Once again, the man before him began to change form. His fair skin, silvery hair and violet eyes darkened. His skin took on a reddish tinge; his hair and eyes turned as black as night. His tall, slender body shortened, and muscles erupted across every inch of the warrior's stocky form.

The king didn't even have to wait for the image to fully transform to realise it was Teo; they'd met during Maelgwn's brief visit to the twentieth century some twenty years ago. This half-caste native American had been Tory's sensei for many years and, as far as the king knew, Teo was the only other man Tory had ever taken to her bed.

'Damn thee.' Maelgwn shook as he lowered the mirror, his worst and only fear realised. 'Damn ye both!'

'Maelgwn, it be not as Mahaud would have thee believe . . .'

'Mahaud! Huh!' Maelgwn backed away from the magician, incensed by his discovery. 'All the forces of the underworld could not defile me as thou hast. How could thou bestow such a beauteous favour upon me . . . when thy true intention wast to covet her at every given opportunity?'

'In the name of the Goddess, Maelgwn.' Taliesin was losing his patience. All he'd ever wanted was the king's greatest happiness and that which was best for Britain. 'If that wast truly the way of it, why would I have bothered at all?'

'Because thou needed Tory to lead Britain, thus thou had to marry her to one of royal blood.' The king stormed from one side of the room to the other, as a complete scenario took form in his mind. 'It did not matter who thou chose — he would die eventually — and as thou art both immortal now, the time before thee could have her to thyself would be relatively short. Aye, now I see it!'

Taliesin shook his head. The destruction of everything they'd worked so hard to achieve was staring him in the face, and it had taken Mahaud all of a week to achieve it. 'Please, Maelgwn . . . deep in thy heart thou must know I could never do what thou art suggesting. And if not I, surely thou must realise Tory would never betray thy wedding vow . . . she loves thee beyond life.'

The king returned to his chair and took a seat. 'And how easy that must be to say, when she hast no fear of losing it.'

Taliesin was at a loss, the king must see reason. 'There will be no advising thee, Maelgwn, if thou dost not listen to me now. Dost thou not see the witch at work here, twisting the truth for her own end?'

Maelgwn thought a moment. 'Aye, that I do.' He leant back in his seat. 'Thus it is that I banish thee from this kingdom, Taliesin . . . and all those lands within the alliance.'

'Be reasonable, think about . . .'

'And if thou ever . . .' Maelgwn stood, spurred forth by his hatred, 'ever, go so far as to even think of my wife again, I shall seek out the services of Mahaud myself, to wipe thee from existence.'

The darkness Taliesin perceived, surrounding the looking-glass, suddenly exploded to envelope the king and its force was so overwhelming that even Taliesin could not avoid it. The Merlin hadn't felt such undiluted evil since his days as Gwion Bach, his former self, before Keridwen transformed him. A sense of deep unrest rushed through his being, for he realised all his years of careful planning had amounted to naught. As his anger built, his form rose into the air, expanding as it decreased in density. Taliesin wailed like a man possessed, and his voice was like thunder to the king's ears:

'This vengeance shall be the end
    of all that we have built.
And if common sense shall allow it,
    then heed this warning.
If thou dost persist in banishing me,
    the Otherworld shall damn thee,
    Maelgwn Gwynedd.'

When the Merlin had vanished, he left Maelgwn maddened and confused. The king knew Taliesin had never uttered truer words than those of his prophecy, for this incident would be their undoing.

Their escape had been almost too easy for Bryce's liking, yet after riding through the night he'd seen no sign of anyone pursuing them.

The sun rose over the wide, open plains and stole away their cover. They had half a day ahead in the saddle to reach the British border and Aella was falling asleep in Bryce's arms. If they rested, it would give the Saxons a chance to catch them up. Still, if they could hide out till nightfall, darkness would increase their chances of making it to the safety of his father's kingdom unseen. 'That will do nicely.' Bryce spied an abandoned property, and headed them off towards it.

There were many such places here, in the no-man's land that separated Saxony from Britain. People from both races had tried to claim the land to farm it, only to be driven out by the opposition. The farmhouse on this property was in a crumbled state of disrepair, but the large barn still appeared to be quite structurally sound. Bryce climbed from his mount, helping Aella down after him, and drew his sword before leading her and his horse inside.

A few birds had made a home in the rafters, but apart from that the place appeared devoid of life.

'We can rest here awhile,' Bryce told her, placing his two hands together at one side of his face and closing his eyes. 'Sleep?'

Aella smiled and nodded her understanding, wishing she spoke just a little of his tongue. *Thou hast risked thy life for me twice now, I have never known a man like thee.* She watched Bryce get himself comfortable against a pile of straw, then walked over to where he lay and sat herself down. The prince didn't stir or open his eyes. Aella hesitated but a moment, before timidly lowering her head to rest on his chest, hoping he would not think her common for wanting to be so close to him. After a moment, his arm moved around her back to cradle her. Aella felt safe here and closed her eyes to sleep, lulled by the sound of his heartbeat.

'Aella.'

She woke to the sound of her name whispered, and was startled when Eormenric went flying over the top of her. Bryce had taken hold of him with his free hand and now had her brother pinned to the ground with a blade at his throat.

'Aella, tell him I come in peace,' Eormenric called to her desperately.

Aella was on her feet now, and in a fluster. 'I do not speak his tongue.'

Bryce raised Eormenric to his feet and thrust him hard against the wall.

'Aella?' Eormenric groaned. 'Do something!'

She paced, perplexed by her brother's sudden appearance. 'What art thou doing here? How do I know I should trust thee? This could be one of the witch's tricks. Thou hast been close to her.'

'Please, Aella,' Eormenric managed to squeeze out as Bryce's elbow pressed hard against his throat, the prince's blade gleaming before his eyes. 'If I wast coming to fetch thee back, why would I be alone and unarmed?'

Aella strode to the barn door to validate what he said. Only his horse grazed outside and there didn't appear to be another living soul for miles around. She returned to where the men were poised, awaiting her word, and stared at Eormenric sternly. *He did try to defend me against the crone, I suppose.*

'My lord.' She resolved to give her brother the benefit of the doubt, placing a hand on Bryce's shoulder. Bryce eased off, allowing her to take the blade from his hand.

The warrior prince took a few paces back and Eormenric slid down the wall, relieved.

'Now explain thyself, before I have him run thee through,' Aella ordered. From now on, she would trust none bar her protector.

As Eormenric raised himself, Bryce took hold of Aella gently and urged her closer to him.

'I am not here to harm thee,' Eormenric emphasised. 'When I spied the two of thee escaping, I wast glad! I told no one. I followed thee because I thought thy friend may know of a way I might dispel the witch from our midst, and release Vanora from her domination.'

'I see.' Aella wasn't sure whether to believe him, or how she would convey his explanation to her guardian. She turned to Bryce who was still observing the intruder very closely. 'Eormenric,' she pointed to her brother, 'wishes to kill . . .' She passed the blade in her hand by her throat, 'Mahaud.'

Bryce looked to Eormenric surprised, and Aella smiled; he understood.

The prince strode forward and gripped hold of Eormenric's head, staring deep into his eyes a moment.

'What be he doing?' Eormenric stared back at him, a little wary of the warrior's great strength and forthright manner.

Aella found this rather curious, too. 'I am not sure . . . perhaps he be trying to work out if thou art telling the truth, so try not to resist.'

'How can he tell that by looking at me?'

Aella smiled, observing the prince's focus. 'Who knows . . . he be a wondrous soul.'

Finally, Bryce let him go and smiled with a nod to verify her brother's claim.

'It would seem he believes thee.' She still sounded sceptical.

Eormenric looked to the Briton, who stood staring at him with his hands outstretched as he focused once again. 'What be he doing now?'

Aella shook her head and shrugged, enchanted by his ways. 'I wish I knew.'

Bryce imagined the white shield of light, already surrounding Aella and himself, expanding to encompass Eormenric as well.

Though he couldn't perceive the man's intent, Eormenric was suddenly swept by a feeling of calm and strength. He'd feared for his life for so many days now, yet suddenly he was not afraid anymore.

Tory awoke with a start, and a strong feeling of foreboding.

'Tory.' Taliesin sought her attention, and her head shot up to view him. 'You must come with me at once. Our work here has been brought an end.'

'What?' Tory was immediately angered. She did hate it when the Merlin didn't bother to clarify himself. 'Would you mind ex —'

'Maelgwn has accepted a gift from Mahaud, and she has gained control of him. He knows of how I appear to thee, and has discovered I was once Teo. Needless to say, I have been banished . . . and you are next,' Taliesin informed her, without so much as a compassionate pause. 'Make haste before he sends a guard for thee.'

'But if I leave with thee, Maelgwn will surely presume we have run off together.'

'Never mind what he will think! Mahaud has hold of him now; hence he is bound to think the worst no matter what happens.'

'I will not leave him and those in our service to Mahaud. Taliesin, please tell me thou art not really planning to forsake Britain like this?'

'This period of history is beyond even my help; the human race is already too twisted and confused. Twice now I have attempted to cleanse the world, using the sixth century as my base in time, and both times I have failed miserably. I believe I must go back further if I expect to have any success.'

Tory pulled on a wrap and climbed out of bed. 'But, I have already seen the future we've created, and it was far more wonderful than the twentieth century reality from which I stemmed originally.'

'You're referring to a reality that we fostered twenty years ago, Tory. But following what has taken place this night, you would find the state of the twentieth century just as reprehensible, if not worse, than the one you first left.' His voice expressed his deep regret. 'Thus I plan to take myself elsewhere and see what I can do about it. Are you coming?'

Tory could hardly speak. She didn't want Taliesin to leave without her; she would surely lose track of him within the complexity of the time–space continuum, and without him she had no vehicle to travel backwards or forwards in time. She'd only just mastered the art of physical teleportation. Time travel was quite a different matter. One needed knowledge of the earth's natural energy fields and the cycles of the stars — things Tory knew very little about.

'You know I would love to, Taliesin, but I cannot,' she resolved. 'I love him.'

'But if you stay, you will be condemned by him, then where will you be?'

All the same, Tory would not sway from her decision. 'Shall I never see you again?' The thought filled her eyes with tears.

'Not whilst Maelgwn Gwynedd still lives and breathes on this earth,' he stated, making his aversion to Maelgwn plain. 'And thou can tell him I have foreseen his end:

It was drawn from four winds
and travels great distances in silence.
It was created from
the darkness of the moon,
the stillness of the air,
the rotting depths of the earth,
the thirst of great drought.
Readied from the worst
in all living things,

*Its wrath will descend upon
Maelgwn Gwynedd!*'

'Taliesin, wait!' Tory moved to grab hold of him, but the Merlin had gone. 'What do you mean?' she mumbled, as her knees gave way and she collapsed to the floor. 'Damn you, Taliesin, come back. You got me into this, you can't just leave me here alone now . . .'

After sobbing uncontrollably for some time, her thoughts turned to how she was going to deal with her unfortunate circumstances.

I'd best dress and ready myself. She could not face the crone in this sorry state.

When Sir Tiernan, accompanied by a half dozen soldiers, came for the Queen, the knight instructed the guard to wait outside and entered the Queen's chamber alone.

He wasn't really surprised to find her fully dressed and awaiting him, yet she was not wearing her queenly attire.

Tory was dressed as she was the day she walked into Maelgwn's life. Only now she wore a different jacket over her T-shirt and jeans; she'd given King Brockwell the original leather jacket she arrived in.

'My Queen.' Tiernan came forward reluctantly, fighting back the tears as he executed his chore. 'I am required to ask thee to — '

'I know . . .' Tory whispered away the knight's rather difficult predicament.

'I am sorry, sensei,' he assured her, knowing that now she was well aware of her fate. 'I do not believe a word of it. Hast the king lost his mind!' He fell on his knees before her. 'What shall become of us once thou hast gone? Please, Goddess, tell me what I must do.'

'Dear Sir Tiernan. I do promise thee that I am not going anywhere. Dost thou think that even banishment could keep me away?'

He looked up to her, more hopeful.

'I can take care of myself, have no doubt of that.' She motioned him to rise and approach, and grasped him firmly by both shoulders. 'Do as thy king hast bid, and speak no more of treason against him.' As Tiernan opened his mouth to contradict her, she added firmly, 'It not be Maelgwn thou art reasoning with at present, but Mahaud. We must play along with her until I can figure a way to expel her from our king.'

Tiernan was most relieved by her explanation; leading an uprising against his king was the last thing in the world he wanted to do, but he would have done so to spare the Queen from this needless ridicule.

'Thou must stay and watch my love, Tiernan . . . surround thyself with white light and be alert. The crone cannot affect thee unless thou dost give in to her anger, hatred, greed and so on. Thy state of mind upon entering this room shows how easily she can cause conflict and dis-ease.'

Tiernan held his head. He felt ashamed in retrospect.

'Do not feel bad. I fear even Taliesin hast been taken in by her cunning. But we shall not. Feel only love and the purest of thoughts, and she cannot mislead thee.'

'I understand, sensei . . . and I shall not fail thee in this.'

'I know.' She smiled and embraced him tightly. 'Thou art a true champion, my friend.'

Besides the clothes on her back and a saxophone, Tory hadn't a possession left to her name. Still, she considered that she was leaving this place a far richer person. She had no plan, just a gut feeling that said she needed to make herself distant from this house. The crone's madness seemed to be spreading itself rapidly across Gwynedd; she must escape Mahaud's reaches if she was to have any chance of outsmarting her.

After one last look around their chamber, Tory calmly and voluntarily accompanied Sir Tiernan to the room of court to face sentencing.

Rhun rode into the courtyard at Degannwy and was met by Sir Angus and Javotte.

'Praise the Goddess.' Angus was beside himself with grief.

'Sir Angus. Javotte.' Rhun dismounted with haste. 'I heard what happened to Lady Alma. I am so sorry.'

'I thank thee, Highness.' Angus struggled to keep his wits about him. 'But another tragedy be about to befall us, if thou dost not make for thy father's room of court at once.'

'The king be banishing thy mother.' Javotte told Rhun as much as was needed to send him racing off through the fort to the aid of his parents.

'Stop!' Rhun slammed open the doors of court and stormed through the gathering, determined to get to the bottom of this outrage. 'What be the meaning of this?' He looked to his father for an explanation, to find none was needed; he at once noted the dark presence that overshadowed Maelgwn. *Nay please, not my father!*

I am afraid so. Tory bethought her son without looking to him. Do not mention to Maelgwn what thou hast seen. It would be better if the dark forces remain ignorant as to the full extent of thy expertise.

'Thy mother hast been proven guilty of treason,' Maelgwn informed his son with regret. 'The details of her deceit, I would rather not discuss with thee in my present mood.'

'But Father . . .'

'But Father nothing! As I can neither contain her, nor execute her for her treachery, she hast been banished. From this moment forth, to speak or look upon her be punishable by death.'

Rhun's jaw clenched.

Calm thyself, his mother instructed. *Do not allow the crone any control over thee. But the common folk art going to interpret this as their king casting the Goddess from the land . . . there will be a rebellion for sure!*

I have already been through all this with him, it be no use, trust me.

After a deep breath, Rhun raised his eyes to view his father. 'I have an urgent message from King Brockwell . . . something frightful hast happened. Queen Katren, Prince Blain, Prince Owen and Prince Cai have all mysteriously vanished.'

'*What?*' Tory couldn't believe her ears, and the concerned faces of all in the room looked to her son.

'I expected thou would still be at Arwystli and so I went there first.' Rhun pretended to ignore his mother's plight, as ordered, which appeared to please his father no end. 'King Brockwell asked that I beg the High Merlin and the High Queen to go to Powys at once.'

Good lad. Tory silently congratulated her son for delivering his message so diplomatically.

'Well, as Britain no longer possesses a High Queen or a High Merlin . . .' Maelgwn's tone was so nonchalant, he near incited the whole room to a riot, 'it would seem the King of Powys shall have to deal with his family dilemmas on his own.'

Rhun heard King Catulus' representative whisper behind him. 'Be he refusing to aid an ally?'

This be madness, suicide! The young Prince of Gwynedd was again forced to calm himself before responding. 'Aye, Majesty, I suppose so.'

'Well, why art thou still here?' Maelgwn cast a cold look at Tory, who was desperately trying to refrain from bursting into tears. She knew there was no point in confronting Mahaud now, as tempting as it was. The witch would not have the last laugh, she would see to that personally.

'Be gone from my sight,' the king demanded, outraged.

'As be thy wish, Majesty.' She bowed her head. *Avoid thy father if thou can, Rhun . . . And if at all possible, meet me at Arwystli.'*

That I will. Tears welled in his eyes. Rhun couldn't bear to stand by and watch his mother shunned in such a fashion. Still, this was obviously not an easy task for any of those present. The prince thought Ione would explode at any moment, and probably would have, had her husband not been present to subdue her.

Do not be sad, the Goddess will prevail, I swear it. If thou hast need of me, at any time, thou hast only to call.

I always have need of thee. Rhun couldn't refrain any longer and turned to view her, but his mother had vanished. The prince looked to his father, trying as best he could not to despise him for his treatment of the Queen, when suddenly the room began to shake and Taliesin's voice thundered from above.

'Primary chief poet am I to Elffin.
And my native country is the place
of the Summer Stars.
John the Divine called me Merlin,
But all future kings shall call me Taliesin.'

Rhun found himself mouthing the words to the prophecy, for he recognised it. He'd come across this piece in one of his mother's books and had made a point of memorising it, for it was said Taliesin had made the address to his father.

'I am the instructor
Of the whole universe.
I shall be till judgement
On the face of the earth.
I continue to revolve
Between the elements.
There's not a marvel in the world
I cannot reveal . . .'

This was where the prophecy had ended in the book, and Rhun was rather alarmed to learn what followed.

Taliesin warned of a loathsome beast, with inflamed skin and glazed eyes that were a ghastly shade of yellow. 'This vile presence will come to haunt the Kingdom of Gwynned,' claimed the Merlin. 'It will spell doom for Maelgwn, High King of the Britons, and all those who still keep his company.'

The courtroom was thrown into an uproar upon the announcement.

The king stormed from the room, angered that the Merlin had cursed him.

'Wonderful!' Tadgh, the king's squire, commented as he passed Rhun in pursuit of his master. 'What was all that supposed to mean?'

'Trouble,' predicted Rhun.

7

THE GRIFFIN'S VOW

With the whole of her consciousness focused on King Brockwell, Tory soon found herself in the sitting room at Arwystli. The king was seated by the fire, unaware of her arrival, his fists clenched in front of his face as he bit at both his thumbnails.

'Calin?' she whispered, so as not to startle him.

Upon sighting her, Brockwell felt all the tension rush from his body. 'What took thee so long?' He raised himself to greet her.

She hugged him tightly for some time, feeling both of them needed the momentary comfort of the embrace. 'My deepest apologies.' Tory drew herself away to look him in the eyes. 'I wast busy being banished.'

'What?' He tightened the grip he had on her arms.

'Taliesin hast been banished also,' she informed him with regret, moving to take a seat by the fire. 'And he hast sworn that he shall not return whilst Maelgwn lives.' The Queen lowered herself onto the lounge and burst into tears.

'Tory . . .' Brockwell came to sit beside her, placing one arm around her shoulder to console her, his free hand resting upon her own. 'Tell me, what hast happened?'

'Mahaud,' Tory sniffled, endeavouring to regain some control. 'I have a few confessions to make.' She looked to Brockwell, a mite ashamed to admit so.

'As do I.'

He sounded as sorry as she did. Had Tory not been so emotionally distraught herself, she would have foreseen his sorry state of affairs. But as her mind was awhirl with a million other problems, she remained blissfully unaware.

Brockwell insisted Tory begin, as he was not yet ready to divulge his own situation. He poured the mead, listening intently whilst Tory conveyed all that had befallen since they'd parted company.

'But I swear to thee: since I married Maelgwn I have neither desired nor needed any other as a lover,' Tory appealed to him in conclusion. 'And certainly not Taliesin . . .'

'Nay, not he,' Brockwell agreed, appearing somewhat puzzled by her story.

'No, not anyone,' Tory said, wondering why he didn't seem to believe her. 'What? Dost thou think I am lying?'

'Nay, I believe thee. If thou wast going to take a lover, thee would naturally have chosen me.'

He joked, or so Tory thought, and she smiled. 'Anyway, enough of my problems . . .'

'Our problems.' Brockwell corrected. 'These events concern us all.'

'Tell me of Katren and thy kin. Dost thou have any clues as to what may have become of them?'

'Some . . .' Brockwell dithered.

'Dost thou suspect Mahaud could have been involved?'

'Maybe . . .' He was awfully vague about it.

'Calin, please. I know thou art worried about them and in shock at this time, but I cannot help thee if thou dost not tell all the facts . . . I am too weary to guess.'

Calin couldn't work out if she was playing him for sport or not, so he thought it best to start at the beginning. 'Dost thou recall how I came to be at the battle of Arwystli?'

Tory's brow became drawn, she was losing patience with him. 'Well, I wast being damned by Mahaud at the time, but it was said that thou arrived upon a griffin.' She didn't understand why he was bringing this up now.

'Aye, 'tis true.' He was saddened by the fact. 'And in return for that passage, I made the griffin a vow.' The king's lips parted to reveal it, when he choked on his guilt and fell silent.

Tory's hands moved to her mouth to cover the look of horror that swept her face.

'Oh, his request seemed simple enough at the time, I was young and madly in love . . . And I do love Katren, still, after all these years, despite . . .' His conscience smothered him to secrecy again and he looked to the fire, every muscle in his face battling to conceal his dread.

'Despite what, Calin?' Tory's tone now boarded on accusation. 'What did thee promise that Otherworldly creature?'

'That I would remain beholden to Katren alone, for as long as we both doth live?' He admitted rather begrudgingly.

'Or?'

'Or the griffin would claim her and all our offspring, and I would never lay eyes on them again.'

The tears ran silently down his face, and her heart went out to him as she could truly sympathise with how he felt. 'But how could this have befallen, unless thou hast —'

'Coveted another.' Brockwell's eyes darted up to catch her reaction.

'Calin, thou did not!' Tory begged him, as she stood up. 'How could thee do such a thing to Katren?' she scolded; hadn't he learnt?

Calin was shocked, speechless, as he watched Tory begin to pace out her frustration with him. 'But Tory, 'twas thee I did forsake her with,' he announced, halting the High Queen in her tracks.

'Come again?'

'The desire thou doth stir in me, I did try to deny.' He rose, his eyes affixed upon her as he neared. 'Katren subdued it for a time, a long time . . . but over the years, more and more, thou hast been a distraction to me.'

'Calin, what art thou saying?' Tory was horrified. 'Surely thou dost not believe it was really I that thee took to thy bed? I just got through telling thee I have slept with none bar Maelgwn.'

'Thou art denying it?' Brockwell was becoming annoyed and confused.

'Aye, I am denying it!' Tory stated with conviction. 'I swear to thee, Calin, 'twas not I!'

Calin stopped still to think; by his memory there was no mistaking her, for the room had been candlelit. 'Perhaps Mahaud bewitched thee, and thus thou hast no memory of the event.'

Tory's heart was pounding in her chest. *Please, Goddess, don't let him be right.* It was not that Calin Brockwell was not an attractive man. He was well admired by many women, both young and old. It was more that he was a past-life incarnation of Tory's brother, Brian, and she'd always regarded him as such.

'When did this . . . episode take place, Calin?'

'Last night, just after sundown.'

Tory breathed a sigh of relief. 'I was discussing matters with Taliesin till well after midnight.'

'Then who was in my bed?' Brockwell became somewhat nauseous at the dwindling possibilities. 'Not Mahaud, please . . . not that foul creature.'

'Well, Taliesin mentioned Vanora also possessed skills of transformation,' Tory put forward.

Brockwell had to sit down before he fell down, his face was as white as his shirt. 'Be that supposed to make me feel better?'

'I suppose not . . . but it was thy choice, Calin.'

'Please.' He held up his hand; he didn't need a lecture.

'Damn her!' Tory wanted to hit something. 'That hag hast managed to expose the weakness in every one of us.'

'The question being, what art we going to do about it?' Brockwell shook his head. What hope did they have against such trickery? 'What can we do?'

'Well, firstly, we had best see to the rescue of thy clan.' Tory's mind shifted into gear. 'And, I dare say, as we shan't be able to rely on Taliesin to aid us, I had best seek out the whereabouts of Selwyn.'

'But no one hast seen the hermit for years?'

'Fear not,' the Queen assured him with a smile. 'We still keep in touch. It be my guess that Selwyn already knows of all that hast befallen, and shall be hard at work on a solution by now.'

'Let us hope thou art right.'

In the wake of his father's disastrous resolve, Rhun pacified their subjects. He proposed that the only way they would overcome the problems that overshadowed them was to have patience and stick together.

Tiernan supported the young prince, claiming that he believed the king had been temporarily overcome by the stress of his troubles and this was affecting his decision-making. Yet he assured the subjects of the High King that the Goddess was aware of this and was dealing with the matter personally.

'So, until such time as we art instructed otherwise, we must adhere to our king's word and speak no treason against him. This be the will of the Goddess.'

'So be it.' The gathering seemed reluctant to agree.

'Thou had best not be lying to us, Sir Tiernan. We art talking about disastrous consequences if thou art making this up to save face.' Sir Guillym, King Catulus' representative, bowed and took his leave.

The rest of the nobles, knights and advisers exited the room after him, mumbling their concerns amongst themselves.

'Well put,' Rhun assured his father's champion. 'Now I need thee to help me persuade my father to let me go to King Brockwell's aid. Mother hast asked that I meet her at Arwystli.'

Tiernan rolled his eyes knowing how difficult the king was to reason with at present, but he would to give it a try.

Before they entered his father's chambers, Rhun paused to instruct: 'Now, no matter what happens, we art not allowed to be angry with him, understand? That will only give the dark forces more power.'

Tiernan nodded, mentally preparing himself for the challenge.

'Nor should we anger him, if we can avoid it . . . save he starts throwing the death sentence about.'

'Aye,' Tiernan rolled his head around to relieve the tension in his neck. 'I am ready.'

Expecting to find the High King alone and brooding, Rhun knocked and entered. He strutted into the room to confront his father and was taken aback to find him in bed, with a maiden near half his age. If not for Tiernan clasping a hand over his mouth in constraint, Rhun's fury would have thwarted him.

'Forgive the intrusion, Majesty.' Tiernan made it sound as if nothing were amiss. 'But we have an urgent need to speak with thee.'

'Now what?' Maelgwn raised himself and the maid moved around to sit behind him, watching the intruders over the king's shoulder with playful delight.

Tiernan had let go of Rhun, but the prince's voice quivered as he struggled to contain his contempt. 'I think I should go to Sir Brockwell's aid. It dost not look good for us to be abandoning our allies.'

The king laughed at this, turning his head to view the girl behind him. 'What dost thou think. Should I let him go?'

The girl toyed with him a moment, giggling now and then as she pondered. 'Nay,' she decided, wrapping her legs and arms around the king's body. 'Keep him close to us,' she urged, in a whisper that was loud enough for Rhun to hear.

This didn't make sense. Rhun knew this girl; he'd pursued her himself for a time. Strange that he'd found the maiden far too chaste to warrant any real interest. Rhun calmed himself enough to focus on her and, sure enough, the evil that shrouded her was even stronger than the forces that had beset his father. *They art purposely trying to disgust me, and be damned if I shall stand about playing word games for their amusement.*

'Well, there be thy answer.' His father's gaze was still caught up in the girl. 'Arianwen wants thee here, thus here thou shalt stay.'

'Of course.' Rhun forced a smile, realising any attempt to reason with his father was going to prove completely futile. 'I am sure that Arianwen hast Britain's best interests at heart.' The prince made for the door before he said something he would truly regret.

'And best assets at hand . . .' the girl giggled as they returned to their mischief.

Tiernan slammed the door closed behind them, then searched frantically for something he could plough his fist into.

'Tiernan, calm thyself.' Rhun prevented him from belting a solid oak door. 'I think I have an alternative means to our end.'

A vague image of a forest took form and then manifested in brilliant colour. Wind rustled through the tree branches above, stirring up the local bird life. Water from the mountains babbled down over the rocks of a small waterfall close by, and the filtered rays of sunlight felt warm against his skin.

'Rhun?'

He turned his head to spy his mother.

'What art thou doing here?' There was a proud kind of laughter in her voice. 'Am I here?' He shuffled his hands up and down himself, feeling a little light-headed from the experience.

'Indeed thou art, Highness. Well done.' Selwyn's face beamed.

'Mother, I am so sorry.' Rhun near flew to embrace Tory.

'Sorry? For what?' Tory couldn't tear him away from her.

'Everything!' He calmed a little as he absorbed his mother's healing energy; Mahaud's forces had him wound up like a coil. 'Father hast . . .'

'I know.' Tory hushed him to a more serene state. The whole sordid confrontation was ablaze in his mind. It was not necessary to make him speak of it.

'Vanora set a curse loose in Gwynedd, and hast instructed it to wreak havoc on thy father,' Selwyn enlightened him. 'They art both merely pawns on the crone's chessboard of deceit.'

The prince finally let go of his mother, feeling his strength returning. 'How did thou find out about this, Selwyn, when the Otherworld hast been in such chaos?'

'Why, the trees, of course.' Selwyn looked around at the surrounding forest with considerable admiration. 'They saw Ossa draw upon the four elements to cast the curse and Vanora direct it toward thy kingdom.'

'It was drawn from four winds and travels great distances in silence,' Tory uttered in recognition. 'That was something Taliesin said after he told me he had foreseen Maelgwn's end.'

'Aye,' Rhun added. 'And after thou left Degannwy, Taliesin returned to voice a prophecy concerning a yellow monster.'

'A yellow monster now?' Tory turned her fear-ridden visage to Selwyn. 'After the destruction of my home, the loss of my mentor, a divorce, banishment and two affairs I never had, not to mention the dear friends I have lost through death or disappearance . . .' Tory paused from her raving and took a deep breath to stop herself from completely losing her mind. 'Why did he do it, Selwyn? Taliesin knew Mahaud's evil forces had hold of Maelgwn. How could he just abandon him in this fashion and then curse him to boot?'

'I believe it was more a prophecy, Majesty, as Rhun said. Perhaps the High Merlin was just trying to warn the king away from disaster.' The bard's sweet, open face confirmed that he shared Tory's pain and confusion. 'Then again, Mahaud may have outsmarted even Taliesin in this case. I mean, what if some of the accusations the High King made against him were not so far from the truth? This would have struck at the part of Taliesin that remains mortal. He said to me once that Gwion Bach still lived within him and worked his own mischief.' Selwyn's unwrinkled brow became drawn. 'To learn that he was not so infallible, not so perfect, would surely have angered Taliesin. After all, if he'd been in the right, he would never have lost his patience with the king, for he knew it could only grant the witch more power.'

Dear Goddess, what if she has infected him too?

Selwyn could feel Tory's mounting panic. 'Mahaud seeks to overwhelm and confuse thee, to make thee scatter thy energies. But do not allow her to convince thee that we have lost before we have even taken the field. We still have a couple of tricks up our sleeve . . . never fear.' He took her hand to encourage her strength. 'I suggest we concentrate on one problem at a time.'

Selwyn sat Tory and Rhun down by the brook with some food and water. This particular place in the forest was empowered with positive earth energies that helped to protect them from the crone's evil eyes and ears.

There was nothing they could do about Aberffraw now or about those who had been lost in the disaster. It worried them all that the High King was surrounded by such evil, but as far as they could surmise he wasn't in any immediate danger. Thus their first priority was to see to the rescue of Queen Katren and her sons, and warn their allies of the impending danger that the witch posed to Britain.

'Rhun, dost thou feel confident enough with teleportation to reach each of the kingdoms within the alliance?' Selwyn enquired. 'They will adhere to thy word faster than a scrolled directive sent via a messenger, which may not reach them at all.'

'Aye, Merlin. If it be only a matter of will, as it was to find thee, my conviction be plentiful at present.'

'Good.' Selwyn reached into the pocket of his robe and pulled out several little pouches which he handed to Rhun. 'Take these, one for thyself and one for each ruler.'

'What art they?' Rhun gave them a sniff and inhaled the pleasant aroma of many a different herb and flower.

'Amulets. They contain small carvings of symbols that ward off disease, mischief and evil spirits. They shall repel all negative vibrations and will enhance one's psychic energy, so that our allies shall be better able to separate fact from fiction.'

'Excellent!' Rhun slung the long leather strap of one around his neck and tucked the pouch inside his shirt, feeling the braid of the Lady Bridgit in his pocket. 'Dost thou have a spare?'

'I have only enchanted exactly as many as we require.'

'Never mind,' Rhun resolved with a smile. 'I shall meet ye back at Arwystli presently.' Rhun kissed his mother's cheek and closed his eyes to concentrate.

'Goddess speed.' Selwyn smiled proudly as the young prince disappeared.

The Queen seemed dazed after her son's departure.

'He shall be fine, Majesty.' Selwyn placed an amulet around her neck, and she smiled faintly at its pleasing energy.

'Let us be gone, also.' Tory took hold of Selwyn's hand and squeezed it. 'King Brockwell shall be beside himself by now.'

Rhun made straight for Dunadd, in the most distant kingdom of Dalriada. Fergus MacErc had only just arrived home from Arwystli to be informed that his brothers, Loarn and Aengus, were besieged by Pictish raiders along their bordering estates.

Rhun promised to see what he could do about sending some legions to their aid, but after informing the ruler of the dreadful state of affairs he'd just left in Gwynedd, thankfully, Fergus realised how difficult that might be.

The leader of the Scotti accepted the Merlin's magic charm, stating he could use all the help he could get. As he reckoned, it was not as if he'd never had to deal with the Pictish before. In parting, Fergus swore his everlasting allegiance to the Goddess, stating he was confident she would see them through the darkness that had descended over Britain.

Rhun left for Dumnonia to address King Catulus, more confident that the alliance would hold firm through this peril; perhaps the witch was not as powerful as he'd first feared.

Unfortunately, the prince arrived to find that the same scenario had erupted in both Dumnonia and Gwent Is Coed, only it was the Angles who plagued their borders. Therefore, Rhun had to conclude that the Saxons had already begun to raid along the borders of Powys and Gwynedd. It seemed Ossa had been forming a few alliances of his own.

Once the amulet had been placed around the neck of each leader, Rhun found them very easy to reason with. They all stated their allegiance to the treaty and to the cause of the common good, each willing to do whatever he must to restore the peace and rule of the Goddess.

It was not long after Bryce had entered the sitting room at Arwystli to greet his father, with the son and daughter of Ossa in tow, that Tory and Selwyn materialised in the middle of the room.

Naturally, Eormenric and Aella were rather startled, and then even more so when Selwyn approached to greet them in their own tongue.

'Eormenric, Aella. So pleased to make thy acquaintance.' The young Saxon warrior was speechless as this strange, yet intriguing individual grasped hold of his hand and shook it firmly. 'I have been expecting thee.'

'Really?' Eormenric smiled, wide-eyed.

'Sensei.' Bryce rushed to Tory and bowed quickly, before giving her a hug. 'Father hast just finished telling me of thy woes. How dost thou fare?'

She squeezed him tightly to alleviate his anxiety, feeling that another in the room strongly envied her position. 'Now that thou hast been returned safely to us, I am fine.'

'I shall never leave thee again.' The young prince took a step back. 'As Ione can no longer watch over thee for fear of the death sentence, I shall.'

'That be not — '

'I want no argument on the subject. It be done.'

Aella was jealous of the obvious devotion Bryce held for this woman. Who was she?

'Eormenric. I am Selwyn, a Merlin to the Druids of Britain.' He led the young Saxon leader to where Tory stood. 'And it gives me great pleasure to introduce thee to our High Queen.'

'The Goddess,' Eormenric gasped, as he bowed deeply before her, overcome to meet the legend at last. 'It be an honour, lady.'

'The honour be all mine, Eormenric.' Tory placed both hands on his shoulders, urging him to rise.

'Nay.' He could not look her in the eye, feeling guilt-ridden. 'It wast I who caused thee all this grief, some of which can never be righted.'

Tory smiled faintly; he was not much older than her own son, and too young to carry such a burden. 'But now thou hast come to seek me out, there be a real chance for peace and trust between our nations that may never have arisen if this had not all come to pass.'

Eormenric finally looked to her, his eyes wide at the wisdom of her words.

'We all have lessons to learn from this experience,' the High Queen assured him. 'Thus there be no blame to be laid, just a challenge to be faced.'

Bryce slapped Eormenric's shoulder with a wink, to loosen him up a little. 'And Aella.'

The Queen approached and embraced her warmly, to the maiden's great surprise.

'I want to thank thee for the deliverance of my Masters from the tower of Londinium. Thou art a brave soul indeed and most welcome in my kingdoms.'

'I thank thee.' The girl curtsied. 'But no thanks be required, it was the just thing to do.'

Tory smiled, looking back to Bryce. 'No wonder thou brought her home.'

The Queen spoke in Bryce's tongue, which Aella didn't comprehend. The young prince blushed all the same — he never could hide anything from his patroness.

'Well, then, let us get down to business.' Selwyn rubbed his hands together and took a seat. 'Let us start with the rescue of thy good Queen.' He looked to Brockwell and Bryce near had a fit.

'Hast something happened to Mother?'

'Thou hast not told him?' Tory appealed to Brockwell, who cringed at the thought of doing so.

'I wast just getting to that, when ye arrived.' The king stood and looked to Bryce, who was poised and ready to hit something. 'Could we have a moment?'

Tory took Eormenric and Aella to the dining room to be fed, whilst Selwyn stayed to ensure Bryce remained civil; this sad news would not be an easy thing for the prince to hear.

It was in the wee hours of the morning that Rhun finished speaking with Vortipor in his court at Castle Dwyran in Dyfed.

As this kingdom was protected from the threat of land raids, being bordered by Gwent Is Coed and Powys on each side and water on the other, Vortipor immediately ordered troops to both his neighbouring kingdoms to help secure their position. The Protector of Dyfed then kindly offered the young prince a bed for the night, as he was obviously weary from all his travels, trials and lack of sleep.

Although Rhun was grateful, he declined, stating he could not rest until he had rejoined his mother and been updated with their state of affairs. The prince felt that Vortipor was relieved to hear this. The memory of Bridgit, in the throes of a heated kiss with such a notorious womaniser as Rhun, still bothered her father greatly.

Even so, Rhun could not bring himself to leave Dyfed without at least seeing her. For as much as he hated to admit it, Bridgit's kiss had lingered long in his memory. Upon disappearing from Vortipor's sight, the prince found himself beholding a vision that was more enchanting and perfect than a scene from a fairytale.

The maiden lay sleeping in a huge, canopied bed of pure white. The blueish light of the moon streaming through the open window reflected off the covers, giving the impression that the whole bed was aglow.

As the prince took a seat beside her sleeping form, Bridgit stirred and opened her eyes.

Outlined against the moonlight, he appeared like an angel. She was not frightened, knowing at once who it was; Rhun had filled her dreams so many days now, that every inch of his fine, vigorous form had been clearly committed to memory. 'Am I dreaming?'

'Nay, Bridgit, I am truly here.'

'Oh Goddess!' She raised herself to hold him fast. 'I was so worried.'

The prince found the lady's energy so potent, so virtuous and true, that it shamed him to think he could have contemplated toying with her affections as he had. She was not some common whore looking for the favours of a man well positioned in society. Bridgit was a well educated lady of royal breeding and hence a treasure to be savoured, not squandered. In fact, he even felt a mite guilty relishing the sensation of her body pressed so hard against his, and so eased her away from him a little.

'I have something for thee.' He lifted the amulet from around his neck. 'It will protect thee in the midst of this chaos.'

Bridgit smiled broadly as the prince placed the charm around her neck. 'With all that hast been taking place in the world, thou art worried about me?'

Oh my, but she was adorable this maiden, and clever. 'There be none more surprised than I,' the prince admitted, but with a remnant of cynicism; he'd no intention of committing himself to one woman just yet. Still, if he didn't claim this bounty soon, another man, most likely one of his best friends, would.

Bridgit knew he was only pretending to be aloof with her now. 'I thank thee, with all my heart,' she whispered, pressing her lips against his. For a moment, the prince felt pleasantly inclined toward her advance. She was so trusting of him and quite willing to take her passion further.

'Stop that.' He found himself on the defensive, and standing in the middle of the room. 'Hast thou no idea what a volatile lover I am.'

'Aye,' she said with a sultry smile. 'But I am fairly confident I could persuade thee to come back.'

'Thou dost not have to persuade me to come back, Bridgit.' Rhun became, for some reason, annoyed with her. 'Be that not obvious by my presence here.'

'Oh, Goddess.' Bridgit sounded rather embarrassed as she shrank back to hide inside her bed. 'Thou dost not want me.'

'Nay!' He climbed on to the bed after her. 'Bridgit, I do.'

'Then please, Majesty, have mercy.' She leant towards him. 'I have spent the last four and ten years in a convent.'

Rhun laughed, she certainly wasn't backward in coming forward.

'What?' She tried not to laugh herself. 'Look, I am inexperienced, I know . . .' she caused the prince to laugh even harder, 'but I am very eager to learn.'

'Thou art way too eager for a lady of thy stature. Face it, Bridgit, thou art the marrying kind.'

'Oh great!' She pushed him away. 'If I must wait until such time as thou art ready to marry, I shall die an old spinster. We art on the brink of war, I know it. I saw Father dispersing his troops. What if something should happen to thee?'

'Never fear, I am a fast healer.' He joked to ease her alarm. 'Ask anyone.'

'I do not find that at all funny,' she scolded him. 'Dost thou not know how worried I have been?' Her tears forced her words to falter. 'And thou can make a mockery of my love, Rhun, but it will not be swayed, not ever.'

'My lady . . .' Rhun's heart sank; surely not even in the Otherworld would he find a maiden so fair as the one before him now. 'I am sincerely honoured and flattered, but I cannot take thee like this. Thy father would have me killed for starters, and then we would have precious little hope of ever being properly wed.'

This made Bridgit smile, for although he still hadn't said he loved her, she was at least steering him in the right direction.

'I have to go.' Rhun reversed off the bed. 'But I shall be back, I swear.' He held a hand to his heart and disappeared.

This stunned Bridgit a moment, as such feats were unheard of by any outside the Druid circle. Maybe this was a dream after all? Bridgit fished for the charm Rhun had given her and kissed it as she lay back down, comforted by its presence. 'I believe you will be, Highness . . . make it soon.'

Once Eormenric's belly was filled with yet another free meal supplied by the Britons, he decided he must clear his conscience and tell the Goddess all he knew.

'Though I know it not be by her own will,' Eormenric was saddened to tell, 'it be Vanora, in the body of another, who seduces thy husband, lady.'

His words snapped Tory from her silent daze.

'But it was Mahaud who gave him the looking-glass,' he explained. 'It was also she who assumed thy form to trick King Brockwell.'

Tory held her head and let out a deep breath. 'Well, best not tell King Brockwell that.' She forced a grin as she paused to consider. 'Dost thou know how the spell over the High King might be broken?'

'Aye, lady.' Eormenric hesitated a moment, then said in a whisper. 'It be said that thou hast only to get the king to destroy the gift he accepted.'

'I see.' Tory imagined this would be easier said than done. 'Did Mahaud say anything to thee of a yellow monster?'

Aella's eyes parted wide at the question, though Eormenric shook his head. 'Not that I recall.'

The High Merlin's prophecy was slowly driving Tory insane. She knew the answer to this riddle; she'd studied Taliesin's works back home in the twentieth century and yet the meaning continued to elude her. The frustrating thing was that she was certain an explanation lay within the pages of her reference books, now buried beneath the rubble at Aberffraw.

8

JUDGEMENT

With the new day there dawned new hope. All those endeavouring to solve the dilemmas that confronted Britain met in the king's room of court at Arwystli come first light. Even Bryce seemed to have calmed a little, though he'd yet to speak a word to his father.

After presenting Bryce, Eormenric and Aella with their amulets, Selwyn instructed them that they must stay at Arwystli whilst he, King Brockwell and Tory saw to the rescue of Queen Katren and her sons.

Of course, Bryce did not take such instruction willingly, but as he was the only other member of his kin who remained he was finally persuaded to see reason.

Rhun was given the task of trying to convince his father to destroy the looking-glass.

'Thy amulet shall grant thee additional influence over the king,' the Merlin advised him, 'and the strength to ignore the influence of the demons who have beset thy father.'

'Good.' Rhun nodded, not mentioning that he'd already relinquished his charm to defend another. He felt well equipped to handle the situation on his own, and so decided that none need find out about his little oversight. 'I shall return as soon as I can.' He closed his eyes and disappeared from their midst.

'Great wonders!' Eormenric voiced the mind of both he and his sister. 'Doth everyone in Britain travel thus?'

'Not everyone,' Tory said, standing to join hands with King Brockwell and Selwyn, the three of them vanishing also.

Eormenric shook his head, dumbfounded. 'I am on their side,' he commented to his sister. 'I think Father had good reason to live in awe of these people.'

'Aye,' Aella agreed.

The court room doors opened wide, a knight entered and bowed before Bryce. 'Sensei.'

'Speak, Sir Lucas.'

'We art besieged,' he explained, his gaze turning to the prince's guests, 'by Saxons.'

Bryce and Eormenric raced to the window to behold the war party massing in the distance. A weird electrical storm gathered above the enemy, the like of which Eormenric had only ever seen at Aberffraw.

'Mahaud,' Eormenric stated, whereby Bryce turned and regarded him suspiciously. Eormenric backed up, shaking his head. 'I did not know, I swear! Tell him, Aella.'

'How do I know that.' Aella came to stand beside the prince. 'All that information thou so willingly offered, hast seemed to have made everyone absent but us. How convenient.'

'We should take him prisoner, Highness,' Lucas advised, 'for bargaining power. The girl, too.' As the prince appeared angered by this, the knight quickly emphasised: 'For her own protection.'

'I shall worry about the Lady Aella.'

'But sensei, there art more impor —'

'And Eormenric shall stay with me,' Bryce ordered over the top of him. 'I shall need all the help I can get.' Bryce turned to the Saxon beside him and held out his hand.

Though he understood naught of the conversation, Eormenric did catch the gist of it. He was overwhelmed that the prince would choose to trust one of the known enemy, despite being advised to the contrary. Thus he took hold of Bryce's hand with both his own, shaking it firmly. 'I wish I could tell thee, thou wilt not regret this.'

Aella was still dubious; perhaps her gallant warrior was too trusting. 'If I live to regret this, Eormenric, I shall kill thee myself.'

Maelgwn woke from a deep slumber, still weary enough to sleep longer. He rolled onto his back, allowing his sight to drift around the dim room. To his alarm, there was his son, down on one knee by the pile of clothes the king had worn the day before. Rhun held a shirt in his hand and his eyes were closed in concentration. This seemed rather curious, as to the best of the king's knowledge the door and all the shutters on the windows were locked. The Merlin's prophecy had scared him into complete seclusion.

'What art thou doing?' Maelgwn's agitated tone woke the maid beside him.

'I am trying to discern if thou dost retain any love for me at all.' The prince looked to his father, who didn't appear at all well. The room was stuffy and the smell of death hung heavy in the stagnant air.

'How sweet.' The girl cuddled up to the king, but he cast her aside to sit upright.

'Rhun, thou hast done nothing to lose my favour.' Maelgwn couldn't believe his son was serious about his enquiry. 'I do not hold thy mother's offences against thee.'

'Then, as thy son, I wish to ask a favour . . . which hast nothing to do with Mother,' he added quickly before his father jumped to any conclusions.

'In that case, ask.'

'Nay, my love.' The girl was seeming a might edgy, but the king's attention was firmly focused on his son.

'The looking-glass?' Rhun asked after its whereabouts.

'Aye, I have it.' His father pulled his treasure from under his pillow.

Rhun smiled broadly, looking to the maid.

'Nay!' she objected. What was his game? He seemed way too smug.

'I would ask that thou view thy lover through it, Father.'

Maelgwn considered this a simple enough request, though he first viewed his son.

Rhun rolled his eyes, knowing his father would find nothing amiss with him. 'Come, come, dost thou not even trust me?'

'I cannot be sure who to trust.' The king swung around quickly to view the girl.

'Damn thee!' she shrilled, as her outer identity peeled away to reveal the face of Vanora.

Maelgwn jumped clear into the middle of the room, the looking-glass firmly clenched in his fist. The maiden's eyes closed as she collapsed onto the bed unconscious, quivering like a leaf in the breeze.

'I cannot believe it.' Maelgwn was horrified. 'Be there no end to the deceit?'

'That not be the worst of it.' Rhun retrieved a mirror that was hanging on the wall and, facing it away from himself, he approached his father. 'Now I would ask thee to view thyself through it.'

'Nay, please.' The king's eyes filled with tears, and he appeared too weary from the betrayal to even raise the looking-glass.

'Do it!'

The king lifted his enchanted gift to view himself, his eyes widening as his facial features contorted into those of a hideous beast with eyes, hair and teeth of yellow. 'Nay,' he cried in dread, casting the looking-glass to the stone floor, where it smashed into a hundred pieces. 'What have I done!' Maelgwn's remorse drove him to his knees and he began to weep bitterly. 'Tory. Tory!'

A wave of fever rushed over the king and every muscle in his body began to ache.

'Help me.' He raised his head to view Rhun, but the strain proved too great and he dropped to the hard stone floor.

The young Merlin had brought them to one of the hundreds of hallways to be found within Taliesin's maze of a house.

In front of them lay a door that was in every way identical to the others that lined the corridor, yet Selwyn seemed confident that this was the right one.

'How can thou tell?' Brockwell couldn't, and he'd been there before. 'If I open this door to find a dragon, demon or the like, we art in big trouble.' There was no telling what kind of company the High Merlin kept hidden within these walls.

'Have no fear.' Selwyn turned the knob and entered. 'I have wandered this labyrinth for near twenty years. I know my way around it near as well as the High Merlin.'

'Dost thou think Taliesin could still be here somewhere?' Tory wondered out loud as she followed Selwyn inside.

'I doubt it. The Chariot of Arianrod be missing . . . I checked. I dare say Taliesin be residing in another millennium by now.'

Once inside, Brockwell recognised the dark, rocky terrain and headed down the torchlit stairs ahead of his companions.

'Oh dear.' Selwyn paused, and closed his eyes to consider the information he was perceiving.

'What now?' Tory came to a stop beside him. The Queen was far too consumed by the events taking place in the material world to perceive any wisdom from the Otherworld at present.

Selwyn waved it off. 'Nothing, Majesty. We must make haste.' He hurried off after the king.

'Nothing, Majesty. We must make haste,' Tory repeated with scepticism. 'Now why do I not believe thee?'

Brockwell reached the large plateau of rock that dropped off to a bottomless cavern on the far side; amidst the shadows there stood two figures. The king slowly approached these to find Blain and Owen frozen motionless in a prism of quartz.

'Nay, damn thee!' Brockwell hammered the hardened stone with both fists. 'Let them free!'

'Father!' Cai came running at him from the shadows. 'Thee must not be angry or the beast will surely turn thee to stone as well.' He jumped up on Brockwell and held onto him for dear life.

'Thou art safe.' Brockwell felt partly relieved. 'And what of thy mother?'

'I am here, Calin.'

Katren came forth out of the shadows some distance from him, yet even in the poor light he could not fail to notice how harrowed she appeared. Brockwell put the boy down, but Cai still clung to his waist, not prepared to let go.

'Tell me it not be true, Calin . . . look at our sons and then tell me the griffin lies. For I would rather live out my days in this wretched place, than spend them with a man who hast willingly betrayed me.'

'It wast a trick, Katren.' Tory attempted to allay her friend's pain.

'Thou hast some nerve, Highness, showing thy face here,' Katren shot back at her. 'When thou wast the other half of this conspiracy.'

The deep resentment her friend felt towards her plunged like a dagger into Tory's heart.

'I saw the two of thee. The griffin showed me in his magic pool.'

'Nay, Katren, 'twas Mahaud.' Brockwell moved to approach her, when the screech of the huge beast was heard from above and the griffin came to land between them.

'Be nice,' Cai quietly told his father, as Tory drew him back out of the way. 'I am not ready to be a king.'

One did not expect to see thee, warrior. Be gone before thou dost anger me, the huge half-lion, half-eagle creature bethought the king. *Thou hast bequeathed thy kin to me, fair and square.*

'Nay, 'twas not fair!' Brockwell protested strongly. 'I was bewitched, and thus my decision was not my own.'

A minor detail, the griffin scoffed.

'I do not think the Goddess would agree with thee.' Selwyn took a stand beside Brockwell. 'Shall we summon her and find out?'

Ha, ha, ha! the creature squawked with laughter. *The Goddess hast no time for the unfaithful.*

'We shall see . . .' Selwyn raised his arms into the air.

'Merlin, wait.' Brockwell delayed him, recalling how he'd induced the creature to aid him in the first place. 'I got myself into this mess, I shall get myself out.'

'As be thy wish, Majesty.' Selwyn politely bowed out of the argument.

Good! The beast didn't like being threatened, it made him angry.

Brockwell looked to his wife, who seemed bewildered, then to Cai, near frightened out of his wits. His sights drifted to Owen and Blain, destined to spend eternity entombed in stone whilst remaining completely aware of their surroundings. Tears welled in the king's eyes, as the horror of what he'd done consumed him, and for the first time in a long while Brockwell allowed himself to feel his pain, his regret, his loss.

Oh no, please . . . The griffin began to sniffle.

As Calin reminisced on the excitement and passion he'd experienced the first time he and Katren made love, tears began to flood down his cheeks. The joy he'd felt at the birth of his sons enveloped his soul, as he relived each event in his mind. But it was the little things his sons had achieved over the years that really set his emotions whirling: the day Bryce had become a master; the first time Blain split a piece of wood with his bare hand; Owen's first kiss; Cai's recital on the harp at only four years of age. 'I shall pay for my own mistakes, if thee please,' the king said. 'I implore thee not to punish my family for my imperfections.'

The griffin was howling now; he could barely breathe for his emotions. *So be it, he blubbered, and the stone surrounding Blain and Owen disappeared. Take thy family and leave this place.* The great, huge beast crawled away to where it could lament in peace.

The king closed his eyes and said a silent prayer of thanks, as he embraced all his sons at once.

'Quickly, Majesty,' Selwyn urged, although he hated to disrupt such a heartwarming scene. 'Arwystli be under attack.'

'What!' Brockwell was floored by the news. 'Why did thou not tell me sooner?'

'Well, despite how gallant thou art, Majesty, thou can still only handle one catastrophe at a time,' Selwyn told him.

'But surely Tory and thyself cannot transport so many of us back to Arwystli.'

'Fear not.' Selwyn remained a calming force. 'I do believe Taliesin keeps a gadget around here somewhere that should serve that purpose nicely. Go ahead of us with the High Queen, and I shall see to transporting thy family when the situation be more stable.'

'Father.' Blain delayed the king. 'I want to help.'

'Then guard thy mother and thy brothers until I send for thee.' As Blain appeared rather disappointed, Brockwell added, 'It be a treasure I hold more sacred than my own life that I place in thy hands, Blain.'

His son nodded his understanding, his conviction plain in his eyes.

Katren came forth to stand behind their sons, her arms outstretched to encompass them all. 'May the Goddess protect thee.' Her eyes drifted from her husband to the High Queen, who smiled.

'May she protect us all, Katren.' Tory motioned Brockwell after her as she took off up the stairs.

'Where art thou going?' the king asked as he pursued her.

'I need a weapon.'

Tory burst through the door that led back into the High Merlin's labyrinth, quickly eyeing the models of warriors that stood between each of the doorways in the corridor. Taliesin had been collecting this wild array of armour and battledress amid his comings and goings through time, and there was not a finer armoury to be found anywhere in history.

Though Tory had mastered the art of wielding a broadsword, she spied another weapon that better suited her fighting style. She approached the ominous exhibit of a warrior's guise and retrieved a long, steel shaft, bladed at each end, which looked as though it might have belonged to someone like Genghis Khan.

'Now this, I recognise.' Brockwell lifted Dyrnwyn, the fiery sword of Rhydderch, from another of the exhibits. 'Come to thy master.' He relished the feeling of again holding one of the thirteen treasures of Britain.

'Now that seems to me just a bit too coincidental,' Tory shouted down the empty hallway. She looked to Brockwell with a smug grin on her face. 'Dost thou think the High Merlin could have had this much foresight, or did he never leave?'

Tory joined her comrade, equipped to depart.

'Seems like old times, ay.' Brockwell took hold of the Queen's hand.

'Goddess forbid.' She rolled her eyes before closing them, her thoughts turning to war-torn Arwystli.

After leaving Aella in the room of court, in the care of her brother and a half dozen guards, Bryce made haste to join the battle that had erupted on the roof. The Saxon fighters had begun to scale the walls in their attempt to penetrate the fortress's outer defenses and raise the portcullis.

'Bryce, wait up.'

His sensei's voice brought the prince to a standstill, and he turned to find the High Queen and his father bounding up the stairs to join him.

'What of Mother?' The prince seemed panicked by their presence.

'She be safe,' his father assured him.

'Then I am glad to see thee.' Bryce directed his address to Tory; it was clear he still hadn't forgiven his father for his unfaithfulness. 'A storm be on our doorstep, the like of which destroyed Aberffraw.'

Tory raised her eyebrows and flung open the hatch that led to the roof, momentarily startled by the enormity and power of the fiery disturbance that was now almost directly overhead.

'Holy shit!' She could only mouth the words, as Bryce and Brockwell bounded out past her and straight into combat. 'Where art thou when I really need thee, Taliesin?'

Tory couldn't imagine how she was going to deal with the abomination, but, as enemy soldiers made to engage her in battle, there was no time to contemplate the issue. She addressed the onslaught with gusto, throwing caution to the wind.

'I shall honor the Goddess who gave me the stability of the earth as my strength.' She lashed out at the first of her attackers, killing him with one fatal stroke and booting him out of her path. 'The passion of fire as my driving force.' She sprang into the air using her long, slender weapon as a support and planted both feet into her opponent's face, sending him hurtling backwards off the roof. 'The air that I breathe for endurance.' She decapitated the next in line then stabbed his companion, bringing him to his knees. 'And the depth of water for clarity and right action.' She swung around 360 degrees to finish him off with a kick to the side of the head. 'For I am forsworn!' Every Briton within earshot shouted in unison with her.

As King Brockwell's clan followed Selwyn through the High Merlin's labyrinth, they were all struck speechless by the huge, warlike figures that lined the corridors and the staircases.

The Merlin had conveyed to Queen Katren the whole sordid story of what had taken place in her absence by the time they reached the corridor that led to Taliesin's room of hexagons.

'I can scarce believe it.' Katren was sick with remorse. 'How hurt must the High Queen feel already, and then I go and accuse her of adultery?'

'The witch's effects have been far-reaching, Majesty.' The Merlin took hold of both her hands to calm her. 'It just goes to show how one's deepest fear can be one's greatest enemy.' Selwyn held out a hand before him, and the two huge doors at the end of the passage parted wide.

'No more fear then.' Katren raised herself up tall, but with her husband, son, and kingdom in such peril, it was hard to fight the rising dread.

'Wow!' Owen emphasised his wonder as he entered the room of hexagons; not in his wildest dreams would he have imagined such a place existed.

'What are all these strange devices, Merlin?' Blain was a bit more wary than his younger brothers, and kept a good distance between himself and the strange objects in the room.

'All the apparatus around the walls be known as processors. They control all the different hexagons in the centre here, via these.' He pointed out the various terminals scattered about the room.

'But what does it all do?' Cai couldn't begin to imagine; it all looked so amazing, with its flashing lights and strange monotone sounds.

'Well, they all have different functions. Which one would thou like to learn about first?' Selwyn put it to the princes and they all immediately pointed to the largest of the hexagons, which stood from floor to ceiling in the middle of the room.

''Twas my choice, too.' The Merlin laughed as he made his way to a smaller hexagon, positioned close by the one in question, only this was more the size and height of a pulpit. As with the base of its larger affiliate, the hexagon Selwyn stood behind was covered with chips of black onyx. Embedded in the middle of the top was a large round dome, glowing in mottled shades of red as Selwyn passed his hand over it.

All eyes looked to the hexagon. Its solid, black onyx base only rose about one quarter of its height, then large glass screens extended to the roof. From within the blackness of the base, inside the glass casing, rose a holographic image of a city in full colour — complete in every detail.

The boys eyes near left their sockets at the sight, and Owen cried out: 'That looks like — '

'Arwystli.' Blain moved closer as he noticed a battle taking place. 'From what I would guess to be a bird's eye view at present.'

'Why be the sky such a strange colour?' Cai drew everyone's attention to it.

'I do not know.' Selwyn came down from behind the control panel to take a closer look.

'It looks like it's on fire,' Owen added, a little fearful.

'Indeed it does.' Selwyn rushed over to one of the computer terminals and took a seat, limbering up his fingers to type. 'And one should always fight fire with water, I say.'

'Art thou going to make a storm?' Cai ran to observe the Merlin's movements, his brothers right behind him.

'Why not?' Selwyn punched a few instructions into the computer to bring up a map of Britain on the display screen. Once he'd acquired the exact co-ordinates for the city of Arwystli, he turned in his seat and smiled broadly. 'Gentlemen, we have the technology.'

The heat from the air above was stifling, and fighters from both sides were starting to tire due to the extreme temperature. The Britons had lost many men to the fiery lightning that lashed at random from overhead, and the bodies of its victims lay smouldering all across the city.

''Tis becoming unbearable, sensei,' Bryce commented over his shoulder to Tory, who was covering his back.

'Then . . .' she panted for breath, fending off an attacker's sword, 'just think about winter solstice, and thou shalt appreciate the warmth.'

The sky above began to rumble louder, as if it was battling to win its own war. With a deafening clap of thunder, a huge, dark cloud burst through the middle of the hell above them and it began to rain.

'Yee-hah!' they all cried, indulging in the sweet, cooling relief of the shower.

'Thou art right, the power of imagination be an amazing thing,' Bryce observed during a brief pause in the action. 'I feel much better.'

'They have raised the gate!' Brockwell went racing past, heading back into the house with a company of soldiers in tow.

'Oh-oh . . . . Aella.' Bryce took off to her defense, motioning Tory after him. 'Come on.'

It was a race to the room of court, for Ossa knew well enough where it was.

'Bryce, I have to get something.' Tory darted off down the hallway in the opposite direction.

'But, sensei?' Bryce had a sudden conflict of priorities.

'Art thou daft.' Tory became frustrated with him. 'Save the girl. Run!' she urged, disappearing round the corner.

'I want to see how my husband fares.' Katren regretted that she'd not even held him before his departure. 'Can any of this . . . apparatus grant me that?'

'We could search for him, I suppose.' Selwyn took up position behind the large hexagon's control panel.

As the Merlin passed his hand over the dome, it changed in colour to a mottled purple and the tone of the machine rose in pitch. The holograph inside the hexagon flipped up to a two-dimensional format, each of its six screens showing a different aerial view of the city below.

'Holy mother!' Owen held his head.

'Amazing!' Bryce seconded his wonder.

'Here we go.' Selwyn took the image on the screens zooming towards the action.

In through the outer bailey portcullis they soared, and over the havoc left in the wake of the fighting there.

'This feels weird.' Cai was viewing the screen that awarded a view of behind. It seemed as if he were flying backwards.

They passed straight underneath the inner bailey gate, across the court-yard and into the entrance hall.

As King Brockwell made haste down the stairs that led to the large entrance hall of the house, he spied Ossa amongst the din below.

'Right, Warlord. Thee and me.' He jumped over the banister to challenge his adversary and activated his fiery blade.

'King Brockwell, old son, so glad thou could make it.' Ossa bowed as he drew a blade of the crone's design with currents of blue energy, like lightning, zapping over it. 'I heard thou wast having a few family problems.'

'Indeed.' Brockwell was angered until he paused to consider. 'But they do seem relatively insignificant compared with thine own.'

The rest of the fighting waned as the opposing energies of their leaders' swords clashed, showering sparks everywhere.

Ongen recruited a small group of soldiers and used the distraction to fight his way up the stairs that led to the room of court, in search of his treacher-ous kin. The witch had told Ossa and himself everything. Ongen could well conceive of Aella falling in love with a prince who was their enemy. What was harder to believe was that Eormenric had turned renegade.

Bryce had only just arrived in the room of court when Ongen and his men came barging through the doors.

'Kill them all,' he ordered, as he stormed forth to challenge Bryce, who hovered in front of Aella. Yet before his sword made contact with the Briton's, it was blocked by Eormenric's.

'Get her out of here!' He barged Bryce aside, motioning with his head for them to flee.

'Traitor!' Ongen cried, thrusting Eormenric backwards. 'Thou calls thyself a Saxon?'

'That I do.' Eormenric regained his balance and stood fast. 'I shall not be the tool of some cursed witch, who would turn brother against brother . . . kingdom against kingdom. I shall not.' He placed the sword in its scabbard.

'Then die.' Ongen swung at him repeatedly, but Eormenric would not engage him. He just kept darting out of the way, which made Ongen furious. 'Fight, damn it!'

'Why?! Thou art my brother, I have no desire to kill thee.'

'Well, I want to kill thee,' Ongen assured him, 'and shall, with or without opposition.'

'This way.' Bryce turned a corner. Aella was near tripping over her skirts as she battled to keep up with him.

'Going somewhere?'

The pair froze at the sound of Mahaud's evil voice, and although Aella and Bryce spoke different languages, it seemed they both understood her perfectly. They slowly turned to find the apparition of the crone floating about three metres behind them.

'I do believe thou hast something that belongs to me, young prince . . . and I would like her back.'

Bryce had heard the tales of how horrific the sight of Mahaud could be, but there were no words to describe the evil of her presence, nor the foul odour.

'For in order to be the daughter of Ossa,' she explained with delight, 'I must first have her corpse to inhabit.'

'Nay!' Aella appealed to her champion, gripping his arm tightly.

The prince hid the terrified girl behind him. 'Thou shalt have to come through me to take her.'

'Oh, come, come, my pretty. Thou can have thy way with her presently.'

The witch sickened him with her suggestive inflection, and beneath her hood she ran her greyish tongue around her wrinkled, disease-infested lips.

'If thou art anything like thy father, I do fancy thou art well equipped to render a girl a good serve of earthly pleasure.' She screeched with laughter. 'And imagine me, a virgin!'

'I think not.'

Bryce and Aella swung round to find Tory at the opposing end of the corridor, her weapon strapped to her back, her saxophone in hand.

'Thou hast but three seconds to withdraw, Mahaud, before I turn thee into fairy food.' Tory raised the saxophone to her lips, but before she'd even begun to play the witch had vanished.

'Hast she gone?' the prince dared to ask the question.

'I seriously doubt it.' Tory picked up the pile of idle torches she'd collected, and ran to hand the load to Bryce. 'Best stick with me, ay?'

He didn't understand; what had her threat to the witch meant? 'But, what . . .?'

'It's the Pan call she fears,' Tory explained as she got them moving. 'Unfortunately, geologically speaking, I do not have the required energy patterns to contain her long enough to banish her. All I can do right now be to scare her off.'

'Sorry I asked.' Bryce was confident that she knew what she was doing. 'Where art we going then?'

'To the roof.'

'Why? There be nothing happening up there now.'

'Oh, do come on,' Tory urged, eager to be done with it. 'We art going to clean house.'

The rooftop was deserted, except for charred and bloody corpses; all the fighting had moved to ground level. The rain shower, which had now eased to nothing more than a light spray, thankfully subdued the smell.

'These had better still work.' Tory pulled a packet of matches from her pocket. 'I have a little bag of tricks I keep for emergencies . . . I believe this situation qualifies.'

When she struck the tiny match to light a torch, the prince near dropped dead.

'Waterproof, windproof . . . beautiful,' she explained with a wink, as the material bound at the end of the wooden pole burst into flame.

'Thou truly art a Goddess.' Aella looked to the High Queen in awe.

Tory was amused. 'Just wait a moment or two.'

The four torches were lit and Tory used her compass to place them in the northern, southern, eastern and western positions on the rooftop, where many mounds for torches already existed. She stood in the centre of the circle she'd cast, and took three deep yoga breaths to calm and focus her mind. *Please, Goddess, hear me now.* She raised her saxophone to her lips to blast out the four note sequence that was the Pan call.

This tune had successfully swept the witch from their midst once before. Arwystli was not marked as a sacred ley line crossing as Aberffraw had been, but there was still hope that the healing forces of nature would come to their aid.

As the High Queen repeated her musical summons over and over, a mist, green in colour, began to converge on the city.

'Sensei, I believe it be working!' Bryce yelled in encouragement. The prince squeezed his lady fair to reassure her, for he could already sense the remedial force behind the impending haze of light and energy.

The mist rolled over the house and then in through every available crevice. It carried a fragrance that was sweeter than the forest in springtime, and its millions of tiny, green spectres enchanted every soldier to calm as they flitted around in droves.

Ongen stood with his sword poised at his brother's chest, having finally cornered him.

'Do not do this,' Eormenric begged, though he could see Mahaud's evil influence in his brother's face. 'Do not place the fate of Saxony in the hands of that witch.'

'I would never . . .' Ongen protested.

'Really?' Eormenric ventured, pretty sure that his end had come. 'So thou dost truly believe Father controls her . . . Look at what she hast done to us!' His eyes motioned to the sword poised at his throat. 'I only sought out the Britons to find a way to be rid of her.'

'Dost thou expect me to believe that?' Ongen scoffed as he spied the strange lights, floating in through every opening in the room. 'What on earth?' His sword dropped from his hand as the spectacular vision moved over him, filling him with a sense of peace, love and wonder. 'For once in thy life, little brother, I believe thou hast done the right thing.' Ongen reached out and took hold of Eormenric around the neck, his eyes never leaving the magic phenomena that now encircled them. He drew Eormenric in close. 'I near killed thee of mine own hand.' The huge warrior began to cry, as a conflict of positive and negative energies took place within him.

'I forgive thee, Ongen,' Eormenric insisted light-heartedly, though inwardly he was still recovering from the shock of his near-death. 'Mahaud hast drawn us all in.'

'Except thee.' Ongen was proud of him.

'Nay, me too. I shall not be so quick to pass judgement on others in future, I assure thee. For I have come to learn that leadership be not about the amount of power one possesses, or how much land one owns, it be about people . . . guiding, protecting, and watching out for the best interests of those under thy rule. The Goddess said we all had a lesson to learn from this, and I believe I have seen the light.'

'Aye,' Ongen confirmed with a smile, still spellbound by the fairy lights. 'I just hope Father hast.'

As the sparkling green haze enshrouded the two great leaders, the witch's enchantment departed from Ossa's sword. However, completely ignoring the amazing occurrence that was talking place around him, he still continued to fight on like a man possessed.

'Give it up, Warlord,' Brockwell advised, having fought him all the way up the stairs. 'The witch be gone, she hast fled. What thou can see around us be the Pan Ray. Mahaud cannot exist in the presence of such harmony.'

'Want to bet?' Ossa coaxed Brockwell into the room of court.

'Do not make me kill thee.' Brockwell gave a final warning. 'Stop now, and walk away.'

'It was thou who challenged me, remember?' Ossa strode into the middle of the huge room, limbering up his sword arm. 'And I never walk away from a challenge.' He turned and grinned, his weapon poised, ready to do combat. 'So let us finish this.'

'Finish what, Father?' Eormenric queried. 'These people have done nothing to us.'

'This city should have been mine, boy!' Ossa cried, his rage causing him to quiver. 'If not for that damned Goddess . . .'

'Who? Me?' Tory entered and took a stand beside Brockwell, hoping she could call Ossa's bluff. For although the divine was not upon her, as the last time they'd met, chances were Ossa would recognise her as the face of the Goddess.

'Aye.' Ossa was dubious; something was different, she looked more human somehow. 'But thou art not floating today.'

Tory served Brockwell a sideways glance before vanishing into thin air.

'Oi!'

Ossa swung round to find the High Queen behind him.

'If thou dost not yield, sir, thou art going to die . . . believe it.' Tory raised both her eyebrows and folded her arms, approaching the warlord confidently. 'So, give up the witch.'

Ossa abruptly began to choke, gripping the sword in his hand tightly.

'O Goddess!' Tory watched the huge warrior drop to his knees. 'He be having a heart attack.' She knelt down to try and help him, her mind a blank in the panic of the moment.

Ongen and Eormenric rushed to his aid.

'Please, Goddess, do not kill him,' Eormenric begged. 'He was not always like this. I swear to thee.'

'I am not doing this.' Tory fumbled with Ossa's armour in an attempt to remove it. 'I only meant to scare him. Damn it!' She became frustrated, he was fading fast. 'Get this off!'

His two boys obliged her at once, and Tory rolled up her jacket to place it behind his neck. She tried mouth to mouth, she tried heart massage, but nothing worked. The warlord had one last gasp at air then stopped breathing.

'Father!' Aella rushed over and flung herself down beside him in a fit of tears.

'I am so sorry.' Tory moved back out of the way.

Ongen looked to the High Queen, his anger returning now that the mist had passed. 'I should kill thee . . .'

'Nay!' Eormenric put his foot down. 'No more killing. No more!' He held Ongen tightly until he was able to reason with him. 'Let us take our father home.'

Ossa's death was the worst thing that could have possibly happened, as Eormenric again viewed the High Queen and her whole race with dubious eyes.

'Please believe this was the last thing I wanted.' Tory tried to reassure him, but Eormenric only gave a slight nod.

'Art thou alright?' Brockwell embraced his friend in the wake of their ordeal, as he thought she would break down at any moment.

The Saxon leader was raised to his feet by his sons as Aella looked on, grief-stricken. Suddenly, her father's eyes parted wide, glowing red like a demon's. The maiden screamed as Ossa lunged forward and plunged his sword straight through Brockwell and into the High Queen.

Goddess no! Tory dropped to the floor beside the king. As she reached out to him, it seemed as if time were suspended. 'Not Calin, please!' She didn't even feel her pain. She was in shock, and by the time it passed she would have healed. However, her friend was losing an ounce of blood a second.

Next thing Tory knew, Ossa wast leaning over her. He raised her by the shirt till she found herself staring into the eyes of the crone.

'I may not be able to hurt thee, but I can hurt those around thee,' she hissed. 'And no matter where thou dost run to, in the whole of time and space, I will follow thee. And just when thou dost believe thou art rid of me, I shall come back to haunt . . .'

The warrior's head suddenly parted from his shoulders. Bryce stood behind the carcass as it slumped to the floor.

'Calin, my love!'

Tory glanced back to find Katren raising her dying husband's head onto her lap. She stroked his face, hysterical with grief.

'Nay, please, do not leave me,' she sobbed, tilting her head back briefly so that she might be able to view him through her tears.

'Do not cry, Katren.' He took hold of her hand then turned to view Tory, reaching out and taking hold of her hand also. 'We shall all meet again . . . in another life.' With that, the warrior's spirit took flight into the Otherworld.

'The king be dead!' Katren cried aloud for all to hear as she slumped over his body, weeping uncontrollably.

Bryce was on his knees beside his sensei, looking at Blain as he approached them through the crowd. 'Long live the king.'

Blain stared back at his brother, appearing distressed by the announcement; he'd not expected his time would come so soon. His father's advisers already hovered around him to whisper their instruction, and Blain's fear overwhelmed him. Tears escaped the young prince's eyes as he looked back to his older brother to implore him in a whisper, 'Help me.'

9

THE YELLOW MONSTER

Much confusion followed the tragic incident at Arwystli. Tory gripped hold of Bryce, feeling that someone must assume control of the situation. 'Have the court room cleared, bar thine own kin and Ossa's.' She remained curled up in the foetal position so none would see that her wound had already healed over. 'And have the bodies of the dead removed.'

As Bryce went about the High Queen's instruction, Katren left the dead body of her love to tend her friend.

'Please, Tory, hold on,' she wept, pulling her exhausted form across the floor to hold hands with her. 'I did not mean the things I said . . . I could not bear it if I lost thee, too.'

'Shh, Katren.' Tory smiled meekly. 'I am not going anywhere just yet.'

Up until now none here had known of Tory's immortal condition, except Maelgwn, Brockwell, and Taliesin, though she suspected her son knew.

Bryce closed the huge doors when only those needed remained present. Silence fell in the huge room as the High Queen stood of her own accord. She displayed a gaping bloody hole through the centre of her attire, and as she turned to make her way to Brockwell's throne, it was clear that Ossa's sword had passed right through her, though no wound or scar could be seen on her skin.

'Goddess!' Katren gasped.

'Ongen, Eormenric. I should like to speak with ye first.' Tory motioned them to approach as she took a seat. *Hold it together*, she urged herself, for her eyes filled with tears as they met with the bloody pool left on the floor in the wake of her dear friend's life.

'Highness.' Eormenric was a little shaky as he came forward to kneel before the High Queen, urging his brother to do the same.

'Dost either of ye still believe it was I who murdered thy father?' The High Queen's voice was stable and calm.

Eormenric had a few quiet words with his brother. Ongen shook his head firmly and lowered his eyes to the floor.

'Nay, Highness, we do not.' Eormenric bowed his head.

'Then, in thy mind, be there any cause for dispute between our two nations?' They again huddled in intense conversation before Eormenric offered their verdict.

'Nay Highness, only that we art back to our original problem of a poor harvest. Which,' he added politely, 'we now realise was not of thy making.'

Tory breathed a quiet sigh of relief; this had not all been for naught after all. 'Then I have a proposition for ye, gentlemen, that should solve quite a few of our dilemmas, and hopefully prevent any incident, the like of this, from ever occurring again.'

In return for the cessation of all attacks on allied Britain, the kingdoms under the rule of the Goddess would provide aid to those kingdoms that had been warring on behalf of Ossa. Those kingdoms that were not yet part of the alliance would then be expected to sign the pact of peace.

As a further token of good faith, Tory was prepared to train Eormenric in the ways of the Goddess, and he could then become the Saxon representative in her 'circle of twelve'. She explained her choice to Ongen, stating that he would now have his father's huge responsibility facing him, and thus very little time to devote to such an intensive training program. But, if he so desired, she would grant Eormenric permission to train others from Saxony, Ongen included, in the warmer seasons.

The two young men seemed very pleased with the arrangement, especially Eormenric, and thus it was agreed.

'There be one other thing.' Tory cocked an eye. 'Tell me, where be Vanora?'

Ongen had forgotten about her. 'She should be awaiting us just outside the walls of the city.'

'Please have her brought to me.'

Ongen left the room to see to the High Queen's wish.

'Now . . . Bryce, Aella.' Tory motioned for them to come before her. Eormenric moved to depart. 'Please. Stay,' she bade him, and he complied.

The maiden came to a stop beside Bryce, and they bowed before the High Queen. As they were standing quite close together, Aella reached across and very discreetly took hold of the prince's hand.

'I have but one question to ask of ye both,' Tory stated in Aella's tongue and then in Bryce's, to ensure they were both following her. 'Bear in mind, Mahaud still be at large and may come after any one of us, at any time.'

When they had both nodded to confirm their understanding, Tory looked to Aella. 'Aella, would thou take this man to be thy husband?'

The maiden was wide-eyed a second, before she smiled and nodded.

'Hold on a moment,' Eormenric broke in with a laugh in his voice. 'I do not know if Ongen would agree to that.'

'Hush up, Eormenric.' Tory waved him off. 'I shall come to thee, presently.'

Eormenric held his hands out before him in truce, stepping back with a grin on his face from ear to ear.

'Bryce.' The High Queen's mischievous eyes turned to the young prince, who was looking a tad confused. 'Would thou take this maiden to be thy wife?'

Aella guessed the question the Queen had asked the prince and thus gazed up at Bryce, praying he felt as she believed he did.

'I have thought of little else since I met her,' he had no qualm in confessing. 'Dost thou really think it could ever be thus?'

'What did he say?' both Aella and Eormenric at once entreated the Queen.

Tory burst into laughter for the first time in ages; this situation was completely ridiculous. 'I can see I shall have to start teaching a lot more language around here. Now, Eormenric . . .' she looked to him, 'thy true motivation for seeking me out was to release Vanora from the witch's spell. True?'

'Oh, I see where this be heading.' Eormenric avoided her question a moment, wandering a small way away from her, his grin ever-present as he mulled over her suggestion. 'And . . . aye,' he announced with conviction as he moved back towards the Queen. 'I do wholeheartedly agree, if she doth.'

Aella had to refrain from clapping her hands, she felt so excited suddenly; how wonderful that such good could come from such evil.

'One of ours, for one of thine . . . very good.' Eormenric was impressed — till the doors parted and Ongen escorted Vanora to the High Queen.

'She claims she had no control, Majesty,' Ongen reported.

He thrust her forward, towards the High Queen. Vanora fell to her knees, exhausted and bewildered by her ordeal. 'Please, Ongen . . .' Tory noted both Eormenric and Bryce becoming disgruntled by his treatment of the woman. 'I see no need for that . . . now, or at any time.'

'Sorry.' He noted the scolding expressions of all those present. 'I got carried away.'

Vanora bowed low to the ground, burdened with the memories of what she'd done. 'Goddess . . . I have no words to describe my shame, or my remorse.' She tried to refrain from sobbing, but the tears just wouldn't stop. 'I have hurt thy family most grievously and wish only to die.'

This was the maiden Eormenric had first met, and he was overjoyed to see her safely returned to her senses. 'Nay, 'twas not thy fault,' he assured, as he moved to console her. 'It wast my father who did it, and he hast paid for his bad judgement.'

'Indeed,' Tory confirmed. 'But Eormenric here hast offered to marry thee,

Vanora . . . thou might want to consider that over a death sentence.' The Queen made light of Vanora's woes; the poor girl had known enough torment in one lifetime.

'But why? I am so old.' Her sobbing subsided as she looked to Eormenric, ashamed. 'And I am anything but virtuous.'

Eormenric slapped himself in the head. Now that Vanora had returned to normal, her dialect was again that of a native Briton; thus he hadn't understood a word.

'Dost thou want me to translate?' Tory suppressed a laugh.

'Nay. I think I can clear up any confusion.'

As Eormenric bequeathed a kiss to the maiden, his brother was baffled.

'Did I miss something? What be the meaning of this?'

'A double wedding,' Aella was delighted to inform him, as she turned to bestow a kiss on her saviour.

'Be everybody happy now?' Tory slapped her hands together and rose.

'Nay, Majesty.' Blain came forward.

'Ah, Blain, just the man I wanted to see.' She threw an arm over his shoulder and gave him a squeeze of encouragement. 'Thou had best pack.'

'Pack, Majesty?' His spirits lifted somewhat.

'Well, the way I see it, thou shalt have to become a master before thy inauguration.'

'Really?' Blain hadn't considered this, but he became very excited by the news.

The truth of the matter was that, once Blain had been crowned, his advisers would want him to marry. The obvious choice for a bride, in Blain's eyes, would be Bridgit, and Tory was fairly confident that this particular maiden's heart had already been stolen. The Queen had another in mind, who was closer to his age and far more suited to his requirements. She decided she must take the young king-to-be back to Degannwy with her.

Tory looked back to Eormenric and Vanora, who now stood in huddled conversation with Bryce and Aella, desperately trying to understand each other. 'Thou may as well come with us, Eormenric, and I shall swear all three initiates in at once.'

'Three?' Blain became curious. 'Who be the third?'

'Majesty.' Selwyn near startled Tory to death when he suddenly appeared beside her.

'Damn it, Selwyn! Hast there not been enough attempts on my life today?'

'Forgive me, Highness. I have more bad news.'

'But I thought we had addressed everything!' Tory racked her brain; what had she neglected? 'Did Maelgwn not destroy the looking-glass? Hast something happened to Rhun . . .?'

'Please, Majesty, allow me to finish.' Selwyn clasped both her hands firmly, his huge, blue eyes filled with empathic feeling. 'The High King hast come to his senses and smashed the cursed gift. But since then, he hast taken very ill . . .' He paused. 'And that be not the worst of it.'

They took a deep breath together.

'Go on.'

'The girl, whom the king took to his bed, hast come down with the same strange sickness,' the Merlin explained, adding hesitantly, 'I fear it could be plague.'

The answer to Taliesin's riddle was now staring Tory in the face. She gazed down upon her sleeping husband, who was obviously running a temperature, and she wondered what it was that prevented her from collapsing into a hysterical mess.

The answer was simple; if there was a way to save Maelgwn, she was the only one who stood a chance of finding it. If she fell apart now, her love and many others would surely perish.

'It be yellow plague.' She confirmed Selwyn's fears rather calmly, considering the implications of what it meant.

One did not have to be a doctor to diagnose this disease, for the High King's skin was literally turning yellow. This plague was how Maelgwn had reputedly died, according to the history books of the time–space continuum from which Tory had originally stemmed. Legend had it that after falling out of Maelgwn's favour and being banished from Gwynedd, Taliesin had predicted the king's death. This was, of course, exactly what had come to pass, though up until a couple of weeks ago, Tory would never have imagined it could.

'It would seem history hast finally caught up with us.' Tory proceeded to open up all the shuttered windows to get some fresh air circulating round the musty room. 'Cover thy mouth with thy robe, Selwyn. Thee can catch this plague by simply breathing the same air as one of the sufferers.'

'Dost thou know something of this sickness then, Majesty?' He raised his sleeve to cover his nose and mouth.

'I tried to find out a little about it during my last visit to the future, but as I was talking about a disease that was fourteen hundred years old, no one could really tell me much.' She wrung out a piece of cloth in a bowl of warm water and returned to Maelgwn's bedside to wipe his brow. 'I know it was one of the most destructive of all the ancient plagues. It will ravage a path across the continent for the rest of this century, and the next, if we do not contain it now.'

'Goodness!' Selwyn looked back to the king, more fearful. 'I had no idea.'

'Who else hast been in contact with the king?' she enquired, as her patient began to stir from his long sleep.

'Only Sir Tiernan, Rhun and Tadgh, his squire, so I believe . . . Oh, and the girl, of course. But I would not worry too much about thy son. His talisman should have shielded him from infection.'

'Even so, they art all to be quarantined to separate quarters, and art forbidden to see anyone until I find they art safe from infecting others. That includes thyself, Selwyn. I shall persevere in finding any others who have come into contact with it . . . and pray to the Otherworld that I cannot carry it.'

'Tory.' Maelgwn smiled, barely able to part his eyelids; still, the sight of her face made his pain seem one hundred times less. 'I can hardly believe thou hast come to my aid after all I put thee through,' he whispered, his voice husky and weak. 'But then, thou hast never ceased to amaze me.'

'Hush now.' Tory helped him take a drink of water. 'Forget this month past, it hast been naught but a bad dream. Thou must concentrate on getting better.'

The king gave half a laugh as his head collapsed back onto the pillow. 'There shall be no recovery for me, Tory. I have resigned myself to the fact that this be what I deserve.'

'I strongly beg to differ.' Now she was angry with him. 'Thy jealousy and guilt be the cause of this damn disease, Maelgwn, and if thou dost not give it up and forgive thyself, as I have, thou art going to wipe out our whole kingdom!' She took hold of his face to will him to fight. 'Please . . . I beg thee, do not let Mahaud win.'

Maelgwn smiled faintly once more, closing his eyes. 'Dear, sweet, Tory . . . if only I could be as strong and fair as she.'

His words brought tears to her eyes. 'Thou art not going to give up on me, damn it. I love thee, Maelgwn. I have never, and will never, love anybody else.'

'Truly?' He opened one eye to view her.

'Oooh!' Tory raised herself from the bed, enraged. 'What do I have to do, huh? What will it take —?'

'Just teasing.'

He appeared rather amused with himself, which Tory saw as an encouraging sign. 'Then thou shalt fight this thing with me?'

The king held out his hand, and Tory rushed over to take hold of it.

'That be the story of our life,' he replied.

There was so much Tory needed to do and so little time to do it in. She had no idea how long it would take for this disease to inflict its ultimate toll upon the king. The only indication she really had was the young maiden, who had also been beset by the disease. The girl, though severely weakened, had yet to pass away, and she was far more fragile than Maelgwn.

Though Tiernan, Rhun and Tadgh all seemed unaffected by their contact with the disease, they were quarantined as ordered. Sir Tiernan's wife, Ione, and a couple of the housemaids that had been tending the sick girl, were also confined to separate quarters for observation.

It proved useless trying to isolate Selwyn, however, for he kept teleporting himself to the king's chamber to soothe his king's discomfort with the melodious strains of his harp. As Maelgwn was most grateful for the enchanting distraction, and Selwyn was careful to keep his distance, Tory allowed it. What choice did she have? All the guards and walls in Gwynedd would not sway such loyalty.

With the king bedridden, and Tiernan, Ione, Rhun and Selwyn all in isolation, the responsibility of keeping the peace had fallen upon the shoulders of young Sir Gawain and Sir Angus. Since the banishment of the Goddess, and all the looting that had befallen Gwynedd since that time, the people of the land had threatened an uprising if something wasn't done. Apparently, the Saxon retreat couldn't have been more timely. Tory sent out messengers to the four corners of the kingdom to advise one and all of the Goddess's return.

A small contingent of men arrived from Powys late the following evening, to present their soon-to-be king to the High Queen for his swearing in to her group of masters. Eormenric accompanied the prince's party as requested, and despite the language barrier he didn't feel at all uncomfortable travelling with the group of Britons. One of Blain's advisers that did speak Anglo-Saxon had been acting as a translator for him, so Eormenric was starting to pick up a few words of the native tongue here and there.

The party was fed in the court dining room, before being shown to their allocated rooms within the citadel. The two initiates were advised that their audience with the High Queen would take place the following morning after the Masters had completed kata at sunrise. Blain was invited to join the High Queen for this exercise, and Eormenric was welcome to observe.

The young Saxon warrior was still rather drowsy as he followed Prince Blain to the great room of court.

They entered to find the Goddess and two of her Masters executing a series of slow, graceful movements in the middle of the huge room. Each position of their routine perfectly mimicked that of each other, and was in complete harmony and time with the group as a whole.

The Briton's referred to this exercise as kata. Eormenric found this quite extraordinary indeed, and as he watched what he was about to learn, his entire being tingled with expectation.

Blain, familiar with the exercise, quietly approached the group and joined in; the thrill of training with the Goddess was so great that it very nearly broke his concentration. But after just a moment or two, his deep breaths calmed his thoughts and his movements began to flow along with the others in the same graceful manner.

As Eormenric was engrossed with the mesmerising exhibition, he hadn't noted someone else entering. When he spied a figure out of the corner of his eye standing beside him, he near jumped out of his skin.

This girl was quite akin to the Goddess, appearing very warrior-like as opposed to the more feminine women he was accustomed to.

She suppressed a giggle upon noting his stunned expression, and wandered over to join the others.

Once their exercise had drawn to a close, the High Queen approached her two new arrivals to welcome them. 'What dost thou think so far?' she inquired of Eormenric.

'I think I have much to learn.'

'Blain.' Tory motioned Javotte to join them. 'Dost thou remember Javotte?'

'We have met before, Majesty,' the maiden informed her. 'It hast been a long time though.' Her gaze shifted from Tory to Blain. 'How fares thy eye?'

Though the Queen did not understand what was obviously a private joke between the two, Blain gave a chuckle of recognition.

'Long healed,' he assured. 'I do swear to thee, I did not mean to kill thy cat. At the time I had yet to perfect the art of wielding a slingshot.'

Javotte smiled at this, placing a hand on her hip and slouching in her stance. 'Well, I would hope thy aim hast improved since then.' She couldn't resist the chance to have a dig.

Blain didn't mind too much, as he did sort of deserve it. 'And I would hope thy aim hast not.'

'Indeed.' Tory interrupted; my, this was going to work out well. 'Javotte shall be thy new sparring partner,' she announced with glee, astonishing them both.

'What!'

'But Javotte be a woman!' Blain protested.

'Brilliant observation,' Javotte taunted, insulted by his attitude.

'I am a woman.' The High Queen pointed out.

'But . . . but . . .'

'Sorry, Highness?' Javotte goaded him further. 'I cannot understand thee with that foot in thy mouth.'

All present had a chuckle at the young prince's expense.

'Let us give it a try, shall we,' Tory suggested. 'If by the end of the day thou dost not feel Javotte a sufficient challenge, then I shall rethink the circle. Fair enough?'

'Aye.' Blain seemed pacified by the suggestion.

'Fine with me,' Javotte agreed. 'But a word of warning, I hit much harder these days.' She wandered off to get prepared.

Blain roused half a smile. 'Great.'

After a workout to warm up, a brief sparring match between Blain and his proposed partner proved the High Queen's judgement quite sound.

'I concede I was severely mistaken about thee,' Blain mumbled, delirious, spreadeagled on the floor after his third knock-out punch from Javotte.

By the Goddess she was good, perhaps even better than Ione, but then the prince had yet to see how well Javotte wielded a broadsword — the thought was rather frightening.

'Oh, come on, Majesty . . . I wast just getting started.' Javotte very courteously lent him a hand to get to his feet.

'Well, I am quite finished, thanks all the same.'

Blain was a little woozy once vertical, and Javotte steadied him. 'I think thee might be right.'

'I am pleased she be thy partner, Highness,' Eormenric commented after witnessing the slaughter.

'I thought thy partner should be Bryce,' Tory advised Eormenric. 'But for the time being, thy training shall be handled by Sir Gawain.'

'Majesty, I am not sure if that would be wise.' Gawain was sporting a look that could kill.

'Why ever not?' Tory enquired, well aware of the reason, though she wanted him to be out with it, so that it might be resolved before it festered into a problem.

Gawain was hesitant to admit his resentment towards the Saxon's presence, yet he stared at Eormenric undaunted. 'I lost both my parents at Aberffraw and my want of revenge dost run deep, sensei.'

As Tory translated her knight's woes to Eormenric, he recalled the sight of the holocaust of which they spoke; he was not proud of what he'd allowed to happen, not even at the time. 'I lost my father in all of this, too.'

Tory had no need to convey the response as Gawain spoke Eormenric's tongue as proficiently as Rhun did, but she translated for the benefit of the others present who did not.

'As did I.' Blain's brain began to function again. 'But creating more trouble shall not bring my father back, nor will it help the future of this fine land of ours.'

'Spoken like a true master,' Tory commended the young prince. 'Thou shalt make a formidable king.'

Blain bowed his head to accept her compliment. 'I hope so.'

'Dost thou see the sense of it, Gawain?' Tory beseeched him, but he was still none too willing to submit.

'For goodness' sake, Gawain . . . what be wrong with thee?' Javotte approached to snap him out of it. 'My mother died at Aberffraw, too. If thou dost not stop this foolishness, thy hatred shall make thee sick.'

'I know, but . . .'

'But, nothing! We have all been through a lot lately, but we must work together.' She grabbed hold of him by the shirt. 'It be the only way to prevent the witch's return. If thou dares provide a channel for her, I shall kill thee myself.'

'Alright! I shall do it.' He surrendered, nearly cracking a smile. 'I just thought I should make my feelings known.'

'And rightly so,' Tory agreed. 'But Javotte be right . . . revenge be not the way of the Goddess, Gawain, it be the way of the witch. It be thine own decision, but thou must choose between us. For one cannot walk two entirely different paths, not even for a short while.'

Suddenly it was clear to the young knight why his sensei had given him the assignment, and as he did honour her judgement above all others, he walked over to Eormenric and held out his hand. 'Then I choose to forgive thee,' he conveyed in Anglo-Saxon, which seemed to excite their visitor no end; Gawain had to admit he did seem a likeable enough character.

'I do thank thee, Sir Gawain, and am most gratified to be able to tell thee so.' Eormenric grasped hold of the knight's outstretched hand and shook it firmly.

'Then it be settled.' Tory was proud of them; hopefully the children would not make the same mistakes their parents had. 'Sir Angus shall begin thy training in my absence.' She looked to Blain and Javotte.

'Where art thou going?' Blain was disappointed; he'd finally got to train under the Goddess and now she was going away.

'Do not fear, I shall not be gone very long,' she stated with a smile, praying on the quiet that she was right.

'How long be not long?'

'A few hours, a few days . . . I cannot say.' Any longer and she might lose her love. 'But I promise, thou shalt not have enough time to even notice me missing.'

'I shall see to that,' Angus assured the prince.

Following a short meditation that concluded a rather eventful morning, Tory ran her new initiates over the laws and pledges of the Masters. Each of them swore to uphold and respect the ways of the Goddess. They vowed to act in a manner reflective of the divine and to disclose nothing of their training to any other living soul without first obtaining the High Queen's permission. For this was the worst crime a master could commit, and it carried a sentence of death.

Eormenric, Blain and Aella were presented with their master's attire, bearing the emblem of the dragon on the back; one uniform of white to wear during their training, and one suit of black for when they trained others in the name of the Goddess.

'On behalf of myself . . .' Tory began, with Gawain repeating her words in Saxon for Eormenric's benefit, 'Maelgwn, the High King of Gwynedd; Vortipor, the Protector of Dyfed; Prince Rhun of Gwynedd; Prince Bryce of Powys; Sir Gawain of Din Lligwy; Sir Angus of Caernarvon; Sir Tiernan . . . champion to the king; and my champion, the Lady Ione, I do welcome thee to our circle.' The beaming faces of her newest students filled the Queen with fresh hope. 'In doing so, remember that thou art a teacher, a protector, and a representative of Britain, the Goddess and her mysteries. I want thee to consider those aforementioned, and those who stand beside thee now, to be more sacred to thee than thy life. Regard them at all times with the same respect thou would want for thyself. This be the will and the way of the Goddess.'

'So be it,' Javotte and Blain said with great enthusiasm.

Eormenric echoed their resolve, as it seemed the thing to do, and his two new comrades hugged him and each other in turn. Their time to prove themselves as one of the elite had finally come.

By the midnight hour of that same evening Tory had addressed all the pressing affairs of state and settled in her new initiates. She'd left strict instructions with the head maidservant at Degannwy of the precautions to be observed when attending to those confined to quarantine. Tory then went to visit each of those in question, before her departure, leaving Rhun and Maelgwn till last.

Her son, to her surprise, was still wide awake, reading a book by candlelight.

'Praise the Goddess. I thought thou would never come.' He rose to embrace his mother. 'How fares the king?'

'He be holding on, Rhun.'

His mother seemed downhearted, which was not like her at all. 'The girl hast died then?'

It was times like these that Tory was thankful she was not forced to explain herself, as maintaining a positive outlook was becoming increasingly difficult. 'Aye, moments ago. Thus, the time I have remaining to find a cure seems to have been considerably lessened.'

'Time be an illusion, Mother.' He smiled, giving her a nudge in encouragement. 'Thou, better than anyone, should know that.'

'Indeed. But, unfortunately, it be an illusion I do not fully understand.'

'Mother, please.' Rhun sat her down. 'I can stand to see anybody else this unsure, but not thee. If thou dost lose hope there be no chance for the king.'

'I know, I know.' Tory thought this rather unfair; she was as emotionally vulnerable as the next person, why was she the only one never allowed to admit when she was frightened or upset. 'I am fine, really.' She smiled to reassure him. 'I just wanted to see that thou still fared well before I left.'

'I am as fit as a fiddle,' he announced, though he did feel a mite lethargic from laying around all day.

'Well, then, I should depart and see Maelgwn before I leave.' She stood and embraced him again.

'Take me with thee,' Rhun begged; he couldn't imagine what life would be like if she never found her way back to them.

'Too dangerous,' she announced, pulling back to view him. 'I could end up with grandchildren from one end of time to the other.' She slapped his shoulder with a wink, before becoming more serious. 'But should something happen and I am unsuccessful . . .'

'I know what should be done.' Rhun didn't even want to consider the possibility. 'But thou shall not fail. Thou never hast.'

'Of course.' She took a deep breath and made for the door.

'I love thee,' he pledged, with a good serve of sentiment.

'And I love thee tenfold that.' She blew him a kiss, closing the door behind her.

Selwyn was still keeping his vigil at the king's side and was softly strumming a tune on his harp when Tory entered.

'How fares our patient?' she enquired of the Merlin in a whisper, closing the door.

'I wish I could say.' He placed the harp aside. 'He hath been sleeping a great deal.'

Tory said nothing in response. She stood staring at her ailing husband from a distance, her thoughts seemingly elsewhere.

'Art thou ready to leave?'

'Aye, I suppose so.' She appeared none too happy about it.

'Where art thou going?' Maelgwn questioned, startling both his wife and the Merlin.

Tory knelt down beside the bed and took hold of his hand. 'Only the Otherworld knows.' She smiled at him. 'Wherever I must, to find a cure.' It was obviously a battle for him just to keep his eyes open, but Maelgwn squeezed her hand with what strength he had left.

'Then take my sword.' His eyes drifted across to where the fine steel weapon lay resting against the wall in its sheath. Vortipor had given the king this sword as a wedding gift. 'I know thou art a fine warrior, but I shall rest easier knowing thou bears a decent weapon.'

'As be thy wish, but thou hast no need to worry . . .'

'I know.' He squeezed her hand once more. He still couldn't help feeling a little concerned. 'What I would not give to make love to thee just one more time.'

'Thou hast a one-track mind, my love.' She patted his hand. 'Thou shalt have plenty of opportunities to fulfil thy wish when I return.'

'Promise?'

'I do.' Her eyes moistened, as the fear of her own doubt consumed her. 'So rest now, and I shall return in time to greet thee when thou dost awaken.' She leant up and kissed his forehead. 'Remember how much I love thee, and all shall be well.' She moved to stand, but Maelgwn gripped hold of her hand to prevent her leaving.

'Please, just stay until I fall asleep.'

Tory climbed onto the bed beside him and resting his head upon her breast, she gently stroked his hair until he'd returned to a peaceful slumber.

'Watch over him, Selwyn,' she instructed, strapping on the belt that harnessed the huge sword about her waist.

'Have no fear of that, Majesty.' The Merlin was rather teary-eyed himself. 'It be thyself that worries me more . . . do take care.'

'Fear not.' She felt her determination and confidence returning. 'I do solemnly swear that I shall walk back through that door before the next sunset.' She hugged him to draw strength, and vanished before another word could be said.

10

DIVINE INTERVENTION

By the light of the full moon, Llyn Cerrig Bach was a hauntingly beautiful place. The soft, blue light filtered down through the canopy of huge trees overhead, falling in shadowy wisps across the temple ruins.

Tory had no idea why she'd decided to start her search here. But then, deep down, she still suspected Taliesin hadn't really abandoned them — or was it more wishful thinking?

Surely the High Merlin couldn't have truly meant what he'd said about Maelgwn; the king had always been like a son to him, his prize student before she had come into the picture.

Upon ascending the stone stairs, Tory entered the inner sanctuary of the Goddess. Here, a circle of statues that represented the nine muses of metaphysical law watched over the stone altar in the centre surrounded by the overgrown exterior foundations.

Although Tory was not a great believer in ritual worship, she approached the altar reverently. The nature of the powerful energies that surrounded this place had remained outside the realms of her understanding — and the understanding of all mankind for that matter. Not to mention the type of phenomena that the earth's natural energy grid spat forth at times. She did realise that the place where she stood was a ley line crossing, and that the local people believed Llyn Cerrig Bach to be a doorway to the Otherworld. Yet the full purpose of such sites remained a mystery. Therefore, it made good sense to exercise a little caution.

'Taliesin?' Tory took a stand on top of the stone altar, as she'd done many times before. 'Taliesin, are you there?'

Her voice seemed to shatter the eerie silence, although she'd not spoken very loudly. It was as if every living thing in the vicinity had suddenly stopped what it was doing to hear what she had to say — even the breeze was taking a silent pause.

'Please, Taliesin! If you are still here, I implore you to make yourself known . . . don't just watch me from the shadows.' She was losing hope. 'I really need your help now!'

'He hast gone,' a woman's voice, soft and sweet, advised her.

Tory spun around, trying to peer into the shadows that seemed to be leering at her. 'Who speaks?' she demanded. 'Show yourself.' Her right hand was poised on the hilt of the sword that hung on her hip.

'You have no need of your weapon with me, Tory Alexander.'

The statue that stood in the central position behind the altar began to glow with a soft purple hue.

'Don't you know me?' the voice questioned with a delighted strain.

A face and then the torso of a woman, who appeared the very image of herself, took form and emerged out of the solid stone.

'What . . . who? . . . I don't understand?' Tory managed to stammer.

'Well, we have never met face to face before,' she explained with a smile of greeting.

'Sorcha?' Tory chanced a guess.

Maelgwn's mother, the Queen of the late King Caswallon, had been killed long before Tory had arrived in the Dark Age. It was true that they had never met. Yet, on more than one occasion, the late Queen had assumed wilful control over Tory's body to execute certain deeds in the physical world. The prophetic dreams and gentle guidance Tory had received from her since the time of those events had also proven invaluable. They had had a fair amount of contact in the years past, and Tory had sensed that Sorcha was never far away, especially in a time of crisis. She had been told many times of the striking resemblance she bore to the late Queen, and viewing Sorcha with her own eyes even Tory found the likeness hard to believe.

'Indeed.' Sorcha's full form now floated completely independent of the statue from which she'd emerged. Her long, silvery hair and her glittering, mauve robes flowed about her gracefully, though there was still not a hint of breeze to be felt. 'But I have become so much more these days.'

Tory thought Sorcha's choice of words rather curious. 'How so?'

'Well, in perfect synchronicity with thou obtaining thy immortal state of being, I have become more than just a past-life manifestation of thyself. I am again part of our total consciousness. You might know me better as thy Higher Self. In fact, every different manifestation of thyself that ever was or will be, be one with us.'

'How awful for you all . . .' Tory felt guilt-ridden by the news. 'I am so sorry.'

'Do not be sorry, my sweet,' Sorcha chuckled. 'I do not mourn physical existence. To tell you the truth, I much prefer the role of guide. I am more than happy to leave the physical experience to thee.'

Tory couldn't understand this at all. 'But don't you miss Caswallon, and . . . you know . . .' she took a modest pause, 'sex?'

'We experience and learn through thee,' Sorcha explained with an echo of laughter in her words. 'And Taliesin was right, thou art the finest physical incarnation of us all, and thus the best equipped for the job.'

Tory was starting to feel uncomfortable about all of this. 'But Maelgwn is your son?'

'Yes, and my husband, and my father, and in the long run myself, too.'

'But how can that be?' Tory was perplexed. 'Are you saying that a soul-mind can split apart and coexist within the same time, space and dimension?' Tory had a sudden burst of awareness and began to pace as she thought. 'Well, why not?' She answered herself. 'If time is simultaneous, and we shall all be part of the one divine consciousness some day, then that has to be the case.' Tory looked to Sorcha, who appeared very pleased with her resolve.

'I think we should aid her. I believe she be ready,' Sorcha announced to the circle of nine.

Before Tory knew what was happening, all nine of the statues began to glow a different pastel shade in a whole spectrum of colours.

'I agree.' The maid in blue, who had the appearance of Katren, voiced her view.

Then, in an anti-clockwise sequence around the circle, the women lay their blessings upon her: Cara, Alma, Jenovefa, Ione, Aella, her Aunt Rose and Tory's mother, Helen.

The poor girl was overwhelmed to see so many she had lost throughout time. But then she realised she hadn't really lost them at all, they were all just an extension of herself. She began to tremble uncontrollably and tears flowed down her cheeks as she felt the awesome power of the force that was bearing down upon her.

Suddenly the nine women merged to become three. They seemed more defined now, one dressed in white, one in red, and the other, the eldest, in black.

The triple goddess! What is going on?

'Do not be alarmed, child,' said the tiny woman in black.

She was of unusual appearance; young of face, her hair long and silver, like Taliesin's. Her features were somewhat pixie-like, as her ears were small and pointed, and her eyes were large, yet slanted.

Could this be Keridwen, the dispenser of the Old Truths?

'Thy instinct serves thee well.' She appraised the subject before her. 'I am just a further extension of thy universal mind.'

Tory's eyes broadened. 'I see the truth of it.' She paused but a moment, to gather her thoughts. 'Maelgwn is dying . . .'

'We know thou dost seek a cure, but we cannot supply this to thee directly,' the woman in red, the warrioress, told her.

This woman, named Rhiannon in local mythology, appeared very much like Tory in build and height, but her hair sat in long, fiery waves. In her capacity within the triple Goddess, she had charge of justice and the airing of the truth.

'We can, however, grant thee passage to a place where such cures abound,' the lady in white, Branwen, added with a smile.

This beautiful young maiden was the teacher of truth and the guardian of righteousness. Her skin was fair, though it did have a slightly golden hue. Her eyes were dark as night, as was her long, straight hair.

'Fair enough.' Tory submitted to the suggestion, not sounding incredibly thrilled; she worried for her love and her people, time was wasting.

'It is all just an illusion in the end, my child. The object be experience, and then to learn from that experience. Thee too must master, and trust in, the universal process.' Keridwen approached her mentally and emotionally exhausted pupil. 'The ability to save a human life is a powerful thing, and cannot be placed into the hands of an amateur. It must be learnt and mastered, the same as everything else. As for finding a miracle cure, thou might get lucky, who knows? But thou must seek thy own solutions. I am not here to give them to thee . . . for what could be learnt from such an act?'

'Is that what you told Taliesin?' Tory sniffled, feeling very put in her place.

'It be exactly what I told him.'

Tory was silent a moment. 'So where be this place?'

Keridwen shook her head. Tory's mind was indeed bleary or she would surely have known. 'Mankind did know a Golden Age of civilisation, back in the Old Land . . .'

'Atlantis.' Tory became excited; this was surely where Taliesin had gone. 'You can send me there?'

'If thou dost wish it.' Branwen confirmed.

'I do.' Tory swore wholeheartedly.

'Now, be warned . . .' Rhiannon moved closer. 'All the rest shall be up to thee . . . we shall offer thee no more aid beyond this point.'

'For, although we owe thee much, for all thou hast done for our cause, and the cause of mankind . . .' Branwen admitted, 'even this favour be somewhat out of line with Cosmic Law.'

'I understand.' Tory stood tall, not to be swayed. She tried not to think about problems before they arose, so as not to jinx herself.

'Well, then,' Keridwen motioned her two associates closer, her eyes still fixed on Tory, 'as thou hast acted as a channel for us so often, allow us to act as a channel for thee.'

The three women began to merge into one angelic being that had no definable shape. Their combined manifestation appeared as a glowing green haze that spoke with the voices of all three Goddesses.

'Be guided, Tory Alexander, for thou hast still much to learn . . . and much to teach.'

The powerful green mass began to approach her and Tory froze, speechless and terrified beyond all reason.

In a flare of light, love and energy, all fear departed from the divine's over-awed subject, and she was swept out of the Dark Age into one that promised great enlightenment.

PART TWO

THE UNIVERSE

CHARACTERS OF ATLANTIS

Shu Sar (supreme king):	Absalom (father of peace)
Shar (prince, 1st born):	Alaric (noble ruler)
Shar (prince, 2nd born):	Turan (bond of heaven)
Shar (prince, 3rd born):	Xavier (bright)
Shar (prince, 4th born):	Gaspard (treasure master)
Shar (prince, 5th born):	Zadoc (just)
Shar (prince, 6th born):	Diccon (firm ruler)
Shar (prince, 7th born):	Seth (appointed prophet)
Shar (prince, 8th born):	Lazarus (helper, seer)
Shar (prince, 9th born):	Jerram (war raven)
Shar (prince, 10th born):	Adelgar (noble spear)
Nin (lady, 1st wife of Shu Sar):	Melcah (queen)
Nin (lady, 2nd wife of Shu Sar):	Orphelia (clever)
Nin (lady, 3rd wife of Shu Sar):	Salome (peaceful)
Nin (lady, 4th wife of Shu Sar):	Kila (earth seer)
Nin (lady, 5th wife of Shu Sar):	Mahar (woman of red)
Chief High Priest/Magi (healers):	Shu - Asa (healer)
High Priestess:	Nin - Bau (lady who brings dead back to life)
Head Truth Seer:	Nin - Sibyl (prophetess)
Lord High Guardian (Sciences):	En - Seba (eminant)
Chief of the Mind sciences:	En - Norbert (bright metaphysician)
Chief of the Body sciences:	En - Darius (preservar)
High Magi, The Orders of Passage:	Shu - Micah (godlike)
Head Healer of Kheit-Sin:	Nin - Lilith (clever)
Head Healer of Khe-Ta:	Nin - Tabitha (gazelle)
Head Healer of Danuih:	Nin - Anthea (lady flower)
Head Priest of Akhantuith:	En - Cato (cautious)
Head Priest of Ta-Khu:	En - Durand (lasting)
Atlantean name for Taliesin:	En - Razu (shining wise lord)
Atlantean name for Tory:	Lamamu (divine master of love and war)
Shar Alaric's Wife:	Antonia (precious)
Chief of the Annunnaki:	Anu (he of heaven)
Wife of Chief Anu:	Keturah (incense)

Son of Anu:	Calisto (most beautiful)
Banished Head of Mind Sciences:	Keeldar (battle)
Antillian name for Keeldar:	Engur (Lord of the Rockets)
Chief of Antillia:	Zutar (leader)
Son of Zutar:	Rastus (staunch)
Rastus' Girl:	Lana (light)
Zutar's Atlantean Prisoner:	Mahala (sweet singer)
Jerram and Adelgar's Scout:	Thais (gift from the divine)

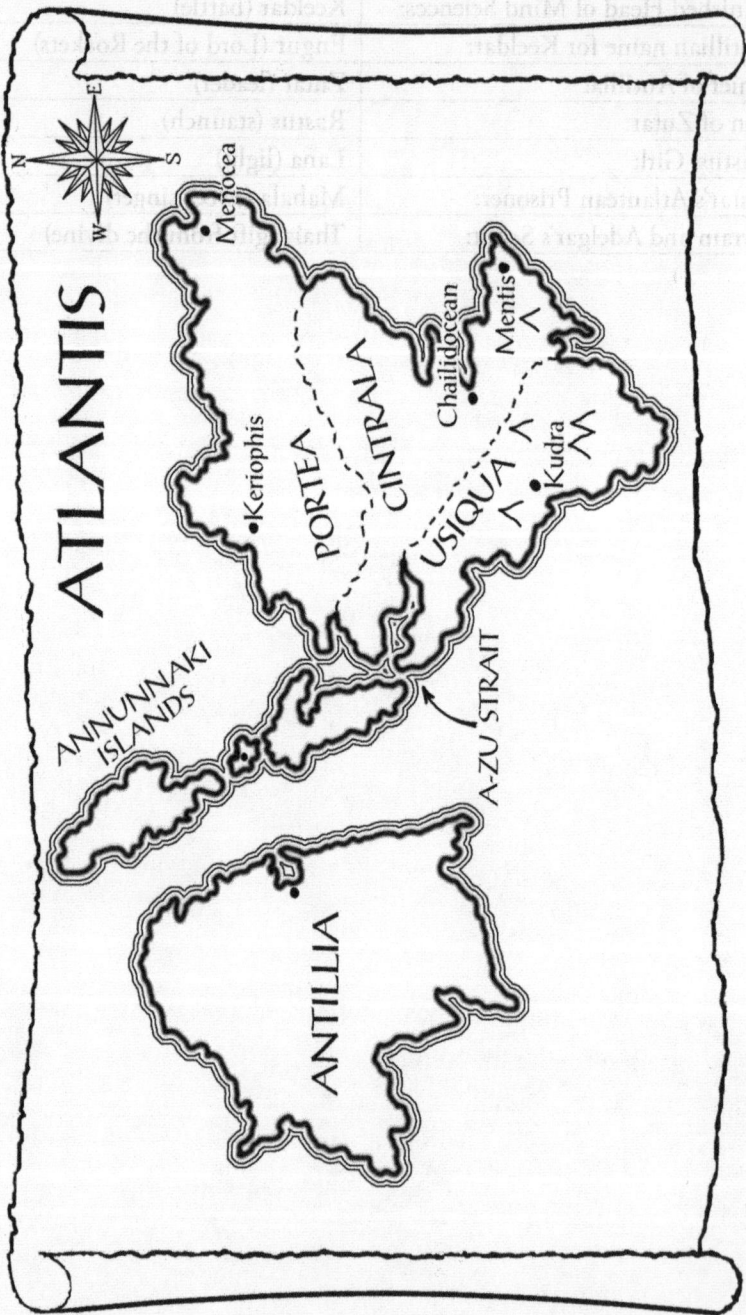

ATLANTIS

Menocea

Keriophis

PORTEA

CINTRALA

Chaliliocean

Mentis

Kudra

USIQUA

ANNUNNAKI ISLANDS

AZU STRAIT

ANTILLIA

11

A HEALING PLACE

Taliesin hurried up the marble stairs into the Shi-im-ti temple, his bare feet preventing any sound as he made his way to the healing chambers of Shu Sar Absalom.

Attending the Sar in his sanctuary for rejuvenation was the Lord High Magi of the Healing Orders, Shu Asa, and En Darius, Chief Magi of the Body Sciences. Shar Turan, the second-born son of the Shu Sar and Head of Technologists, was present to assist with the operation.

It was the young Shar Turan who moved to greet Taliesin as he entered. *En Razu.*

This was the name the Merlin had been given here; it meant 'shining wise lord'. It was, coincidentally, the same name the Britons of the Dark Age had given him; Taliesin meant 'shining brow'.

I am sorry I am late. Taliesin slowed and calmed himself to greet his colleagues. En Durand and En Cato detained me with their comments on the extraordinary energies disturbing the circuits of time at present.

So they have felt it then? Turan appeared vaguely pleased with himself.

You have been alerted to it, too? This was intriguing.

Of course. Turan was very matter-of-fact about it. I have felt a huge build-up of feminine energy within the continuum.

That's a highly unusual observation for you, my Shar. Taliesin nearly dragged a smile out of his friend, who was far too serious.

Will you all stop discussing science for a moment, and come and do something about this beastly headache of mine! the normally good-natured Sar Absalom entreated his subjects impatiently.

A thousand apologies, Highness. Taliesin approached the thick, marble healing tablet upon which the Shu Sar lay. We shall not delay another moment.

Under normal circumstances, there were several healing processes a patient was required to go through before the healing of the physical body took place; the etheric and mental state of being of the patient needed to be balanced and cleansed first. Though, in the Sar's case, because his pain was so unbearable, he was undergoing a kind of emergency surgery. When he was more at ease to be receptive to the rest of his treatment, his etheric and mental bodies would be addressed.

Shu Asa and En Darius, the two finest healers in the known world, assisted their Sar to a comfortable, workable position. En Darius then placed a large emerald jewel upon the forehead of their patient.

Breathe steadily, my Sar, Taliesin instructed with his sweet, tranquillising voice. He then moved to the end of the marble tablet and took hold of Absalom's feet, sending healing energy up through his body.

Shar Turan, who had taken up a position beside the psychokinetically operated control panel, opened and adjusted a porthole in the domed ceiling to align the sun's rays with the healing stone on his father's forehead. A beam of sunlight crept across the white marble floor as it honed in on its designated position. It was mid-morning, so when the light met with the stone it shone in at a sixty degree angle from behind the Sar's head.

The stone began to glow as it absorbed the sun's healing energy, and after a moment or two the Sar gave a great sigh of relief. *That feels wonderful!*

But no sooner had Absalom thought so than the thin beam of light flared to a blinding green flash.

The sudden phenomena took Taliesin off guard and he was flung backwards to the floor.

'DANUIH!' the Sar cried. This was the name of the Earth Goddess, the divine mother of creation.

When all present had had a moment for their eyes to re-adjust after the flash of light, they beheld a young woman resting comfortably against their patient.

Oh my. Absalom didn't quite know what to think as the lovely young girl in his arms began to stir.

'What happened?' Tory raised herself, feeling awfully groggy.

She is armed. Shar Turan raised a hand to claim the weapon from her, but Taliesin prevented it.

No, it's alright . . . He stared at Tory, rather amazed she'd found him again. I know this girl.

As Tory peeked out from underneath her drowsy eyelids, her eyes came to focus on Renford, her father. 'Dad?'

What did she call me? Sar Absalom wanted to know.

'It means father or pa,' the Merlin explained.

'Taliesin?' Tory's head shot around upon hearing his voice. Yet the sight of Maelgwn, floating beside the Merlin, was too much for her and she passed out cold on the floor.

I don't care what anyone has to say about it, Sar Absalom insisted, as he passed through the lovely gardens in the courtyard of the Shi-im-ti temple with En Darius in tow.

But my dear Sar . . .

No, I do not want to hear another word. The Sar stopped by the fountain to pick a few of the rainbow-coloured flowers that grew by it. *I had the stone of the Goddess Danuih upon my forehead at the time, and I saw her divine presence with my own eyes! Then the girl's first word to me turns out to mean father . . . you were there, you heard her. What further proof do you need?!* the Sar asked.

But if I could just run a few simple tests to confirm . . .

Do whatever tests you like. My view shall not change. The Sar strutted merrily through the entrance that led to the part of the temple where his new child had been taken to rest; he was feeling much improved since her arrival.

The Shu Sar entered the recovery room to find his dear adviser, En Razu, still watching over their mysterious visitor and his son, Turan, observing her with a kind of clinical interest.

How fares the dear child? The Sar passed his small bouquet to a temple novice to put in water; the junior orders of the priesthood were easily definable by their pale green garments.

She is resting peacefully, Highness. Taliesin rose to address the Sar.

Absalom approached the healing cubicle where Tory lay sleeping, gazing upon her with considerable pride. *Typical, is it not, that my first child not born of a mortal woman is neither male, nor a twin?*

The Shu Sar had taken five wives in his desire for children, for every woman was only allowed by law to give birth once. Each of these fine women had borne him twin sons. After the fifth set, the Sar had given up all hope of ever having a daughter.

What do you think of your little sister, Turan?

As his father appeared in such wonderful spirits, Turan didn't wish to dampen his mood. *She appears as fine as any other of her gender.*

The finest! Absalom corrected him with glee, before frowning slightly. *Though she is rather short. But never-to-mind,* he shrugged off the observation. *Her good looks and fine form make-up for that . . . wouldn't you say, En Razu?*

Indeed, Majesty. Taliesin had to smile. *You have no idea.*

Yes, well . . . Absalom looked back to his divine little girl, dressed in unusual attire, complete with weapon and all. *What are we going to name her?*

Taliesin released a slight chuckle at the notion. *I have a fair idea.* But he waved off suggesting it. *I think you should wait for her Rights of Passage. Let En Micah and his council decide what is suitable.*

The ceremony of which Taliesin spoke was usually held when a child reached three years of age. At this time, the Priests of the Orders of Passage would measure the individual's sonic, particle and auric frequencies. This enabled the child in question to be guided into the areas of study for which his, or in this case her, talents were best suited. A name appropriate to each individual's destiny was also given at this time.

You're right, of course, Absalom conceded with a beaming smile on his face. *I am just so excited . . . you understand.*

Rightly so. Taliesin humoured him.

Well, I must be off. The Sar headed for the door. *But you will send for me when she wakes.* The leader paused in his tracks and turned back to seek confirmation.

Of course, Highness. Taliesin bowed slightly, as did Turan, and the Shu Sar took his leave of them.

I have never heard anything more ridiculous in my life! Turan was pleased to be finally able to voice his mind. *Do you think my father is finally going senile on us?*

No comment. But I do suspect both your science and the priesthood are going to have a hard time disproving his claim.

Taliesin considered that if Shar Turan felt his father's idea preposterous, he'd best not mention to him that Turan had probably been married to the girl in more than one lifetime. For Turan, whose name meant *in the bond of the divine,* spent most of his time studying the mind sciences and had precious little time for anything as trivial as the opposite sex. Besides, the young Shar had managed to raise his personal vibratory rate to such a level that it was akin to the mental plane of thought. Hence, his body lacked the required density for any physical relations to occur.

Taliesin had learnt to do the same thing himself, but he maintained his physical existence most of the time as only it held the key to true experience. Turan, on the other hand, clung to his higher consciousness, for as long as he maintained his semi-physical state he did not age and he could not die, feel pain, or any other emotion for that matter, but he could study, create, theorise and explore the universe all he liked.

Well, Turan began his analysis, *if she is truly of the divine Mother, explain to me how her emotional and mental state became such a mess?*

Turan could readily assess this, as he was perceiving Tory from an etheric level.

I mean just look at her heart chakra. It has a dark patch covering it the size of a melon! And . . .

Taliesin politely motioned the Shar to pause, as he noted Tory stirring from her coma. 'Lady?' He sat himself down on a chair that was right next to her healing chamber; this was all going to be a little strange.

Her eyes wavered open, just long enough to determine who addressed her.

'Taliesin.' She smiled, still very sedate. 'I found you, thank goodness.'

'Indeed you have.' He reached into the solid amethyst cubicle and took hold of her hand.

Tory's eyes ventured to part again, and she cast her sights around the strange, walled bed in which she lay. The smooth, purple stone exuded the most potent calming energy, and positively glowed with a splendid radiance that was in no way hurtful to view. 'Is this crystal?' She sounded enchanted as she reached out with her spare hand to touch it.

'Yes it is.' Taliesin gently took hold of her chin, guiding her sights back towards him. 'You'll find this interesting,' he commented, as he eyed her face over. 'Your eyes have changed colour since last we met.'

'They have?' She rolled them around in her head a second, as if trying to view them for herself. 'What colour are they now?'

'Violet, like mine . . . that will serve you well here.'

Tory let out a half laugh and waved it off; there were other matters more pressing on her mind. 'Why did you leave me, Taliesin?' She squeezed his hand tight. 'I really could have used your help.'

'Why . . .' Taliesin's brow became drawn. 'Because you instructed it, Lady. You said I was to seek out Keridwen, so she could send me back to Atlantis to learn the sacred mysteries from the Old Ones.'

Tory held her head as she sat upright. 'Oh . . .? You're that Taliesin.'

This was not a past-life incarnation of the Merlin, this was his younger self. Tory had sought him out during a visit to the twentieth century, for she'd been told by Taliesin's older self that she would. For the Merlin's travels, backwards and forwards through earth's history, had been rather extensive, and thus at any given time one could never be sure which evolutionary stage of Taliesin's self one was addressing. He didn't appear any different to the Taliesin who'd abandoned her so abruptly in the Dark Age. Though one could surmise by his manner that this soul hadn't been in existence for anywhere near as long as the Taliesin more familiar to her. At this stage of his growth, he was more naive and humble.

'Have I forsaken you in some way?' The Merlin was deeply concerned.

'No, no.' Tory didn't see any point in pursuing it further at this time. 'I am sure I have just misunderstood.'

You two seem to know each other well. Turan made both his curiosity and his presence known.

'Maelgwn!' She gasped faintly under her breath.

He was easily over two metres tall this man, and a band of silver was bound around his forehead. His straight, plum-black hair was much longer than Maelgwn had ever worn his, as it fell to his waist. His eyes were not brown, as her love's had been, but a grey-violet colour that was completely mesmerising. The long robe of pure white he wore was bound at the waist with a royal blue sash that was entwined with another of purple. On his left hand he wore a ring that bore a large sapphire, but set in the ring on his right hand was an amethyst.

Tory's heart skipped a beat as she noted that his legs just disappeared into the solid crystal bed on which she sat. 'Is he a . . . ghost?' she quizzed the Merlin, more than a little uneasy.

'Nay, Lady.' He assured with a laugh. 'Shar Turan maintains a very high vibratory rate, that is all.'

'Shar Turan?' Tory repeated in an inquiring fashion.

'Indeed. The second son of the Shu Sar, the Supreme Ruler, or High King, if you like.'

The Shar bowed slightly to confirm his status, and Tory managed half a smile. 'I see.'

So the sleeper has awakened. En Darius entered. A white, marble tablet floated silently in behind him, carrying his instruments.

Holy moley, it's Rhys! Tory felt a wave of panic pass over her, realising that he hadn't moved his mouth when she heard him speak. It must be telepathy!

'Indeed.' Taliesin confirmed her thought.

'Is there anyone here I don't know?' Tory wondered out loud.

'I doubt it.' Taliesin said simply.

'Well how . . .' Tory paused, deciding to rephrase her question. 'What is he planning to do with all that?' She motioned to the floating table of utensils.

I am just going to examine you. En Darius bethought her, wearing a smile of reassurance.

'Over my dead body!'

Tory absolutely hated doctors and believed very little of what they had to say. She knew sickness was all in the mind, and unaware that this was also what the doctors here believed she wasn't about to let him anywhere near her.

'Tory please.' Taliesin attempted to calm her. 'Your spirit is in great need of cleansing, thus En Darius needs to measure your sonic, particle and auric frequencies.'

'Will it hurt?' She still observed all the strange equipment warily.

'Not in the least,' he emphasised. 'I shall stay, if it will make you more comfortable.'

'Yes do.' She glanced at Turan, then at Darius, for although in the Dark Age she had known them both well, they were total strangers to her now.

Tory marvelled at their style of doctoring, which was more akin to body reading sciences of the twentieth century than the accredited medical profession.

En Darius checked her eyes and the palms of her hands very closely, then carefully measured her hands and the size of her head. The frequency tests were carried out with different hand-held devices that, as they were passed over her body, made a variety of amusing sounds whilst registering her vital statistics. He took both a skin and a blood sample, utilising two other strange little devices that felt as if they'd barely made contact with her body.

The Head Healer of the Body Sciences made notes as he continued his examination, grunting now and then when he made an interesting observation. He was attired in much the same fashion as Turan, though his sash of royal blue was entwined with one of dark green. The headband Darius wore was of a strange pinkish-gold substance. On his left hand was a ring that featured a sapphire, and the ring on his right hand bore an emerald.

Taliesin was attired in exactly the same fashion as Darius, barring the headband, as the Merlin's appeared to be made of solid gold.

When Tory enquired as to the significance of the use of colour, metal and jewels in their attire, Taliesin explained it was just a practical way of identifying who was who.

For example, the white robe told you that the wearer belonged to one of the High Orders of the Priesthood or Sciences. The different sashes and rings identified what Deity's doctrines one had studied. The Goddess Philaeia for example, whose Orders were those of philosophy, science and architecture, was connected to the colour of deep blue, hence her sacred stone was that of a sapphire. The Earth Goddess, Danuih, was naturally associated with dark green, hence her stone was emerald, and so on. Headbands, however, were special awards. A gold headband told you when someone was in the service of the Shu Sar, whereas a band of silver indicated a healer specialising in the field of mental or psychological research. The strange pinkish-gold metal En Darius wore was orichalchum and signified a healer of physical medicine and surgery.

When En Darius had taken his utensils and gone back to his laboratory, a small ball of light entered in his wake. It flashed the three primary colours, in due sequence, until it came to encompass Taliesin's head and turned white.

'What is it?' Tory gaped at the phenomena; it looked just like the cosmic anomaly scientists of the twentieth century referred to as 'earth lights'.

A message. Turan obliged her with an explanation. From the Shu Sar, I imagine.

'Oh . . .' She implied her understanding, even though she couldn't really fathom the idea.

Taliesin's eyes were closed as he perceived the instruction.

Absalom voiced his regret that he could not make himself present to greet his daughter, as he'd been detained at the palace with a problem of a political nature, and as En Darius refused to let her leave the Shi-im-ti Temple before she'd been fully cleansed, their meeting would have to wait a few days. But he instructed that the girl was to be treated in his own personal healing chambers and extended every possible comfort as befitting a child of Shu Sar.

Hence the Merlin guided Tory to the Sar's private sanctuary, explaining that she would probably be spending the next few days there.

Tory was about to protest when she beheld the luxurious abode, and decided that she might never want to leave.

The walls of the large, round room were made of a shiny, smooth substance the like of marble, only it appeared to illuminate its own gentle light. The floor was made entirely from amethyst, as was one of the two pools of water that steamed with a heavenly scent and a healing cubicle the same as the one in the room Tory had just left. The other pool was of fresh stream water that flowed underneath the Shi-im-ti temple, its purifying waters being an essential tool to the Orders of Healing. All manner of plant, both flowering and non-flowering, thrived in the powerful healing energy of the tranquil chamber.

'The Gods?' Tory motioned to eight large, gold statues that stood round the walls. These figures, all roughly two metres in height, were akin to Turan's proportionate stature.

'Indeed. The Shining Ones, as they are known here.' Taliesin indicated a long robe and towel, pale pink in colour, from the wall beside the door. 'I shall leave you to bathe, first in the stream, and then in the pool. Afterwards, you shall be required to wear this.'

'Oh not pink . . . please!' Tory screwed up her nose. 'I hate pink'

'Exactly!' Taliesin emphasised, handing the bundle to her. 'So no arguments. One of the priests will be sent to speak with you presently.' Taliesin headed for the door.

'So please try to accommodate him, and we shall see if we can't get you out of here within a week.'

'A week!' Tory objected, but the Merlin had gone. Her attention turned to the glistening pools of water that awaited her. 'Ah well . . . I'll just have to make the most of it, I guess.' The suggestion made her smile.

12

TO DELVE BEYOND

Tory floated on the surface of the crystal clear spring that had water the colour of brilliant blue. This pool was somehow lit from beneath, and appeared to go to a depth far beyond that which she cared to investigate at present.

A large, round window in the domed roof allowed the afternoon sun to stream in upon her naked body, soothing her being with energising rays. The earth's solar orb lacked the golden hue Tory had come to associate with sunlight; its rays were much whiter here. Still, the water on her skin acted like a conductor for the pure energy, and Tory imagined the experience was like how it might feel to be set adrift on the astral plane.

As she floated into a shady area she opened her eyes. The roof of this delightful dwelling was made from the extraordinarily beautiful metal they called orichalchum. Like polished gold, this pinkish counterpart to the latter was very reflective.

Tory observed her slightly obscured reflection in the dome above, marking how tiny she appeared in the huge space, whereupon she spied two other reflections entering on the other side of the room. Tory moved immediately into a tuck position. *Thanks so much for the warning guys.*

She recognised Turan at once as he floated his way towards her. But she did not identify straightaway the other young man, who walked on his own two feet.

Come, come. There was a mocking tone in Turan's thoughts and gestures. We are your brothers.

'I beg your pardon?' Tory nearly choked.

Have you not heard? Turan came to a stop beside the pool, his hands interlocked comfortably in front of him as he gazed down upon her. Our father, the Shu Sar, thinks you're his daughter. . ... begotten from the divine Mother, Danuih.

'But that's ridiculous.'

That's what I said.

Tory was rather insulted that Turan was so quick to agree. 'Well, let's hear your theory then?' She tried to be modest as she made for her towel. Turan was making her uncomfortable with his probing eyes; she felt like a bug under a microscope.

No, let's hear yours, he suggested firmly.

Tory reached the pool stairs that led up to her towel, but she still had the problem of how to get to it. 'Would you please do me the courtesy?'

Whatever for? Turan made it sound as if she were being childish. I certainly have no physical interest in you.

'Then you won't mind turning around.' She forced a smile.

Allow me. The other young man bethought her, a little appalled by his brother's behaviour. He made haste to fetch her towel. He turned his sights away from her as he walked down the stairs and into the water, holding the sheet of fabric out like a screen.

Once she was safely wrapped up, Tory looked up to the man to thank him. 'Tha . . . *Cai?*' She was taken aback. It was him, only he was much older, not to mention taller. 'Look at you!' She had to smile. 'You're all grown up.'

Yes, Nin. For several hundred years now.

Tory's jaw nearly hit the floor. 'Come again?'

Isn't that funny. His expression changed to one of wonder. *I do feel I know you, too.*

That's wonderful. Turan interrupted the heartwarming scene. Then you'll have lots to talk about. He waved to them as he floated towards the door. *I will expect a full report.* He turned to view his brother, then disappeared through the wall.

'Your brother gives me the creeps,' Tory commented, as she trudged up the stairs.

'He's very clever.'

Though there was a fondness in his voice, Tory nearly jumped out of her skin; he was the first person, apart from Taliesin, who'd used his voice to communicate with her. 'You speak English?'

'No.' His tone was rather comical. 'You just think I do.' As Tory appeared perplexed by the notion, he explained: 'It's still a form of thought projection, only you're perceiving the image of me moving my mouth and words coming out . . . because that's what you feel comfortable with, and I want you to be relaxed. Now, Turan on the other hand . . .' He took a seat on the side of the pool. 'He's what you might call an intellectual.'

'Yeah, no shit.' Tory grinned.

'But he does not realise he is intimidating you . . . he's blissfully unaware of human emotion. He perceives only thought.'

'Why?'

'Because there are fewer distractions between himself and the divine. Turan's perception of information is more attuned to the common good . . . the big picture, you understand.' He shrugged with a smile, and a sigh. 'I wish I could be so disciplined.'

'So what do they call you?' Tory motioned him to turn around, so that she could put on her robe.

He swivelled himself round to face the opposite direction. 'My name is Lazarus. It means helper, or seer, because that is my calling. I investigate that which is ailing people, and then help those people realise and release their dis-ease . . . on an etheric level, that is. Their are others who specialise in the mental and physical levels of sickness.'

'Are you saying I'm sick?' Tory pulled on the weightless garment that felt absolutely wonderful against her skin.

'Quite obviously so, I'm afraid.'

'But that's impossible.' She came to sit beside him. Then, thinking twice about disclosing her secret at present, she corrected herself. 'I mean it's silly . . . I feel fine.'

'That's because physically, you're in wonderful shape. But emotionally and mentally,' he shook his head slowly, 'you're a mess.'

Tory hadn't considered that, although her immortal state of being prevented her from any physical ailments, her subtle bodies could still be prone to dis-ease. 'How can you tell?'

'Your aura and your energy centres say it all,' he informed. 'You have a huge blockage over your heart, another that encompasses both your root and spleen chakras and a small obstruction over your third eye.'

'Really?' Tory was fascinated.

'Yes, and until all these have been worked through and cleansed, you cannot be permitted to leave this temple.'

Oh dear, Tory mused. How on earth was she going to clear these blockages without giving too much away?

Shar Turan had been requested by En Darius to meet with the other members of the High Order of the Shi-im-ti temple.

He arrived in the room of conference to find only Taliesin, En Darius, and Shu Micah, High Magi of the Orders of Passage, in attendance.

Turan thought it unusual for Shu Micah to be interested in what was to be discussed this afternoon, for what possible interest could he have in the girl at this early stage?

Ah . . . Shar Turan. The magi grinned broadly, peering out from under his large hood. Lovely day, isn't it?

I suppose . . . Turan shrugged, rather impartial. This seemed to amuse the old magi somewhat, for he began to chuckle aloud.

Gentlemen, it's amazing! En Cato announced as he entered with En Durand. *The girl is going to have a profound effect on this planet.*

Durand expanded on his colleague's statement. *Yes. According to her chart, her destiny is so immense that it could only be compared to that of En Razu, or yourself, Shu Micah.*

I couldn't agree more. Darius sat back on the large, round conference lounge, its base moulded out of the floor of amethyst.

Surely there is some mistake? Turan interjected. *She is fully human, I'll grant, but there is nothing at all exceptional about her.*

You think so? Darius broke into laughter, Shu Micah along with him.

Here, take a look for yourself. En Durand handed Turan the charts, walking down the stairs to take a seat in the circle with En Cato.

Has anyone found out about her origins yet? Darius was interested in knowing.

I know a little. Taliesin spoke up, immediately gaining the attention of all in the room. *I met her once, in the twentieth century . . . that's about fourteen thousand Earth orbits from now. That's where she was originally born, so I believe.*

Are you sure? En Darius sounded rather sceptical.

My good man. Taliesin seemed surprised by the question. *What have you discovered?* En Darius did not respond. His eyes were focused on the doorway, and he stood as Shu Asa entered.

Everyone present followed suit once they were alerted to the arrival of their Chief High Magi, barring old Shu Micah who merely bowed his head slightly to greet him.

Relax gentlemen. Shu Asa motioned them all to sit as he descended the stairs and seated himself beside Shu Micah. *You must be very excited.*

The old magi nodded, smiling broadly, and Turan had to wonder what on earth had everyone so worked up. He moved down into the conference area to take up a position beside his current instructor, En Durand, and floated cross-legged just above the cushioned seat.

Well, now we are all present, will you please put us out of our suspense, En Durand implored the Chief Healer of the Body Sciences.

Yes, Taliesin added. *Why do you doubt my story of the girl's origins?*

Darius raised his eyebrows, rather perplexed. *Because her physical make-up would seem to indicate that she does stem from our Shu Sar's gene pool.*

Most of the men where taken aback by the statement, especially Turan.

What! No, no, no, there must be . . .

That's not the all of it, Darius advised. *Hear me out. Now, I must admit, some of her genes are of an unknown origin to us, but I can safely confirm that this girl is only second generation from Shu Micah's gene pool as well.*

With this, everyone in the room was thrown into confusion. For Shu Micah was a direct descendant of 'the Shining Ones'. Micah was one of the few of his people who had mastered existence on the earth plane. Still, due to the discomfort and danger of physically manifesting himself on a planet that had an atmosphere so vastly different from his home, he usually employed a subtle form.

En Darius, that's impossible! Turan hated to state the obvious. My father is not even as closely related to the Shining Ones.

You're not listening, my friend. Darius could feel the young Shar's resistance. I said she comes from your father's gene pool . . . but not directly.

So you believe she belongs to the fourth great race of mankind, as opposed to the fifth that inhabited the earth by the twentieth century. Taliesin showed his understanding.

Perhaps both . . . En Darius tried to continue.

That would mean that the Shu Sar's bloodline is still existent some fourteen thousand years from now! Durand could not readily accept this. I'm afraid I find that very hard to believe.

Please gentlemen. Darius was getting tired of being interrupted. Do let me finish. He looked toward the Head Priest in the field of Chaos. Now, as for agreeing with your calculations regarding her destiny, En Cato, the cell activity of the skin sample I took from her is proving rather interesting, in that . . . he paused to take a breath, the cells are still reproducing themselves upon separation from the subject's life force.

Taliesin's eyes parted wide. *But that would mean . . .*

Indeed, Shu Micah confirmed with a smile. Immortality. Like you, En Razu, she has been touched by the divine. We suspect her to be the second of the 'Chosen Ones' to be sent to us for instruction.

Shu Asa stood to resolve. *And thus the prophecy unfolds, gentlemen.*

Lazarus spent an hour or so running through the possible causes behind the particular blockages that Tory's etheric body was experiencing.

He'd started with the largest blockage located over her heart chakra, advising her that this indicated she was pining for a loved one.

Maelgwn, Tory surmised. Or was it mourning Brockwell that had caused it?

Lazarus went on to suggest that perhaps somebody that she'd loved and trusted had let her down; broke her heart so to speak.

This seemed to suggest that Taliesin might have been at least partly the cause of the problem. Lazarus had seemed to hit the nail right on the head with all of his guesses, thus Tory had to consider that he was rather good at his given profession.

He said the blockage over her spleen chakra that extended down to her root chakra, usually pointed to either sexual repression and guilt, or stifled creativity.

This had been a bit of a puzzle to her. Tory had never really been very artistic, though she did express herself through music. She certainly couldn't recall a time when she'd ever felt sexually repressed or guilty, but then she remembered Miles.

Like Turan, Miles was another earthly incarnation of Maelgwn. Tory had met him in the twentieth century about twenty years before, and although she'd willingly admitted to loving him she refused to become intimately involved with Miles whilst she was still married to Maelgwn. She'd felt at the time that an affair would only confuse the issue, but Tory still hoped she would see Miles again at some point in the future.

The dark patch that penetrated Tory's third eye area did so only on the left side of her forehead.

'I would say,' Lazarus summed up. 'That you are allowing some pretty negative force to play on your psyche.'

'Mahaud,' Tory concluded most assuredly.

No matter where thou dost run to, in the whole of time and space, I will follow thee. The witch's last words came back to haunt her.

'Yuk.' Tory shivered. The thought of the witch made her skin crawl.

'Who is Mahaud?' Lazarus enquired, perceiving the dark patch on his patient's forehead expand upon the mention of the name.

'An evil sorceress you don't wish to know about, let me assure you.' Tory shook off the memory.

'Evil?'

'You know . . . harmful, destructive, morally abusive . . .' Tory attempted to make herself clear.

'No,' Lazarus appeared rather perplexed. 'I do not understand these words.

O-oh. If these people literally didn't understand the meaning of the word evil, that left them wide open for attack from the likes of the witch. Tory prayed to the Goddess that Mahaud had not followed her here.

'Well, I guess you'd see her as a very negative person,' Tory began again, 'only she's spirit mostly . . . like Turan but completely opposite in her intent.'

'Oh, I see.' Lazarus smiled broadly, though when he realised the implications of what this meant, his expression collapsed into a frown. 'That's not good.'

'Excuse me.'

Tory and Lazarus turned to see who had entered.

Rhun. Tory's heart leapt to see him.

'Xavier.' Lazarus rose to greet him. 'Tory, allow me to introduce one of our older brothers. He is Head of Research here in the Shi-im-ti temple.'

'That's wonderful . . .' Tory was in shock, and didn't quite know what to say. 'I am pleased to meet you, Xavier.'

'Likewise. I have already heard so much about you.'

Turan had had Xavier summoned to the meeting in the conference room to be briefed before attending their subject. She was, as it turned out, proving to be a woman of major historical significance.

'Lazarus, Turan wishes to see you. I'll take over from here.'

The beaming smile on his brother's face puzzled Lazarus. Xavier was known to be of a cheery disposition, but he appeared completely ecstatic about something.

'Am I healed then?' Tory was disappointed that Lazarus was leaving; she was just starting to feel really comfortable with him.

'I was just here to help you realise the cause of your blockages. Now I will leave you in Xavier's very capable hands.' He smiled as he began to depart. 'I'll see you when you get out of here.'

Tory waved after him then looked to Xavier.

He was dressed just as Darius had been, in a robe of white, a sash of royal blue and one of green. The rings on his fingers were those appropriate to these orders and his headband was made of orichalchum. His hair was long, straight, and as dark as Turan's, but Xavier wore his back off his face in one tidy braid that fell the length of his spine. She noted his eyes were violet, as was the case with everyone else she'd met thus far, and he was about two metres in height. 'So what does your name mean . . . giant?'

As he gazed down upon her, Xavier had to chuckle. 'No, Nin, it means bright.'

'Please, call me Tory . . . nobody else does.' In fact not one person had even bothered to ask what her name was.

'What does that mean?'

'I have no idea.' She shrugged. 'I don't think it means anything.'

'Well, it's totally unsuitable then. En Micah shall give you a proper name, no doubt.'

'What do you mean it's unsuitable.' Tory let out half a laugh. 'It's my name.'

Xavier turned her around and walked her towards the steaming, scented pool made of amethyst, massaging her shoulders gently. 'But one's name should be attuned to one's own sonic frequency to enhance one's personal potential . . . reinforce it.'

'I suppose,' Tory murmured, not really catching his drift, or even caring to. The energy Xavier was channelling into her body was so tranquillising she could barely walk.

'Now into the tub.' He directed her to the steaming pool.

She was so sedate that she automatically followed his instruction and began to untie her robe. 'Hold on a minute.' Tory finally acknowledged her actions and tied the belt back up. 'While you're here?'

'Well I'm going to have a lot of trouble trying to cleanse you from outside the room.' He seemed amused by her protest. 'Trust me . . .'

'If you say, I'm a doctor, I'll hit you.'

'Well, no . . .' Xavier took a serious pause. 'I'm the best, is more what I had in mind.'

He seemed quite serious about the claim, and Tory reached the conclusion that Xavier was every bit as cocky and impressed with himself as her son had been. Needless to say, she felt all the more uncomfortable about disrobing in his presence, Rhun being the philanderer he was. 'Aren't there any women around here?'

'Yes, indeed, I treat several of them every day. But there are none in my profession, if that's what you mean. If being naked around me bothers you, I can remove my — '

'No, really . . .' Tory insisted. 'It's fine.'

'Well, then.' Xavier raised his eyebrows, as he again motioned her to the pool. 'Let us get you cleansed.'

Tory wouldn't have thought twice about undressing for a masseur or a doctor, and as neither Lazarus or Turan seemed even mildly interested in her feminine attributes, Tory figured why should Xavier prove any different. Hence she dropped her robe and descended the stairs into the steamy pool.

Holy Mother! Xavier could hardly believe his eyes.

'I heard that,' Tory warned, gliding along the surface of the scented water that felt kind of silky against her skin.

'I do apologise.' The Shar gave half a laugh, surprised by his own lack of professionalism. 'It's just that I have never seen a woman with such a muscular physique . . . you are truly a warrior.'

'Have you been speaking to Taliesin?'

'No, Nin . . . not he.'

'Who then?'

'That is not your concern at present.' Xavier wandered over to the steps of the pool and took a seat in the water, still fully robed. 'Come.' He motioned her to sit before him.

'Why?' She hesitated.

'Because otherwise I'll have to come to you, and I don't feel like a swim at present.' He again motioned her closer. As she cautiously approached, the Shar turned her around so that her back was to him. He supported her torso between his knees, placing one hand over her third eye and the other palm upwards towards the sunlight.

Tory was forced to close her eyes at this point, his calming energy was so intense. 'That feels unbelievable.'

'Yes, well . . . there is some work involved for you, too.' Xavier spoke ever so softly now. 'I want you to turn your attention to where my hand is placed. Breathe deeply with me, feeling your breath rushing through and cleansing this area on the inhale . . . and as the blockage is released on the exhale, I ask you to envisage the darkness dispersing through your fingers and toes into the water.'

'To prevent you from absorbing it.' Tory had experienced Reike healing before, and this seemed quite similar.

'Indeed.' Xavier was surprised that she knew. 'Now, as you do this, I want you to think of what has caused this blockage.'

'But then you shall know.' Tory ruled that if they could pick up on each other's thoughts from the other side of the room, Xavier would surely know everything, holding her as he was.

'Yes, but I am not permitted to discuss your case with anyone without your consent.' He could feel her tensing up. 'You must trust me, Nin. You shall never get out of the Shi-im-ti temple until we work through this.'

She drew a deep breath in resolve. 'Alright . . .' She let go of the fear; at least it wasn't

Turan treating her. 'But just remember, you asked for it.' She got comfortable again.

'I think I can handle it,' he assured, still blissfully unaware of the complicated history of his patient.

After the conference had adjourned, Shar Turan accompanied En Durand to the Temple of Dur-nu-ga.

This was the main astrological observatory in the city of Chailidocean, and was located across the canal from the circular central island that housed the citadel. All the temples of the Higher Orders were located on the first of the ringed islands that encompassed the royal city, along with the abodes of those who studied there. This meant there was little cause for the scholars and priests to venture far from their well isolated inner sanctum of learning, and most liked it that way.

As Turan entered the temple, he was pondering the Elders' peculiar behaviour towards him during their meeting this afternoon; what had been amusing them so?

What has this girl to do with me? the Shar inquired of his mentor.

Durand came to a complete standstill, stunned by Turan's art for getting straight to the heart of the matter. He tried to be just as straightforward in his retort. *I have been advised not to discuss that with you at present. But, believe me when I say, you are smart enough to work it out for yourself.* Durand was thinking that if the Elders did not want Turan to know of his destiny in this affair, then they should not have been so obvious when vexing him about it.

Could you possibly be a bit more specific? What's come over everyone today? Turan continued towards the observatory.

You're going the wrong way, Durand hinted, *glancing around the large foyer to make sure there was no one to overhear him. If it's answers you seek, try the Hall of Records.*

Why? What am I looking for exactly? Turan returned to Durand's side, and the priest thought hard before resolving to take action. *Follow me.*

Durand spread Tory's chart out on one of the huge study benches, whilst Turan entered one of the many long rows where the astrological charts where filed systematically for easy reference.

Why am I looking for my birth chart? Turan willed the old scroll from its place on the shelf, then directed it towards En Darius. The scroll floated towards the study table and came to rest gently upon it.

All shall be made clear, Durand assured, *as he pinned the last corner of Tory's chart down securely. Now, it has been decided by En Micah, En Cato, Shu Asa and myself, that this girl's name shall be Lamamu . . . guess why?*

Divine master of love and war, Turan surmised, *looking to the girl's chart. Well, 'divine master' comes from what we have already learnt of her.* Turan motioned to the chart. *And as both the planet of war and the planet of love are positioned in her first house, I would gather this is where the rest of her name was derived. The first house in one's chart pertained to one's self.*

Indeed, Durand confirmed. *Now take a look at where these planets are positioned on your chart.*

The seventh house — which normally pertains to one's business partners, lovers and marriage partners. So, it's just a strange coincidence. Turan shrugged.

Yes, but her birth sign is the virgin, Durand pointed out, *which also occupies your seventh house.*

Another coincidence. Turan was sounding a little uneasy now.

Yes, well, that's what I thought, but take a look at what sign occupies her seventh house.

Turan looked closer. *Oh no.*

It was the sign of the Goat, which was the Shar's birth sign.

But you may be right. Durand assured his pupil. *It may not mean anything.*

How on earth did you discover this? Did you go through everyone's chart, or just mine? Turan sounded a tad annoyed, which was very unlike him as he rarely showed any sort of emotion at all.

Just after the girl arrived, En Razu came to give me her details, so that a chart could be drawn, Durand confessed. *He was the one who suggested I might want to compare it with yours. I asked him why, but he only explained that he guessed I might find it interesting.*

Is that so, Turan pondered. *It would seem his friend knew more about this girl than he was letting on. But surely many of the same planets feature in Alaric's chart.*

Alaric was Turan's elder twin brother.

No, as he was born earlier, his chart is quite different.

Of course. Turan wanted to hit himself. He knew this had to be the case. *So, you have obviously told the Elders of this.*

Not as such, Durand was hesitant to admit. *You know they have their own avenues to source information. En Micah has always preferred psychic hypothesis over scientific fact.*

This thought served to bother Turan even more; what kind of ludicrous scenario were they all dreaming up about him?

It was quite late by the time Xavier had heard Tory's whole sordid tale. They had finished in the pool hours ago, and when Tory was robed she had felt comfortable to sit and chat. The healer's mind boggled at what this poor girl had been through just prior to her arrival in their midst, not to mention the silent anguish she must have felt since landing here, recognising everyone and knowing no one. Not even En Razu was truly who she thought he was.

'Wow.' Xavier sat back and poured himself a glass of water.

'I warned you, didn't I.' Tory bit into a piece of melon that was a strange purple colour and tasted rather like passionfruit. She felt absolutely fabulous to have gotten the whole tale off her chest. 'So, what would you advise I do now?'

'Well.' He let out a heavy exhale. 'All things considered, that's quite a question. Your two main problems would seem to be finding a cure for your husband and getting back to him without causing a shift in dimension.'

'They didn't call you bright for no reason.' Tory gave him a gentle nudge of encouragement.

'Why, thank you, Mother.' He made jest of her claim that he would be her son in a little over twelve thousand years from now.

'Don't laugh,' Tory cautioned. 'You sound just like him.' She placed aside the rind of the fruit and washed her fingers in the bowl of water provided. 'So, can you help me?'

'Not I, I'm afraid.' Xavier sat upright. 'But there are quite a few men here that could.' He paused to consider. 'On the healing side of things . . . Shu Asa, En Darius, or even En Razu.'

'Taliesin, good.' Tory's mind ticked over.

'En Durand and my brother, Turan, are the highest authority on the time–space continuum.'

'Great.'

She sounded discouraged. Xavier wondered why. 'Do you feel anything for Turan . . . knowing he will be your husband some day?'

Tory shrugged, a little overwhelmed by the question. 'Do you feel any differently towards him, knowing he will be your father?'

'Sorry.' He could tell by her tone that she felt his question rather personal. 'I shouldn't have asked.'

She shrugged again. 'The truth is, no . . . I don't think so. Mind you, that's what I said about Miles.'

Xavier.

Tory and Xavier were both startled by Turan's voice, and looked to the entrance of the chamber to find his upper body protruding through the door.

Time to let our patient get some rest, don't you think?

'Indeed.' Xavier raised himself, helping Tory to her feet as he did. He paused to look at her . . . 'Well, it's been a real education.' He gave her a hug of reassurance. 'I shall come back tomorrow, and we shall talk again.'

'I'd like that.' Tory observed him fondly as he left.

'Sweet dreams.' He pressed the button that opened the door and it slid aside so fast and so silently that one would have thought it had merely disappeared. 'You're safe here.' Xavier closed the entrance behind him, turning to his brother who waited in the corridor. 'Fascinating woman,' he commented to Turan as he began to walk off.

Why did you imply I would be her husband one day?

'You know I can't discuss a patient's case with you.' Xavier seemed to revel in the fact. 'That would be unethical.'

I feel these are extenuating circumstances.

Xavier laughed. 'I don't see why? Do you have some special interest in our sister?'

What do you mean?

'Well, she is a very attractive woman . . . intelligent, strong, and forthright to boot.'

So?

'So!' Xavier shook his head. 'Sometimes I feel very sorry for you, my friend.' He walked away from the conversation, enjoying having one over on his brother for a change.

Likewise, I'm sure. Turan let him go, as he was obviously not going to be of any help. If he was going to find out anything at all, En Razu was the man to speak with.

13

THREE WISE MEN

For two days, Tory did nothing but swim, sunbake, eat tropical fruit and drink her fill of fresh spring water; doctor's orders. This was their customary way of cleansing the body, along with the hands-on healing and counselling she received from Xavier.

The Shar had successfully calmed her state of being to the point where nothing seemed to bother her. For, as he'd pointed out, time wasn't imposing itself upon her any longer. At this perspective point in history, the Dark Age wasn't going to happen for thousands of years, thus there seemed little point in rushing back there. He advised she could learn much here that would aid her in the future, wherever it may lead her.

Tory had been mulling over the nature of time a good deal lately. By her reckoning she could live a whole lifetime here in Atlantis, which according to Xavier averaged around a couple of thousand years, and still pick up in the Dark Age where she'd left off. This was provided she didn't meddle too much with history. Still, Xavier had said his people could figure out a way around even this problem.

All the answers she was seeking were here, along with a few she didn't even have the questions for yet, thus she felt at ease to relax and enjoy herself.

On the eve of Tory's third day in the Shu-im-ti temple, when she'd finished with Xavier for the day and it was still too early for bed, she sat herself down by the pool and dangled her feet in the cool water, staring up at the night sky beyond the domed ceiling. What was it like out there, she wondered? The peace and isolation of this chamber were wonderful of course, but she yearned to get out there and explore.

'My, but they have done a good job with you,' Taliesin exclaimed upon sighting her. 'You are the very picture of health and radiance, Nin.' He took up her hand and kissed it.

'I feel much improved.' A smile beamed upon her face; she was pleased to see him.

'Sorry I've been away so long.' He picked up on her relief as he sat himself down. 'I've been in conference with the High Priests of the Shu Sar for days . . . deciding what's to become of you.'

'Of me?'

'Well, don't sound so surprised,' Taliesin laughed. 'It's not every day that an immortal warrioress from the future drops out of inner space and into the family of the Shu Sar.' He tamed his amusement somewhat. 'The island hasn't seen this kind of event since, say, the day I arrived.'

Tory giggled; Taliesin was more charming this way, more human. 'They're going to make me a goddess or something, aren't they?'

'Something to that effect . . .' He raised his eyebrows. 'It certainly makes one wonder where some of the old Greek legends came from, that's for sure.'

'So what did you all decide?'

'Well, that's a rather good question. According to your chart you have such a varied array of potential that I dare say the final decision shall be left up to you. You see, the rite of judgement usually takes place at the age of three; thus the child is simply guided by the High Priests to study that which will help fulfil his or her karmic debt. However, as you are immortal . . .' He paused and smiled; she had not told him this, nor how she'd become thus.

'So you know.' Tory had already considered that, with the level of technology they had here, it wouldn't take them long to figure it out.

'It's something I hope we can discuss one day.' He smiled, acknowledging his curiosity. 'But not today. Now, as I was saying . . . as you are immortal, your tests and chart encompass all your karma, making it very hard to decide what field would serve you best. For only you know what purpose you are here for. So, some of the members of the council would like to meet with you in the morning to discuss your options, if that suits you?'

'Well, I'll have to check my schedule . . .' Tory joked, but then became more serious. 'Are you kidding me? That would be wonderful.' She seemed overawed.

'What's the matter?'

Tory shook her head and gave a shrug. 'Everyone is so helpful here, so extremely hospitable.'

'Oh yes,' he assured her with all sincerity. 'The city of the golden gates is a most splendid place . . . especially for scholars, like ourselves.'

'I imagine it's beautiful.' An air of fascination came over her as she looked again to the starlit sky out the window.

'Splendiferous, in fact.' He spoke like a true patriot. 'Take your scenario of beauty, times it by ten, and you might come close to the serene majesty of

Chailidocean. But I shall not spoil it for you.' He patted her knee and stood up.

'Are you going?' She was disappointed.

'Regrettably, I must.' He bent down and took up her hand to kiss it. 'You should get some rest. You'll need your wits about you tomorrow.'

'Taliesin, I'm immortal. I don't need to sleep . . . don't you find that?'

'Ah!' His eyes parted wide as he pointed out. 'Rest and sleep are not the same thing now, are they? That's why you've been in the Shi-im-ti temple so long.'

Tory rolled her eyes; she'd walked right into that one. 'Alright.' She dismissed him with a shrug.

'Learn to relax!' He emphasised on his way out.

'Will you be present tomorrow?'

'You can count on it.' He closed the door and was gone.

Tory leant back onto her elbows, smiling broadly with satisfaction. 'Excellent!' She voiced her enthusiasm softly. 'I couldn't have planned it better myself.'

En Razu.

Taliesin paused on the temple stairs to wait for Turan to catch him up; he'd anticipated that the Shar would be seeking an audience with him by now.

Where have you been? I've been looking for you for days! Shar Turan stated in a way that demanded an explanation.

I'm so sorry, Taliesin began, *carefully considering his response. But I've been in conference with Nin Bau, Shu Micah, Shu Asa, Nin Sibyl and En Seba.*

Holy smoke! Turan was taken aback by the prestigious list. *What could have prompted such a gathering?* He fished for information, but Taliesin wasn't biting. He merely laughed and continued on his way towards the main promenade that led to the citadel bridge.

Those ripples in the continuum since the girl's arrival? Turan had caught up to Taliesin; he wasn't about to let him get away without getting some kind of a clue as to what was going on.

What about them?

They wouldn't have anything to do with all this?

Oh! . . . Most certainly!

How so? Turan pushed his luck.

My dear Shar . . . En Razu paused, as smug with his hidden knowledge as Xavier had been. You are the expert on the time–space continuum . . . we were hoping you'd tell us. The Merlin suppressed a laugh and walked away before he said anything too clever and gave the whole scheme away.

Not you, too! Turan was disappointed; he'd felt sure that En Razu would enlighten him a little, but it would seem everyone was in on the conspiracy.

After her morning swim and a breakfast of fresh fruit and water, Tory waited impatiently for the imminent arrival of her distinguished visitors in the Shu Sar's healing chamber.

I wonder if I'll know them? she speculated, wandering slowly to and fro.

Tory stilled herself, as the sound of her door vanishing alerted her to company.

'Tory, good morning.' Taliesin strode in ahead of everyone to do the introductions. He took hold of her hand and led her to the lounge by the door where his associates were waiting to be seated. 'These are the three gentlemen I was telling you about.'

Tory almost froze in her tracks when she spied the face of the hooded man in the middle, who seemed to be the shortest of the three, though perhaps that was because he was rather stooped. His features were like Keridwen's, only he appeared to be mortal. His huge, long, slanted eyes nearly wrapped around his enlarged head to meet with his temples and were grey-green in colour, as was his skin. He had barely any nose at all and a tiny little mouth, but despite his strange features he was rather beautiful in that he was emitting the most lovely energy.

Do not be afraid, child. He smiled as he addressed her, bowing slightly.

'I am not,' Tory assured him politely. 'Just a little . . . astonished.' She looked to Taliesin; he could have given her some kind of warning.

'This is Shu Micah,' Taliesin merely smiled as he picked up on her annoyance. 'He is the Chief Magi of The Orders of Passage here in Chailidocean.'

Tory bowed slightly to the holy man; deciding to seek an explanation later. 'I am pleased to meet you, Shu Micah, sorry if I seemed rude.'

Not at all . . . it is to be expected. He raised what would have been his eyebrows if he'd had any, having an amusing thought. You should have seen the look on En Razu's face the first time he laid eyes on me.

All the men present chuckled at the recollection. Tory's eyes were drawn to the man furthest from her, for she recognised him.

Yes, well. Taliesin sounded quite embarrassed. That was a long time ago. He conveniently directed his colleagues attention back to their meeting. As Tory was staring at En Durand, Taliesin decided to introduce him next. 'This is En Durand, who is in charge of the Orders of Time, Space and Etheric Frequency study.'

Durand was one of the men Xavier had named as being useful for her to know. Xavier had also named him as Turan's mentor, so Tory was not surprised to find the scientist was in fact Sir Tiernan.

I am honoured to meet you. Durand bowed politely to the putative daughter of the Shu Sar.

'And I am pleased to meet you, sir.' Tory emphasised the fact.

'And this is Shu Asa. He is the Chief High Magi of the Healing Orders, both animal and mineral.'

Another of the men Xavier had told her to look out for, but this man she did not recognise. He did rather remind Tory of the stereotypical image of the prophet Noah, as he'd been depicted in the storybooks she'd read as a girl. His hair, beard and moustache were snowy white, though he did not appear so old for his hair to warrant such a colour. His eyes were bright blue and light seemed to shine from them, as was the case with his whole being.

'I am very pleased to meet you too, sir.' Tory bowed her head as the Magi took hold of her hands and guided her to a seat beside him.

The pleasure is all mine, child. Shu Asa assured, *as the rest of the men were seated. Xavier has told me you are doing splendidly, and in his opinion, you are ready to be socially activated.*

'Yes, Taliesin mentioned I would be allowed to study here.'

Indeed, Shu Asa confirmed. And that is why we are here . . . to explain the different Orders you may enter and help you choose the one that will suit you best.

'Only one?' This was most disappointing; from what Xavier had told Tory, she needed access to at least two.

Well, this is usually the case, as it is unwise to scatter one's energy and concentration. But, he emphasised, as you are more spiritually mature than the average novice, we might just make an exception.

There were eight major deities one could choose to serve, pertaining to the eight golden statues that stood around the chamber. Three of these were mainly associated with the Orders of Healing, whilst there were three that encompassed the Orders of Science. The two deities remaining dealt with the Orders of Passage, where both healing and science fused.

The Orders of Passage that were affiliated with the solar deities Helio and Heliona, were Shu Micah's department. His initiates saw to the sacred rites of birth, judgement, maturation, union, and the passing of the spirit. He was responsible for the prophets cum advisers, in the service of the Shu Sar and indeed all the truth seers in the community.

En Durand explained that the Orders of Science were under the guidance of one En Seba, who could not be present due to other business. The deities concerned with the Sciences were the Orders of Akhantuih, where one could study Astrology, Astronomy and the principles of Chaos. Or there was the Order of Philaeia if one was more interested in the subjects of Philosophy, Humanist Science, Technology and Architecture. And lastly there was the Order of Ta-Khu, where the time–space continuum and etheric frequencies were studied.

The Orders of Healing, headed by Shu Asa, were more extensive and diverse than the other orders and encompassed many things. He made it clear that, although the orders had their different deities to appease, they all intertwined and depended on each other in many ways. The Orders of Danuih were dedicated to healing the human body or healing the earth. The Order of Khe-Ta studied the healing of domestic animals, but also encompassed those who studied the arts. In the Orders of Kheit-Sin one could learn how to heal or train wild animals. Those who wished to serve in the Courts of Justice and study law, or those who wanted to learn the warrior arts, would also enter the Order of Kheit-Sin.

When the three learnt men had departed, Tory meandered around in a daze, feeling as if she would burst with joy. 'Can you believe this?'

Taliesin smiled broadly, understanding her excitement.

'This is the kind of university I've always wanted to attend.' Tory threw her arms in the air, spinning round, before coming to a complete halt. 'Trouble was, it didn't exist.' She had a laugh. 'I love my life.'

'That is why you've been given so much of it.' Taliesin thought he'd best endeavour to calm her down. 'Now let us talk about what you shall do with it, shall we?' He took her by the arm and sat her on the lounge again.

'But I already know exactly who I wish to study under . . . Shu Asa and En Seba.' Her decision was resolute. 'But I would like to talk to you about why I'm here, as I believe you should know.' She would leave out the part about him abandoning her, and just stick to the quest at hand.

'Well, I'm happy to listen.' He offered politely. The Merlin couldn't let on that she'd told him before as Tory would want to know when, and this he was not allowed to tell her just yet.

'Well, in that case,' Taliesin commented when the saga was over, 'Shu Asa and En Seba are sound choices, and what's more, I will get to see you quite often.'

'So you will help me?'

'Of course!' He could hardly believe she'd even felt she had to ask. 'Everyone here will be happy to help. But ah . . .' Taliesin scratched his head. 'I think it best not speak of Maelgwn to Turan.'

'I had no intention of it . . . though Xavier knows about the connection.'

Taliesin waved off that concern. 'Xavier is very tight-lipped, he shall say nothing without your permission.'

The thought of Xavier reminded Tory of a question. 'Taliesin, why is it that I recognise practically everyone here?'

'Well, as everyone lives for thousands of years these days, there are more souls incarnate than in the following epochs, where the normal lifespan was considerably shorter. Thus, the greater probability of bumping into those you've known, know or will know again.'

It made sense. 'So what happens now?' Tory was eager to get on with her quest.

'Tonight you will be taken to the Great Temple of Chailidocean, where all the High Priests and Priestesses shall give you their blessing. They will present you with the colours of your chosen Orders, and pronounce to you your given name.'

'Which is?'

'You'll find out tonight,' he teased. 'Then afterwards, I've heard that the Shu Sar is giving a huge feast in your honour.'

'Good Lord!' It all sounded a bit awesome. 'You could have told me sooner.'

'Why? There is no need for you to prepare. As I said, this rite is usually performed when one is three years of age . . . ergo, a child could do it.' He mocked her dismay.

'But what am I to wear to this hullabaloo?' Tory motioned to the rather sheer pink robe she wore at present. 'I am not leaving this room wearing this.'

Taliesin burst into laughter. 'No, no, no. You shall be brought a robe the like of mine, only it will be of pale blue. The High Priests all decided that you are a bit too experienced to be considered a novice, and not yet experienced enough for the white garment of the High Order. Thus, yours shall be the garment of the middle orders.'

'Hold on, if Turan has hardly ever lived in the physical world, how experienced could he be?' She didn't understand how the system worked.

'Well, Turan's rank was earnt through spiritual attainment and technological advancement. For in these, his chosen fields of study, he has excelled beyond even his mentors.'

'So I would be considered of the High Order of Kheit-Sin, if the warrior arts were one of the fields I had chosen.'

Taliesin nodded to concede. 'As I have heard that you are a fine warrior, I suppose so.'

Tory forgot this Taliesin didn't know her as well as his older self. 'I don't suppose there is much call for that sort of talent here.'

'Not in this city. But in Keriophis to the north, and Kudra to the South, there is a growing need.'

Tory was interested to learn this, but Taliesin rose to prevent further enquiry.

'Anyway . . . I can't sit around chatting all day, I have much to do before tonight.'

'You will be there,' she beseeched him with a smile. 'To hold my hand.'

'I shall always be there, Nin.' He was very sincere about the pledge. 'I hope you don't mind . . .' his tone became more humorous, 'but I am assuming the role of one of your parents, along with the Shu Sar. You may remember seeing him briefly when you first arrived.'

Tory shook her head with a perplexed look on her face. 'I do not recall anything before waking up with you.'

'Ah . . .!' He sighed light-heartedly. 'It sounds so lovely when you put it that way.'

Tory could have sworn he was flirting with her, and she could feel herself blushing. 'You know what I mean . . .' She smiled coyly before frowning again. 'Though I do recall having a dream about my father.'

'That would be he.' The Merlin clicked his fingers.

'What? Are you saying my father . . .'

'A past life incarnation of,' Taliesin corrected.

'Is the supreme ruler of Atlantis!' Tory couldn't believe it. 'All these sons are his!'

'Yes, ten in all.'

'Ten!' Tory held her head. 'His poor wife.'

'Wives, the Shu Sar has five.'

'Five!'

'Melcah, Orphelia, Salome, Kila, and Mahar — in that order. They bore him one set of twin sons each.'

'Just like Plato's legend of Poseidon.'

'Just,' he agreed. 'Now I really do have to go,' he implored her. 'I shall arrive before sunset, so don't worry about a thing.'

'Hold on.' Tory wasn't quite finished with him yet. 'Shu Micah?' She paused to consider how to phrase the question. 'Is he an . . . extra-terrestrial, or a fairy, or . . . what is he, exactly?'

'Well, it all means the same thing . . . and yes, he is.' He waved on his way to the door; he did hate being late, and he was fast becoming so.

'Are there a lot of beings like him here?' She went after the Merlin.

'No, not any more. He's what you might call a missionary. But he is in touch with his race.' Taliesin took hold of her shoulders. 'There is nothing for you to fear here.'

Tory gave a mild nod to confirm she trusted in his word, then he departed. She had much food for thought; the enigmas of Atlantis were really starting to get interesting.

14

NIGHT OF THE SOUL

At sunset, when the liturgy was due to begin, Taliesin arrived to escort Tory to the temple. He found her standing in the middle of the chamber, her arms outstretched, gaping at the garment on her body.

'I feel like a monk,' she laughed, raising the large hood up over her head and crossing her arms deep inside the huge sleeves.

He humoured her. 'It's just for tonight. We'll see to your fashion preferences tomorrow. Besides, I think it's rather becoming.'

'You're too kind.' She rolled her eyes.

But he wasn't joking. She was tanned and vibrant from her rest, and the pale blue of the robe only enhanced the colour of her lovely, violet eyes. Her long, fair hair was in brilliant contrast to the golden colour of her skin as it hung softly round her shoulders before disappearing inside the hood.

'Are you ready, Nin?' He held out his hand to her.

'As ready as I'll ever be.' She interlocked her arm in his, expectation beaming from every fibre of her being.

They moved into the beautiful hallway of the Shu-im-ti Temple. Consistent with the rest of the structure was the amethyst floor and the luminous walls of white marble. The roof was curved, and featured large windows, so you could stare straight up at the stars. Off to one side of them was a long window seat, where patients and staff could sit and look out over the garden courtyard. Featured on the sill of the long window were small domed objects, metallic in colour. Tory slowed down to observe a temple novice drawing back the metal sheath to uncover a glowing blue ball.

'Solar-charged crystal,' Taliesin explained. 'Now you can't get cleaner energy than that. They will light this whole area come nightfall.'

Between the doorways on the other side of the rather wide corridor stood beautiful crystal and marble sculptures of the human body. There were

139

fountains here and there, each featuring a different kind of stone: quartz, rose-quartz and aquamarine amongst others.

They turned a corner to descend the wide staircase that led to the foyer, when Tory spied Xavier speaking with a young woman on a lounge close by.

Upon sighting his sister, the Shar excused himself and approached Tory. 'I wanted to wish you luck.' He gave her a flower. 'You've done very well.'

'You're the one who's done well.' She gave him a squeeze, which he returned with fervour. 'Thanks so much, for everything.'

'Do come on, Tory.' Taliesin urged from the bottom of the stairs. 'We'll be late.'

'I'll see you at the celebration afterwards.' Xavier watched Tory make haste down the stairs.

'Please do.' She waved back at him.

The Merlin guided her across the grand foyer where they bumped into Lazarus, who also gave her a flower and wished her luck.

'Must we address all your brothers before we get there?' Taliesin ushered her outside.

'Oh my!' Tory came to a halt, the sight of the sun setting over the city was absolutely glorious.

Hundreds of exquisite temples and majestic buildings were laid out before her, mainly white in colour. The streets were beautifully paved in white sand-stone, and the entire place looked immaculately clean. Lamps in the mode of the solar ones inside the healing temple were being turned on throughout the city, only they were long and thin in structure. These shed a bluish light that was quite like that of the moon, only brighter.

'Is it real?' she asked, frozen to the spot, her eyes glued to the mountain peaks on the horizon.

'I've asked myself that same question every day since I arrived.' Taliesin caught her sense of wonder and paused to appreciate the moment. The breeze was warm and sweet with the scent of gardens, which were everywhere, and, in the distance, Tory could hear the sound of voices chanting to the sound of pounding drums.

'Where's the music coming from?' She felt drawn to it and descended the stairs to seek it out.

'It's coming from the temple.'

Tory came to a standstill, deciding to wait for her escort. 'That's funny . . . I feel like . . .'

'Like they're calling you,' Taliesin said. 'They are. The composition has been specifically written to attune to your personal sonic.'

He guided the wonderstruck girl by the hand down the main promenade to the citadel bridge, which was guarded by eight huge men all dressed in red and gold.

As Tory and the Merlin approached, the large golden gates were opened and the guards moved aside. All eight men bowed deeply to them, granting them passage without question. Tory felt rather like she was in the land of the giants, as they all stood at least half a metre taller than she.

In the middle of the canal bridge, Tory paused to look back at the ringed island from which they'd come, then to the circular central city that they approached. 'Plato was right again.'

'Yes, indeed.' Taliesin guided her away from her sightseeing. 'But your observations can wait until tomorrow. Let's not keep those on the High Council waiting.'

At the far side of the bridge was another guard of eight, who parted the large, golden gates at their end and bowed as the Shu Sar's adviser led the young initiate into the royal city.

'Taliesin . . .' Tory gaped at the road before them. 'It looks as if it has been paved with gold.'

'All the way up to the temple.' He winked at her. 'So just follow the yellow brick road.' He skipped down it with her, which made Tory laugh.

The chanting and the drums were louder now. Tory could hear tambourines and other percussion instruments. There was also some sort of tightly strung string instrument with a very high pitch, weaving a melody over the rhythms.

When they'd passed through the large outer buildings of the royal island, they came to an extensive garden. The golden pathway continued through the lovely park and in the centre, at the top of a large mound, stood the Great Temple silhouetted against a backdrop of stars. Torches burnt brightly down either side of the path that led to the temple stairs, where the musicians and choir were playing.

Butterflies began to flutter in Tory's stomach, though she did not waver from her course; as a Queen of twenty years, she was well used to pomp and pageantry. The music consumed her, heightening her senses and calming her mind.

The structure that lay before them was completely circular, as all the buildings appeared to be. Marble stairs spiralled their way round the huge mound towards the plateau upon which the temple had been constructed.

The temple itself was octagonal. Taliesin explained that the structures here were all of a rounded shape because sharp angles were not harmonious to the human spirit — or any spirit for that matter.

They ascended the stairs to the shrine, and with one final pound from the drums, the music stopped and all was silent.

Tory looked to her escort, curious as to the delay. He was smiling at her, one eye cocked in anticipation.

A woman's voice that was stronger and more compelling than a tenor, yet sweeter than any soprano, rung out in the night. Again Tory felt the hypnotic allure of the chant tugging at her heart, alleviating her fear as it beckoned her forth.

Upon reaching the summit they passed under the giant marble pillars trimmed with gold, and came to two huge doors made of orichalchum that were already parted wide to grant them entry.

The floor of the inner sanctum was solid gold, and the silver tiles that covered the walls sparkled in the flaming light of the torches and candles. In fact, everything within sight glittered, as it was all made of one precious metal or another. The foundations that supported the roof were set with jewels, some as large as your average soccer ball; not in all of Tory's travels, nor her wildest dreams, had she ever seen anything like this.

In the centre of the shrine was a raised platform, about nine metres round. This platform sat directly underneath the centre of the dome overhead and was only the height of a couple of stairs. The area that was located in the semi-circular apse at the opposing end, however, was raised much higher, as it housed the altar. The holy symbol hanging in pride of place in the apse was three entwined rings. The central ring at the top was of orichalchum and it passed through the lower two rings of gold and silver. Tory guessed this represented either mind, body and spirit or the triple Goddess, or maybe both.

The Shu Sar, Shu Micah, Shu Asa and Turan awaited her on the central platform along with one other man she hadn't met, and two women whose faces were completely veiled.

One of the women was dressed entirely in shimmering silver from head to toe, though her veil was of a sheerer material than the rest of her attire. Around her head was a band of platinum that featured a large pink diamond in the centre. The other woman was the one chanting, and she stood in the middle of the semi-circle. Tory guessed her to be the High Priestess for her head-dress was rather ornate and strikingly similar to those worn by the pharaohs of ancient Egypt. Her veil glittered white, and her dress glistened with the colour of the sky on a clear day. This woman's voice filled the space inside the house of worship, empowering the atmosphere within it to the point that Tory thought her feet would leave the ground and she would simply float away.

Taliesin brought Tory to a stop before the council. The Shu Sar came to stand to one side of her, or at least she was presuming he was the Shu Sar.

Daughter, he acknowledged with a smile as he lifted the hood that shrouded her face.

Father. She nodded slightly, flashing a smile as she took his hand. This felt completely natural to Tory, as, apart from the extravagant attire, he appeared the very image her father.

This made the old ruler very happy indeed. She'd already accepted him and thus he felt a lot more comfortable with his parental claim.

The High Priestess finished her summons and the temple fell silent.

'I, High Priestess to Chailidocean, Nin Bau, welcome this initiate into our midst. May the divine bless her, on this her day of judgement.'

'So be it,' all present replied aloud and in unison.

Nin Bau was handed a headband from Shu Micah, which she placed around Tory's head. 'Yours will be a band of silver, gold, and orichalchum, as your destiny encompasses every aspect of our culture. Let it be known from this day forth that your name shall be Lamamu, the Divine Master of Love and War.'

'So be it,' they all responded again.

The High Priestess then directed Tory's attention to Shu Asa, who held a green sash and an emerald ring in his hands.

'I welcome you, Nin Lamamu, into the Orders of Healing.' The Magi slipped the ring onto the ring finger of her left hand and presented her with the sash of his Order. 'During your service to Danuih, I have assigned you to En Razu for instruction, though my time and knowledge shall always be at your disposal.' He kissed both her cheeks then stepped back into formation with the others, a huge beaming smile on his face.

'I thank you, Shu Asa, you are most kind.' Tory felt overwhelmed.

The High Priestess then motioned to the man Tory had not yet met. He stepped forward and politely introduced himself.

'My name is En Seba . . . and I do welcome you, Nin Lamamu, to the Orders of Science.' He placed an amethyst ring on the ring finger of her right hand, and presented her with a purple sash. 'During your time in the service of Ta-Khu, I have assigned you to the instruction of Shar Turan. However, I too make myself available to you at any time.' He kissed both her cheeks before returning to his spot.

'I do thank you, En Seba. I very much look forward to the opportunity of studying the doctrines of your Order.' Tory bowed in gratitude.

'Oh, mighty forces, guardians of time and space,' Nin Bau beseeched the heavens. 'I ask you to vest this dear soul with your wisdom and virtues, so that she may have the spirit to complete her karmic destiny.'

'So be it.'

'Stay put,' Taliesin whispered, as everyone else turned and departed from the platform. 'Good luck.' The Merlin smiled, as he too abandoned her.

'Good luck for what?' She whispered after him. 'Where's everybody going?'

The sound of moving metal drew Tory's attention upwards, where she saw the huge dome above partially open outwards with the ease of a camera shutter. A bright light beamed down onto the platform, blinding everyone and everything from Tory's view. Nin Bau resumed her chant, and Tory began to feel very sedate. Because she trusted Taliesin, she opened herself completely to the experience and stood inhaling deeply, her mind focused on the Priestess's voice. Before long her whole body began to tingle, until it reached the stage where it felt comfortably numb. By this time, all fear had left her body and, although Tory was relaxed, it was no effort to support herself for it felt as if the energy of the light force was lifting her. In fact, it rather felt as if she were floating, and looking down Tory could no longer see the golden floor beneath her feet — just light, light everywhere. With the return of her fear, she stopped rising and began to twirl.

Goddess give me strength! She didn't want to be afraid. Nothing can hurt me, Tory assured herself, whereupon she stopped spinning and again started to rise.

She felt as if she had soared beyond the height of the temple when she finally became stationary. Through the light Tory perceived beings with features like Shu Micah peering back at her, only they were glowing white in colour and thus barely definable from the lustre of the great energy source. Strangely enough, this did not alarm her, she felt completely safe, surrounded by love and goodwill. *The Shining Ones?*

The beings encircled her, their smiling faces conveying their kind sentiment. One by one they touched her forehead, before transforming into a ball of light.

These tiny spectres gravitated around her and Tory allowed herself to spin inside the whirling vortex they created, being empowered and exhilarated by the ecstatic experience.

For a moment, she lost herself completely.

By the time Tory realised she'd stopped spinning she was kneeling down on the golden floor of the temple. Her eyes caught sight of the shimmering silver-blue dress before her, and she looked up to the veiled face of the High Priestess.

'You are truly one of the chosen,' she advised.

As the initiate appeared to be in a state of shock following the event, the Shu Sar had her taken back to the palace where she could rest awhile before the feast.

Tory bathed, then dressed herself in the clothes that had been laid out for her, too dazed to acknowledge the grandeur of her chamber or the beauty of her attire.

The sound of the door disappearing registered in her brain, and a voice from Tory's distant past brought her attention to the fore.

So this is Lamamu, the divine child of the Shu Sar. The woman gave half a laugh.

Tory turned to see four women had entered. Three of them Tory did not recognise, but the woman who had spoken was her mother, Helen.

'Who are you?'

Well, quite obviously, no one.

There was a deep resentment in her voice. Helen had been known to adopt such a tone when everything wasn't going her way.

'If you have a gripe with me, feel free to voice it.' Tory folded her arms, defiant. She felt rather powerful at present and wasn't about to take this kind of shit from anyone, least of all an incarnation of her mother.

It's just that our husband, the Shu Sar, is making such a fuss over you, explained the woman who appeared the youngest and fairest of the four.

Fuss! Helen scoffed at the understatement. You'd think the Goddess Danuih herself was coming to dinner.

She is rather short for a daughter of the divine, wouldn't you say? A woman with long dark hair posed this question to the others, who chuckled.

'Do I detect a hint of jealousy in the air?' Tory harassed them in turn and the young, fair woman suppressed a laugh.

Helen's bright blue eyes, a stunning contrast to her fair skin and flaming auburn hair, flared wide. 'How dare you . . .'

'No! How dare you!' Tory stated emphatically. 'What right have you to judge me, or blame me for your own shortcomings?'

As Tory approached them, she appeared to grow larger and began to glow like an angel.

This mystical quality had been a gift from the Goddess many years ago for services rendered. Tory hadn't had just provocation to use it in many a year, but these women obviously needed a wake-up call.

'You create your own reality, Melcah.' This was just a good guess on Tory's part. She recalled Taliesin naming the Shu Sar's wives to her and, as her mother was so outspoken, Tory figured her to be the Shu Sar's first wife. 'If you're unhappy with your lot, I feel quite sure that I am not to blame.'

The women backed up towards the door — all except the youngest.

I shall give that some consideration. Nin Melcah and the other two women made a hasty retreat, closing the door behind them.

'Well done.' The woman who remained applauded her while Tory resumed her normal appearance. 'I am Kila, fourth wife of the Shu Sar, and mother of Seth and Lazarus.'

'I have met Lazarus.' Tory took hold of her outstretched hand.

'Yes, I know. He's told me all he was permitted to about you.' Kila smiled. 'My son is very much in awe of you, Lamamu, as indeed everyone who has met you seems to be . . . well, almost everyone.' She gave a chuckle in the wake of Nin Melcah's performance. 'Ignore her, she's a self-centred old hag at times.'

Tory boggled at her words, for none of the women really appeared much older than herself. 'It takes quite a bit to faze me.' Tory assured Kila.

'I can see that.' Kila held out a jewelled pouch made of purple velvet.

'What is this?' Tory smiled broadly as it was dropped into her hands.

'Why it's a present, of course.' Kila sounded eager for her to open it, her beautiful, soft blue eyes beaming with anticipation.

Two bands of silver were inside the offering. Kila explained these were worn around the top of the arms, as she put them on Tory. Kila thought the gift appropriate, as all the finest warriors wore them.

'They suit you very well.' Kila stepped back to take a look then frowned. 'Allow me to fix your attire.'

Kila removed the white tasselled scarf that was bound around Tory's waist. She folded it slightly short of center, corner to corner, so the tassels hung in tiers, then wrapped it around Tory so that it crossed in the front and tied at the side in the proper fashion. 'There,' said Kila and directed Tory to look into the mirror.

This outfit was both unusual and comfortable. Entirely white and of a soft hemp-like fibre, the top sat off the shoulder. The sleeves flared wide, then gathered at the bottom, and were slit from the shoulders to her wrist; thus the silver armbands were well exposed. The body dropped straight into harem pants, which also had a slit down both sides from her waist to her ankles. The large waist scarf, now properly bound, made the outfit more modest. Tassels the same as the scarf, some made of fibre and some of feather, were repeated around the neck of the garment giving the whole outfit a rather exotic appearance which Tory very much fancied. The best thing of all, though, was that now that she belonged to the Orders she was expected to go barefoot, as they all did.

The door vanished and Taliesin entered. 'Ah, Tory. You appear much improved.'

'En Razu.' She near lost her temper at the sight of him. 'Just the man I wanted to see. Would you mind?' Tory looked to Kila.

'Of course not.' She backed up a couple of paces and gave a slight bow. 'I shall see you downstairs, Lamamu.' Kila left them gracefully, acknowledging Taliesin with a slight nod as she passed him on her way out.

Tory waited until the door had closed to voice her mind, yet, as it turned out, she was not given the chance to say a word.

'I just want to say in my own defence . . .' Taliesin became very sincere in a cocky kind of way, 'that I knew from my own experience that you would have panicked if I'd told you.'

Tory stood stunned for a moment, her fury preventing her from commenting. 'You knew I was to be hoisted up inside an alien spacecraft and you didn't see fit to let me know?! Why do I trust you?'

She was becoming hysterical. The Merlin grabbed hold of both her wrists. 'Tory, listen to me. In the universe there are no aliens. We are all one,' he stressed. 'And besides, your body never left the ground.'

'What?' She stopped struggling, though she still trembled.

'That's right. Only your subtle bodies ascended to the etheric level. At no time were you in danger.'

Tory was overwhelmed. 'Astral projection.' She'd never experienced it before. 'It felt so real.'

'As real as the earth plane.' He let her go. 'Forget the alien abductions you remember from the twentieth century, Tory . . . as with the human beings of that time, other beings will also become influenced by negative forces. But the beings you are dealing with here are a race apart, I assure you. We have them to thank for the hospitable conditions of this planet, and for the physical and intellectual advancement of our race.'

Tory held her head, this was all too much. 'Taliesin, I really don't think I could cope with a party right now.'

'Now, don't be like that. The hard part is over — now it's time to enjoy yourself.'

'But what did it all mean?'

'We can talk of it tomorrow. But tonight,' he took up both her hands, 'is for celebration!'

The palace dining room was a real sight to behold with its mottled mauve and white marbled floors and pillars, set against marble walls of pure white. Tory imagined the roof was probably domed, but as it was opened wide to expose the starry sky above she could not say from what material it was made. Large candelabras, holding tens of candles each, burnt brightly around the perimeter of the room. Other candles floated amongst the water-lilies in a little pond in the centre of the table, both of which were circular. This was positioned in the middle of the huge round room, and instead of chairs there was one large, round velvet lounge that encircled the banquet table, where everyone lay about feasting. Feet to the outside, the guests picked from the array of food in the centre; this was rather more informal than Tory was accustomed to. Still she quite liked the idea.

Not everyone was at the table, however. Novices stood around the walls, keeping an eye on the proceedings at the table. They ducked over to fill a glass here and there, or to take an empty platter away and replace it with another. They were so merry as they went about their duty, talking amongst themselves, having a nibble here and there or a drink, that one could hardly consider them servants.

'Dear Daughter!' the Shu Sar exclaimed with delight as he slid off the couch to greet her. 'Come sit by me.'

'Yes, do,' Xavier, who sat to one side of his father, encouraged as he rose. 'We've been saving a spot for you.'

'Well, it looks like I'm outnumbered.' Taliesin gave her a wink as she was led to her seat by the royals.

The Merlin went and took up a place by his friend, Shar Turan, who was seated at the other side of the table from Tory. Turan did not eat; he just came to dinner for the conversation.

Ah. En Razu. Turan called to him through the music and conversation. *His father had insisted that everyone talk aloud in his daughter's presence so she wouldn't become confused or feel uncomfortable. Hence Turan could barely hear himself think. The other poor soul who has to lead her around by the hand.* The Shar sounded none too pleased about En Seba's decision.

'Believe me,' Taliesin assured, 'leading Nin Lamamu around by the hand gives me the greatest pleasure. I think you shall find she is full of surprises.' Taliesin knelt down between the Shar and En Durand.

But, why me?! I have study to do, projects of my own I am working on. I just don't need this right now.

Taliesin and Durand were rather amused by his frustration.

'I cannot say I'd mind.' Durand looked to the tiny warrioress directly across the table from them, sitting cross-legged between the Shu Sar and Xavier.

Then you do it, Turan suggested.

'I'm afraid En Seba has spoken. I'm sure he had his reasons.' Durand sidestepped his plea. 'Perhaps because she's from the future — '

'I have seen glimpses of the distant future,' Turan interjected, 'and none of it is good.'

'Then you didn't go far enough,' Taliesin commented. 'What goes around comes around. I should like to seek out that utopia one day, for I feel sure it does exist. But right now, I am quite happy here in this one.'

'Me too.' Durand flopped onto his back, pleasantly sedated by the spicy elixir he was drinking.

Well, I'm not. Turan appeared perplexed, looking across the table to the cause of his woes.

Tory had been left with Xavier, as the Shu Sar had been called away from the feast. Thus far, the Shar had been explaining the dietary laws to her, which varied according to one's calling. Red meat of any kind was strictly forbidden. In fact, to kill any animal was a legal offence. Seafood or pheasant was partaken by the common folk, but to those in the priesthood this was also prohibited. Only fruit, vegetables and some dairy foods were allowed.

'Well, it looks like I've just become a vegetarian.' Tory stared at the fresh king prawns with relish.

'I am sure that tonight the High Orders would make an exception.' Xavier offered the seafood platter to her.

'No, no,' Tory insisted. 'A law is a law.'

As she sipped the heady brew from a silver goblet, Tory noted the antagonistic look Turan was serving her across the table. 'I don't think Turan very much likes that I have been put in his charge.'

'Oh don't worry about him.' Xavier waved it off. 'He's got a natural aversion to anything female.'

Tory lay on her stomach to question him more intimately. 'How long has he felt that way?'

'Most of his life. See, Turan and his twin brother, Alaric, fell in love with the same woman about a hundred years before I was even born. She's Alaric's wife now.'

'I see.' Tory thought the tale rather sad. 'Do they still get along then . . . Turan and Alaric?'

'Oh yes. Now that they have both found their own niches in life.'

As she gazed around the table there were several faces Tory recognised: Bryce, Blain, Gawain, and her dear old friend, Selwyn. She got to wondering which of them was the oldest son of the Shu Sar. 'Point Alaric out to me.'

'I can't, he's not here yet.' Xavier filled her glass again. 'But over there,' he motioned to Gawain, 'is my twin brother, Gaspard. He's Treasure Master here in Chailidocean.'

Tory considered that made sense; in the Dark Age Gawain and Rhun had often been mistaken for brothers.

'That's our mother, Orphelia.'

The Shar pointed to the dark-haired woman who had vexed Tory earlier about her height.

'Her name means clever, which she is. Zadoc over there, is head of the Courts of Justice.' Xavier drew her attention to Bryce and then to Blain. 'And Diccon, his twin, has charge of the Kingdom of Cintrala, but our elder brother, Alaric, governs the actual capital of Chailidocean.'

'I follow, I think?' Tory raised her brow. 'But tell me, who might that be, strumming on the lyre over there.' Tory pointed Selwyn out.

'That's Seth, Lazarus's older twin. He heads the creative arts of Khe-Ta.'

How apt, Tory thought; art, poetry, music and dance were all right up Selwyn's alley.

'Hey, there's Alaric and Antonia now.' Xavier's eyes were fixed on the doorway where Tory witnessed Caradoc and Vanora enter.

Back in the Dark Age, Caradoc had been Maelgwn's younger brother. He'd not been content to wait his turn for the throne of Gwynedd, and with Vanora's aid, he'd tried unsuccessfully to take the kingdom by force; this act of treachery had eventually been the death of him.

'Oh dear.' Two of her greatest adversaries together again, and even allowing for their entirely different set of circumstances, Tory couldn't feel comfortable about their presence.

15

CITY OF THE
GOLDEN GATES

As the first rays of dawn streamed through the large circular window of her room, Tory lay wide awake in her huge round bed, which was sunk into a staired platform that rose out of the marble floor. She was admiring the silver dome that hung overhead, from which a large, sheer net dropped to encircle her.

She hadn't lasted long at the banquet after Alaric and Antonia's arrival; with all those faces from her past, it was just too weird. But she'd remained long enough to be formally introduced to all her brothers, bar the youngest set of twins — Jerram and Adelgar — who were not in the city at present.

Xavier had informed her that these two had been born of a native red-skinned woman, Nin Mahar, and thus they were looked down upon by some in the royal city. The Shu Sar had wanted to ally his central kingdom, Cintrala, with the native kingdoms of Portea to the north and Usiqua to the south. For although Absalom ruled these kingdoms, appointing one of his own race to govern had proved most unwise, as they didn't understand the native ways. So, once Jerram and Adelgar had grown, Absalom sent Jerram to rule in Kudra, the capital of the cooler, mountainous land to the south, and Adelgar to Keriophis, the hot, tropical capital of the kingdom to the north. The Shu Sar prized his two youngest boys dearly, for they'd managed to bring peace to all the people of his nation. And, up until the recent raids of foreign tribes, all had been very harmonious.

Tory wrapped herself in the silken sheet and crawled out from under the netting to look out over the city.

From the height of her window, she could make out three rings of water channels that separated one circular island from the other. The narrowest ringed island was also the closest. It was here that all the temples of learning stood, but on the larger ringed island that lay beyond the second circular canal was what appeared to be a stadium and a track. Further beyond was another waterway. The bridge across this waterway lead to the outer city markets, mountains, harbour and to a wider channel that led out to sea.

Incredible!

The sound of bells chiming filled the air and below her in the city people began to flood into the streets. They all carried little mats, which they placed on the ground facing the sunrise. They then knelt upon them with their forehead and palms to the ground. After a moment, and in perfect time with each other, everyone raised their faces and palms towards the sun.

'It is lovely, no?'

Taliesin startled Tory, near causing her to drop her sheet. 'I wasn't expecting to see anyone up this early.' She secured the piece of fabric around her, somewhat discomforted by the handsome young Merlin's alluring smile.

'Well, as you can see, *everyone* is up this early.' He came to gaze out the window beside her. 'What you're witnessing below is known as the bringing down of the sun.'

'It's lovely.' Tory noted everyone below change position, crossing their arms at their chest and bowing their heads.

'They are requesting guidance and blessing from Helio and Heliona. And see the people in the parks and gardens; they have their palms to the ground . . . this is so Danuih partakes of their essence, adds to her own energies, and then returns them to the healer with her thanks and blessing. These are the Earth Healers of her Order, and they are the reason that the plant life here flourishes so.'

Tory was staring at Taliesin now; he had such a beautiful understanding.

'Well . . .' he snapped out of it, 'as the Dance to the Rising Sun is the official start of the day, you'd best get dressed and we'll be off.' He walked over to the wall and pressed a button to reveal a large walk-in wardrobe.

'That was solid marble.' Tory rushed over to investigate. 'How does it do that?'

'It's a simple form of particle control.' He eyed over the garments in the wardrobe. 'How do you think the pyramids get built?' He emerged with a loose-fitting, sleeveless garment of pale blue. 'How about this? It's of a very light fabric, and it does get very hot come midday.'

'It's a bit short.' Tory cringed. 'Where are my clothes?'

'Here.' Taliesin pulled them from the shelf, rolling his eyes. 'They've just about had their day.'

'Rubbish! I'll just cut the legs off my jeans and they'll be right.' She gave him the thumbs up. 'Have you got a pair of scissors?'

Taliesin dug into his pocket and handed her what appeared to be a small metal torch. 'It's a laser knife . . . here, I'd better do it.' He took the pants and knife away from her.

'So what's the plan?' Tory slipped the garment Taliesin had selected over her head. As with most of the daytime attire here, this garment had a large hood to shade one's face from the sun.

'I thought I might take you to see En Darius this morning, in reference to the cure you seek. Then, after lunch, I am to deliver you to Shar Turan for the afternoon.' As Tory became discomforted by the thought, he added, '. . . Which will be the perfect opportunity, if I may say, to figure out how you are going to get back to Maelgwn and avoid a time warp.'

The research laboratories of the Shi-im-ti Temple were rather remarkable, as they were far more orderly than those of the twentieth century. Most of the work was carried out on a form of computer, yet this equipment was far superior to anything Tory had ever seen. There were no keyboards, but there were screens — liquid crystal, perhaps?

All the strange devices that Darius had tested Tory with were plugged straight into the hardware where the information was sorted and made ready for observation and diagnosis. The command centre was of a psychokinetic variety, and quite similar to the apparatus in Taliesin's room of hexagons, which the Merlin claimed to have acquired in the years beyond 3000 AD. Yet the machinery before her was not as cumbersome as Taliesin's paraphernalia, being more slimline and quiet. It seemed that mankind in the thirtieth century had still to better their achievements here in the Old Land.

Another very pleasing difference, Tory discovered, was that there was no animal testing here. Taliesin explained that not only would this be considered ridiculous, as the human system functioned entirely differently, but criminal as well.

En Darius was most curious to see En Razu and his new pupil, and took time out from his heavy workload to take tea (of the herbal variety) with them in the serenity of the temple garden's courtyard.

Before Tory would say a word, she made En Darius swear an oath of secrecy; Mahaud's vow seemed reason enough to exercise a little caution.

The scientist laughed at this, explaining his Order's code of ethics ensured complete confidentiality.

Darius was like Rhys; perhaps a bit less self-centred and chauvinistic, but a man of honour. Thus, for the third time since she'd arrived, Tory retold the calamity of her life to date, with Taliesin clarifying things here and there, as he'd heard the tale twice before.

As busy as he was, Darius was so enthralled that morning tea turned into lunch. 'But how did you become immortal?' He had to ask, for it seemed the only question she'd left unanswered.

'Yes, how did that come about?' Taliesin's brow became drawn as he leant his elbow on the table, placing his head in his hand as he looked to her.

Tory smiled. 'No comment.'

'For the sake of science?' Darius implored her.

Tory shook her head. 'So, can you do it?'

'Well, I certainly could, if you'd answer my question . . . or let me run some more tests on you.'

When again she motioned strongly to the negative, Darius gave in and resigned himself to the matter at hand. 'In that case, the answer is no.'

'No!' Tory couldn't believe with all the technology to be had here that they couldn't solve this.

'Not without some samples, anyway.' He sat back in his chair, having finished his fruit salad topped with honey yogurt. 'If you can figure a way to get back to your husband, I shall teach you how to use my devices to retrieve what information I need . . . that's the best I can do.' He shrugged, wiping his hands with a napkin.

Tory looked to Taliesin to see if they were still hopeful, and as he was smiling she figured they were. 'Thank you, En Darius, that would be wonderful.'

'My pleasure.' He looked to the sky noting the position of the sun. 'Good heavens, is that the time? I must go.' He rose, as did his companions.

'Indeed.' Taliesin hadn't realised it was so late. 'We must get you to Shar Turan.'

As Taliesin led the way to the Temple of Dur-nu-ga (astrology and astronomy), where he'd arranged to meet the Shar, the bells of the citadel tolled and once again people flooded into the street.

'What's going on?' Tory asked, as the Merlin pulled her off to the side of the walkway and bowed his head.

As before, everyone lay their mats on the ground. Their arms were crossed at their chest and their heads were bowed low. All flung their arms open wide, tilting back their heads as far as they would go, their eyes closed in silent prayer. After a time, their heads lowered as they knelt and placed their palms on the ground.

As one by one they rose and went back about their business, Taliesin took off down the promenade to make their appointment.

'Dance to the High Sun?' Tory caught him up.

'Close . . . Hymn to the High Sun.' He raced up the stairs of the Dur-nu-ga temple, striding two stairs at a time.

They found the Shar impatiently awaiting their arrival in the foyer of the Astrological Centre.

A thousand apologies, Shar Turan. Taliesin bowed. *The time just got away.*

Never-to-mind, we're late. Turan motioned Tory to follow as he turned and floated off down a corridor.

Tory gave a shrug and a wave to bid Taliesin farewell.

'I shall come for you later,' he assured in parting.

Tory bolted after Turan, excited by the prospect of somewhere new to explore.

Please don't run. Turan paused to look at her. *It's considered the height of bad manners.* He assumed his course.

'So sorry.' Tory forced a posh accent.

And must you talk aloud all the time? He frowned in disgust. *It's very disturbing to those trying to concentrate on anything other than what you have to say.* He walked through the door in front of them, leaving Tory to press the button and enter of her own accord.

What a sweetheart this guy is turning out to be. Tory entered a huge lecture hall where En Seba was giving a lesson, and upon noting that it was already well in progress she quickly sat herself down.

The large black and white mottled marble stairs descended in a circular fashion all the way down to the central platform where En Seba was giving his address. These stairs served as seating for those attending the lecture. The room's large, domed roof served the function of a screen, depicting the movements of the planets against the stars of the night sky. En Seba stood behind a holographic image of the solar system that tracked in fast motion the movements of the planets around the sun. She was surprised to note a couple of smaller planets that had never been on any map of the solar system that she'd ever seen, one of which had an orbit that was in complete contradiction to every other planet in the twentieth century system.

This must all seem very primitive to you, Nin Lamamu.

Tory looked to discover En Durand beside her. *No, not at all! Quite the contrary really.*

So the future is as bad as they say?

The distant future. Tory specified. *But who knows what lay beyond that.* She smiled.

She is supposed to be listening.

Tory and Durand turned to find Turan frowning down at them.

She'll never pick this up without some prepping. Durand looked from Turan to Tory. *Come on.* He took up her hand, serving the Shar a scornful look. *Allow me to show you around.*

Where do you think you're going with my fledgling? Turan followed them out into the corridor.

Well . . . Durand paused and looked back to his associate, *I think a cup of iced tea might be a good start. Then I could explain what goes on here, before I show our new recruit where everything is*. Durand's tone implied that this was what should have been done in the first place. He considered that he might have made an error himself. Perhaps if he hadn't pointed out his observations concerning the birth charts to the Shar, Turan would not be so wary of the girl.

They sipped their tea as Durand gave Tory the guided tour at a very leisurely pace. This drove Turan nuts, as he neither drank tea, nor went about anything at this speed. Turan had tagged along on the premise that his sister was his responsibility, but Durand suspected an ulterior motive.

This is the main observatory. Durand activated the door.

Holy smoke! Tory wandered into the large circular room, awed by the magnitude of the operations here.

Above the dome was a giant screen, like the one she'd seen in the lecture hall only much, much larger. Light beams of different colours extended across the map of the heavens above her. Durand explained the beams were tracking movements and collecting data. Psychokinetic computers were positioned by the study tables and chairs in the centre of the room, and around the perimeters stood what looked to be periscopes.

Durand invited Tory to have a look through one, and although it was still daylight outside she could distinguish the constellations above as clearly as if it were night; Durand accredited this to certain filters they'd developed.

How do you harness enough solar power to run all this equipment?

Set in the sun temple — the Great Temple of Ap-su — is a very powerful crystal, Durand explained, as their party wandered back into the corridor to continue the tour. The concentration of the sun's rays through this prism creates a tremendous amount of power, that is, in turn, distributed throughout the city.

But how? I've seen no wires or —

Wires! Durand chuckled, somewhat amused by the concept. No, no . . . via waves.

Oh, I see . . . clever, she conceded with a nod.

Tory was treated to an insight into her birth chart, though neither Durand nor Turan mentioned the coincidences they'd noted on their last visit to the hall of records. Durand noticed how on edge his associate seemed to be while they were in the charting room, thus he did not linger there.

So tell me, Nin Lamamu. Durand sought permission to pry. Why did you choose to serve in the Orders of Ta-Khu?

Tory looked down the corridor both ways to ensure they were alone. *If the truth be known, I'm on what you might call a mission.*

A mission. For whom? Turan was most interested to know.

As a couple of novices were walking past them down the hallway, Tory hesitated to answer.

In here. Durand directed Tory into a small conference room, sealing the door behind them. *Feel free to speak your mind, no one can hear us in here.*

A mission for who? Turan persisted with his interrogation.

Tory was tempted to say, *Yourself,* but refrained when she recalled Taliesin's caution about mentioning Maelgwn to the Shar. *For the Goddess, who is the guardian spirit of my adopted homeland.* Tory seated herself and looked to Turan. *You see, a great king, or Shu Sar as you might call him, is dying . . . from a dis-ease he was tricked into catching. I am here to seek a cure.*

Turan didn't understand. *So what's the big secret?*

Ah! Tory raised her eyebrows. *The negative force that victimised the king, and many others, would very much like to stop me.*

What's it like, this negative force? Turan moved closer to her, his curiosity struck. *Could you imagine it for me?*

What on earth for?! Tory was repulsed by the thought.

The Shar has been having visions of something that might be perceived as negative, Durand explained. *I'd say he's just interested in making a comparison.*

You have? This was a worry. *What do you want me to do?*

Just place your arms so, Turan demonstrated, resting his elbows close together on the table, his forearms, palms and fingers touching in a horizontal position before him.

Alright. Tory complied. *Now what?*

Just concentrate on an image of the force of which you spoke.

It has many images.

Well, please, don't hesitate to include them all. He walked through the table to get closer to her, then kneeled down in the middle of the solid marble bench, placing his elbows parallel to either side of hers. Slowly he closed the gap, his forearms enveloping her own. Tory's eyes grew wide at the sensation. *Concentrate,* he advised.

But she could not. Tory could sense Maelgwn's personal essence flowing through Turan, which brought with it so many sweet recollections of their intimacy that all she could think of was making love to him.

She quickly withdrew from Turan's reach. *Could we do this some other time?*

Alright.

He sounded a bit fazed, which led Tory to wonder what he'd made of her reluctance.

Durand, who'd been quietly observing their interaction with some interest, decided to pursue the other matter. *So you still haven't explained why you wanted to join the orders of Ta-Khu.* Durand took a seat beside her. *How can we help you in this quest? I would think En Darius was your man.*

Well, I spoke to En Darius this morning, and he needs samples from the king to have any chance of giving a diagnosis or figuring a cure. Thus, I'm needing to get back to the same interdimensional reality that I left . . . Is that possible? She aimed the question at Durand.

He, in turn, looked over at Turan, who was the real expert.

I doubt it, the Shar mused. *From this point in time and space, anyway. You've already been here a week or so. You may have already done something to effect causality.*

But! What if we could take her back in time, Durand speculated. *To, say, before she arrived, and then send her forth to the king?*

Turan nodded, interested by the notion. *Theoretically, that could work . . . but how would we do it?*

The council might be persuaded to utilise the power of the Shining Ones. Durand looked to the Shar in hope. *Or there is always your project.*

Forget it. Turan refused to even consider the possibility. *It is nowhere near complete . . . and anyway, the energy source involved would kill her.*

Ah . . . I hate to state the obvious to two such learnt men as yourselves, Tory grinned, *but you can't kill someone who's immortal.*

That's right. Durand was excited.

True, but with the oscillation of wave frequencies involved there is a risk of psychological fragmentation. Turan dampened everyone's spirits again. *It wouldn't be much fun being an immortal vegetable, I can assure you.*

Could I take a look, in any case, Tory appealed to him. *I'd be most inter —*

Heavens no! Turan protested. *It's not ready to be viewed.*

Look, I promise I won't touch a thing. She knew what Maelgwn was like about his study area; he hated it when something wasn't where he'd left it.

The Shar was staring at her with a stunned look on his face; she'd seen right through him — metaphorically speaking.

Alright, he resolved, finally.

This rather amazed Durand, as every time he'd requested admittance the Shar had flatly refused. Turan never let anyone see anything he was working on until he was quite sure he could make it work. And as he'd made many astounding discoveries if left in peace, his peers questioned him little.

They entered a completely white room. A desk, a lamp and a computer were the only furniture Tory could see. There was a large round window at the far end of the room that looked out over the channel towards the citadel. Many strange-looking tools were lying about the place, and bits of scrap metal were neatly stacked around the walls.

In the centre of the room stood an object, the size of a small car, covered by a glittering golden cloth; Tory experienced deja-vu as she observed it. She looked at Turan, who was intently watching her with no expression whatsoever on his face. His eyes motioned her back to his project, and, with a thought, he raised the veil from it.

'Oh my god!' Tory cried out loud, slapping her hands together. 'You're building the chariot of Arianrod!'

The what? Turan was quite confused by her hysterical outburst.

'Well, that's what they called it back where I come from.' She circled it, feeling a sense of ease following the discovery. 'It takes one quickly to the place of one's desire.' She recited the legend. Looking back to Durand and Turan, Tory realised they weren't following her line of thought. 'Don't you get it! I've used this to move through time already . . . I know you make it work.'

Really! You have? I do!

As the Shar was sounding much more accommodating, Durand quietly left them to it.

Tory told Turan of her adventures involving the chariot. And, as she was so intimate with its function, Turan felt obliged to explain the setbacks he'd encountered since its conception.

Quantum mechanics had never really been one of Tory's stronger interests. Even so, she sat and listened to him speak of it for hours, although not comprehending even half of what he said. She learnt that the particle manipulation function of the doors here and the psychokinetic control panel employed to run the computers, had both been Turan's projects. She understood that he sought to combine these two inventions in the hope of being able to manipulate matter at will for the purpose of interdimensional teleportation.

No wonder you resent having to drag me around. Tory sympathised with his predicament. You've obviously got enough to cope —

I don't resent it, he politely interjected. I'm just not sure I am the best choice of instructor, having so little regard for the physical condition and you being eternally so.

Well, what you lack in sentiment, you make up for with focus. She grinned.

I must say . . . Taliesin stood in the doorway, his head whirling around in an attempt to take in everything in the room at once; he'd obviously never been granted admittance to the Shar's private lab either. I am surprised to find you in here.

'Taliesin, look!' Tory excitedly motioned to the chariot.

'Yes, that is impressive.' He folded his arms. 'What is it?'

'Oh. Never mind!' She rolled her eyes; would she never cease to confuse Taliesin with his older self? At this stage of the Merlin's evolution he'd probably never even heard about the chariot, let alone seen it. 'It shall, one day, be one of the thirteen treasures of Britain.' She sighed, eyeing it over fondly.

'The thirteen treasures? That Myrddin boasted he had collected and hidden away?' Taliesin inquired.

'Indeed!' She was pleased to learn he had some knowledge of it, as this confirmed her story to Turan. 'Myrddin was my father.'

The Merlin's jaw near hit the ground.

I thought my father was supposed to be your father? Turan found her confession rather curious.

'He's an incarnation of my father's physical self, where Myrddin is the manifestation of my father's immortal selves.'

Taliesin looked as if his brain was going to explode and he held his head to prevent it. 'Of course! That would explain the roots of your unusual gene pool, as Myrddin's father was said to be of the Otherworld,' he mumbled aloud, though neither Tory nor Turan were really following his line of thought. 'That still doesn't explain how you got the Shu Sar's genes though.' He scratched his head.

'Earth to Taliesin,' she jested. 'What are you talking about?' She shrugged to emphasise her lack of comprehension.

'Not to worry. Are you ready to leave? I am sure you'll want to refresh yourself before dinner. The Shu Sar is expecting you.'

'Not another feast, please!'

'No, no. Just you and the Shu Sar, so I believe.'

'When do I get time to do the things I want to do?' She faked a moan, taking hold of Taliesin's outstretched hands. 'You said we could talk today, *and* you were going to show me some of the city.'

'Well, I could come and speak with you after dinner, then I could show you some of the city tomorrow morning.' He gave her a hug. 'How about that?'

They were made for each other, these two travellers from the future, Turan thought. He'd never seen En Razu so enchanted with anyone of the female persuasion before. In Turan's opinion, it was En Razu's birth chart they should be matching up with the girl's, not his. Watching them laughing and toying with each other filled the Shar with a rather unpleasant emptiness.

I shall see you tomorrow then, he directed, dismissing his student for the day. On time, preferably. Turan directed this comment to En Razu, giving a mild wave as he watched them depart.

On the way back to the citadel Tory witnessed the last solar rite for the day, which Taliesin named as the Prayer to the Setting Sun.

As the bell tolled, the sun was low on the horizon. The people in the streets all faced the golden orb. They kneeled upon their mats, their arms outstretched before them and their palms upright as if accepting a gift. Then, as with the other rites she'd seen, each bowed low, head and palms pressed firmly to the ground. A few moments later, everyone kissed the earth beneath them, before rising and returning to their normal routine.

The next morning, Tory rose and dressed to practise Kata before Taliesin arrived to fetch her; just because there was no call for her skills here, it was no excuse to be lax in discipline.

Dinner with her father had been lovely. Absalom had apologised profusely that he'd not had more time to spend with her, but the eight-day Festival of Air and the Divine Ancestor, Ta-Khu, was less than a week away. The theme of this celebration was communication; hence it was also a time of conference for the leaders of his lands. Absalom seemed pleased to inform Tory that he expected his youngest two sons, Jerram and Adelgar, any day now. He so looked forward to their visits, as they brought gifts of all manner of wild beast to honour Chailidocean's stadium and law courts. Tory understood what wild animals might be doing in a stadium, but in a court of law? Apparently, the larger varieties of the cat family were specially trained to be the jurors in cases where the truth was in question, for the big cats could always sense the fear that accompanied a lie. The cats' reaction, either positive or negative to the person in question, would determine their innocence or guilt.

Unfortunately, Jerram and Adelgar would also bring news of the raids on their lands. Tory had wanted to talk more of this, but Absalom insisted that he had ten sons to take care of such problems. And, as he was obviously unaccustomed to discussing such matters with females, she didn't push the issue.

Her stroll with Taliesin through the extensive gardens of the palace after dinner had also proven to be rather enlightening. They'd walked the length of the Shu Sar's swimming pool, which wound its way throughout the entire garden. They talked of Tory's close encounter during her rites of passage, which Taliesin explained was nothing more than going to visit her grandparents really. It occurred to Tory that her father had never really spoken about his parents or his childhood, and she resolved that if she ever did make it back to the twentieth century she'd have to question him about it.

And the Merlin had drawn her attention to something about the Old Land that she'd failed to notice; there was no moon. Earth had known another smaller moon many eons ago. The smaller moon had eventually been drawn down out of its orbit around the planet; this catastrophe had ended the great civilisations of Mu and Lemuria around the end of the last Scorpionic age. Taliesin had then pointed out a star twinkling brightly in the night sky, stating this would one day be the moon she'd known at birth. When this tiny planet was eventually cast into the earth's orbit, it would cause the earth to tilt on its axis and all this would cease to exist. However, they were currently in the Virgoan Age, and this particular catastrophe was not expected until late in the Cancerian Age, which was over three thousand years away.

Tory had finished her exercise by the time the Dance to the Rising Sun commenced, and Taliesin arrived on cue to collect her.

There seemed to be a lot going on in the city this morning, and as they made their way over the second canal bridge Tory could have sworn she heard an elephant.

'Is the circus in town?' She'd always been wary of animals.

'Something like that,' he answered, his attention fixed on something ahead.

A woman approached, unlike any other Tory had seen here. Her skin was red, her eyes ebony. Her long, thick hair, jet black in colour, fell straight down her back to her knees. The woman was no taller than Tory in height. She wore a band of gold around her forehead, in the centre of which was a large ruby. Her dress was a simple robe-like garment of deep-toned red, trimmed with gold and bound at the waist by a sash of the same colour. This attire was of a soft fabric that flowed about her as she walked. She did not employ the large hood of the garment, though she did cool her face with a flat, woven fan.

She waved to Taliesin when she spotted him and excused herself from her entourage. 'En Razu. How lovely to see you.'

'Nin Mahar, how magnificent you look.' He kissed her hand. 'I am so pleased you could grace us with your presence at the festival this year.'

'You're good for my spirit.' She gave a laugh. 'Who is your young friend?' She served him a wink, motioning to Tory.

'Nin Lamamu, daughter of the Shu Sar.'

'So you're the one.' Her smile filled with warmth, as she took a step back to view Tory. 'You'd best keep her away from my boys, En Razu.' Her eyes skipped back to her party a second. 'I should keep moving.' Mahar looked to Taliesin with regret.

'Then I shall look forward to your company this evening.' He bowed to her.

'Most certainly.' She looked at Tory with a smile, before resuming her walk to the palace, her entourage falling in behind her.

Taliesin looked to Tory, who hadn't said a word.

'She spoke English aloud. Are the native folk trained in the art of thought projection?' Her eyes were still fixed on Nin Mahar's party.

Taliesin was amused. 'No. I taught Nin Mahar and both her sons to speak English.' The recollection was pleasing to him. 'And now I can speak, read and write Lemurian.'

'But wasn't Lemuria destroyed thousands of years ago?'

Taliesin threw an arm over her shoulder and they resumed their course. 'Aye, but Mahar's people must have migrated sometime before the island continent sank.'

When they passed through the golden gates, Tory could hardly believe her eyes; it appeared things got a little wilder out here on the third island ring.

People of varied hue, red, black, and white mainly, intermingled with each other, and as everybody spoke aloud it was much noisier. Elephants, horses, wildcats and other livestock added to the commotion. Directly in front of them was a large racing stadium, about the width of a football field, that ran full circle around the island. Large walkways passed over the arena and led to extensive gardens on the far side. The colleges of veterinary and botanical studies, and the school of the warrior arts, which encompassed sport, were found here also.

The walkway offered a splendid view of the stadium, and Tory observed the athletes working out below her with relish.

'You might be interested to know,' Taliesin directed her attention to a huge building ahead of them on their left, 'that we have a gymnasium.'

'A gym . . . really!' She was prompted to race off towards it.

En Razu.

Tory halted in her tracks to another voice from the past. She turned to find Ione giving Taliesin a wave as she made haste to greet him.

What drags you out here? She shook his hand.

I came out to see how you were. He sounded sympathetic. You must be having a fine time this morning.

It's the same every year. I do wish the natives would get over their fear of our hovercraft, or think up some better way of transporting these animals . . . three days in a crate across country wouldn't do anything much good.

Nin Lamamu . . . Taliesin held his hand out to Tory. Come and met Nin Lilith. She is in charge of the healing of wild animals here in Chailidocean.

I'm pleased to meet you. Tory was most sincere in her feelings. Ione was one of her dearest friends and they'd been through much together.

Ah, Nin Lamamu, the warrioress. Ione shook her hand firmly. I should like to see you compete sometime.

It would be a pleasure. Tory noted how fit the woman was, wondering at the same time if Nin Lilith had ever met En Durand; Ione and Tiernan had been happily married for seventeen years in the Dark Age.

As Nin Lilith continued to tell Taliesin of her woes, Tory's attention was distracted by something going on in the stadium below. Next time Taliesin turned around, Tory was gone.

She was here a moment ago. He spied her heading down the stairs towards the arena, where some animals were being unloaded after their long voyage. Oh my. You might get to see our young warrioress fight a bit sooner than planned, Nin Lilith.

Tory was experiencing the strangest pull on her mind and body.

Only once before in her life had she ever felt any real affinity with an animal. This had been an Otherworldly creature, a unicorn, that had visited her at a time when she'd badly needed reassurance. From the walkway, she'd recognised the beautiful white beast as it was unloaded out of a crate. It was putting up a hell of a fight, and the two native men who had hold of ropes tied around the animal's neck were pulling in opposite directions.

Tory's heart pounded in her chest and she felt as if she would choke as she ran across the field as fast as her legs would carry her. 'Stop it.' She surprised one of the men as she barged into him, snatching the rope from his hands as he was cast aside. She then ran to boot the other man out of the way, claiming the second rope. At once, Tory stopped choking and leant forward to catch her breath; as she calmed the animal did also. She gave the handsome creature a reassuring hug around the neck, and turned to seek an explanation for such handling. 'You were choking this animal; such treatment is an offence.' Her eyes met with Brockwell as he raised himself, brushing off the humiliation.

'We were not!' he insisted, sounding pretty angry until he got a good look at his assailant.

'But I felt it . . .' Tory mumbled. Her fury departed; she'd missed Calin so since his death. Her sights drifted to the second man she'd accosted, who was also back on his feet. *Teo!*

Like Nin Mahar, these two men were Tory's height, although they were not as dark-skinned as their mother. The dark eyes and long, straight, dark hair were the same in both Jerram and Adelgar, and, besides the odd braid here and there, they wore the bulk of their hair loose. Their garments of red were shorter than those of the other males Tory had met, and this was obviously more practical for their line of work; it seemed that most of the people who frequented this third island employed shorter attire.

'I do believe we have found our new sister.' Teo noted her headband; there was no other like it.

'Most impressive. I thought she'd be a baby.' Brockwell seemed pleased that this was not the case, as both he and his brother closed in on her.

'Then you must be Jerram and Adelgar,' Tory managed to stammer.

'And you must be the Divine Master of Love and War, Lamamu.' Teo said her name with fervour, licking his lips.

It was becoming apparent to Tory that the natives of this island had a healthy interest in pursuits of a more primal nature.

'Lovely indeed.' Brockwell ran his hand over her behind. 'My size and all.'

Tory clenched hold of Brockwell's wrist and twisted it quickly around, holding the Shar in a position that threatened to break his arm. 'You'd best believe the war part, too,' she warned, as he groaned for mercy.

Teo surprised Tory from behind, grabbing hold of her around the neck so she was forced to let go of Brockwell. She reached back and bore her fingertips into the pressure points in Teo's upper arm. His grip on her loosened and she flung him over herself to the ground.

'Well, raise my ancestors! . . . This girl really can fight.' Brockwell gave a laugh as he nursed his ailing arm.

'You don't say.' Teo looked up to his brother from the ground.

'Well, you shouldn't gang up on people like that.' Tory held a hand down to help Teo up. 'You could get hurt.' She suppressed a laugh. Teo batted away her hand and rose of his own accord.

'Teach me to do what you just did, and I'll give you this beast.' Brockwell motioned to the unicorn. 'Helio knows you're the only one who's been able to control it.'

'Can I do with it as I please?' Tory inquired.

'Of course.'

'Then you've got a deal.' She shook on it. 'Now, I want you to take my payment back to wherever it was that you found it and let it go.'

'What!' both brothers exclaimed at once.

'Which word didn't you understand?' Tory placed her hands on her hips defiantly. 'Have you got any idea what we went through to catch this beast?' Brockwell protested.

'Well, the only task worth doing is the one you do for the sake of it.'

'You've met Jerram and Adelgar, I see.' Taliesin finally reached the scene.

'I still don't know which one's which . . . No, let me guess.' Tory stopped the Merlin before he enlightened her. 'What does the name Jerram mean?'

'War raven,' Taliesin advised. 'And Adelgar means noble spear.'

'I see.' She grinned, as did both her brothers, amused by the game.

'You are Jerram.' She pointed to Teo with both her index fingers, and then to Brockwell: 'And you are Adelgar.'

'How do you know that?' Adelgar entreated her.

Tory could tell by the stunned expression on their faces that she'd guessed right. 'I know everything about you,' she teased, 'so just watch yourselves.' Actually, she'd recalled that Adelgar ruled in the hot region; thus Adelgar was obviously the one with the better tan.

Nin Lilith was beckoning Taliesin from the walkway above, and rather than be left alone with these two Tory headed off across the field after the Merlin.

'Hey!' Adelgar called after her. 'What about my lesson?'

'How long are you here?' she stopped to ask.

'Twelve days.'

Tory shrugged. 'Come see me before you leave.' She turned and took off in pursuit of Taliesin again.

The suggestion brought a smile to Adelgar's lips. 'If you insist.'

16

THE MORTAL VIEW

The rest of the morning had been pleasantly spent in the wild animal nursery. Nin Lilith showed off her new babies, the pride of which was the first-born of the elephant calves. Personally, Tory thought the lion cubs were the cutest.

Taliesin dragged her out of the animal sanctuary before the midday solar rite took place; today of all days, he didn't want to be late in delivering her to Turan.

Tory was disappointed that they hadn't had the chance to check out the gym, but there was always tomorrow.

The Merlin walked faster than usual on the way to the Temple of Dur-nu-ga, his mind preoccupied.

'Is something the matter?' Tory picked up on his strange mood.

'Not at all.' He was quick to respond, coming to a stop at the bottom of the stairs.

'Aren't you coming up?'

'Not today. You run along. Turan will be awaiting you.' He moved to walk off.

'Are you meeting me afterwards?' He certainly was in a hurry, and her question seemed to catch him off guard.

'Ah . . . yes.' He smiled in an odd fashion, as he strode off down the promenade.

The afternoon hours flew by. Shar Turan taught Tory how to use his tools so that he didn't have to compute and phychokinetically control equipment at the same time. Tory enjoyed the hands-on aspect of the manual labour, as it was giving her a good insight into how the chariot would function. Surprisingly enough, she was enjoying Turan's instruction, but then she'd worked well with Maelgwn and Miles before him; thus it seemed to her that they were predestined to get along.

'I'm sorry to disturb you, Turan,' Durand's voice came through the intercom, 'but Nin Bau is requesting an audience with you at once.'

Is something the matter? This was rather unusual, Nin Bau hardly saw anybody these days.

'She wants you to bring Nin Lamamu with you.'

Turan looked to Tory, concerned by the request. *Alright. You can tell the High Priestess we're on our way.*

What do you think she wants? Tory removed her protective clothing.

I'm sure your guess would be better than mine. The Shar's lovely mood disappeared, and again he seemed wary and distant.

She followed the Shar to the High Temple of Chailidocean, up the stairs, under the pillars and into the entrance foyer. Here Turan turned and came to an old-fashioned door of solid gold, which he passed through. As Tory reached for the handle the door swung wide open before her. Stairs led down to what was a whole community unto itself existing within the huge mound supporting the high temple. A great number of the populace here were female, though Tory didn't recognise any faces as the women were veiled.

Tory was asked to wait outside another door, and Turan entered the council chamber of the High Priestess alone.

The Shar was most alarmed to find En Razu, Shu Micah, Shu Asa and En Seba also present in the room.

My dear nephew, do not be alarmed. Nin Bau motioned him closer from her seat in the middle of the gathering. *I have need to ask you a favour.*

Anything, he declared, going down on one knee before her.

Best that you hear my request before agreeing to it, she advised. *I shall understand if you wish to refuse.*

Turan stood, nodding for her to continue. He'd pondered for too many days what the council had been scheming; it was high time he was enlightened as to their intent.

We have decided to utilise the powers that be to aid Nin Lamamu in her quest. I believe she must return to the time she arrived here, before attempting to retrace her steps further.

Yes, Nin Bau, if this will work at all, that has to be the case, Turan agreed.

Then, as the council will have to be rallied at Mount Dur-an-ki upon her arrival in our past, it is the wish of this council that you accompany her for the first leg of her trip.

But that would mean . . . Turan paused as the thought horrified him.

That you would have to allow yourself to reconstitute into your physical form, the High Priestess decreed from behind her veil.

Could I not just meet her there?

We don't want to risk the two of you becoming separated, En Seba explained.

Please, Turan, Nin Bau beseeched him. I know it is a lot to ask, but it would only be for a few days.

No. I will not, the Shar protested very strongly.

Nin Bau sympathised with how he felt. She knew the affair with Antonia and Alaric still haunted him, though Turan hid it well. Hundreds of years had passed since then, and his isolation didn't seem to be healing the wound. *Dear boy, tell me what you fear?*

What does any mortal man fear? Turan questioned rather boldly. Why me?

Because when she came back, you were with her, En Razu informed him, in no uncertain terms.

Turan looked to his friend, wide-eyed now. *So that is the secret you've all been keeping from me, not that . . .* The Shar cut himself short, not wishing to voice his misunderstanding.

Why, of course it is, Taliesin stressed his words. What did you think?

The situation made more sense now. Why would En Razu be trying to match him with a woman he so obviously fancied himself. Turan waved off an explanation. *If it will please the council, I will do as you ask.*

Splendid! Nin Bau sounded most relieved. We would be very much in your debt.

Patience had never really been one of Tory's stronger virtues; it seemed as if Turan had been hours in there. A veiled woman was seated on a chair by the door, but she wasn't saying much. This could have been the silver woman Tory had seen in the temple on her night of judgement. Her hair was the same, hanging in long, thick masses of brown curls, but as the women's entire face had been masked on both occasions, who could tell?

Why do you all cover your faces? Tory's curiosity got the better of her. Have you all been horribly disfigured? Or —

The woman suppressed a chuckle, as the door at last opened and Taliesin, Shar Turan, En Seba, Shu Asa and Shu Micah emerged.

'What's going on?' It seemed that she'd asked that question a lot lately.

'Grand news, little one.' Shu Asa placed both hands on her shoulders.

Tory looked to Turan, who actually smiled at her which made her all the more wary.

'Nin Bau shall tell you all about it.' The Magi ushered her into the room, closing the door behind her.

The round chamber was dimly lit and cosy to the senses. Most of the furnishings had a very rustic quality about them, dyed in dusky shades of red, brown, green and blue. Nin Bau was seated in the middle of the room on a large throne-like chair, carved from timber and lined with fur.

Come, take my hand, child. The Priestess bade Tory in a tender voice, so compelling that Tory nearly ran to oblige her. Tory knelt down at the feet of Nin

Bau and took hold of the holy woman's hand, looking up to her veiled face. You are a brave girl . . . I know all about you, you know?

Really. How? Taliesin?

No. The Priestess's tone tickled with laughter. *You told me, the day you arrived.*

Tory was puzzled by her words; she could not recall this.

The council decided to aid you in your quest before you even woke from your journey from Gwynedd . . . How do I know this?

Tory's eyes parted wide as she understood. *Because if I do successfully go back in time to when I first got here, in your reality it must have already happened.*

Nin Bau patted her hand to confirm Tory's guess. *You brought me a message that I wrote to myself in explanation, that I shall again give to you to give to me at the appointed time.*

Which will be?

On the feast day of Ta-Khu, the Lord of Time and Space, which is in the middle of the eight-day Festival of Air, seven days from now.

That's wonderful! Tory was overjoyed. Thank you so much.

Do not thank me child, thank Turan. He's the one who will organise it. For it was my nephew who first brought you to me, and it was he who rallied the council on your behalf.

Does he know this? Tory sounded doubtful, as Turan certainly hadn't seemed that disposed towards her an hour ago.

The Priestess was amused by Tory's perception. *Turan has already agreed to accompany you, even though it means returning to a physical state of being for a time.*

He can do that?

Oh yes, Nin Bau stated with certainty. Though as you might imagine, with his lack of physical experience, this does leave him very vulnerable to be hurt . . . in every sense of the word.

Yes, it would. Tory was rather amazed he would do this for her.

So you must be very patient with him, for, although he has the mind of a genius, he has the emotional understanding of a novice.

After Antonia married his brother, Nin Bau had guided Turan toward the Mind Sciences as he'd needed something to absorb him. The Priestess hadn't foreseen just how absorbed he would eventually become until it was too late. Yet, when Turan entered her chambers almost a week ago to plead Lamamu's case, for the first time in hundreds of years Nin Bau saw a glimmer of hope for him to achieve happiness; she saw an avenue that might deliver her nephew from his spiritual isolation back to the land of the living.

During the days leading up to the festival, Tory spent her mornings in the Shi-im-ti temple with En Darius, learning the idiosyncrasies of his devices.

In the afternoons, as Turan was in isolation to reconstitute, Tory was assigned to En Durand, who'd been instructing her in the use of etheric vision and hearing.

He explained the etheric world as being all of invisible space. Etheric world atoms, vibrating at varying rates, formed seven different layers of energy that each had a distinct characteristic and function, though they interpenetrated each other.

Tory had learnt about the seven different planes of existence back in the twentieth century. The first was the earth plane (experience), then the astral plane (love), the mental plane (thought), the buddhic plane (wisdom), the spiritual plane (will), monadic plane (involution), and totality (perfection or god-consciousness).

Her instructor went on to explain that the etheric world was made up of four essential kinds of vibrational frequencies: warmth ether, light ether, chemical ether and life force ether, which combined to form the differing planes. Once one learnt to exercise etheric sight and hearing properly, one could perceive and communicate with creatures of a non-human nature that lived just outside the normal range of vision. The music of the spheres, beautiful, indescribable sounds, were forever there for one's leisure, if one knew how to access them.

But the thing that intrigued Tory the most was that one could tune into the auric field of any physical object, living or no, and understand all its counterparts in the etheric realm. This was accomplished by staring at the object in question until the object disappeared and one perceived only the astral counterpart. She deemed this ability could come in very handy when seeking out Mahaud, for it also enabled one to define any undesirable beings that might be clinging to a particular physical form.

Thus, by the eve of the festival of Ta-Khu, after a long meditation, Durand had Tory sitting in the gardens across from the astrological centre, staring in wonder at the fauna's brightly coloured auric energy.

When she finally looked from the tree and flower bed to her instructor beside her, she nearly jumped out of her skin. For a brief moment, Durand appeared to be wearing Tiernan's guise — the very image of her husband's champion was smiling back at her.

'Is something the matter, Lamamu?' Durand wondered why he'd startled her.

'I knew you,' she confessed, 'in another time.'

Durand appeared intrigued, stunned and quite delighted all at once.

'The dying king I spoke of. You are his champion and most trusted adviser.'

'Really?' He gave a chuckle. 'Fancy that.'

Tory nodded with a smile. 'En Darius, En Razu, the Shu Sar, and all my brothers, I recognise as others who are connected to the king in one way or another.'

'How awfully strange that must be,' Durand sympathised. 'And this king, have you seen him here?'

Tory stared at him a moment then nodded.

Durand could feel her sudden resistance to his line of questioning, thus he was all the more compelled to pursue it. 'May I ask who he is?' As her large, violet eyes appeared to fill with dismay, he swore, 'If you wish to tell me, Nin, it shall go with me undisclosed to the next life, I assure you.'

Durand was very much like his sixth century counterpart; although Tiernan had been Maelgwn's champion, he had always been one of Tory's closest confidants. 'Shar Turan.'

Durand was thoughtful a moment. 'Then it makes perfect sense that he should aid you, if the quest is to save himself.'

'I suppose so.' Her mood lightened.

'So what was your relationship to the king . . . if you don't mind me asking?'

That was the horror question, and Tory guessed that this was probably made plain by her expression.

'I am sorry.' En Durand stated with great sincerity. 'I shouldn't pry.'

'No, that's alright.' She let go of her fear. 'I trust you, Durand. Truth be known, I was his wife. Of twenty years, in fact . . . which in that day and age was half a lifetime.'

'I shouldn't have asked.' Durand felt for her.

'Please don't feel bad, I'm fine about it, really I am.' She sounded quite convincing. 'I've had this problem before.'

'My, but you must have led a wondrous existence,' Durand philosophised, as he lay back on the grass.

'But still, in all, I have not lived even one tenth of the time you have.'

'Don't rub it in.' Durand gave a chuckle at her gall, purposefully confusing the innocent intent of her comment.

He was very handsome when he laughed, which made Tory wonder about his marital status. 'Well, now you know all about me, how about you tell me about you? Do you have a lady, Durand?'

The scientist looked rather fazed by the question. 'There's nothing to tell.'

'I don't believe you.'

'No, really.' He sat upright. 'People here tend to couple with others of their given profession, and there are no women in my chosen field.' He shrugged. 'I really don't have that much time to spare on a relationship, though I suppose I could make the time if the right woman came along.'

A cheeky smiled formed on Tory's lips, she couldn't prevent it.

'What?'

'I don't know if you really want to know.' Tory hesitated, still frightfully amused.

Durand cocked an eye. 'Can you give me a hint?'

'Do you ever get out to the third island ring much?'

'No, why?'

'Because a few days ago, I met the woman you married in the age from which I came.' Tory watched his interest snowball.

'On the third island ring?' He never would have thought to look there. 'Who?'

'I thought you'd want to know. She's the Head Healer of Kheit-Sin.'

'Nin Lilith!' he exclaimed, sounding both bemused and enchanted.

'You know her then?'

'Yes, I tutored her in etheric sight when she was a mere novice,' he informed her in an abstract manner, caught up in recollection. 'That was hundreds of years ago now. She is a graduate of the warrior arts. What could she and I possibly have in common?'

'I am a warrior,' Tory reminded him. 'And we don't seem to lack for conversation.'

'Your name does suit you.' Durand gave a chuckle as he stood. 'I think the reason we have so much to discuss is because you're a time traveller.'

'As are we all.' Tory stood up. 'It's just that I consciously remember my travels. If you could, sir, your view might be quite different.'

'But who's to say it's meant to be, this time round?' He began the walk back through the gardens to the temple. 'You loved your king in one life, yet you claim to feel nothing for his counterpart in this one. Why should we be any different?'

The scientist had her there. 'I didn't say I didn't feel anything for him. Perhaps if I wasn't still bound by a wedding vow I made to the king, and Turan was even slightly interested in me, things might be different.'

'Sorry?' Durand stopped in his tracks to look at her. 'Do you realise how ludicrous that sounds?'

'That's my life for you.' She shrugged.

'No, seriously,' Durand appealed in all earnest. 'You would deny your love for him here, because you loved him there? I can't see how that could be good for you . . . or right, for that matter.' He continued to walk at a very leisurely pace.

'Do you really think so?' Tory caught him up, fascinated by his view. Indeed, he was the second person to offer that opinion on the matter. Rhun had also thought this when she'd told him about Miles. 'I figured I was better off just trying to live one life at a time.'

'But you're not living one life at a time.' He turned to face her as they reached the promenade, where they were to part ways.

'That's a good point,' Tory conceded. 'I shall bear that in mind should the situation ever arise.' She tried not to grin, as her intended pun seemed to embarrass him.

'All I'm saying,' Durand summed up, 'is that you should keep yourself open to the will of the universe.'

'That sounds like good advice for both of us.'

On the third evening of the festival holiday, the Shu Sar threw a huge feast to honour his two youngest sons. As the whole family would be there, Tory decided not to attend. She wasn't sure she could handle all her brothers and their mothers at once, so she ate alone in her room and had a long hot bath ahead of a cool swim.

As it was a rather warm night she lay naked under her silken sheet, feeling fresh and cool in the wake of her dip. Her mind's eye was picturing images of those that had helped her in her quest thus far; they'd all been so incredibly good to her and she wished there was some way she could repay their kindness. Her thoughts then turned to tomorrow, and the four different trips she was to make through the time–space continuum. The initial trip would take her back to her first day here, and Turan would accompany her for this leg. The second part of her journey would take her back to Llyn Cerrig Bach. From there, she would teleport herself to Maelgwn's side (though she'd not mentioned this ability to anyone here) and take the samples required. She would then return to the temple in the valley to rendezvous with the channel created by the council of the Old Ones. This would bring her back to the point in time when she'd first arrived in the Old Land, where she would meet up with Turan. The final leg would hopefully bring Turan and herself back to the present, to complete the time loop.

Impossible? The council, who'd already witnessed the whole event, didn't seem to think so.

The door of her room opened and someone entered. In the darkness, Tory couldn't tell who it was, she saw only a silhouette before the door closed.

'There you are.' The intruder moved through the shadows towards her. 'Why were you not at our feast?'

Well, it's Jerram or Adelgar. Adelgar was her guess. She wrapped the sheet firmly around her and sat upright to confront him, as he crawled through the part in the netting that surrounded her bed. 'What are you doing here?'

'I'm here for your tutorial.'

Dark as it was, she saw his grin as he stretched out on the bed to face her.

'I could teach you how to kill a man, one-handed.' She smiled sweetly. 'And I'll use you to demonstrate.' She backed as far away from him as she could, but there was little chance of escape. The netting surrounding her was firmly attached to the floor and only had one place of entry, which Adelgar now lay across. She could try and rip through the netting with her bare hands, but there was the distinct possibility that she could lose the flimsy silk sheet bound round her in the process.

'Now don't be like that.' He took hold of her around the ankle and dragged her towards him, the silken sheet beneath her aiding his cause somewhat.

'Let go.' Tory kicked herself away from him, using his stomach muscles as a springboard as she clung to the sheet around herself with both hands. 'What are you doing? I'm your sister!'

'No, you're not.' He reached for her again, only he raised himself this time, sliding her into position and pinning her beneath his body weight. 'You're only my half-sister.'

'Damn it.' Her legs were firmly trapped, thus she attempted a one-handed strike which Adelgar blocked. Before she had the chance to retaliate, he had both her wrists clamped down to the bed. 'Shit.' She resigned herself to the fact that she couldn't break free, it would seem Adelgar had Brockwell's strength too. This was her cue to teleport herself elsewhere, if she could just concentrate long enough to do so.

'Now we can do this the hard way, or we can do this the easy way.' Adelgar leant forward and took hold of the sheet with his teeth, slowly drawing it down.

'You're going to regret this,' she cautioned, expanding her chest to fill the fabric and hindering his attempt to expose her breasts.

'Not fair,' Adelgar joked, but the next thing he knew he was airborne. 'Put me down,' he demanded, floating just high enough for Tory to be beyond his reach.

'I'm not doing it.' She laughed, bundling up her sheet and escaping through the net.

'Get back here!' Adelgar was losing his good humour.

Well, well, well, if it's not my little brother . . . Turan came forth out of the darkness and turned Adelgar's floating form around to address him face to face.

'Put me down, Turan,' Adelgar snarled. 'Or I'll break every bone in your body.'

'You're the one who's going to need medical attention,' Tory commented, having thrown on her clothes.

Turan guided his captive out from under the netting and into the room. *What would you like me to do with him?*

Tory smiled at the question, staring up at her assailant. 'Well, I think he needs cooling down, what do you think?'

I think you might be right.

Tory's window opened and Adelgar began to float towards it, kicking and yelling in protest.

'What are you doing?! . . . I'll kill you, Turan, I swear it.' Adelgar tried to cling on to the window frame, but his brother's will was too strong.

As he disappeared outside, Tory rushed to the window. 'Don't hurt him,' she pleaded, once the warrior was out of earshot.

I won't. Turan let his hold over his prisoner lapse, and Adelgar dropped into the canal. Someone will fish him out, sooner or later.

Since justice was served, Tory had to chuckle. 'Lucky you came by, I . . .' Tory paused as she noted the tears in Turan's eyes. 'Is something wrong?' She approached him, but the Shar backed up.

'I think I've had a nightmare,' he confessed, then forced a smile. 'It's so long since I've had to sleep, I'd forgotten how real dreams can feel at times.' He wiped the tears from his face. 'I wouldn't have disturbed you, but I wondered if the negative entity you spoke of might be the same detrimental force I've seen in the visions that plague my sleep.'

Tory's jaw dropped, for he spoke aloud. He did not float as she'd known him to, but walked. 'Turan.' She moved nearer to him, and reached out her hand to make contact with his. 'You're real!' She near choked on the words as she held his huge hand in her own.

'I always have been,' he informed, withdrawing from her touch. 'Will you help me with this, or not?'

The Shar's moods were quite obviously all over the place; hence Tory thought him in no state to be introduced to Mahaud. 'Turan,' she released a heavy sigh, 'please, come sit down.' She took a few steps toward the lounge, holding her hand out to him, but he was hesitant. 'Come on.'

He allowed to her take up his hand and lead him to a seat.

Tory leant over and pulled back the metal sheath of the solar lamp, to shed a little light on the subject, which caused them both to squint.

'Ouch!' Turan rubbed his eyes as they adjusted. 'Pain,' he explained. 'I'd forgotten.'

'I'm so sorry.' She closed the cover three-quarters.

'That's fine.' He assured, his eyes wavering open. 'Really. Let's just . . . proceed.'

'Before we do . . .' Tory stalled, getting herself comfortable, 'I want you to tell me how you're feeling?'

'You sound like Darius . . . I feel fine!' He became annoyed and rose to depart.

'Well, if you feel fine . . .' Tory stood also, remaining very calm, 'why are you getting so angry?'

'Because I fear Chailidocean could be in great danger, and you're not helping me any,' Turan snapped.

'Well, why don't you tell me what you've seen, and I might be able to help!' Now Tory was losing her cool.

'All I want from you is a picture, that's all!' He stressed the point. 'If you would be so kind!' The lash in his voice made her jump; even when Maelgwn had divorced her his words had not seemed so cutting. 'Alright,' she decided, clenching her jaw to control her urge to thump him. 'If that's what you want, then that's what you shall get.' She plonked herself down on the lounge, holding her arms together as required, and closing her eyes to concentrate. 'Come on . . .' she urged, 'while I'm still in the mood.'

Turan sat, clasping her hands between his own, and closed his eyes.

Tory focused on her memories of Mahaud from the first time they'd met at Arwystli, where the witch had terminated the life of her first unborn child, to the ordeal the crone had put her through with Teo in the twentieth century. Next came the apocalypse she'd witnessed at Arwystli just recently, where Mahaud had made a threat of vengeance against her on the deathbed of Calin Brockwell.

'Dear Gods! I am so sorry.' Turan let go, the tears streaming down his face now. 'I had no idea.' He was ashamed of the demands he'd made on her.

Tory suddenly felt a mite guilty herself. She'd known Turan was in no emotional state for such a shock and now she'd hurt him through her impatience; this was the one thing she'd promised Nin Bau she wouldn't do.

'Was I any help?' The damage was done, best to try and make amends.

'It's hard to say.' He tried to gather his thoughts. 'Maybe. The many images you put forward are different to what I have seen, but as you've said, this force assumes many different forms.' He paused to consider then shook his head and stood, frustrated.

'Maybe,' Tory rose, taking a firm hold of both his arms, 'you should relax. Remember that . . . relaxation?' She smiled as she felt his tension ease.

'Perhaps you're right,' he conceded. 'I do apologise for my irrational behaviour.'

'It's not irrational to be afraid for those you care about, Turan. I just think it might be best to talk about this in the morning, when you've rested a little. Okay?'

'Yes, of course.' He made a move for the door.

'Ah . . .' She called after him. 'Thanks for coming to my rescue, both tonight and tomorrow. I know this whole affair has been very difficult for you, and I just wanted you to know I appreciate everything you're doing for me, really I do.'

This made him smile. 'Well, what is family for after all?'

He left her in peace, via an open door for a change, and Tory closed and locked it behind him.

'What a night!' She picked up her sheet on route to bed, and collapsed onto it.

It was hard for Tory to conceive that Mahaud could manifest herself here in such a positive environment. She'd met no one thus far that was evil enough for the crone to latch onto, nor had she even felt an inkling of her presence. Still, she would talk to Turan in the morning and find out exactly what he had envisioned.

What did he mean Chailidocean might be in danger? What kind of danger? Tomorrow . . . She encouraged herself to rest, as the day ahead was shaping up to be a long one.

As usual Tory didn't get much sleep. Since she was up and about so early, she wandered down to the kitchens to investigate what she could rustle up for breakfast.

Upon filling a tray with fruits, a large bowl of yogurt, fruit juice, water, sweet breads and herbal tea, Tory inquired after the whereabouts of Shar Turan's chambers and headed off in that direction.

'For me?'

She passed Xavier on the stairs, who tried to take the tray from her.

'If you'd told me you were coming, I would have stayed in bed.' He grinned.

'What is it with you lot?' She jested, steering well away from him. 'I think you need more women around here.'

'Whatever do you mean?' He seemed intrigued. 'You wouldn't know anything about Adelgar's little swim round the citadel last night, perchance?'

'Well, it was a nice night for it.' She grinned.

'I see, no comment.' Xavier motioned to the breakfast tray set for two. 'So, if this is not for me, who's the lucky recipient?'

'Never you mind who it's for.' Tory made haste to depart.

'In other words, Turan.' He chuckled. 'You know it's painfully obvious to me, that you are not the slightest bit interested in him.' He made jest of her previous claim, as he strolled off down the stairs.

'It's not what you think,' she called after him.

Xavier turned back to look at her, faking a serious stance. 'I'm sure I believe you.'

'Think what you like then.' She decided to ignore him. 'I am in perfect control,' Tory stated, but just who was she trying to convince?

Turan was awake when she entered. He sat quiet and still on the seat of the large, rounded bay window, gazing out over the city below.

His room was much like her own, though by her understanding Turan didn't stay in the palace very often. It was said he preferred his quarters in the Dur-nu-ga Temple, away from the disruptions of family life, where he could study in peace.

'Hey partner, how are you feeling?' She spoke and moved quietly, so as not to alarm him, placing the tray on the seat at his feet as she sat herself down.

'This was nice of you.' He looked to her offering and selected a piece of fruit. 'I'm famished.'

'All we need now is the Sunday paper,' she amused herself, and although Turan didn't understand the joke, he smiled anyway. 'You seem in much better spirits today.' His smile broadened. This was too much!

'You handled me very well last night, I apprec —'

'Please!' She appealed. 'You handled Adelgar very well, so let's call it even.' Tory took up her tea and got comfortable. 'Instead, why don't you tell me about your nightmares?'

'There's not that much to them really.' He shrugged. 'But for what it's worth, I'll tell you what I've seen.'

He told of an old mentor of his, Keeldar, who'd been a pioneer in the field of identifying, manipulating and transporting matter via sonic frequency and psychokinesis. Keeldar got himself banished from the continent by the council for what Turan would only describe as sedition. Before this, he'd held a high position in the mineral department of the Order of Danuih, as well as holding En Norbert's position as the Head of the Mind Sciences. Still, the way the Shar envisioned Keeldar now, he was not at all the man of science he remembered.

'He appears kind of . . .' Turan searched for the right word, 'feral. But then the world outside our lovely continent would tend to have that effect on you.'

'So how does this Keeldar place Chailidocean in danger?'

Turan seemed slightly vexed by the question. 'I wish I knew. In my visions he's laughing, but there's a distinct echo of insanity about his presence. Then there's this huge explosion, ten times the brightness of the sun . . . heat upon heat, upon heat. When I snap out of the trance, I'm left with a distinct sense of dread.' He poured them both some juice. 'Keeldar was an accomplished telepathist; in fact, he taught me the art. So, if these images are sent from him, my perception of them is quite purposeful.'

'When did the visions start?'

'A couple of years before you arrived . . . around the time the raids began in Portea and Usiqua.'

'So you think Keeldar could be behind the attacks?'

Turan drank his juice down in a few gulps and shrugged. 'It's as much a possibility as it could be a coincidence, I guess.'

Tory was contemplative. Surely Mahaud couldn't be behind this if it had been going on since before she'd even arrived. 'The council knows?'

'Oh yes, and they are mindful of developments,' he informed her, sounding not too thrilled by their seemingly complacent ruling on the matter.

Tory looked to the door as the sound of the particle manipulation function alerted them both to company.

Turan's mother, Nin Melcah, stood in the doorway, tray in hand, wearing the most astonished look on her face upon spying her son and the daughter of Danuih having breakfast together in his room. 'It would seem you've already been indulged.'

Tory burst into laughter at the misguided accusation behind her words. When she saw Turan's horrified reaction, she laughed even more so.

'Surely you don't think that we . . .'

The Shar, too, was forced to laugh, which, although Tory found it rather insulting, she had to admit was wonderful to see.

'Lamamu and myself are working on a project today, which we were just discussing over breakfast.' Turan motioned his mother to approach. 'But we can discuss it later, do join us.'

'We are in the middle of a festival. I've not got time to be sitting around.' She seemed put out. 'No, if you have eaten already, then I shall go.'

'No.' Tory stood. 'I shall go. I'm sure you don't get enough time alone with your son to pass up an opportunity.' Tory smiled as she passed the stunned woman, and reaching the door she looked back to Turan. 'How about lunch at the Shi-im-ti?'

'That would be fine.' Turan replied; Darius would want to see them both before they faced the circuits of time.

17

TIME LOOP

The Festival of the Air was the second seasonal rite of the year and was held at the time of the equinox. It was one of four solar festivals that took place at each quarter of the Atlantean year, which was Sothic (based on the star Sirius), as would be the later Egyptian calendar — a year consisting of 360 days.

For the first four days of the festival the leaders of the land had been in council. The principal members of the council were: the Shu Sar, supreme ruler of the continent; Shar Alaric, ruler of the city of Chailidocean; Shar Diccon, ruler of the state of Cintrala; Shar Adelgar, ruler of the state of Portea; and Shar Jerram, ruler of the state of Usiqua. The Shu Sar's advisers were also present, including En Razu, plus the rulers of the other major cities like Mentis to the east, and Menocea to the northeast. Yet, aside from communication on a physical level, this festival also encompassed communication with the cosmos and its divinities; hence the leader's parleying would cease before sunset to allow the celebration to truly commence.

The ceremonial rite to Ta-Khu was always held in a high place, and performed on the fourth day of the eight-day festival. The priests of Ta-Khu held ceremonies high in the mountains outside the city for the common folk. These commenced at sunrise and continued until just after dark, so one was at leisure to attend at any time and could stay for as long as one chose. This pilgrimage was to offer gifts to the divine ancestor, which had been made by one's own hand, and were blessed by the priests and kept in the temples to be given later to those in need. The High Priests of the order performed a special service for the Shu Sar and his subjects in the High Temple of Chailidocean after sundown. A great feast was held afterwards, and the four days that followed were for games, rest, and recreation.

Taliesin briefed Turan and Tory over lunch with En Darius in the courtyard of the healing temple.

He advised that just before midnight, the members of the High Council would meet them at the site on the Mount Dur-an-ki plateau. This was in the mountain range to the east of the city, but there was an underground passage that ran from the High Temple. Turan knew the way and would accompany Tory there at the appointed time. Should anyone need an excuse to leave the feast, they were to say that Nin Bau had summoned them; no one questioned the High Priestess' will. If all went to plan, they would be back at the celebrations before anyone even missed them.

En Darius handed over a fully equipped belt of the apparatus that Tory was to take with her. Everything was strapped in good and tight, fully loaded, and ready to use. As Darius would not be present on Mount Dur-an-ki tonight, he wished Tory well in her quest. He was confident that tomorrow they would start work on the cure.

Come evening, Tory dressed herself in the long, pale blue robe of the middle orders, and was escorted by En Razu to the Great Temple for the service of Ta-Khu. She carried a beautiful bouquet of mixed flora, in various shades of purple, to offer to the divinity of time and space on his feast day.

Along with the family of the Shu Sar, everyone of the Higher Orders of learning was present for the rite. Tory gathered this from seeing all the white attire, for most had their hoods drawn well over their heads to concentrate on the ceremony.

Nin Bau lead the liturgy, most of which was sung in a language foreign to Tory's ears, that in an aesthetic sense was very inspiring. There was music throughout the entire service that went for a little under a couple of hours, upon which time everyone adjourned to the banquet.

The dining room was adorned with flowers, candles and stones of purple, the colour of Ta-Khu. This room was open to the stars and the extensive gardens; musicians, dancers, and guests alike spread themselves throughout.

Tory had wandered down along one side of the pool to where the first of its seven crystal fountains were positioned. There she stood admiring her old friend Selwyn (Shar Seth), as he strummed out a tune on a lyre, when she felt the warmth of someone's hand taking hold of her own.

'Adelgar.' She was surprised to find it was he, especially after last night's episode, and she withdrew her hand abruptly.

'I want to apologise . . .' he began, but Tory was already way ahead of him.

'Why? So you can try your luck again as soon as you get me alone? Oh no.'

The young warrior was rather stunned that she could know him so well, as she turned and made for somewhere more crowded.

'I shall formally ask the council for their consent if I must.' Adelgar came after her, unaware Turan was within earshot.

His older brother and Durand were seated just to the other side of the tall hedge, by which Tory and himself passed, and Turan politely motioned Durand to quiet so that they could listen.

'For their consent to what?' Tory was curious enough to stop and inquire.

'Why . . . to join with you, of course.' He took hold of her hands.

'Join with me!' she echoed, unable to believe how casual he was about it. 'I'm not joining with anyone,' she instructed him as she freed herself.

Shouldn't we do something? Durand bethought his associate.

Presently. There was mischief in Turan's smile.

Durand had never seen Shar Turan behave so, not in many a hundred years, so he played along just for the entertainment value.

'But you'll have to sooner or later. Every woman is required to give birth once,' Adelgar informed Tory. 'And Turan is not so inclined towards breeding as I, if that's what you're hoping.'

Let's face it. Turan conveyed his view to his companion on the quiet. *No man alive is as inclined towards breeding so well as he.* Durand near burst out laughing at the comment. But Turan anticipated the event and clasped a hand over his friend's mouth before he gave them away.

'Look Adelgar, I hate to tell you this, but I have already had a child, to a man I am very much in love with.'

Durand looked to Turan who appeared to be of mixed emotions about the news. Turan was, in fact, wondering if En Razu knew.

'No, that can't be.' Adelgar didn't understand.

'I'm sorry, but it's true. They're both waiting for me back in the future.'

The young Shar was at a loss for words, wandering to and fro in a daze. 'So you're not planning to stay long.' He sounded so disheartened. 'I wanted you to teach me your way of defense . . . I wanted to show you Portea, and . . . and . . .'

'As much as I would dearly love to stay awhile, I have to get back.' She placed a hand on his shoulder. 'Someone of great historical significance shall die if I don't.'

'I could change your mind, I know it.' He pulled her close to maul her neck.

'Goddamn you, Adelgar.' Tory attempted to push away, but he wasn't letting go. She dug her fingers deep into the vital points in both his shoulders.

'Aw!' Adelgar again found himself airborne. 'Turan!' he yelled in vengeance.

Tory grinned at this, looking round to spy Turan and Durand come walking through a gap in the hedge up ahead.

'Don't you dare,' Adelgar warned, as he floated over the swimming pool.

'Are you alright?' Durand was amused that she'd not really needed their help to control the situation.

'Whoever said history never repeats was an idiot!' Tory shook her head. 'But that's another story.'

182

'Now I thought I'd warned you about accosting our little sister,' Turan teased his brother from the side of the pool, lowering and raising Adelgar above the water.

'Turan don't!' Tory implored him, noting they were drawing a crowd. 'Put him down on the ground.' As he seemed surprised by the request, she added, 'Please.'

Turan gently set Adelgar down on the far side of the pool, as it was quite a hike either way round to reach them again.

Adelgar stomped off on his trek, mumbling curses in the native dialect.

'Can I be of assistance.' Nin Lilith, who'd noted the goings on, approached to investigate.

'Ah, a healer of wild beasts . . . just what we need.' Tory welcomed her warmly, turning back to serve Durand a wink as she walked over to meet Lilith halfway.

The scientist felt himself blush at her inference, and thanked Ta-Khu for the poor light.

Tory made sure everybody knew each other before she announced her departure. Her date with destiny was drawing closer, and she needed to change.

'I'd best keep an eye on her,' Turan explained, as he took his leave of them also.

'Well, then . . .' Durand looked to the lovely lady beside him, not too sure what to say to her.

She smiled at his dilemma. 'Could I tempt you to a stroll, perhaps?' Lilith suggested.

'Nothing would please me more.' Durand resolved with a smile, interlocking her arm in his.

The old jeans, which were now shorts, T-shirt, jacket, and steel-capped boots were pulled out of the closet for the expedition.

Tory wrapped her hair in a tight bun, strapped on Maelgwn's sword, then slung Darius' tool belt over her head and shoulder. 'Ta-da!'

She let Turan know it was safe to look; however, he'd been quietly observing her reflection in the window for some time. When he turned she had her arms parted wide.

'Well, I think I'm prepared for just about anything.' She placed her hands on her hips when she got tired of waiting for his opinion. 'Shall we go then?'

The Shar was just staring at her, appearing somewhat overawed. 'You're not afraid of anything, are you?'

'Should I be?'

Turan refrained from answering, then smiled meekly. 'No. Our flight is in the best of hands.'

The Shar led Tory through the golden door in the foyer of the Great Temple and ascended the long staircase to the communal dwellings underneath. There was hardly anyone about, due to the hour, thus their passage to Nin Bau's council chambers was swift.

As they approached the throne of the High Priestess, Tory noted that the large marble block at the base of the chair had been moved forward to reveal a staircase hidden underneath. This led to a dimly lit tunnel that was tubular in shape.

As the passageway seemed to go on forever, Tory made conversation whilst they walked. 'So what does Dur-an-ki translate to?'

'The meeting place of heaven and earth.'

'Whoa, really?' Her thoughts were in motion. 'So your name must mean something similar.'

Turan smiled at her interest. 'In the bond of the divine, or heaven.'

Tory chuckled at this, and Turan looked mildly offended until she explained. 'And I am the divine master of love and war . . . is it any wonder you got lumbered with me?'

This connection hadn't occurred to Turan, but he smiled as he conceded she might be right.

'What's that?' Tory referred to the beautiful purple-pink light beyond where the tunnel ended, and began to run towards it. 'Sorry.' She slowed down, recalling how Turan disliked boisterous behaviour.

'We've reached the mountain.' He sounded, on the contrary, delighted by her excitement.

'Good heavens . . . just look at this!' Tory's eyes scanned the expansive underground deposits of crystals; they were everywhere. Large stalactites of quartz, rose quartz, and amethyst hung like icicles from the roof of the cavern. Stalagmites rose like daggers from the floor, occasionally uniting with the stalactites overhead to form one splendid, long column.

'It's beautiful.' She stepped out of the tunnel and onto a pathway that wound upwards between the glittering clusters of stone, to an exit at the top of the mountain.

'Come on, we're nearly there.' Turan headed off up the pathway ahead of her.

This place was just one marvel after another. 'Can I take one?' Tory spotted a large amethyst wand laying by the side of the path.

'Feel free.' He'd reached the stairs that disappeared into an opening in the wall.

Tory placed the wand in her pocket and made haste to catch up.

From a high vantage point the cavern below appeared rather like a huge power conductor, and upon mulling this notion around for a moment or two she considered that this might not be so far from the truth.

As they scaled the narrow stairway inside the mountain, Tory became aware of the strong energy currents that pulsated around her. *A ley crossing,* she surmised as a warm breeze swept over her; they must be close to the top.

A door opened onto a large marble plateau that must have been about forty-six metres round. Upon this was a stone circle, that consisted of nine of the largest hunks of polished crystal Tory had ever seen. Positioned just in front of her, in the same proximity to the stone circle as, say, the King Stone at the Rollright site would have been, was a box the size of an alter that was made of pure gold.

The symbol of Caduceus (a winged rod with two serpents entwining it in opposing directions) was engraved upon all sides of the golden feature. The serpents represented negative (the chaotic principle) and positive (the orderly principle). The wings of the rod personified the transpersonal self, suggesting that the mind is capable of bringing these opposing forces into balance.

'The guest of honour.' Taliesin approached to welcome Tory. 'Fascinating, isn't it?' he commented, noting her preoccupation with the glistening golden box. 'I bet you'll never guess what it is.'

As there was a distinct ring of challenge in his tone, Tory cocked an eye and had a guess. 'It's a control mechanism of some kind.'

'It's not just a control mechanism. It's *the* control mechanism . . . does the Ark of the Covenant ring any bells?'

'What?' Tory was confused. 'Wasn't that the box Moses was supposed to have stored the ten commandments in?'

'Hardly. Though the Bible was right in so far as it was a means of communication between worlds. Inside this golden shell are many crystals, but they are not of this world. They come from a place that is within the fourth dimension, a region of anti-matter, or chaos if you will. Unlike crystalline structures more well known to us, these stones are pentagonal and therefore have a fivefold symmetry.' As Tory appeared to have totally lost track of the conversation, the Merlin clarified: 'In other words, they give off a charge of anti-matter necessary for the gravity control needed to create a doorway into the time–space continuum, along with the natural earth energies of this site and the crystal conductors that are required to harness the vortex.'

'So what's it doing here?'

It's my means of transport to and from home. Shu Micah joined them. *It was only after I got here to your third-dimensional concept of time, that I realised I could not only dimension shift using this form of gravity control, but time travel as well. For where I come from, there is no time.*

'If you don't mind me asking, Shu Micah . . .' she couldn't pass up the perfect opportunity to inquire, 'where do you come from?'

From within the region of Nibiru, the brightest star in the night sky. He pointed it out.

'You might know it better as the binary star, Sirius,' Taliesin whispered.

Tory wanted to ask what Shu Micah had meant by 'in the region of', but Nin Bau summoned everyone to take their places for the operation.

'I'd wish you luck, but I already know you don't need it.' Taliesin turned her to face the centre of the stone circle where Turan was already in position, and gently encouraged her to head that way.

Turan was feeling a little edgy as he'd never travelled the circuits of time in a physical form before, and what was worse, somebody else was manning the controls.

'Well, here we are.' Tory came to a stop in front of the Shar, marking how perturbed he appeared. 'There's nothing to worry about . . . I've done this lots of times, even before I became immortal.'

Nothing to worry about! he thought to himself.

She obviously had no notion of the potential danger of becoming trapped in a time warp, which could involve being in a limbo of spiritual isolation for centuries of earth time.

If only I could be so blissfully naive. Turan smiled and took up her hands.

'Oh dear!' Tory panicked suddenly. 'The letter from Nin Bau.' She went to run off, but Turan prevented her.

'I have it,' he informed her, looking to the key mechanism for the site around which Nin Bau, En Seba, Shu Asa, Shu Micah, and En Razu were gathered.

Out of the golden base of the control panel rose a cylindrical dome of a shiny metallic colour. All the members of the council placed their hands on the conductor, as Nin Bau began chanting her summons.

A turbulent cloud erupted in the sky overhead, its core alive with electro-magnetic activity. A bolt of lightning lashed down to make contact with the dome and a glowing white mist began to rise from the centre of the stones where Tory and Turan stood.

'Don't let go.' Tory tightened her grip on him.

'I've got you,' he vowed, as a great whirlpool of light engulfed them.

When Tory next became aware of the world around her, she was standing in the middle of the Dur-an-ki plateau. She wasn't holding Turan's hands any longer; rather, her arms were wrapped tightly around his huge form and her head was pressed against his chest.

As Turan came to realise he was embracing his companion, he ceased to do so at once. 'Ah . . . I do believe we're here,' he announced, looking around the darkened site that was completely abandoned.

Having lost her means of support, Tory staggered about readjusting to the gravitational pull. 'So, where to from here?'

'Nin Bau.' He fished the scroll from his pocket. 'We shall find her in her council chambers.'

Taliesin was in the chart room of the Dur-nu-ga Temple, informing En Durand of the exact time Tory had appeared during the Shu Sar's healing session. He'd left their sleeping visitor with Shar Turan watching over her. The girl was in a deep sleep state and the Merlin did not expect she would awaken for some time yet.

What does Shar Turan have to do with our mysterious guest? En Durand wanted to know.

Taliesin did not feel at liberty to say. *I just think if you compared their charts, you might find some interesting analogies,* he advised with a grin.

A thought form floated into the room and settled upon Taliesin's shoulders. Durand watched En Razu absorbing the message, curious as to the sender. As the transmission vanished, the recipient appeared rather astonished. *Is something amiss?* Durand enquired.

Quite the contrary. Taliesin broke from his thoughts to look to Durand. *It would seem there is much afoot.*

Did anyone else note it? En Cato hurried into the room, carrying a hand-held device from the bioelectronics lab.

What was going on today? Chaos reigned supreme. *I'm sorry? Note what?* Durand questioned his excited associate.

The latest ripple in the continuum. En Cato passed Durand the device so that he could view the relevant information for himself. But as you may note, this charge was completely polarized.

My apologies gentlemen, but I must go. Taliesin took his leave. Nin Bau seldom called an impromptu meeting of the High Council, and curiosity alone would not allow him to delay.

En Cato appeared most disappointed. *But I wanted to discuss the implications of this.*

Taliesin politely shrugged. *Tomorrow perhaps. Right now, however, Nin Bau is awaiting my presence.*

Nin Bau?! Both Cato and Durand exclaimed in unison.

Relax gentlemen, the Merlin advised. *I'm sure she wishes only to know of our guest.* Deep down, however, Taliesin expected different, and made haste to find out.

Upon entering the council chamber of the High Priestess, Taliesin found En Seba, Shu Asa, and Shu Micah already in attendance. The Merlin noticed that the large stone tablet underneath Nin Bau's throne was in a forwardly position, meaning the trapdoor that led to Mount Dur-an-ki was open.

You sent for me, Nin. He bowed to her. A matter of some urgency, you said?

Yes, indeed, dearest adviser, she sounded absolutely delighted to announce.

Early this morning, there was another interesting development with our young visitor from the future. She motioned to behind her where Tory and Turan emerged on cue from the tunnel hidden by her seat.

Taliesin's jaw near hit the floor. 'When did you awaken?' He could hardly believe Tory could have recovered already, and even if she had, she should still be in quarantine.

'About two weeks ago.' She informed, gratified to have the chance to confuse him for a change.

'Pardon?' Taliesin baulked.

'This cable . . .' the High Priestess handed the scroll to him, 'written in my own hand, is fairly self-explanatory.'

The Merlin unrolled the message and read it. The situation was briefly explained prior to the instruction on how to proceed, which was not to be questioned.

'When?' the Merlin quizzed, as he continued to read.

'Late tonight,' Nin Bau answered.

Taliesin looked to Tory, whom he'd only once had the pleasure of consciously addressing. As that conversation had changed the entire course of his existence and, most likely, the course of history for the better, he figured he owed her a favour or two. 'I shall be more than glad to help.'

'Thank you, my friend.' Tory smiled at him warmly. 'I knew I could count on you.'

'Well, now that we are all together, do fill us in on your quest, child, and how you came to be in our midst.' Nin Bau requested from behind her veil.

Tory took a deep breath; this was absolutely the last time she was going to tell the tale of her trials. Again she was careful not to mention that Taliesin had abandoned her, but rather said that he was elsewhere in time at the time of her departure.

The members of the council left at mid-afternoon to go about their normal routine, so that none might be alerted to their unexpected task. They would meet late tonight to execute Nin Bau's instruction as per her letter.

The High Priestess had a large tray of food brought to her council chamber and left Turan and Tory alone to eat and relax awhile before this night's episode took place.

They ate in silence for a time. Tory's mind was focused on her trip home. Turan, however, was mulling over the tale of her origins; he'd learnt much from her most recent version of it.

'You didn't mention before that you were wed to this king, whose life you seek to save.'

'It didn't seem that important,' she replied. 'The reasons I gave for my quest were not false, so what difference does it make?' She threw the ball back in his court, as she bit into a very large apple.

'None,' he was quick to concede. 'En Razu obviously knows . . .' The Shar voiced his train of thought, as he gave a shrug.

'He's known since the moment I met him. In fact, if it wasn't for Taliesin's intervention I never would have met my husband at all.'

'That's odd.' The Shar was baffled. 'It just seemed to me that En Razu was very fond of you.'

'Well he is, and I of he.' She melted into a smile as the memories flooded back. 'We've been through chaos and back, he and I. And we've found paradise a couple of times, too. He's like my godfather, a guardian through time and space . . .' She paused and her expression suddenly saddened. 'Or at least he used to be.'

'Used to be?'

She took a deep breath and let it out again, her heart heavy with the secret. 'He was present when Mahaud broke loose to wreak havoc on Gwynedd.' Her eyes filled with tears. 'Only Xavier knows about this, and I want you to swear not to say anything to En Razu . . . as I haven't quite decided if I should tell him yet.'

'Well, maybe I can advise?' Turan lay on his side, propping his head up on his hand to listen.

This was just as Maelgwn used to do.

Tory closed her eyes a moment, not wanting to see her husband in the man before her, and focused on her anecdote instead.

The more the Shar came to learn of the daughter of Danuih, the more he admired her. For although he was well learned, he couldn't even dream of surviving some of the trials this girl had been through. The tiny amount of emotional hurt he'd felt when Antonia married his brother all those years ago seemed a mere trifle in comparison.

'Well . . .' Turan voiced how he perceived the situation. 'If you tell En Razu what has happened, you could arrange for things to unfold that way . . . and then there would be no question in your mind as to why he left.'

'That's interesting.' Tory smiled. 'After all, I did come through it okay . . . and who's to say that Brockwell might have been spared had Taliesin stayed.' She gave a heavy sigh in mourning.

'Well, that would depend on if the event of your friend's death was time-asymmetric — irreversible. Or time-symmetric — reversible.'

'Oh dear.' Tory gave a thought to the history books of the twentieth century, all of which clearly stated that Maelgwn had died of yellow plague. 'What if my husband's death is asymmetrical? Correct me if I'm wrong, but that would mean that no matter what I do, something will prevent me from saving him?'

Turan sat up and placed a hand on Tory's shoulder for reassurance. 'There's only one way you'll ever know, isn't there?'

Nin Bau had entered so quietly that neither Tory nor Turan had realised she was present. She watched the two of them having a picnic on the floor of her chambers from the doorway. Her nephew had not looked upon a woman thus for hundreds of years, and it seemed the gods had answered her prayers by sending this girl their way. The Priestess silently took her leave without disturbing them, for such a miracle was not to be disturbed; she would speak with their time traveller later, for indeed, they had much to discuss.

That night, the council gathered in secret and called on their allies in the fourth dimension to send Tory back through the continuum to Llyn Cerrig Bach.

Tory stood on top of the alter stone in the temple, barely able to believe she was home. Everything was just as she remembered, not a stone was out of place.

'Alright!' She readied herself for phase three, immediately focusing on the bedside of the High King. For here in the Dark Age there was no time to waste; Maelgwn's biological clock was ticking away rapidly.

Tory was surprised to find Maelgwn alone when she arrived in their bedroom at Degannwy; she'd thought at least Selwyn would be with him. But this made her task easier in a way; thus she removed Darius' belt from her person and took the samples from Maelgwn as the Head Healer had instructed her to.

Once this was done and the devices were strapped back in the belt for cartage, Tory kissed the forehead of her love, placing the amethyst wand still glowing with healing energy in his hands.

'Tory,' he mumbled, having barely enough energy to smile.

'Yes, my lover, it is I,' she whispered with adoration.

'You look so lovely in this light.'

He must have been delirious; his eyes were closed and it was dark out. She was going to inquire as to what he referred, but the sound of several people hurriedly approaching up the corridor outside caused her to make a quick departure.

'Hang on, my dearest.' She kissed Maelgwn and made her leave.

'Wait!'

Tory heard a voice cry, and strangely enough it sounded quite like her own.

She stood on the alter stone at Llyn Cerrig Bach, debating whether or not she should return to Degannwy to investigate the matter, when the light mist that was her ticket back to the Old Land began to rise from out of the cross engraved at her feet.

'Too late now.' The decision was made for her. And as she took one last sweeping look around the familiar place, her eyes met with a horrible sight.

Mahaud, no! Tory protested, as the light of the vortex consumed her.

Turan had been pacing up and down since Tory's departure.

Taliesin had been watching the Shar's private turmoil with some amusement. *You're going to wear a hole in the ground if you keep that up*, he commented to his friend in jest.

It's not funny, it's been too long. Turan looked to Nin Bau who had her hands resting on the dome of the site's control mechanism and was deep in concentration.

Taliesin had a quiet chuckle at this. *Lamamu has only been gone a few moments. Give her time.*

The Shar didn't share his friend's chirpy view, and walked away to where he could pace in peace.

Again the Merlin chuckled, amused by the thought that in less than two weeks Turan would change so much; this was going to be fun to watch.

'Gentlemen.' Nin Bau summoned them to take their stations by her.

Turan stood just outside the circle to catch Tory should she faint upon arrival; her molecular structure had been transposed so many times in such a short period of time, it would be surprising if she had the faintest idea where she was.

A cloud mass burst forth out of the night sky and lightning shot from within to make contact with the key. The centre of the circle glowed, as mist swirled out of the ground and up to meet with the swirling vortex above. The claps of thunder were almost deafening, and anyone who didn't know better would have thought half the continent would know what they were up to.

But, thinking back to this night two weeks ago, Turan recalled the quietest of evenings. He'd observed Tory sleep most of the day, all that night, and into the following morning. He'd certainly not suspected all this was taking place, proving all etheric occurrences are directional phenomena and are, therefore, experienced only by those intended to perceive them. For not even the Shu Sar knew what took place on the sacred mountain half the time.

The disturbance died away and Tory's tiny form was left trembling in the middle of the plateau. Turan rushed to support her, and she murmured as her eyes rolled round in her head.

'She . . . she saw me.' Terror had a firm grip on her being, she was hyperventilating and in shock. *Must stay awake, must tell them.* Her vision was hazy.

Must tell them what? Turan perceived her thought before she blacked out and he caught her up in his arms.

18

THE MATING GAME

When consciousness took hold once more, Tory found herself moving through the crystal cavern beneath Mount Dur-an-ki. It was Turan who carried her, and they were alone.

'When are we?' She was seized by panic.

'Everything is fine. We're back in the present. It's over,' he was happy to announce, and was surprised when Tory sprang from his arms to land on her feet.

'No, it isn't. This is very bad.' She stumbled to and fro. 'Damn it! If I'd told them back then, Nin Bau never would have permitted the time loop to take place and she wouldn't know.'

Tory near collapsed again, but Turan was quick to intercept her fall. 'You're not making any sense, you realise.' He swept her back up into his arms, and resumed their course. 'We have the samples and are on the way to the Shi-imi-ti to give them to Darius. Our quest has been successful, what more — '

'Mahaud!' Tory explained in a word. 'On my way back, she saw me.'

'So.' Turan was very casual about the news. 'That doesn't mean she knew where you were going, or that she could get here if she did.'

'But I know she must have a means of transporting herself through time. She's done it before,' she postulated.

'I think you need to relax,' Turan commanded. 'Let us get you to the Shi-im-ti Temple. You'll think more clearly given time to rejuvenate.'

The sun was rising in the morning sky by the time the Shar left Tory in the Shu Sar's healing chamber to bathe and relax. Turan roused up Xavier to check on their sister's state of being, and then sought out Darius as requested.

'What on earth happened to you!' Xavier exclaimed upon sighting Tory. For a dark patch of negative energy had attached itself to her third eye area, near covering one side of her head.

'Thank goodness you're here. I've got the most splitting headache.' She sat with her feet in the heated spa pool, supporting her head in her hands.

'Well, I'm not surprised.' He made light of her ailment, knowing he'd soon have it cured. 'Come on then, clothes off, and into the water.'

He spurred her to action, but although she was eager to be rid of the pain, her limbs were slow to respond. Tory couldn't understand how she, as an immortal being, could feel so drained.

Xavier assisted her to release the negative force back into the universe and replenished it with a more constructive energy.

'I have to say, Lamamu, if you don't stop giving this entity so much power, you shall never be rid of it.' Xavier bathed his hands and arms after the session.

'I know, I know!' She tried not to be cross with herself as she pulled on a robe of purple — the colour that pertained to the third eye area. 'She took me by surprise . . . I didn't expect it.'

'No excuse.' He was firm with her. 'Remember that every emotion or feeling you have, or pick up, is only energy particles on loan to you from the cosmos. Hence, the energy you employ and promote is entirely of your own choosing.'

'But I don't want to be afraid of her,' Tory insisted.

'Then don't be.' Xavier came to sit beside her at the pool.

'I don't fear for me,' she spoke up in her own defense. 'I know Mahaud can do me no harm, and she knows it too. It's those around me that are more the concern.'

'Don't you dare give me that,' he scolded. 'Don't you see . . . by fearing for those you love, you're assisting to place them in peril, which is just what this entity wants you to do.'

Tory's brow became drawn in defeat; she understood what he meant, but it was human nature to want to protect those you cared about.

'Look . . .' He decided to continue. 'Any thought is composed of highly complex energy particles that draw their reality from that energy. Therefore, if you think clearly fearful thoughts you are transmitting to the cosmos a well defined signal that you expect the worst . . . and believe me the universe shall be swift to oblige. Creation does not question, it merely processes our instructions.' As she was becoming a little more receptive, Xavier advised further: 'So, if you really want to thwart your opponent, you'll believe she has no idea where you are, or what you're doing, and leave it at that.'

'That's more or less what Turan said.' Could she dare to believe the resolution of the problem was so simple.

'Turan's a smart man.' Xavier stood; the sun was swiftly making its way towards the midday rite and he had many other patients to see today. However, when the door opened before him and Adelgar stood poised in the doorway with a huge bunch of flowers in hand, Xavier postponed his leave. 'I'm sorry

Adelgar, but I can't permit you in here. Nin Lamamu needs to rest.'

'Please, Doc. Just for a little while. Adelgar and I do have a thing or two to discuss.' She gazed up at him with her large soulful eyes.

'Oh, alright. Till midday.' Xavier advised his brother sternly on his way out.

Adelgar was more cheery upon discovering he was welcomed, and strode over to present the flowers to their intended recipient. 'I was sorry to hear you were feeling poorly . . . what are you in for?' He crouched beside her.

She accepted the bright bouquet from him with a smile, and breathed the many different scents contained therein. 'I've contracted a horrible sexually transmitted disease,' she stated, very matter of fact.

Adelgar appeared horrified. 'You're joking!'

'Yes, I am.' She laughed at the expression on his face. 'The truth is, I had a headache.'

'Phew . . .' He grinned at her folly. 'I suppose you think you're clever.'

He took the same position Brian or Brockwell would have when tricked, and she saw both of these other selves in the one confronting her.

'I am clever,' she told him surely, placing the flowers aside. 'And I have a great need to tell you something.'

Adelgar seated himself properly to listen.

'Has anyone told you where I'm from?'

He shrugged. 'It is said you are from many different lands in time.'

'That's right. Good . . .' She paused to consider her approach. 'Now, many of the people I have met here, are people I have known in these other lives.'

'Are you trying to say we've met before?' Adelgar made it sound as if this was quite an obvious assumption to reach.

'That's exactly what I'm trying to say.' This was easier than Tory expected.

'We were joined, no?' He posed with confidence.

'No.' She broke it to him gently. 'You were my one and only brother.'

'No!' he protested, springing up to stand over her. 'Why me?'

'I don't know.' Tory shrunk from him.

'In all these lives or just one?'

'Just the one I was born into.'

'Damn it!'

'But, listen to me,' she rose, imploring him. 'I know for a fact I am not the woman you seek. You've joined with the same girl in both the lives I've known you in, and I can assure you, it wasn't me.'

This news seemed to capture his attention, and his mood took a swing for the better. 'Who then?'

'Well . . .' Tory was hesitant. 'I'd know her if I saw her.'

'Aw.' He waved her off, disappointed.

'Look I'm sure she's here.' Tory pleaded for his patience. 'Everybody else is.'

Adelgar waved his head about, finding it difficult to accept her view. 'What if she isn't?'

'She will be, I know it.'

Adelgar didn't have the patience for such a quest as true love, especially when there was a perfectly adequate substitute right here in front of him. 'She'd want to be really exceptional this girl.'

Tory grinned, confident he would think so. 'She's managed to keep you faithful to her and her alone, for two lifetimes. You be the judge.'

Adelgar dwelt on the claim. 'You must help me look then. And don't forget you owe me that lesson.'

'I promise. If you agree to no more visits in the middle of the night . . . or any form of sneak attack upon my person.'

Again he paused to consider. 'Alright.' He shook on it. 'You're on.'

After delivering the samples and being given the physical 'all clear' by Darius, Turan made for his quarters in the Dur-nu-ga Temple in the hope of avoiding questions from his family about his whereabouts last night. For, in addition to his unexplained return to a physical form, both Lamamu and himself had disappeared from the feast at approximately the same time; hence, he had a fair idea of what all those in the palace would be thinking.

There was something about this scenario that made him smile, and Turan considered it must be that good old ego kicking in. If he didn't work on resuming his etheric form soon, chances were the desires of this physical body would make it increasingly difficult.

The Shar bathed and changed before retiring to the temple dining room. He spotted Durand seated in a corner on his own, reviewing his students' assignments.

Can I join you? Turan enquired, taking a seat in any case.

Where have you been? Durand was in a most jovial mood. You're the talk of the town this morning. He chuckled.

I can imagine.

The Shar tucked into the tray of food before him, and Durand couldn't help but stare; it was so strange to see him eat.

So why are you here working, instead of at the games?

I'm just finishing these last two papers, then I'm off . . . I'm meeting Nin Lilith. Durand smiled. Afterwards she's treating me to dinner at the Temple of Kheit-Sin.

Turan stared at his mentor a moment, a smile frozen on his lips. *Well, it couldn't happen to a nicer chap. He shook his hand. Congratulations.*

Well, let's not get ahead of ourselves. Durand tried to downplay his excitement; seven hundred years was a long time to live alone. Tell me about you then?

Turan's good mood evaporated and he went back to his food. *Nin Lamamu and I were just working on a project.*

You're not being straight with me, Durand insisted. It was quite obvious to him how Turan felt about the girl.

I am. His voice shrunk to a whisper. I'm not supposed to tell anyone, but we performed the time loop and it worked. You were right.

That explained why Turan had reconstituted. *So why wasn't I told. I am Head of Time and Space studies, you know.*

Because you weren't involved originally. Only the High Priests of the council and Nin Bau knew, for only they were required to perform the task.

I suspected something was going on.

Turan shrugged in resolve. *What's done is done. Darius has what he requires to aid Lamamu's husband, and I suspect once she has the cure she seeks, she will return from whence she came and all shall get back to normal around here.*

You sound as if you won't be sorry to see her go?

She should be with the one she loves. Just as you should. Turan attempted cheer. *Leave the damn papers. Go, have fun.*

Durand could hardly believe these words were coming out of Turan's mouth; Lamamu had had a profound effect on him. He so wanted to tell Turan that Lamamu's King and the Shar's good self were one and the same person, but he'd vowed he would not.

You know, it was only because Lamamu mentioned to me that she'd known me in another life, that I even considered Nin Lilith and myself might be compatible. Durand thought he might be able to drop a hint somehow. *She told me we'd been happily married once before.*

Did she now? How fortunate. The Shar seemed more interested in his meal.

Durand tried to make his clues more pointed. *She's known lots of us before, she told me.*

What are you trying to say, Durand?

I can't say. I promised I wouldn't tell you.

I see. Turan was rather amused by this game. *Well, it would seem to me that you're inferring that she's known me before.*

Could be. Durand raised his eyebrows. *I gather from what you've said that Lamamu has already told you she's married to this King Maelgwn of Gwynedd.*

Did you say, Maelgwn?'

Indeed I did. Durand was hopeful they'd had a breakthrough.

That's what Lamamu called me, the first time she laid eyes on me. Turan pondered the implications of this.

Funny about that, Durand commented, as he quickly gathered up his things.

Are you saying . . . Turan's words were seized by a burst of joy that near choked him.

I'm not saying anything. Durand was very noncommittal, though he winked at Turan in parting. I shall see you later.

Tory was doing laps in the sunlit pool, having finally persuaded Adelgar to leave, when it came to her attention that she was not alone. She brought her exercise to a halt as the sound of sweet laughter reached her ears.

The veiled form of the High Priestess stood poolside. *I thought the idea was to relax.*

'Nin Bau, this is a surprise.' Tory hurried from the water to dry herself and greet the holy woman.

Take your time, child. There is no hurry. The Priestess sat herself down on the lounge. How are you feeling in the wake of your little adventure?

'Much improved after seeing Xavier.' Tory pulled on her robe as she took a seat beside Nin Bau. *Is that why you're here?*

No . . . She paused a moment.

Tory couldn't see the Priestess' facial expression, but she had an air of great anticipation about her.

I wanted to ask you about the one called Myrddin. What was he like?

This was the last thing Tory was expecting her to ask, though the inquiry warmed her heart and made her smile. 'I know he was very wise, both in his mortal and immortal state. But En Razu is probably more of an expert on the Merlin's greatest historical achievements.'

Where and when was he born? Nin Bau seemed most eager to know.

'Well, let me see.' Tory had to think about that one, it had been a long time since she'd studied British history. 'It was said Myrddin was born and raised in the British town of Carmarthen, at around the middle of the fifth century AD. In other words, about a hundred years prior to the time you have just sent me to, but the same country.'

And his parents? What was said of them?

Tory was becoming most curious about this line of questioning, but obliged the Priestess with what she knew. 'Legend had it that Myrddin's father was of the Otherworld, an etheric being you might say.'

Yes, yes, go on, Nin Bau urged, excited.

'However, his mother was said to have been a nun, a woman dedicated to the pursuit of the higher mysteries, much like yourself.'

Then it was as Darius claimed; Nin Bau could hardly contain her excitement. *You have made me very happy, child.*

'I don't understand.'

The Priestess rose with her back to Tory as she pondered whether or not to tell her what was now, in her mind, confirmed. Nin Bau set her veil back over her head. *Do you recognise me, Lamamu? She turned to face Tory.*

The Priestess had skin as white as snow, with cheeks flushed red like a young girl. Her hair was black as night, though two patches of pure white sprung from her temples, and her eyes were violet.

With her appearance being as breathtaking as it was, Tory felt she would surely have remembered if they'd met before. *I'm sorry, Highness, but I can't say I do.*

Wait, Nin Bau instructed, as she slowly began to age her physical appearance. And now?

As the lines and wrinkles beset the Priestess' face, Tory's eyes grew wide. 'Aunt Rose, Lady Gladys,' she exclaimed. 'So that's why you wanted to know about my father . . . in the twentieth century, you were his sister. Yet . . .' Tory paused, considering what she'd learnt of her father over the years, 'there is increasing evidence to suggest that he may have been adopted in that time, rather than actually being born there.'

I suspect you might be right. Nin Bau smiled broadly, as if withholding information. She returned to her younger self and took a seat.

'What makes you say that?'

I am with child, she beamed, though I have not joined with any mortal man.

Tory could feel her jaw drooping. 'Are . . . you saying, you're carrying my father!'

The Priestess nodded, amused by Tory's flabbergasted expression. *According to Darius, that is correct. For he has shown me the genetic proof that I am indeed, your grandmother.*

'That explains how I ended up with the Shu Sar's genes,' Tory mused out loud. 'But how did you come to be in fifth century Britain, then?'

Nin Bau gave half a laugh. *Only time will tell. But what you have told me complies with what I have already foreseen. In his mortal form, your father appears much like my brother, no?*

'That he does.' Tory nodded; there truly were no coincidences. 'So my grandfather is from the fourth dimension.' She raised her brow. 'That news should knock my brother on his ar. . . sorry.' Tory remembered the rank of the woman in her presence.

You must not tell anyone here of this. Nin Bau was deadly serious. Only En Darius knows and, for the present, I feel it wise to keep it that way.

The Priestess was very mysterious about her reasons. She would only say that this was as her head truth seer had advised, for she'd been so elated by the news that she'd had trouble thinking with any clarity on the matter.

Tory swore by the elements she would not tell a soul. 'Your secret is safe with me.' She couldn't help but grin. 'Grandmother.'

Nin Bau laughed at this; she hadn't even become acquainted with the title of mother yet.

Tory was dying to ask about the conception of the Priestess' babe, but she refrained from prying; sometimes her curiosity went too far and, fortunately, she recognised that this could be one of those times. If Nin Bau wished to speak of it, she would.

Later that afternoon, Xavier gave Tory the all clear to leave the Shi-im-ti Temple, but while she was in the building she thought she'd duck round to see how Darius was going with her miracle cure.

As soon as I have a breakthrough, I'll let you know. He became quite testy at being disturbed. Until then, go and enjoy the festivities of the holiday. Darius looked back into the microscope that interfaced with his computer.

I'm sorry I'm making you miss the celebrations. Tory thought that perhaps this was why he seemed on edge.

My other half shall tell me all about it, no doubt. He rolled his eyes at the thought. I find this far more interesting, truly.

I didn't know you were wed? Tory wondered if perchance his wife would turn out to be the woman she'd known as Jenovefa.

Long time. He seemed proud of the fact. Her name is Anthea. We went through the university of Danuih together, she heads the Earth Healers here.

'Anthea,' Tory echoed. 'Pretty name.'

It means 'woman of flowers' and that's no understatement. Believe me, you ought to see our home. He chuckled.

Their conversation ended there, for Adelgar had managed to track Tory down to start the hunt for his intended.

They exited the Shi-im-ti to find Shar Jerram awaiting them on the stairs. Adelgar explained that he'd told his brother of their quest, and Jerram had asked to come along on the off-chance Tory could match him up with his perfect partner.

'I should start charging.' She didn't sound too thrilled, for the only woman Tory knew that Jerram (as Teo) had truly been serious about was herself.

'Although I have known you before, Jerram, I wasn't associated with you long enough to discover whom you eventually wed.'

'I see.' He sounded rather nonchalant about it. 'Well, tell me — if Adelgar was your brother, what was I?'

Tory grinned as the three of them slowly made their way out to the third island, where most of the festivities were taking place. 'You were my sensei, my instructor . . . it was you who taught me how to fight.' She gave him a nudge on the shoulder as if to say 'Good on you.'

'Was that all I taught you?'

There was a sultry connotation in his tone; did Jerram already know he'd been her first love? Again she grinned, remaining as calm as she could with those large brown eyes seducing her. 'You didn't like to mix business with pleasure.' This was not a lie; she'd just failed to mention that he'd made an exception in her case.

Jerram smiled, cocking an eye. 'But the inclination was there?'

'Hey!' Adelgar pulled Tory away from his brother. 'Stop flirting with my sister.'

'Well, someone's got to do it.'

Tory laughed; this whole scenario was like a mad case of deja-vu. 'Oh, listen.' She had suddenly remembered something. 'Do you know En Darius' wife?'

'Nin Anthea? Yes,' Adelgar confirmed.

'I want you to point her out to me if you see her. I figure if she is the same woman Darius matched with where I came from, then that will substantiate my theory concerning you,' she put to Adelgar, who gave a firm nod to second her reasoning.

An hour or two into their search, Adelgar spotted Nin Anthea. Despite being fearful of his own expectations, he directed Tory's attention to a fair-haired woman seated not far from the Shu Sar, who was in his private stalls watching the javelin throwing competition taking place in the stadium below.

'That's her alright.' Tory was excited for Adelgar, and they resumed the search with renewed enthusiasm.

They passed over one of the stadium bridges to start combing the gardens on the far side, when one of Adelgar's novices came racing up to him in a panic.

'My Shar,' he bowed. 'I'm sorry to disturb you, but . . . it's the panther. She's going to have her cubs.'

'Well, have you notified Nin Lilith?' Both Adelgar and Jerram appeared concerned.

'Yes, my Shar.' The young man humbled himself before conveying the bad news. 'But as one of her elephants is having a breach birth, Nin Lilith and most of her chief students have their hands full already.'

'Damn it!' Adelgar began to pace. 'So who's the head of Domestic Veterinary since En Demetrius' passing last year?'

'Nin Tabitha,' advised his pupil. 'Nin Lilith highly recommends her.'

'I seriously doubt she is qualified for this,' Jerram scoffed.

'Well, what choice have we got?' Adelgar entreated his twin. 'Fetch her, quickly.' He motioned to his novice to do this. 'We will meet you down there.'

Adelgar led the way to the animal stalls underneath the stadium. The beasts were only confined to these quarters for the duration of the games, or in this case, labour, as there were large natural wildlife sanctuaries just outside the city limits.

They came to a stop outside a sandstone cell, and through the barred window Tory could see the panther laying on her side, panting through her pain. The dim light and coolness of the holding chamber must have seemed a blessing to the animal.

Without the slightest hesitation or fear, Adelgar entered the cell and closed the door behind him.

The panther half-raised itself and snarled, as if threatening an attack, and Tory gripped hold of the bars on the window, afraid for her brother. Adelgar halted and let out the same snarling roar, which astounded her somewhat. *Good God! Could he have the ability to converse with such a beast?*

'Now, Selina,' he cautioned the big black cat. 'You just behave yourself. It's not my fault you're in this mess, now is it?'

Tory couldn't believe her eyes when the beast sank back to the ground, appearing all sorry for itself.

'That's better.' Adelgar rang out a rag in the pool of water and sat himself beside the cat to wash and cool its head.

'Did somebody call for a vet?' The novice had returned with Nin Tabitha. *It's her!* It was Katren.

'What a big pussy cat,' Nin Tabitha remarked with a smile, as she entered the cell.

Adelgar stood, but near fell on his butt again upon his sighting of her. 'You must be Nin Tabitha?' He gazed upon the lovely woman, who, like himself, appeared to be a half-caste; a mixture of the red and white races of the continent.

'And this must be Selina.' Her attention immediately focused on her subject, and she crouched down beside the huge cat to check its vital signs.

'Thank you for coming.' Adelgar squatted close by her, contentedly watching every move she made.

'It's my pleasure,' she assured the beast as she stroked its swollen belly. 'Its not often I get to treat one as exotic as yourself.' Her beaming face turned to Adelgar, who suddenly looked tamed.

Perfect. Tory delighted in watching them together; what a lovely way to meet.

Four hours later, two cubs and a new romance had been born.

Nin Tabitha left them with little protest from Adelgar, for he was meeting her later to check their new panther family.

As Adelgar exited the cell, leaving mother and cubs in peace, he and Tory looked straight at each other.

'That's her.' They laughed together.

As the festivities would continue well into the night out at the stadium, there was no official feast to be held in the palace this evening. Hence, Tory, having had more than a full day already, decided to spend a quiet night in her room. Yet, before her evening meal had arrived, Shar Turan fronted in for a visit.

'You've been living up to your name, I hear . . . we have romances bloom-ing all over the place. In fact, I believe Xavier is now seeking to employ your services.' He seemed to be conspicuously joyful.

'I've been looking for you.' Tory broke from the kata she was performing.

'Well, you've found me.' He smiled broadly. 'Have you eaten?'

'Well, no. I —'

'Good.' He took her by the arm. 'Allow me to introduce you to the Temple of E-hulhul.'

She smiled, noting how playful his manner was. 'What does E-hulhul stand for?'

'Temple of Joy. It's the recreational centre here in Chailidocean,' he enlightened her, as he led her out the door. 'There's aroma tubes, flotation pools, anti-gravity chambers . . . you'll love it, trust me.'

Over the course of dinner, Turan proved to be such captivating company that Tory didn't know what to make of this sudden swing in his attitude. Had he not been so like Maelgwn there wouldn't have been a problem, but she was a sucker for his smile, his voice, his manner. Tory was very tempted to tell the Shar what she was feeling and why, especially after her talk with Durand about being open to the will of the universe, but then, to do so seemed a rather selfish act. She would be leaving here soon, and from her understanding of what Nin Bau had said, the last thing Turan needed was more heartache.

'So, how was your husband faring when you saw him?' the Shar enquired politely as he poured them both a cup of herbal tea.

The question floored her. *Please don't let him be reading my mind.* She didn't think she was projecting her thoughts, but Tory wasn't that perfect at the craft for her to be sure.

'As well as could be expected, I suppose.' She was a bit disheartened about it. 'But I left with him the crystal wand that I took from the cavern. Hopefully, it will give him a little more staying power.' She grinned, forcing herself to better spirits.

'My apologies. I shouldn't have brought it up.' *That's what I get for trying to be clever.* He was rueful; they'd been having a wonderful time and now he'd spoilt it.

'I just miss him.'

'He must be a truly remarkable man to warrant such devotion.' *There was that ego again.* The Shar just couldn't help himself.

'Yes, he is.' She stared at Turan a moment, feeling that this could be said of every incarnation of his that she'd had the pleasure of knowing. She gave half a laugh. 'You and he would see eye-to-eye on most things, I'm sure.'

Her comment amused the Shar. He didn't have to read her mind to know how she felt about him. The energy around her heart chakra had increased fourfold during the course of the evening, and now encompassed all her lower chakras. Should he be straight with her and tell her what he knew? *Not here.* 'So, are we finished?' Turan motioned to the almost empty platter.

Tory nodded. 'I couldn't even look at another piece of food.'

'Then let us go. I have a surprise for you.'

Turan moved his eyebrows up and down a few times, sporting the same cheeky expression Maelgwn did when he was up to mischief.

He led her down one of the four long corridors that shot out in different directions from the central chamber of the temple, where the dining room was located.

'This is it.' Turan came to a stop and activated the door in front of them.

They entered a circular room that was entirely composed of polished black marble. Four stairs rose out of the floor in the centre to form a mound-like structure, atop of which was a round platform about four-and-a-half metres wide. There was a lounge and table of white to one side of the room, and a small spa pool to the other.

After closing the door, Turan placed his hand on the control panel beside the mound.

A beam of light, not much smaller than the platform itself, began to glow in a cylindrical form between the ceiling and the mound.

'Excellent!' Tory greatly approved. 'What does it do?'

'Step into it and find out. It's perfectly safe.'

But Tory was already halfway up the stairs. She reached into the glowing beam and her arms disappeared before her, feeling as if they'd been liberated of all stress. A little braver, Tory jumped straight into the huge beam and was immediately swept upwards. 'Whoa . . .!' She settled to a stable floating position about two metres from the ground, and could thus tumble, twirl, or just relax and drift. This was very like her experience in the High Temple on the night of her judgement, but in this case she was positive her physical form was still with her. 'This is fantastic!'

Turan was pleased. 'Not everyone is susceptible to it, but I had a feeling you might be.'

'I love it!' she cried out, and screeched with laughter.

Tory certainly sounded as if she was having a good time in there. Turan, employing etheric sight, perceived a clear image of Tory moving about gracefully in the void. Her golden hair flowing around her added to the lustre of his vision. *Leave*, he cautioned himself.

'So,' Tory called out to him, daring to be so bold. 'Do they build these things for two?'

Could that be construed as a proposition? he wondered, stepping up to enter the anti-gravity beam to find out. 'They have been known to accommodate more than one person.'

Tory regretted her rash invitation as soon as Turan entered the light-field. She watched him float upwards to take a position opposite her, deciding it was time to level with him. 'I have a confession to make. You see — '

'I know about us,' he admitted. 'I know your husband and myself are one and the same.'

Hearing his confession, a tear escaped her eye. 'I can't promise — '

Turan silenced her with a kiss, soft and long. 'No promises required. This is unconditional,' he whispered, admiring the one he would take as his concubine. 'You look so lovely in this light.'

'What did you say?' She held herself apart from him, stunned by the statement.

Turan smiled. Unused to paying another such intimate flattery he felt embarrassed by the query. 'I said, you look so — '

'That's what I thought.' She spared him from repeating it all, staring at him in wonder. At this moment Maelgwn could see her, she knew it. Perhaps her husband's ailment had brought him closer to his source and he had thus become in tune with simultaneous time and his other earthly manifestations.

'Sorry. Was I too forward?' As Turan hadn't had much experience with women, he was afraid he'd upset her.

'Not at all.' She wrapped her arms around his neck and her legs about his waist to reassure him. 'You're the best friend I ever had. And no matter what may become of us throughout the whole of time and space, just remember that I love you — always have, always will.'

As she pleasured him with a kiss, Turan assumed a crossed-legged position to cradle her body against his own. He became so caught up in the sensation of physical arousal that he failed to notice that they'd come to rest in a seated position on the ground.

'I'm very sorry, Turan, I presumed you were alone in here.'

Turan was roused from his state of ecstasy to find the light beam off and his brother in the doorway. 'Alaric.' He stood, lifting Tory with him and placing her on her feet. 'Why should you be seeking me out at this hour on a holiday?'

'Well, actually . . .' Alaric had to grin at the question. 'I wanted to ask if you knew where Lamamu could be found . . . and as I can see, you do.'

Tory was still wary of Alaric, as her memories of Caradoc were not pleasant ones. Still, he seemed a far more obliging character in this lifetime. 'Why are you seeking me, sir?'

'The Shu Sar is requesting an audience with you at once.' He became more solemn. 'If you would be so kind as to follow me.'

Tory gripped hold of Turan's hand.

'I think Alaric meant alone.'

'You may come, Turan,' Alaric added. 'It looks as if this may concern you, too.'

19

CALL OF THE UNKNOWN

The holiday tradition of complete recreation was broken on account of a communication from Atlantis' warring neighbours, the Antillians.

The island continent of Antillia lay beyond a few small islands off the west coast of Atlantis, and was almost as large as the continent it had been waging war upon these last few years. Its people were tall with dark red-brown skin. A primitive people, of a precariously wild nature, most Antillians were taller than those of the white Atlantean race, making them at least two-and-a-half metres in height.

Zutar, supreme ruler of Antillia, had finally agreed to meet with the representatives of Shu Sar Absalom to discuss peace and trade between the two great nations.

'That is wonderful news, father,' Turan allowed, standing before the governing body of Atlantis. 'But how does this concern Nin Lamamu?'

There was a long pause before the Shu Sar informed. 'Zutar will only negotiate with her.'

'But how does he even know of her?' Turan voiced his concern. *Keeldar perhaps? But how would he know?*

Not Mahaud, Tory pleaded with the cosmos on the quiet. Xavier promised if I didn't conceive of her presence she couldn't find me. Tory had broken into a sweat when it occurred to her that she could be being tested. After all, she had no proof of Mahaud's involvement, so why feed the fear by thinking such thoughts.

The Shu Sar's advisers were not at all happy to admit that they could only speculate as to how Zutar had learnt of Lamamu, for they knew very little about the ways of the Antillian people.

'It is irrelevant how they know.' Tory interrupted all the conjecture. 'I am well used to dealing with those of a hostile nature, and, as I cannot be permanently harmed, then I am the perfect candidate for the job in any case.'

'I don't think you understand, child.' Absalom was concerned for her. 'These people are not civilised like the native races of our colonies. They are barbarians who commit unspeakable acts of cruelty and defilement to obtain what they desire. I shall not have you exposed to such danger.'

'I agree.' Turan seconded his father's view.

Jerram stood. 'It is alright for you to protest, living all the way over here in Cintrala, but this truce is very important to the people of my kingdoms.'

'Here, here.' Adelgar voiced with conviction. 'Besides, Jerram and myself shall not let any harm befall her.'

'Really?' Turan forced himself to contain his amusement. 'And who shall protect her from you? If she goes, I go.'

'I think not.' Jerram was cool, yet firm in his objection.

'I just got through saying it is out of the question!' The Shu Sar pulled them both up rather bluntly.

'Excuse me, gentlemen . . .' Tory was beginning to fume, 'but I believe the decision is mine.'

Absalom looked to her, a little surprised, as, normally, nobody overruled his judgement. 'My dear girl, you don't — '

'No, Father, with all due respect, it is you who does not understand,' and she faded from sight.

Psychokinetic teleportation. Turan was so stunned he could only smile; he never would have guessed her to be so accomplished.

'Good heavens! Where's she gone?' the Shu Sar questioned. His astonished colleagues looked around for her. 'Did you know she could do that?' Absalom aimed his query at Taliesin this time.

'I had no idea, my Sar,' Taliesin confessed, as they became aware of Tory's laughter.

'There's lots you don't know about me.' She appeared in front of her father. 'Like how good I am at taking care of myself.' Absalom moved to speak, but Tory cut him short. 'You've all been so good to me since I arrived, now this is something I can do in return . . . please, Father,' she pleaded, going down on one knee before him. 'I shall make you proud, I swear.'

Absalom gave a heavy sigh as he gazed down upon his daughter. 'I was under the impression I'd had a little girl,' he grumbled, 'but this is just like having another son! Oh . . . alright,' he resolved in a huff. But he soon lost his bad mood when Tory hugged him, excited by the prospect of venturing outside the city.

'Yes!' Jerram was pleased.

'I am going with her,' Turan insisted.

'No.' Jerram was most displeased. 'You've never left the inner sanctum of this city, Turan. I will not be held accountable for you.'

'The day I need your aid, Jerram, I shall gladly surrender my life.' Turan expressed himself with a cool, cutting edge to his tone.

'Please.' The Shu Sar stood to finish their quarrel. 'What is wrong with all of you?'

'Father, he's not qualified.' Jerram put forward his case.

'Jerram is quite right,' Absalom admitted. 'If our problem was with another dimension, I would honour your involvement.'

Turan tried to appeal: 'But what if Keeldar — '

'Keeldar is, more than likely, dead,' Jerram contested. 'We have no reason to believe he is in any way connected to this affair. This is a diplomatic mission, not a scientific one.'

'En Razu.' Turan looked to his friend in the hope he would take his side; he knew about the visions he'd had.

'Jerram is right in that we have no proof of a connection,' Taliesin was sorry to concede. 'And, even if we did, to send you to deal with him in your current state, may only serve to make the situation worse.'

'Thank you very much.' Turan was overwhelmed by their confidence in him, or rather their lack thereof. 'I fail to see how my constitutional status has any bearing on my capabilities in this affair.'

Alaric had to laugh at this. 'I do. I've never known you to be so irrational.'

'Irrational!' Turan neared Alaric to quietly ask him: 'Let us send Antonia to face Zutar and see how rational you are?'

'Enough, Turan.' His father gave a last warning. 'What says the rest of this council?' Absalom looked to Shar Diccon and Shar Adelgar, who both shook their heads to make the decision unanimous. 'Then it is final. You stay. If you don't trust Lamamu in the care of Jerram and Adelgar, I shall send Alaric — '

'No!' Tory interjected rather abruptly, quickly rationalising her outburst. 'There's no need to risk your heir on my account.'

Turan was surprised by this. 'Lamamu, you don't know these two — '

'Yes, I do.' Adelgar and Jerram appeared most impressed with themselves, as Tory insisted: 'Well enough to know that they would never purposefully cause me harm, and would fight to the death at my side.' Tory choked on the memory of Brockwell's lifeless form, but resolved with a smile: 'I shall be fine in their charge.'

'So be it.' The Shu Sar concluded.

Turan was excused from the conference, and Tory remained to be briefed by the council.

Both Jerram and Adelgar spoke every native tongue in the known world, hence they would act as her translators. The Shu Sar ran through what they were permitted to agree to, which, basically, wasn't much until such time as the whole council had heard Zutar's terms.

The meeting adjourned with roughly three hours remaining till dawn, when they were scheduled to depart. Tory had been hoping to find Turan waiting for her outside the conference room, but, alas, he was nowhere to be seen.

'Well, it looks like I get my wish after all.' Adelgar snapped his sister out of her daze with a whack on the back. 'Two days from now we'll be in Portea . . . the most beautiful place on earth.'

'You wish,' Jerram interrupted. 'Usiqua is far more breathtaking.'

'It's cold, is what it is,' Adelgar scoffed.

'Guys!' Tory had heard enough disputes for one night, even if it was in fun. 'I'll see you later.'

She made for her quarters to prepare for the journey, but Jerram pursued her. 'Lamamu . . .' He pulled her up. 'I'm sorry about Turan. I realise you and he have become good friends. It's just that I wouldn't function at my best with him along. He has this way of using up my energy.'

Tory nodded with a smile of understanding. 'I know what you mean. But he's a good man underneath, as are you. I just wish the two of you could see each other as I see you.'

Maelgwn and Teo never got along either and Tory had always believed she was the cause. That was obviously not the case in this scenario, however, which she would investigate further at a more apt moment.

'Well, Rome wasn't built in a day.' Tory put an end to the silence, for Jerram had gone rather quiet.

'How do you see me, Lamamu?' The young Shar was suddenly rather serious. 'Does my colour repulse you?'

Tory found the question almost offensive. 'Is a panther any less magnificent than a lion? Of course not! The beauty in any man is found within. And, just for the record, I happen to find coloured men very attractive.'

Jerram smiled. 'You are truly extraordinary for a female of your breed.'

'Oh come on . . .' Tory faked a modest tone as she departed down the hall to escape a sticky situation. 'I'm just extraordinary, period.' She laughed and waved him goodbye.

On the way back to her chamber Tory called in to see if Turan was in his palace quarters, and finding the room empty she assumed he'd gone to the Dur-nu-ga.

He's not mad with me, she convinced herself as she entered her darkened chamber, though she felt quite sure Turan would be wondering why she hadn't insisted he go with her to Antillia.

The truth was, she had to agree with Taliesin's remark concerning Turan's present state of being. Although the Shar could still psychokinetically control his physical surroundings without the aid of any machinery, he was exceptionally vulnerable to emotional confusion and blackmail. Tory figured that the further apart from the situation Turan was, the more help he would be.

She withdrew the metal sheath of the solar lamp on the table to find Turan silently watching her from a position by the window on the other side of the room.

'You'll be leaving at dawn, I presume.' He sounded hurt by the notion.

'I'm so sorry this happened now.' She did not approach, but rather waited for him to close the distance between them. 'I'm not like you, Turan, I'm a born adventurer. How could I possibly say no to the chance to explore the ancient world beyond these walls? And besides, diplomatic relations are my forte. Please don't be mad at me because I want to help.'

'But it's an obvious trap, can't you see that?' Turan neared. 'There are negative forces at work here, I can feel it.'

Tory rose up tall in her stance. 'Well, then, I'll just stay here, huddled in a corner in fear and wait for them to come to us, shall I?'

'Oooh, you are so stubborn.' Turan was frustrated.

'That's why you love me,' she interjected with glee, and his anger was immediately appeased.

'Yes, I believe I do.'

The sincerity behind his confession moved her deeply. 'Then don't fear for me. If anything disastrous should happen, I promise I shall be back here in less than the blink of an eye.'

Turan could feel himself succumbing to her will, and he lifted Tory up to stand on a small table, so that she was more his height. 'Will you visit me?'

'Name the hour and I shall be there,' she vowed in a suggestive fashion, interlocking her hands behind his neck.

'Midnight,' he elected. 'Every night. Then I will know all goes well with you, but if you do not show — '

Tory kissed him before he could conceive of the worst.

'Excuse I.' En Razu sounded most uncomfortable interrupting. 'I am sorry, but the council of the High Priestess would like to see Nin Lamamu in the High Temple before she departs.'

'Of course they would!' Turan was annoyed; could they not have even a few moments alone without somebody requiring her presence. 'How did this continent ever function before you got here?'

Tory shrugged, as reluctant to comply as he. 'Would you go and see En Darius for me? Explain my situation and . . .'

'I know.' The prospect of what would happen if Darius found the cure Lamamu sought disturbed Turan more than this voyage she insisted upon making.

210

'I'll meet you in your quarters in the Dur-nu-ga before I leave.' Tory stepped down off the table to join Taliesin.

Turan gave a slight shrug, then a nod in confirmation. 'I'll be there.'

In the presence of the great elders, Tory was presented with the white robes of the High Order; evidently Taliesin had spoken to the council about her incident of teleportation in the conference room earlier and they'd decided she was more advanced than previously imagined.

As she was going to be representing her father in this affair, Shu Micah also presented Tory with a band of gold that clamped around her waist, to distinguish her rank.

Tory was blessed and thanked for her courage, for no female of their race had ever undertaken such a calling. This was not because political vocation was forbidden to Atlantean women, but it was considered one of the warrior arts and women usually found other avenues to be more beneficial to their karmic purpose.

Tory changed into her new whites, choosing to wear harem pants and a sleeveless, hooded robe that fell past her thighs, feeling this to be both modest and sensible travelling attire.

By the time she'd made it to the Temple of Dur-nu-ga, the sun was shedding its first rays across the darkened sky on the horizon. The bells of the citadel would toll before long, calling all to perform the first solar rite of the day.

Upon entering the entrance foyer Tory realised she'd never been to Turan's private quarters in the Dur-nu-ga, only to his work station. Luckily a few keen novices were already up and about and she was able to ask directions.

She found the door open, and was about to enter when she spied Nin Melcah in the room beyond. Tory ducked to the other side of the doorway, curious as to why the first lady would be up and about so early.

Alaric found you together, that's what he said. Nin Melcah seemed quite irate.

I thought that you would be happy for me. Turan was both surprised and annoyed with her. Isn't this what you all wanted?! . . . For me to come down to earth, meet a nice girl . . .

Yes, a nice girl. Melcah's inflection was very harsh. Not this, this . . . abomination! She's already twisted your father around her little finger, and now you . . .

Melcah was heard to weep, though Tory felt her performance less than convincing.

Don't you see . . . Melcah expanded upon her melodramatic drivel, sounding every bit the concerned mother. She's just toying with you . . .

Mother, I don't want to hear any more of this.

Well, you must hear it. It's not just you she's bewitched; it's every male she's come into contact with. Xavier, Lazarus, Adelgar, Jerram, your father, even En Razu! Am I the only one who sees?

Tory was dumbfounded and quite hurt. She could barely believe this woman, who in some distant lifetime would be her mother, could think such malicious thoughts about her.

Out. Turan advised rather sternly.

Tory dashed for the inset of the next doorway up, flattening herself up hard against the door.

Listen to me. There's something not right about her, I believe she's much more powerful than she lets on, Melcah persisted as she was shown the door.

Goodbye, Mother.

Tory heard the door close. After waiting a moment, she chanced a peek. Nin Melcah was briskly making her way down the corridor in the opposite direction.

'Such hostility.' Tory attempted to make light of it, but she couldn't deny that the ill-will bothered her.

'Knock, knock.' Tory entered the Shar's chamber, which was much smaller than his palace quarters.

'Stop right there.' Turan bade her from his window seat.

This request startled her in the light of what she'd overheard, but she complied all the same. 'What's wrong?'

'Nothing.' He gazed at her, all dressed in white, with silver bands around her arms, and gold bands around her forehead and waist. 'You are a vision,' he explained, sounding far-away. He motioned for her to approach.

'I'm sorry it took me so long to get here. I've left us a little short on time.'

'You overheard her, didn't you?' He sensed the awkwardness in Tory's manner.

Tory dropped the carefree front, she wouldn't insult his intelligence by playing games. 'I didn't realise it was a crime to get along with people. I have made female friends here, too.'

Turan laughed as he reached out to take hold of her hands. 'I do realise that. The trouble with my mother is her mind is too idle. She has to create these little dramas every once in a while to keep her life interesting. I'm sorry if she hurt you.' He hugged her tightly, 'She's just a bit over-protective at times.'

Tory gave half a laugh at this, as her mother, Helen had been no different. 'Tell me . . .' Tory cradled his head against her chest, stroking his long, dark hair. 'Do you perceive anything unusual hanging around in Nin Melcah's energy field?'

Turan was bothered by her query and pulled back. 'She has a few shady patches here and there . . . but everyone gets a bit that way at festival time. It's nothing that a few days in the Shu-im-ti won't fix.'

All the same, Tory was starting to feel uneasy about leaving Chailidocean; there was trouble brewing.

'I will personally see to it that my mother is cleansed within the next couple of days.' Turan noted how doubtful Tory still appeared. 'It's nothing to worry about, I assure you.'

She knew she would be meeting with the Shar every night and he would let her know if anything out of the ordinary took place. It seemed more important that she got to the bottom of how and why Zutar had sought her out.

The bells of the city tolled and the Dance to the Rising Sun commenced. Turan and Tory were out of time; the royal party's departure was imminent.

'Come on then.' The Shar was reluctant. 'I'll walk you down.'

As they made their way to muster on the forth island ring, Turan filled Tory in on what was happening on the cure front.

Darius had said that her husband's tests showed an excess of yellow bile pigment in his blood, hence the appearance of the yellow staining in his skin and the whites of his eyes. This meant that the virus was probably attacking his liver cells, leaving them unable to cope with the normal amounts of pigment from red cell destruction.

Tory raised her eyebrows, none the wiser. 'How does one treat that?'

'Well normally one couldn't, not without having the patient here, yet Darius believes he may have another solution. He hopes to have more of an idea in a couple of days.'

'I see.' Tory struggled to stay positive. 'Do thank him for me, won't you? I know he's been working very hard.'

'It looks very promising, that's what he said.' Turan stopped Tory and turned her to face him. 'So don't be distracted by negative thoughts. Stay focused on the desired outcome of your actions . . . your wellbeing is more the concern at present.'

'How nice of you to join us.' Jerram called out to them through the golden bars of the gate ahead. 'Would you please . . . before somebody changes their mind.'

As Jerram didn't wait for a response, Tory looked back to Turan. He appeared to have a bad taste in his mouth, as he watched his brother disappear into the commotion up ahead.

'What is it with you two?' She had to know.

'You'd better go. I'll see you tonight.' Turan made a move back towards the citadel.

'Oi!'

The Shar turned to find Tory appearing rather surprised at him. The morning breeze played with the golden wisps of hair around her face and as the sun was rising in the sky behind her, her auric field sparkled with a greater lustre than ever before.

I love you. She projected with all her might.

Turan found himself unable to maintain his bad mood. 'It shows.'

'Good.' She nodded assuredly, wanting so much to embrace him. But as the Shar was quite obviously not the exhibitionist her husband had been, she watched him depart without incident.

'Nin Lamamu!' It was Adelgar who hounded her this time. 'Will you please get your politic presence out here.'

As was usual for this time of year, there was not a cloud to be seen in the clear blue expanse of sky above. Even at this early hour, the harbour port of Chailidocean was alive with the hustle and bustle of trade.

Hundreds of seagoing craft, entering and exiting through the canal that lead to the sea, crowded the great waterway. Native men loaded and unloaded merchandise from vessels already docked, and market stalls lined the streets to barter the wares fresh in from abroad with those grown, mined and made locally.

The large animals strapped to carts, that were used for heavy lugging and transportation, were a vast contrast to the streamlined and near silent hovercraft that congested the streets.

Tory wandered past the street vendors, not realising that females of the city did most of the bargaining here. There were short red-skinned men and women jabbering at her in one dialect, and extremely tall, lean men of a deep brown complexion raving to her in another.

'Amelu du!' Adelgar's voice dispersed the crowd, but not without much complaining from the locals.

'Shar lil,' he warned those who were resisting, and they fled from him.

The Shar chuckled at this, and turned to Tory. 'What is that?' He referred to the sword and scabbard strapped to the gold band around her waist.

'Why, it's a sword.' Tory explained, and drew the mighty steel weapon to display it.

In the blink of an eye, tens of the native soldiers had surrounded them.

Oh shit. Tory froze.

'Shar lil du, munuz din gaz.' Adelgar set them at ease, shaking his head; her naivety did amuse him at times. 'That's not a sword.'

Adelgar reached for a hand-sized cylindrical object of metallic colour that was clipped to his belt and pressed a button on the side. A long thin laser, ultraviolet in colour and roughly the same length of her blade, extended from it. 'This is a sword.'

The sword of Rhydderch. Tory considered as she viewed the weapon, greatly in awe of it. *This is where Myrddin acquired it.*

'Igi, du!' Jerram demanded, motioning the soldiers to return to their stations by the convoy that was preparing to leave. 'It would be good to get moving sometime today.'

'You have got to be kidding.' Tory gaped at the elephants before her, with canopied carriages strapped atop of their backs. 'I'm not expected to handle one of those things on my own!'

'Hardly,' Jerram informed with a grin. 'Mother is travelling with Adelgar, therefore you will ride with me.'

Tory looked to Adelgar, who shrugged. 'This way, I'm bound to behave myself.'

She forced a laugh. 'That's very comforting.'

After a few last words of wisdom from their father, Jerram stepped onto the trunk of his elephant and it elevated him up onto its shoulders.

'Do take care.' Taliesin approached to assist Tory up, for she was looking rather wary of going anywhere near the huge creature.

'You know what a cautious person I am.' She obliged him with a bleak smile, as she got a foothold on the animal and it raised her up to Jerram's reach. 'Piece of cake,' she assured, climbing into the shaded basket behind her travelling companion.

Jerram had charge of the expedition, and so remained seated on the elephant's shoulders outside the sheltered enclosure. 'Igi e-ri Portea, du.' At his word the caravan started to move.

'Whoa!' Caught off-guard, Tory was flung back into the scatter cushions on the perfectly level floor of the transport. 'Good grief.' She got herself more comfortable, and watched out of the drawn flaps on both sides of her as they slowly made their way towards the lands north-west of the city.

Tory thought the terrain and weather conditions of the continent they crossed were very reminiscent of Australia, the land of her birth.

This central region, Cintrala, was comparable to northern New South Wales, in that the landscape was more mountainous towards the coast and flattened out as you moved further inland. The vegetation was lush — rolling green hills separated huge expanses of forest, that gave way to rainforest as you neared the more tropical conditions in the north. In the hot season, temperatures normally peeked at over thirty degrees in Cintrala. Though north-west in Portea it was not uncommon for the temperature to hit the forty degree mark.

At the coolest time of year temperatures would drop to a pleasant twenty degrees in Portea, ten degrees in Cintrala, but south in Usiqua, minus five degrees was the average low in the highlands. Taliesin had previously suggested that Tory may know these ice capped mountain ranges better as the Azores. If this was true, at sometime in years to come, the Earth would indeed tilt severely on its axis. For back in the twentieth century these islands were located in the northern hemisphere, off the coast of Portugal, yet the continent they were on was definitely located south of the equator.

They passed over a wide stretch of rolling green fields, which had only small pockets of forest to negotiate around. As this was a very leisurely leg of their journey, Jerram left his post to join Tory in the carriage.

'This is not so bad now, is it?' The Shar reclined alongside her, at which time she immediately sat upright.

'No. It's quite pleasant really.' Tory tried not to sound as uneasy as she felt. 'Once you get accustomed to the swaying motion.' She cautiously assumed a cross-legged position, facing Jerram.

He grinned at her discomfort, reaching out to retrieve a piece of fruit from a pouch that was strapped to one of the wooden supports of the canopy. 'So, what shall we do with the day?'

'Let's talk.' She let him know she was intent on doing so, though Jerram didn't seem overly thrilled by the suggestion.

He gathered his long dark hair and tossed it backwards, taking a huge bite out of the apple in his hand. 'About what?'

'Um?' Tory rolled her eyes around and gave a shrug, as if picking a topic at random. 'Why don't you tell me about you and Turan?' She raised her eyebrows, eager to hear.

Jerram sat upright, disgruntled by the subject. 'I'd rather not. We just don't like each other . . . end of story.'

'But you're so much alike.' She ventured an opinion that Jerram quite obviously didn't agree with. His eyes, as dark as a raven's, bore into her own. But as the animal beneath them suddenly came to a halt, Jerram refrained from commenting and moved out front to find out why they'd stopped.

Next thing Tory knew, Adelgar had climbed up to join her. 'I've got a surprise for you.' He motioned her to follow him outside.

'Adelgar!' Jerram protested, as he watched his brother help Tory down from her transport.

'This won't take long, I swear.' Adelgar quickly withdrew towards the back of the caravan, with Tory in tow.

Five elephants back in the train, they came to one that was pulling a large wooden crate. As Adelgar led Tory to the back of the container, the doors were flung wide as soldiers set a ramp in place.

'Never let it be said that I am not a man of my word.' The Shar swung her round to find the unicorn.

'We are setting it free!' Tory became high-spirited at the notion and when Adelgar nodded to confirm, she squeezed him tight before she raced up the ramp to encourage the animal to come out.

As she did, she discovered the magnificent animal knew well enough what was happening; it must have sensed her excitement. *Good luck, my friend. It allowed her to approach and stroke it. Steer clear of my brothers in future . . . and when Noah asks you to get on the ark, do it.* She kissed its muzzle.

The unicorn reared up a few paces, making a couple of grunting sounds as it seemed to nod. Then, backing up to the back wall of the large container, the beast began to charge for the door.

Tory reached out and ran her hand down the body of the animal as it passed. With an almighty bound, it leapt clear over the ramp, straight into the field beyond. Tory raced to the opening to watch its departure.

When it had reached a safe distance, the unicorn stopped to look back at them.

'He says, thank you,' Tory announced, her eyes still fixed upon it as it began to frolic about in a cheeky fashion.

'Get going, go on,' Adelgar encouraged it to flee, 'before I change my mind.'

Tory jumped out of the trailer to join the Shar on the ground. 'Aw, it was a lovely thought.' She nudged his shoulder with hers, before lightly kissing his cheek. 'Bless you.'

'Well, you still owe me that lesson, don't forget,' Adelgar grumbled, as he felt himself blush.

'Tonight, I promise . . . you deserve it.' Tory threw an arm about his shoulder, proud of him, as they watched the unicorn flee into the safety of the outlying forest.

The party travelled for the remainder of the day until just prior to sunset, when they stopped and set up camp for the night. A tent was raised to accommodate Nin Mahar, Tory, and the other women in the royal entourage. Jerram and Adelgar chose to sleep out under the stars with their troops.

After they'd eaten and all were being entertained by the native musicians, Tory took Adelgar and a portable solar lamp further down the clearing to commence his long-awaited lesson.

She began his instruction by running him through the vital points (kyusho) along the meridians of the body, explaining that when these were struck correctly it could inflict severe pain, loss of consciousness, or even death. She then ran through the different parts of the body considered as weapons, then the different strikes, explaining which were most effective to use on which kyusho and why.

'See . . . now that's the trouble with our culture!' Adelgar emphasised his woes. 'I learnt all of those vital points and which parts of the body are most resilient during my time in the Order of Kheit-Sin. But our instruction was purely from a healing perspective. No one even suggested that they might also be used to inflict pain.'

This statement shamed Tory somewhat. 'No, Adelgar, that's not the trouble with your culture. That's the beauty of it.'

'I disagree,' he put forward light-heartedly, before assuming a more serious tone. 'We are dealing with a hostile enemy now. The centuries of peace we once enjoyed are gone! We, too, must strengthen our resolve, or we shall lose this fair land.'

Tory didn't want to agree with him, though the history books did. 'War begets war, peace begets peace.' She had to smile, remembering she'd had this same conversation with Brockwell not so long ago.

'How can you say that when you have been to war? You have seen the debauched acts men are capable of. They shall destroy us . . .'

'Perhaps. But by thinking thus you're assisting them.' Tory decided to remain true to her beliefs. 'If there's one thing I've learnt here, it's the power of attitude. For heaven's sake, you're supposed to be on a peace mission . . . you don't know what might be achieved. Have a little faith in yourself.'

Adelgar felt his negativity dropping away and grinned. 'I do very much like your attitude, Lamamu . . . you do your mentors proud.'

'As do you, sir.' She gave a slight bow. 'Now. I immobilised Jerram, the first time we met, with a move known as a major hip throw. Would you like a demonstration?'

'Most certainly.' He was eager, until he found out she intended to use him as her victim. Still, Adelgar was enticed by the prospect of being so close to her. Concentrating more on her body than her words, Tory's demonstration took him off guard. Before the Shar knew what had happened, he was flat on his back with the wind knocked out of him.

'You could have warned me.' His voice was strained, due to the lack of air in his lungs.

'I asked if you were ready.' She placed her hands on her hips and shook her head; he obviously hadn't heard a word she'd just said. 'Shall I run through it again?'

Adelgar peeled his body off the ground. 'Ah, I'll give it a miss.'

The sound of laughter was heard coming from the vicinity of the forest. Tory spied the culprit as he came forth from the shadows and nearly fainted as she was awarded a clear view of him. For he had the head and torso of a splendid native man, but the body of a black stallion.

'Adelgar.' Tory whispered, as she backed up nice and easy.

'Oh no,' Adelgar gasped, making fun of her alarm. 'It's . . . it's, Thais.' The Shar broke into a huge smile and approached his friend to greet him.

Tory had always presumed that centaurs were mythological creatures, rather than a species that actually existed. But then, she'd seen a dragon, a griffin and a unicorn in her time, so why not a centaur?

'And who might this stunning piece of anatomy be.' Thais voiced Tory's very thought as he circled around her once, admiring her form.

Adelgar came to stand beside her to do the introductions. 'This is my sister, Lamamu.'

'Unlucky!' Thais teased.

Adelgar responded with a glare, then informed his bedazzled sister: 'This is Thais, the best scout on the island . . . the smartest, too.'

'At your service.' He bowed in a very gallant fashion, which delighted Tory.

She was quietly admiring the creature's dexterity, wondering how on earth he managed to control all four of his legs with such apparent ease.

'Well, you must have impressed her. She's never been this quiet.' Adelgar's words jogged Tory out of her daze.

'I'm so sorry.' She realised how rude she must seem. 'I am delighted to meet you, Thais.'

'The pleasure is all mine,' he insisted.

Although her first sight of Thais had been a shock, ten minutes in his presence and he felt like a dear old friend. To say he was smart was an understatement; he was downright wise. It was little wonder really, for he'd been around longer than he could recall. By Tory's understanding of the ageing process, however, the centaur looked to be in his prime — say, early thirties. That's when Adelgar pointed out that Thais and Tory had something in common; they were both immortal.

This information led Tory to wonder why centaurs were virtually unknown in the years beyond the birth of Christ. She did not voice an inquiry, but was obliged with an answer just the same.

'We were there, though my kind did not much like that period of evolution. Luckily it was short-lived.' He smiled at the bemused expression on the querist's face; so many questions whirled inside her head that she couldn't decide which one to ask first. 'Surely, as an immortal, you realise that we can assume any form we please. As a scout and a protector of wildlife, the form I was born with suits me best here. Around the time of your origin, however, to appear thus would have seen us hunted. We assumed a human form to set up sanctuaries and take action against the senseless slaughter of the animal kingdom.'

'So you've obviously time-travelled?' Tory put forward.

Thais gave a laugh at the notion. 'No offence, but you're really not very well informed, are you?'

Tory endeavoured not to be offended, as Adelgar broke into laughter. 'How do you mean?'

'Well,' Thais inquired coyly, 'if you don't mind me saying so, it seems that, although your physical body is attuned to a higher state of consciousness, your mental bodies are not. I don't understand how that could be, for I have always been led to believe that one went hand in hand with the other.'

Tory found his observation very interesting and as Thais obviously knew much that she did not, she decided to confess. She told of the events leading up to what should have been her death, and of the immortality potion Taliesin had given her. The fact that she hadn't had to reach a higher plane of consciousness to achieve her everlasting state probably explained why she lacked the spiritual awareness usually possessed by those who had taken the proper evolutionary channels to obtain immortality. 'So, in other words,' she concluded, 'I am a cosmic accident. I have not the slightest idea of my true purpose . . . or, indeed, if I have one at all.'

Again Thais was amused. 'I know your purpose. But first, let me assure you that every tiny particle in every universe exists for a reason, and in creation there are no accidents. If you have obtained an immortal state, it's because you are worthy and it was meant.'

'Really?' Tory found his view comforting.

He nodded. 'As for your purpose, dear Lamamu . . .' He was rather surprised she hadn't guessed. 'You are a protector of mankind . . . a creator of peace and destroyer of those who resist it. For you breathe fire and courage into the hearts of men and encourage warriors to gentleness. You are the perfect affirmation that there is no limit to what a human being can do with intellect and willpower.'

Tears had welled in Tory's eyes, she was so overwhelmed by his words. 'How can you say that? We've only just met.'

'I perceive information from a level of awareness beyond the time, space and causational elements of this third-dimensional reality,' Thais modestly enlightened her. 'You have only skimmed the surface of the knowledge available to you in the fourth dimension and beyond. In time, you too will learn to fully utilise the planes above the one on which you exist.'

'How about that?' Adelgar slapped her on the shoulder, naively pleased for her. He gazed up at the night sky. 'It's getting late.'

'Oh, my stars! What time is it?' Tory was thrown into panic.

Adelgar shrugged. 'Close to midnight, I guess?'

'I have to go.' She turned to Thais. 'I wish we could talk more. Are you staying with us long?'

He shook his head. 'We'll meet again. Our cosmic paths run parallel.' Thais extended his two arms out in front of him to illustrate. Tory took hold of both his hands.

'Well, I look forward to that time,' she pronounced. 'It has been both an honour and an education. Any last words of advice before I face Zutar?'

Thais grinned. 'I cannot advise you on your quest. The outcome will depend on how the preceding situations are handled. But the trials ahead may not be quite as they seem, so it will be best not to be too judgemental. That which you find hurtful, may be a gift of love. That which might seem generous, may be given out of greed. View each instance through the eyes of those concerned, and the truth will make itself known.'

'Thank you, Thais. I shall remember that.' Tory withdrew a short distance.

'Hold on, where do you think you're going?' Adelgar protested, as she began to fade from view.

'I'll see you on the morrow.' She disappeared completely.

'Lamamu, wait!' The Shar thumped his foot down hard, throwing his arms into the air. 'That's just great. How am I going to explain this to Jerram?'

20

WORTH KILLING FOR

Turan's room in the Dur-na-ga Temple took form and materialised around her. Tory had been looking forward to their secret rendezvous all day; time alone when no one would disturb them.

'You're late.'

She turned to find Turan behind her, though he did not appear as annoyed as his voice implied. 'I still know nothing of astronomy, so I'm hopeless at telling the time here.'

Turan burst into a huge smile. 'You'll never believe what happened today.'

'You got Nin Melcah to the Shi-im-ti.'

Turan frowned. 'Well, no, I got distracted.'

'Darius found the cure!'

'No, no, that's not it.' Turan calmed her. 'But this is almost as good.'

'What then? Tell me?' The suspense was killing her.

Turan's excitement returned, but just as he was about to let the cat out of the bag he refrained. 'Come with me.'

When they entered the Shar's work station, Tory had a better idea of what had Turan so excited.

'You got it working.' Tory knew she was right. 'You solved the power problem, didn't you?'

He raised his eyebrows, and a cheeky smile of confidence beamed on his face. 'I believe so. But I can't take all of the credit, it was Shu Micah who was the catalyst for the breakthrough. This morning, after you left, he brought me a crystal . . .'

'Of course!' Tory couldn't believe they hadn't considered this before now. 'The like of the ones in the control panel on Mount Dur-an-ki . . . the crystals from the fourth dimension with the chaotic symmetry.'

'Exactly.' Turan took a seat behind his computer. 'I've already installed the stone. However . . . as you know, to do away with the need for fourth

222

dimensional interaction to accomplish time travel, we have synthesised their particle manipulation process, at least in part, with man-made circuitry. We are also dealing with a previously unknown power source that is expected to produce indeterminable amounts of electromagnetic energy . . .'

'What you are trying to say is, you haven't tested it yet and you need a guinea pig.'

'No, I don't think so.' Turan, unsure of what a guinea pig was, guessed she spoke of some sort of critter. 'Animal testing is forbidden, you know that. What I really need, is some generous immortal to test it for me.'

Tory was amused by the misunderstanding, although adjusting the particle manipulation function on a time-machine was not really how she'd envisaged they'd spend this time alone together. Still, it obviously meant a lot to Turan, so she volunteered. 'Where shall we start?' She climbed on board the silver transport, placing her hands upon the psychokinetic control panel.

The following hours passed quickly and as the first few tests took Tory minutes or hours into the future, time for her literally disappeared.

'It didn't work.' Tory climbed out of the chariot, most dissatisfied, after the first attempt at a time span longer than a few minutes.

'What do you mean?' Turan grabbed hold of Tory to squeeze her tight, hysterically happy. 'You were gone so long, I started to worry.' He laughed at his folly now. 'How do you feel? Are you alright?'

'I didn't feel a thing!' She was stunned. 'Truly, I didn't think I'd left.' She tightened her embrace on him. 'Congratulations, the ride is as smooth as silk.'

They stayed as they were, wrapped round each other, until they were calmer.

'You know, this wasn't what I had planned for tonight,' Turan admitted.

Tory cocked an eye, looking up into his. 'So what was the alternative?'

His grin broadened. 'Well, if I could persuade you to accompany me back to my quarters, I shall be more than happy to demonstrate.'

She raised her eyebrows, most agreeable to the proposition, though she was a tad surprised. 'Before we even test the time reversal function?'

'Could we?' He was inspired by her suggestion, not realising it was in jest. Turan left her to resume his seat behind the monitor. 'You're right, it won't take long.'

Me and my big mouth. Tory wanted to hit herself.

'Who could we send you to see to confirm the test for us?' Turan pondered. 'It should be someone who shall be in no way interested in what we're doing, but reliable all the same.'

'What about Xavier?' Tory mused. 'He seems to be able to keep a secret.'

'Perfect. Xavier it is.'

They nominated the previous night as her desired destination, and with that suggestion implanted firmly in her brain Tory concentrated on Xavier.

The room was rather dark until Tory's eyes adjusted to the light, at which time she moved to identify the sleeping figure in the bed.

'Xavier.' She sat beside him, giving him a gentle nudge. 'Wake up.'

'Lamamu?' He whispered in surprise, as he raised himself onto his elbows. 'I thought you'd left . . . I've been looking for you.'

'Yes, you were, weren't you. Turan did mention that.' Tory smiled meekly. 'I can't really help you, I'm afraid. I haven't seen hide nor hair of the girl you seek.'

'But, in your son's life, there was someone special?'

Tory smiled. 'I believe so.'

Xavier was most relieved to hear this. 'What was she like, was she beautiful, intelligent?'

'You'll have to judge for yourself.' Tory was hesitant to put any preconceived ideas into his head.

'But you would let me know if you saw her here in Atlantis, wouldn't you?' He rubbed one eye with his hand and gave a yawn, still half asleep.

'If you want me to, yes. But now I need to ask a favour of you.'

'Name it.' His eyes wavered closed. She took Xavier's head between her hands in the hope that her instruction would sink in. 'Before dawn tomorrow, I want you to meet me in Turan's lab in the Dur-na-ga . . . have you got that?'

'Meet you in Turan's lab, tomorrow before dawn,' he mumbled in response.

Not completely confident that he would remember, Tory added a little incentive. 'If you do this for me, Xavier, I promise you I'll find your lady love.'

His eyes parted wide, as consciousness got a grip. 'Dur-na-ga, tomorrow, before dawn . . . count on it.'

'I am.' She rose and disappeared into the shadows. 'Sweet dreams.'

Upon returning the chariot to the lab, Tory found Turan hunched over his desk fast asleep.

The poor Shar hadn't closed his eyes in days, and was exhausted. As he wasn't used to such physical fatigue she decided to leave him to rest; they would see each other tonight.

Xavier arrived to keep his appointment, thereby confirming the test had been successful. 'I thought I must have been dreaming.' He was rather confused to find Tory present, knowing she'd left Chailidocean the previous morning.

As dawn rapidly approached, Tory had no time for explanations. She thanked Xavier for his participation, explaining he was free to go.

This puzzled him, for surely in return for the woman of his dreams a task of some kind was expected of him. But when Tory insisted that his presence was all she'd required, and that the promise she'd made him would be kept,

Xavier left in the best of spirits, warmed by the knowledge that his mission had been accomplished.

Tory recorded a note in the computer to inform Turan of her findings when he awoke. She also left him a note of a more personal nature, in anticipation of their next meeting.

She took one last look at the chariot before departing, and a wonderful sense of reassurance accompanied the realisation that she now had the means to return to her husband, son and kin, at will.

'You have truly outdone yourself this time, my love,' she whispered, kissing Turan's forehead ever so lightly. 'Until tonight then.' She stood clear of him, focusing her thoughts on Jerram and Adelgar.

There was a young lady of sight,
Who could travel faster than light,
She set off on a quest,
Her intentions the best,
To meet with a terrible fright.
Her love — a man of grace,
Was trapped in a physical space,
His desire so great,
It sealed her fate,
And she was wiped from the human race.

Lamamu! Turan woke abruptly in a cold sweat, the riddle of his banished mentor still ringing in his brain. Another nightmare. He supported his ailing head with both his hands.

When he finally raised his sights and spied the chariot returned, he checked the computer to find Tory's notes. Naturally, he was pleased their directive had been achieved, but the message of love she'd left him caused him to grieve.

How selfish I have been. How stupid! he scolded himself. *The rightful action to take in this matter was plain. I will need help.*

The journey to Portea proved an interesting one to say the least. Shar Jerram was furious about Tory's unauthorised departure from the party the night before, and hadn't spoken to her all day.

It wasn't just that she'd defied Jerram's command that had him so riled. The incident had bruised his ego in more ways than one. Only yesterday afternoon Tory had avoided Jerram's ardent advances, stating she was still bound to her husband and the wedding vow she'd made him. The Shar respected her feelings; thus he'd politely ceased his pursuit of her favours.

Unfortunately, Jerram had a nose like a bloodhound; upon her reappearance at camp this morning he could smell Turan's scent all over her. Jerram was enraged beyond reason and refused to accept Tory's claim that she'd been working on a project with Turan all night; in the heat of the moment he'd called her a liar and a cheat. Although Tory was aware Jerram knew nothing of the connection between Turan and Maelgwn, she was offended all the same. Thus, she told Jerram that he could think what he liked, but as he had no need of her between the hours of midnight and dawn, and she had projects elsewhere that did, she would continue to make use of this time as she saw fit and challenged the Shar to stop her.

How very diplomatic. Tory regretted that she'd succumbed to her anger, but she did hate being chastised for something she hadn't done. Admittedly, if she'd had her way, Turan would have been her lover by now. I should've just told Jerram the truth, and I would have, if he hadn't been so quick to condemn me.

'Lamamu, come see.' Adelgar entered the sheltered transport in which she lay. 'We are approaching my city, Keriophis.'

'That's good news.' She gave a bleak smile, trying to sound enthusiastic.

The excitement he felt was dampened by her mood. 'You're not still brooding over that argument with Jerram, are you?' He sat himself down, concerned for her. 'I'm sure my brother has long forgotten it by now . . . he never holds a grudge for very long.'

'You believe me, don't you?' Tory righted herself to a seated position.

'Well . . .' He shrugged, not sure.

'Smell.' Tory held the palms of her hands under his nose.

'Xavier?' He frowned, not understanding.

'That's right,' Tory confirmed. 'So if I was making love to Turan all night, how did I get Xavier's scent on my hands?'

'I don't know. How?'

'Because we were working on a project, just like I said!' She was losing patience again.

'I believe you.' Adelgar held both his hands out before him in supplication. 'It's Jerram you should be confronting with this, not I.'

'I'm sorry, Adelgar.' She rubbed his shoulder fondly. 'I'm just mad because I handled the situation so badly.' She sank away from him, disappointed in herself.

'Hey . . .' He moved closer. 'I'm sure Jerram feels exactly the same way. When we reach the city, go and speak with him. I'm sure you'll find he's most apologetic.'

Perhaps he was right, and this could be resolved amicably without further dispute. For if their quest was as dangerous as they imagined, they couldn't afford to be divided over such petty matters — her own experience had taught her that.

Although Portea was nowhere near as grand as Chailidocean to look at, it had a profound natural beauty about it, as it had been built in the midst of a great rainforest. Now Tory understood Adelgar's eagerness for her to see it.

Only the local temples of the city and the royal house were built out of marble. These striking examples of Atlantean architecture sat upon large, round mounds to prevent them from being flooded in the rainy season. But the majority of the abodes in Portea, still of a round structure, were built high upon stilts and were made from the more abundant materials to be found in the rainforest. Hence the village was in perfect harmony with its lush surroundings — a little cultural oasis, deep in the forest.

The local people, male and female alike, wore little more than elongated loincloths due to the extreme heat, and were as warm as the weather in temperament. Tory's blonde hair, violet eyes and fair complexion was somewhat of a rarity to the red-skinned natives, who weren't shy when it came to satisfying their curiosity. They gathered around to touch Tory's skin, or take up a piece of her hair, as if making sure that she was real. Akin to the native Indians of the Americas, these were a good-looking, gentle people, whose attentions she found in no way threatening.

With a small child rested upon each hip, Tory was accompanied to the palace stairs by half the village. It delighted Adelgar to see her thus, and he chanced a glance in Jerram's direction to note that even his brother's frown had momentarily lifted.

It was their mother, Nin Mahar, who eventually assisted Tory to bid farewell to her admirers, before leading her away to a room inside the palace where Tory could bathe and change in the wake of her two days of travel.

A cool, freshwater stream channelled into a huge pool inside the palace brought welcome relief from the heat for Tory, Nin Mahar and the ladies in her service.

The native women awaiting their emergence from the water chatted and giggled amongst themselves as they observed Tory's unusual appearance. This didn't bother her as she was well used to being the odd one out.

As Nin Mahar had been travelling with Jerram all day, Tory swam over to do a little snooping. 'Jerram's still mad with me, isn't he?'

The petite woman's large brown eyes filled with empathy as she smiled. 'Turan is the thorn in his side, child, not you.'

'But why?' Tory waited breathlessly for an answer.

Nin Mahar looked saddened a moment, though the smile never left her face. 'Some at the palace never really approved of my union with Absalom, despite all the good that came of it. They wanted to keep the Shu Sar's gene pool pure.'

'Turan is one of those?' Tory couldn't believe it; Maelgwn had never been a racist.

'It's not his fault. He was influenced by his mother and Absalom's other wives. All except Kila that is, she's always been very sweet to us. I have to confess, I could hardly wait for my boys to come of age, so I could escape from Chailidocean . . . I do believe Jerram felt the same.' Nin Mahar mounted the stairs to leave the pool, her long, dark hair near touching the floor. 'The animosity never bothered Adelgar. Most of it was beyond his understanding, and he's so rough and tumble he'd bounce back from anything.' She smiled as two native women draped a large piece of cloth about her shoulders. 'But Jerram took to heart every little sideways glance, every taunting comment.'

'I get the picture.' Tory knew what Jerram must be thinking; that she favoured Turan because of his colour, but nothing could be further from the truth.

One of the women in attendance approached Nin Mahar coyly, motioning to Tory as she uttered a few words.

'What did she say?' Tory stepped out of the pool, wringing all the water from her hair.

'She wants to know if you would like her to braid your hair.'

Many of the men and women wore their hair in tiny braids, weighted at the end with ornate silver beads, as their long masses of hair were easier to maintain this way.

The offer was very tempting indeed. Tory's hair, when loose, was like a blanket, and in midday heat it had just about driven her nuts. 'How long would it take?' She had to meet Turan at midnight, and if what Nin Mahar said of him was true, it would be interesting to see how he'd react to her new hairstyle.

The native girl assured her that, with a few of the other women helping her, it would be done before the moon was high, thus, Tory agreed.

Nin Mahar instructed that food from the banquet be brought up to her. Tory's absence from the feast tonight would give Jerram a little more time to cool off.

As it turned out, Jerram didn't front up at the dinner either, on the premise that he had much to organise before their departure at dawn.

Adelgar, disappointed that neither his brother nor his sister had shown, caused one hell of an uproar when he invaded the ladies chambers to speak with Tory. As he was the ruler of Portea he could get away with this, and the female elders granted him permission to stay.

Fortunately, Tory was dressed. Her attire, in much the same style and colour as what she'd worn before, was of a lighter fabric. Fine tassels fell from the sleeves at the shoulder, and more of the same trimmed the hood and around the bottom of the shirt.

Tory explained to Adelgar that she hadn't wanted to ruin his banquet by creating another scene, upon which he settled down beside her and was quite pleasant company. She inquired after what tomorrow had in store and Adelgar advised that, with any luck, they'd make it to the Annunnaki Islands that stood between Antillia and Portea. On the west coast boats were waiting to take them across the A-zu Strait, a short ride from Keriophis. The inhabitants of the Annunnaki Islands were a mixture of the native races of both the bordering continents. Adelgar warned that their appearance was more warlike than his people, for they were accustomed to Antillian attacks. But the Shar assured Tory that there was no need for her to fear, as the Annunnaki people were allied to Atlantis.

Tory manifested in Turan's quarters at the appointed time. 'I like what you've done with your hair,' Taliesin said.

Tory swung round, surprised to find him there. 'Thank you . . . Where is Turan?'

'Now, don't be alarmed,' Taliesin advised. 'He asked that I meet you in his stead.'

'Why, what has happened?' She rushed to the Merlin's side.

Taliesin took a deep breath. What he had to impart wasn't going to be easy. 'Another nightmare,' he simply explained.

'Is he alright?!'

'Yes, he's fine.' Taliesin took hold of her hands and led her to a seat.

'So, where is he then?'

'My dear Nin. If you would be so kind as to allow me, I shall tell you.' He was not thrilled by the task the Shar had assigned him. 'In Turan's dream last night, Keeldar indicated that you might be in danger.'

'But surely Turan knows that is quite impossible. It could have been his subconscious playing tricks on him.'

'That is exactly what I said. But the Shar has decided to return to his etheric form, all the same.'

'What?' Tory felt her heart split in two. 'Surely not.' She reflected on the last time she'd seen Turan, then stood frustrated. 'Where is he, Taliesin? Let me talk to him.'

Taliesin closed his eyes a moment; he'd anticipated this reaction. 'The Shar left strict instructions that no one was to disturb him . . . not even you,' he added firmly. 'For the truth is, nothing you could say would make the slightest difference now.'

'Why do you say that?' The tears began to well in her eyes, and she sank back into her seat.

Taliesin took up her hands once more, wanting to soothe her hurt. 'The attraction Shar Turan felt for you was proving too strong to permit him to transcend back to his higher state of awareness.'

'Yes. And . . .?'

'Under hypnosis this morning, the Shar had all intimate memory of you erased. He asked only to be able to recall that, as his novice, he is bound to do all within his capabilities to protect you.'

This news came as a real shock. 'So we just go back to the way we were before the time loop?' She brushed away her tears, suppressing her hurt and disappointment. 'Who is this Keeldar, Taliesin? What did he do to warrant banishment?'

The Merlin stood, not at all disposed toward enlightening her. But he continued nevertheless. 'For the sake of science, Keeldar disobeyed a direct order from the Shu Sar . . . therefore he was exiled for sedition.' He moved to pour himself a glass of water.

'Yes, but what did he do?'

'Why, he was the greatest authority in the field of identifying, manipulating, and transporting matter using sonic frequency and psychokinesis.' Taliesin eluded the issue, taking a sip from the goblet.

'Tell me something I don't know.' Tory became annoyed; Taliesin was seeming more and more like his old self all the time. 'If this man has nominated himself as my adversary, it would be nice to know a little bit more about him.'

'It is not you he seeks vengeance on, it's Turan.' Taliesin spoke bluntly. 'And in my personal opinion, if Keeldar did make such a threat, he is bluffing. He's just trying to sabotage, firstly, these peace talks with Antillia, and secondly, any chance Turan might have for happiness. Thus Keeldar gets his revenge on both Chailidocean and the trusted pupil who, in his mind, betrayed him.'

'Betrayed him how? What the hell happened?' If she had to ask again she would explode.

The Merlin's brow became drawn as he considered whether or not he should divulge such information. For unlike most here, Tory would fully understand the dangerous implications of Keeldar's act of treason. 'Think back to the twentieth century,' he began. 'Do you recall a place known as the Bermuda Triangle?'

The question brought a perplexed look to her face, as she failed to see what bearing this could have on her query. 'Yes, I do. Like the Dragon's Triangle, it was a site renowned for unexplained disappearances, electromagnetic anomalies, mysterious weather conditions, even UFO sightings. The Bermuda Triangle was located in the Atlantic Ocean, between Bermuda, Miami, San Juan and a small part of the Gulf of Mexico.'

'Indeed. And for at least a thousand years prior to the twenty-first century, many a vessel went missing in that area. Some of these were destroyed by the strange electromagnetic phenomena in the region and sank to the bottom of the ocean, but others passed through the thin veil in the time–space continuum to be dumped randomly at differing points in earth's history, both past and future.'

'Are you trying to tell me some of these vessels were deposited here?' Tory's eyes were wide with fascination.

'In the waters far west of here, yes, as this is where the Bermuda Triangle is located.'

Though the Merlin's tone was light, the implication in what he said was like a sharp slap across the face. 'Oh, my god. Keeldar found himself some relic of the nuclear variety, didn't he?'

'As interesting as the discovery was, I was obliged to advise the Shu Sar against allowing any such antiquities to be brought onto the continent for examination. Ergo, Absalom denied Keeldar permission to do so.'

'But Keeldar disobeyed.'

'He brought a fully functional nuclear warhead into our capital city!' Taliesin was annoyed by the stupidity of the act. 'But Turan found out about it, thank goodness, and the council took the aforementioned action against Keeldar and his research.'

'So where is the warhead now?' The prospect of its existence made her edgy. 'Dismantled, and hidden in a safe place,' he reassured before changing the subject. 'But all is not completely grim in wonderland. I do have some good news for you.'

'Be out with it, then.' She gave a sigh. 'I could sure use some.'

'Darius is waiting to speak with you in his lab,' he announced, watching Tory's face light up in anticipation.

'He has found the cure?'

'So he says.' The Merlin grinned, pleased to have raised her spirits. 'Shall we go see him?'

'Is there really any need to ask?'

En Darius was impatiently awaiting their arrival in his laboratory in the Shi-im-ti, and strangely enough he appeared rather stressed.

'Come in, come in,' he bade them, as if their meeting was a matter of some urgency, and checked the corridor outside. 'Does anyone else know you're here?'

Taliesin had never seen the scientist behave so. 'No. Is something bothering you, Darius? You don't appear at all well.'

'I am not surprised.' He motioned them to take a seat.

'Is it true, you've found a cure?' Tory complied with his wish, seating herself.

Darius looked a little put out by the question. 'Well, yes and no.' He plastered his hair back off his sweaty brow. 'You see . . . as Turan probably explained, your husband's illness could have been caused by one of three different defects: either malfunctioning liver cells, red blood cell destruction or a blockage in his bile duct. Each one of these ailments has a different treatment, therefore I cannot safely diagnose or treat him without having him physically present.'

'So what's the big breakthrough?' Tory couldn't imagine.

Darius raised his eyebrows, releasing a heavy sigh. 'Well, my dear Lamamu, the answer to our dilemma lies with you.'

Tory's eyes opened wide. 'Me! How?'

Darius checked the corridor outside to ensure they were alone, and even when convinced they were, he still spoke in a whisper. 'Remember the tests I ran on you the first day you arrived?'

Tory nodded.

'Well . . . upon re-examination they proved rather interesting.' He smiled, rather smitten by his own brilliance. 'I know how you became immortal.'

'Come again?' Tory was sceptical; how could he possibly know that?

'It was an elixir of sorts, was it not?' Darius decided the amazed expression on her face was enough of an answer. 'There are traces of it still in your blood,' he explained. 'This formula caused a mutation of your genetic code at a molecular level, thus causing the atoms in your body to resonate at a higher vibrational frequency than is possible in this physical plane.'

En Razu seemed to be following, though Tory looked a little hazy.

'The ability of mundane material to return to its original shape after being deformed is possible, because molecules have a memory.'

'DNA,' Taliesin added for Tory's information.

'Minor injuries to the human body heal without a trace, thanks to our molecular memory . . . but in your case, this process is speeded up. Not to mention the virtual impossibility of any virus being able to penetrate your immune system.'

'Well, that's very comforting, but how is this going to help Maelgwn?'

No sooner had Tory asked the question, than both Taliesin and herself grasped the answer.

'No!' Taliesin stressed, happy and horrified all at once. 'You haven't.'

'I have,' Darius confessed, fearing their wrath. 'I isolated and synthesised the chemical formula that mutated the strand . . . and here it is.' He handed Tory a small bottle and smiled. 'That is the only sample I shall make and once you have safely departed with it, I intend to destroy all my notes and tests pertaining to this affair . . . I do not have the desire, nor the nerve, to play god in this fashion.'

'This shall make Maelgwn an immortal like myself.' Tory's voice faltered in reverence at the miracle she held in her hand. 'How does one express thanks for a gift such as this?' She was nearly moved to tears.

'There is just one thing I would like to know.' Darius sought permission to pry in return for his labour. 'Where did you obtain this work of biological genius?'

Still overcome by what had been achieved, the question startled Tory. Her sights darted from the bottle in her hand to Taliesin, and although she desperately wanted to retract the glance, it was too late. The Merlin knew. '*Shit*,' Tory scolded herself.

'That's why you wouldn't tell us when we asked you before.' Taliesin voiced what he had already suspected. 'Because I gave it to you.'

This revelation made Darius even more wary of his discovery. 'Then where did you get it?'

'Good question.' Taliesin referred it back to Tory, who shrugged.

'You never said.'

They all stared blankly at each other as they pondered the paradox, until Taliesin finally voiced what they were all thinking.

'So what came first . . . the chicken or the egg?'

Tory was concerned. 'One thing's sure. Even here in Chailidocean there must be those who would kill to be immortal.'

'I dare say you are right.' Darius' new knowledge played on his conscience like a curse. 'No offence, but the sooner I see you safely depart with that, the easier I'll rest. Until that time, I have a safe place to store it, but not a word of this must leave this room. Agreed?'

Taliesin and Tory nodded in accord. 'Agreed.'

At muster the next morning, Jerram kept himself preoccupied organising their departure, so Tory didn't disturb him; she would have opportunity enough to make her peace with him throughout the day.

In a way, Tory regretted having committed herself to this mission, now she knew that she possessed the cure for Maelgwn and the means to get it to him. Still, she did owe these people something for all their help. What was a few more days, when she had the whole of eternity to be with the man she loved?

Adelgar was well pleased to find his sister's spirits improved. Lamamu was far more receptive to tales about his kingdom, admiring the beauty of the lush terrain along their route to the A-zu Strait. In her absence the night before, there had been a huge storm in Keriophis; the landscape sparkled in the early morning sunlight and its inhabitants were lively.

By midday, however, there was not a cloud to be seen in the strip of sky above the rainforest canopy. The temperature that Tory imagined had hit the thirty degree mark raised the humidity factor to nearly unbearable proportions, and she thanked the merciful heavens for her new hairdo.

All at once, there came a great cry from the ranks of soldiers and the native men escorting the party on foot began running to the front of the caravan.

What's going on? Tory wondered as she observed the commotion to each side of her.

'Lamamu.' Adelgar called to her from his seated position between the elephant's shoulders. 'Come see.'

Tory raised herself to her knees, crawling forward to find out what all the fuss was about. Adelgar pointed to where the jungle parted up ahead to expose the bright aquamarine of the strait.

'Paradise,' Tory enthused, as Adelgar helped her down from the elephant onto the fine, white sand of the long beach. Off in the distance, she could see the little sea port where their transport was docked offshore. Most of the native soldiers had taken to the water to swim the distance remaining, some heading towards the village and the rest towards where the tall ship was anchored.

'Fancy a dip?' Adelgar scooped her up over one shoulder and made for the water with her.

With the flood of water came sweet relief from the heat exhaustion, and Tory sprang to the surface revitalised. 'Fantastic.' She spread her arms wide, tilting her head back to welcome the warm rays of sunshine against her skin.

After his swim, Jerram stood on the water's edge observing her. How lovely she was, so much more akin to his tribe than Turan's; Lamamu belonged in the wild. It was amusing to watch his brother attempt to flip Tory off-balance; he wasn't having much success. It was clear that Adelgar no longer lusted after the daughter of Danuih. Nin Tabitha, Lamamu's match for him, had won his brother's heart swiftly and completely. 'Keep moving.' Jerram motioned the pair towards their destination, heading off in that direction himself.

The inhabitants of the seaside village, a mixed bag of races, hailed the two youngest sons of the Shu Sar. To these people, Jerram and Adelgar were gods — the last bastion between their life of freedom, and a life of servitude and victimisation. The two young Shars didn't seem at all affected by all the adoration. They carried out the duties of their birthright not for the glory it brought them, but to ensure the continued prosperity of their race and those who were their allies.

Tory followed her brothers through the commotion on the waterfront to where the royal party's supplies were being unloaded onto boats and taken to the mother ship.

She was enjoying this leg of the trip immensely; the scenery was just magnificent. The deep green of the jungle, the white sand, the aqua-blue of the water, and the azure sky above were all in brilliant contrast to each other. All the healthy, well tanned, half-naked men carousing about her added to the already intoxicating surroundings.

Once on board the tall ship, Tory found herself a position in the ship's bow, out of the crew's way, and settled herself to await their departure. Suddenly, she wasn't in such a hurry to get back to the formidable British weather. Tory had missed her sunny Australia, and she found the conditions here even more favourable.

'So, how are you finding the wilderness?' Jerram took a seat beside her as the boat took to sea, casting his sights over the crystal clear tropical waters abundant with marine life. 'Do you miss civilisation?' He looked directly at her.

Jerram cast spells with those dark hypnotic eyes of his, thought Tory. She imagined that many an unsuspecting maiden had succumbed to the siren presence that beckoned from behind the cool facade. 'Your allegiance is what I miss . . . and surely we can't afford to be divided when we face Zutar.'

'I am the last person on earth who would want that.' His tone was serious, though one half of his mouth curved to a smile. 'I was wrong to judge you. I do not see through your eyes.'

'I wish you could.' She smiled briefly before her sights were conveniently drawn away to a huge school of dolphins keeping pace with their craft. 'Good heavens, just look at all of them.' Tory sprang to her feet, enchanted.

Jerram, who'd risen behind her, turned Tory back around to look him in the eye. 'No, look at me. You're in love with Turan, aren't you?'

'No.' Her voice was resolute.

But her eyes slid from his as she pulled away, which led Jerram to suspect another lie.

She decided to come clean: 'I'm in love with a future incarnation of him. Maelgwn of Gwynedd, my husband. And yes, I probably would have fallen in love with Turan, too, had circumstances not been as they are.'

'How do you mean?' Jerram quizzed, for she and Turan had seemed to be getting along well enough the last time he'd seen them together.

'Shar Turan is resuming his subtle form. All feelings he may have held for me have been eradicated from his memory,' she was a little sad to say.

'I always knew he was mad.' Jerram thought the news was too good to be true and couldn't keep the smile from his face.

She served him a look of objection. 'I think it's more that Turan is afraid he won't be able to protect me.'

This was a curious statement, considering her everlasting state. 'Protect you. From what?'

Tory shrugged. 'Keeldar? Zutar? I don't know.'

Jerram shook his head. 'In all my travels and dealings with neighbouring lands, no one has seen or heard from Keeldar since before I was born. He was just a crazy old scientist, who is more than likely dead by now. As for Zutar,

I think Adelgar, all these guards, and myself should prove to be sufficient protection.'

'From what I understand, Keeldar was rather proficient in the mind sciences.' She questioned his logic, politely. 'This man was capable of building a whole temple by the power of thought; thus I seriously doubt he would perish in any manner of climate or circumstance.'

Jerram looked slightly perturbed, but as he was being summoned to the stern of the boat by one of his men he waved off her fears. 'No, think positive . . . he's dead.'

Though Jerram was taking a happy-go-lucky stance, Tory could tell the notion worried him. She decided she must know more about Keeldar, and as Turan was indisposed and Taliesin had told her all he was going to, Nin Bau seemed the logical answer. Tonight, after she'd met with Taliesin to confirm all was well, Tory would seek an audience with the High Priestess, for at the very least a little advice from someone so wise could never go astray.

21

THE QUIET ART
OF DECEIT

Nin Melcah silently made her way through the E-abzu Temple, which was dedicated to the study of the Mind Sciences and the goddess, Philaeia. In one of the isolation rooms contained therein, Turan was resuming his divine state. A smile graced Melcah's lips, for she was most gratified by her son's decision to emotionally detach himself from the daughter of Danuih.

The large hood of Melcah's plain, white robe was pulled well over her head, making her unidentifiable from any of the Order's elders as she headed for the laboratory that had once been her mentor's workplace. It was located at the end of a long, curved corridor that gradually spiralled downward, in a wing of the temple that had long since been locked up and abandoned by the Order. Melcah proceeded as silently as possible, checking behind her often to ensure that her passage hadn't been noted. Inaccessible as this area was to most, being the first wife of the Shu Sar did have its advantages. The door opened immediately upon scanning her hand print. She entered, securing the door behind her.

Underneath the large solid bench in this chamber lay a passage that led to another laboratory deep beneath the temple. Once inside the tunnel that only a few people knew about, Melcah felt more at ease. She dropped her hood to rest about her shoulders and activated the solar torch to see her way down the slightly curved tunnel.

Keeldar? She opened the door to the lab. I must speak with you at once. When there came no response, Melcah added: Your riddle worked like a charm on Turan, just as you said it would.

Was there ever any doubt?

Melcah spun around, bursting into a huge smile when she found Keeldar's ghostly image behind her. *No, she granted, marking how drained of energy her*

237

accomplice appeared; his image grew a little fainter each time they met. I trust the task was not too taxing, Keeldar.

I do not count the cost of your will, Nin Melcah. He bowed his head to her. *I live only to serve it.*

She was charmed by his enduring devotion to her. *And how fares the other half of our scheme?*

Everything is in place, Highness. Lamamu shall not be a concern to you much longer.

Splendid. Her eyes narrowed as she pondered their plan. *And you are quite sure that none of the seers will foresee this?*

Quite sure. He grinned. *And as long as you wear the charm I gave you next to your skin, none shall gain any insight from you.* Nin Melcah seemed relieved, so Keeldar politely inquired: *Now then, there was another matter?*

Yes. Something has come to my attention, that I would very much like you to investigate.

Of course, Majesty. He was eager to learn what had been so important as to risk an impromptu meeting.

Even though Melcah was sure they were alone, she took the extra precaution of closing the door before she disclosed her mind. *It has been suggested that En Darius may have discovered the secret to immortality, and I need you to get inside his head to find out if there is any truth in the rumour.*

Keeldar appeared a little sceptical; Darius was not the kind of man to boast about a discovery like that. *Forgive my reserve, Nin Melcah, but who told you this?*

Her smiled broadened, as she felt her source a reliable one. *Nin Anthea, his wife. It would seem her dear husband, of whom she loves to boast, talks in his sleep when something is troubling him.* Melcah was very nonchalant as she explained. *Apparently the ability to play god weighs heavy on his conscience.* She smiled confidently.

Is that so? Keeldar was inspired by the possibilities this presented.

If this elixir does exist, I shall reward you handsomely for it. Melcah was not getting any younger; she had perhaps a hundred years of life remaining and this was not enough. *Darius will have hidden such a treasure well; thus I need you to locate it for me.*

As you wish, Majesty. Keeldar bowed as he departed. *Consider it found.*

As evening fell, the main island of the Annunnaki people was in sight off the starboard bow of their craft. A mist hung like a mysterious veil over their destination; only the peaks of the lush green mountains could be seen amidst the haze, and an eerie silence came over the crew as their vessel approached.

The anchor was dropped just short of entering the fog. Jerram and Adelgar stood on the bow, their eyes scanning the misty waters ahead.

'What are we waiting for?' Tory felt obliged to whisper her inquiry and Jerram nodded to his point of focus out front. Long, ornately carved canoes began to silently emerge from the haze in a bright red glow due to torches to the rear of their vessels.

Jerram smiled, unconcerned. 'A welcoming party. To set foot on these shores unannounced is considered an act of war. See there?'

Jerram motioned to a young man who sat upon a large throne-like chair built into the stern of the closest boat. A large spear rested in his hand, its arrowhead pointed towards the sky. He was easily defined as the leader of the party by the beaded breastplate and other jewellery he wore. His long, dark hair, shaved down both sides of his head, was plaited back in a long braid that fell down his bare back. The warrior's face and torso were painted, as were all the Annunnaki in the half a dozen large canoes that converged upon their ship. The design of their bright facial make-up was not warlike; it suggested more a celebration — as did the pandemonium that arose from the greeting party upon sighting Tory's brothers on the ship's bow.

'That is Calisto, the son of the elders of this island, Chief Anu, and his concubine, Keturah. So be nice,' Jerram advised Tory, before moving to greet his consort.

Both her brothers seemed to be welcomed by the island's officials as they chatted excitedly with them in the native tongue.

'Come, Lamamu.' Jerram motioned her to approach. 'Only the three of us need go ashore. Calisto's party shall take us.'

Adelgar had already lowered himself into the main canoe, and as Tory joined him there, he introduced her to the Chief's son and others of significance.

Calisto, who was taller and darker than either of her brothers, eyed Tory over with proper reserve, but was delighted. He conveyed his mind to Adelgar, who smiled and shook his head.

'Lamamu kin gu Shu Sar, Zutar en lil.'

'What are you saying?' Tory quizzed, for Calisto looked disappointed by the Shar's response.

'Calisto offered me ten of his women for you,' Adelgar informed, sounding as if he were passing up a bargain. 'But I told him that you are the great messenger of the Shu Sar, and that Zutar insists on dealing with you.'

Calisto made additional comment, which Adelgar conveyed.

'Calisto said he can see why.'

Tory bowed her head to the Chief's son and served him with a gracious smile for the compliment, whereby he reached out with his free hand and rested it against her cheek.

'Sa shu nu,' he stated, motioning to the darkening sky above. 'Ra sag munuz.'

'Oh, brother!' Adelgar rolled his eyes, obliged to translate Calisto's words. 'I'm not going to tell her that,' but when Tory and Calisto both protested with a glare of warning, he obliged them. 'He says . . . your beauty lights up the night sky, and that you are a shining example of a woman.'

'Alright, that's enough of that.' Jerram guided Tory away from Calisto, jesting with his friend in the native language.

Whatever words passed between them, Calisto found them hilariously funny and sat back in his seat to enjoy his amusement.

After Jerram had seated Tory safely in front of him, she had to ask, 'What did you say to him that was so funny?'

'I told him you were mine, and thus he didn't stand a chance.' Jerram wrapped his arms about her shoulders, urging her to lean back against him, and considering the tale he'd spun about them she complied.

'What is so amusing about that?'

'Well,' he gave her a slight squeeze, 'either he considers me little competition, or he finds it rather unbelievable that I would claim any one woman as a permanent concubine . . . Calisto has known me a long time.'

'Oh.' She considered the latter was more like the truth, for two reasons. One, because Teo had also been such a free spirit when it came to women, and two, Jerram looked every bit a warrior to be reckoned with, despite his height.

About twenty yards from shore they penetrated the island's misty shield. In the last rays of daylight, Tory beheld a huge mountainous island of dense tropical terrain ahead. The beach was alight with torches, as more of the Annunnaki people waited to escort the representatives of the Shu Sar to Chief Anu and Keturah.

Jerram stayed very close to Tory as they disembarked, watching her like a hawk, for her colouring and vigour would make her somewhat of a prize in these parts.

The native women showered their visitors with brightly coloured leis, which they placed around their necks. The party was then accompanied up a jungle path, the sweet scent from the flowers they wore filling their senses with a heavenly aroma.

Tory glanced back towards the beach, unable to see their ship beyond the misty veil. 'How is it that the mist cover doesn't engulf the land?' she whispered to Jerram.

'The Annunnaki find it a necessary defense these days,' he shrugged, 'with all the Antillian raids.'

'You mean they manipulate it?!' Tory was stunned; how did such a seemingly primitive race manage what much more scientifically advanced civilisations had not?

Jerram nodded to confirm. 'These people keep in close contact with the earth and her elementals, and utilise that alliance to their mutual advantage.'

'Brilliant!' Tory conceded.

She had learnt to do this herself to a degree, with the Pan Ray, but she'd not conceived what could be sought from the deva kingdoms beyond this.

'But how did they know we were here, if they couldn't see us coming?'

'Keturah, Calisto's mother, sees everything.' He smiled a knowing smile. 'You shall understand well enough once you've met her.'

They followed the pathway through the rainforest, and came to a set of stone stairs which had been carved into the rock face of the mountain. Upon scaling these for some distance, they came to a large plateau.

'Holy smoke.' Tory came to a standstill, observing a huge construction dominated by a large ziggurat at the far end.

'Pretty impressive, huh?' Adelgar commented, admiring the city that illuminated the darkness with hundreds of torches ablaze throughout.

The architectural design behind the structure before them was indicative of those ruins to be found in the twentieth century at places like Teotihuacan in Mexico or Machu Picchu in Peru. A long pathway, paved in stone, led to stairs that ascended all the way up to the huge, three-tiered ziggurat at the end. Other staircases branched off the long walkway, granting access to temples, shrines, plazas, dwellings and workshops.

'It is beyond my wildest expectations,' she mumbled, in awe of the great feat of engineering, for its situation would make it virtually impenetrable to raiders.

They passed through a large, stone doorway into the huge mound, where the pathway began to slope downwards. Carved into the walls and roof were all manner of hieroglyphics, similar to those of the Egyptians.

Calisto noted her interest and spoke to her: 'Ru la ab, du en si.'

Tory looked to Adelgar for translation.

'These walls tell the story of Calisto's ancestors, from their first settlement through to now.'

'He must be very proud to have inherited such a beautiful culture.' She addressed Calisto directly. 'I am envious.'

Adelgar conveyed the message to Calisto, who laughed as he voiced his reply. Jerram lashed out at Calisto for his words, though it was only in jest.

'What?' Tory hated to be left out of the joke.

Jerram grinned as he watched Calisto resume his course. 'He said that, any time you like, he'd be more than happy to make you a part of it.'

'Sure am glad I left my woman at home,' Adelgar chuckled, as he fell in behind their guide.

Up ahead, two large doors parted wide to reveal the enormous central chamber of the structure, where a lavish feast was taking place. Long tables, no higher than your average coffee table, were set up in a square formation, leaving a huge entertainment area in the centre where native musicians and dancers were performing. Calisto led them to the prominent table, situated on a platform that rose above the other tables, at the far end of the room.

The old man seated in the centre was adorned in jewellery and paint that was even more opulent than Calisto's. Tory guessed this must be Chief Anu. The elder clapped his hands and all the entertainers ceased their activities, moving aside as the Shu Sar's party were brought forth.

Jerram and Adelgar were greeted warmly by Chief Anu as, thanks to Keturah, he was already well aware of their mission and was most thankful for their attempt to make peace with the waring Antillians. Calisto introduced Tory as daughter and messenger of the Shu Sar and Jerram's concubine. He seated Tory between her supposed lover and Keturah, as the Chief's wife was most interested in her.

Both Chief Anu and his wife appeared older than any Tory had met in this time zone thus far. Keturah, though red-skinned and dark haired like the rest of her people, had the eyes of an albino, white within white.

The merriment of the feasting resumed and Tory was enjoying the musical spectacle immensely. Yet the pearly gaze of their hostess, which had remained intent on her, was becoming a little offputting. Still, Tory smiled politely at the wise old woman's attentions, sure that she didn't mean to make her feel so uncomfortable.

When most of the food, fruit and seafood had been cleared from their table, Chief Anu motioned to the native who attended him. At his word, a large pipe was brought forth. The Chief lit this, using a long stick which he ignited from a torch close by, and after having a few puffs he passed the smoking pipe to Adelgar, who accepted it graciously. From here it was passed to Keturah, who indulged in the smoke before handing it over to Tory.

Tory forced a smile as she took possession of the pipe, looking to Jerram. 'I don't smoke.'

'You do now,' he instructed firmly. 'To refuse will not only insult our hosts, but their gods as well.'

'Oh.' She forced a smile once more, raising the pipe to the Chief and his wife before lifting it to her lips. 'In that case, cheers.' She inhaled the smoke deeply, as the others had, exhaling it out her nose. 'Good grief, that's not tobacco, that's hemp.' She suppressed the tickle in her throat that was urging her to cough.

Jerram smiled, knowing the effect it would have on her. 'They smoke this to promote communication with the great spirit.'

'That's not surprising.' Tory raised her brow. The smoke tasted strong enough to induce an out-of-body experience.

'Du, du.' The Chief smiled, urging her to have more.

It wasn't too long before the effect of the dope took hold. In her euphoric state, Tory's mind drifted from thought to thought without anxiety or care.

Keturah took hold of her hand. 'Keturah la he na, Lamamu.'

Jerram was quick to right himself from his relaxed position across the cushions beside Tory to translate. 'Keturah said she can see much confusion arising around you.'

'Bad pa.' Keturah added for Jerram's information, whereby he looked to Tory a mite concerned.

'The source of which is your father.'

'What?' Tory didn't understand. 'Does she refer to Shu Sar Absalom?'

Jerram inquired for her, and conveyed her response. 'She would suppose so.'

'Antillia ap nu nun, Engur, igi gi pa, gaz.'

The Shar near turned white with Keturah's words. 'In Antillia, there is a dark lord who watches your father and wishes him dead . . . the Antillian's call him Engur, meaning, Lord of the Rockets.'

Tory's eyes opened wide, her euphoric state quickly departing. 'Keeldar . . . so Turan was right after all.'

'We don't know that.' Jerram tried to calm her.

'Well, who else would it be?' Tory challenged him, but when he did not answer she composed herself. 'Please, thank Keturah for the warning, and ask if she knows of anything else that may aid us in our mission.' Tory paused breathless as Jerram imparted her words to the wise woman, praying to god no mention of Mahaud arose.

Keturah smiled broadly as she spoke her mind to Jerram, who seemed delighted by her words. 'That is all she sees on that subject, but she urges you not to worry, as the righteous ones shall overcome. On a more personal level, however, she said that coming into contact with your first love has disconcerted you. But Keturah advises you not to fret, for true love awaits him elsewhere,' Jerram was pleased to announce. 'I told you Turan wasn't for you.'

Tory had to smile at this. She knew it was not Turan, or Maelgwn, of whom Keturah spoke, for it was Jerram, as Teo, who had been her first love. 'Please thank Keturah for that knowledge. I shall bear it in mind.'

As the hour approached for Tory to check in with Taliesin, she urged Jerram to find out where she was supposed to be sleeping this night.

One of the native servants escorted her and Jerram to a private chamber. The Shar thanked the servant of the Chief, before lowering the curtain behind them.

'I'll be fine now, there's no need for you to stay,' Tory assured Jerram, who was gazing at her with desire.

'Oh, but there is,' he corrected, with an amorous smile. 'As your alleged lover, I have my reputation to think about. Besides, if I am here, you won't have to worry about any unexpected visits in the middle of the night.' Jerram took up both her hands, kissing one and then the other.

'Please, don't.' She took a step away, but the Shar grasped her hands firmly and wasn't about to let go.

'I have never longed for any woman, as I long for you.' His dark eyes were intense. 'How happy I must have been as your instructor.' He closed the gap between them, letting go of her hands to take hold of her face, of the mind to kiss her.

'I have a confession to make.' She pulled away before he could. 'Turan, or rather Maelgwn, was not my first love . . . you were.'

The Shar, though pleased by the news, was not inclined to believe it. 'Then why did you not tell me before?'

'Because I was afraid something like this would happen, and I didn't want to falsely encourage you.' She wasn't really sure if she should be telling him this now, either.

'So, you are saying . . .' He eased his way closer to her, backing her up against the large hammock that was stretched out between four posts in their room, 'that you feel nothing for me any more.'

'Yes.' She had no choice but to climb over the unstable obstruction to escape his advance. 'That's absolutely right.'

'Is that so?' He grabbed hold of the arm supporting most of her weight and pulled it towards him, collapsing her into the hammock beside him. 'Then why should it bother you to be this close to me?' Jerram gently caressed her face with his hand, feeling her whole body tremble at his touch.

'You heard what Keturah said, I'm not the one for you.' She stopped his hand before it encountered her breast.

'I don't believe that any more than you do.' His lips pressed lovingly against her neck.

'But I do believe it,' she said, becoming aware of how wonderful his touch made her feel. 'Really I do.' She forgot for a moment what they were talking about. But, as his hand passed over the dip in her waist to rest upon her thigh, gently encouraging her body to press against his own, a surge of awareness came over her and she leapt out of the hammock. 'No.'

'What do you mean, no?' Jerram sat upright.

'We've been through this before, and it doesn't work.' She stressed. 'I will not make the same mistake twice.'

Though he didn't understand her reaction, he was not angered by it. 'How could something that feels so right be a mistake?'

'It's hard to believe, I know!' She was frustrated by her own good sense.

'But you must trust me. A love affair will completely crucify our friendship, and that really means something to me.'

'Me too, but this is a whole different set of circumstances.' He made a move to pursue her, but she held out her hand motioning him to stay put.

'No, not so different.' She shook her head, before closing her eyes and centering all her concentration on Taliesin.

When Jerram realised what she was doing, he clambered off the hammock to stop her. 'Wait, Lamamu. Please!' But he was not swift enough to reach her, she'd gone. 'Curse this other incarnation of mine, for whatever he did to make you so fearful of me.' His aggravation dissolved into a new sense of purpose. 'But I shall make you see, it can work between us.'

After meeting with Taliesin to let him know all went well with her, Tory teleported herself inside the underground dwelling of the Great Temple of Chailidocean to seek Nin Bau.

On her approach to the council chambers of the High Priestess Tory encountered Nin Sibyl. She was veiled as always, but her long, thick masses of soft, brown curls gave her away.

Nin Lamamu, what are you doing here at this hour? She sounded most surprised to see her. I thought you were on a diplomatic errand for the Shu Sar.

'That I am.' She confirmed with a smile. 'But I have need to speak with Nin Bau. Could you please tell her I am here?'

You should have let us know. Her voice implied she was sorry to have to tell her: Nin Bau is not here.

'Where is she then? It is most important that I speak with her.'

I am not at liberty to say. Perhaps tomorrow night . . .

'But tomorrow may be too late. I need to see her tonight.' Tory was beginning to panic.

What is the matter? Nin Sibyl was concerned for her. Perhaps I can help.

'No, I don't think so.' Tory took a seat, disheartened. 'Not unless you know anything about Keeldar.'

I am afraid not. The veiled woman sat down beside her. He was banished before I was born.

This statement made Tory rather curious. 'So you could not be very old then?'

Nin Sibyl shook her head. *I have been alive barely three hundred years.*

Tory guessed this made her about the same age as Jerram and Adelgar. 'Oh. Well then, comparatively you're just a baby. Do forgive me, but it's hard to tell when I've only ever seen you veiled. You never did tell me why that is?'

It is to shield me from the eyes of men and any lustful intent they might have that would lead me astray from my said vocation. There was a time when the female seers of our order went unmasked, but they were too easily distracted from pursuing the inner sight by male suitors, union and children.

'And you do not desire these things?'

Nin Sibyl forced a laugh. *As I am to succeed Nin Bau one day, such things are not an option for me.*

Tory drew her brow, rather annoyed. 'That's ludicrous! Surely everyone has the right to choose in such matters. Anyway I can't see that loving someone should make you any less of a seer than you are.'

Nin Sibyl shrugged. *I am not beautiful as you are, Lamamu.*

'I don't believe that for a second, and neither should you.' Tory stated in no uncertain terms. 'Why don't you lift your veil and let me see your face —'

No, I could not. She stood, alarmed by the notion. It is strictly forbidden.

'But I am no threat to your vows, and after all, I have even seen the face of Nin Bau herself,' Tory boasted, in the hope of setting her at ease.

You have? Sibyl questioned in disbelief. For in all her years of studying under the High Priestess, she'd never glimpsed her face. Not used to the prospect of mischief, the young priestess was excited by it. She closed the door to the small waiting room outside Nin Bau's council chambers. You must promise not to tell a living soul of this.

'I do.' Tory crossed her fingers behind her back, just in case.

Sibyl hesitated again before lifting her veil. *Now, you will be perfectly honest with me, won't you? You wouldn't tell me I am beautiful, if I am not. I assure you, it will not bother me either way. A priestess knows no such vanity.*

It was becoming increasingly obvious as the conversation progressed that this poor girl was simply screaming for some attention. 'Have no fear of that. I am renowned for being frank.'

Alright. The girl took a deep breath, lifting the veil from her face.

I knew I recognised that hair, Tory thought to herself, as she beheld the face of Bridgit. At least now Tory knew she could fulfil her promise to Xavier, for all the good it would do him. 'You may rest assured, my friend. Had you not been veiled all your life, you would have more suitors than you would know what to do with.'

Really! Do you think so? Sibyl tried to be modest.

'I know so.' Tory smiled, unable to resist the question. 'Tell me, do you know of the Shu Sar's son, the one they call Xavier?'

Oh dear Heliona, it does show on my face! The girl was thrown into a state of panic and fell on her knees before Tory. I only ever saw him once, and I do swear to you, I have tried to put him from my mind.

'Calm down. It's alright. It doesn't show, Sibyl . . . it was merely a guess.' The girl stopped being hysterical, looking up at Tory with a stunned expression on her face. 'Really . . . I just thought you'd make a handsome couple.'

You do? Sibyl burst into tears.

Oh dear. Tory had not expected such a strong reaction; when was she going to learn to keep her big mouth shut. 'Have you told Nin Bau how you feel?'

Heavens, no! The girl sobbed. After all the years she has invested in my training, I could not disappoint her so.

Tory gave half a laugh at this. 'I doubt that anything that would bring about your ultimate happiness would be a disappointment to her. For, if you truly feel something for the Shar, to continue this masquerade is ultimately only deceiving yourself . . . after all, you can't hide from the universe, or escape the inevitable.'

Oh please, don't say that. Sibyl rose, weary from her outpouring of emotion. What would I know of love . . . I have barely even met the man. He may be nothing like I imagine.

'Kind, gentle, clever, discreet, understanding, loyal . . .' Tory paused to smile, 'not to mention extremely good-looking. And available. Funnily enough, Shar Xavier just hasn't found the right woman.'

Stop it! Sibyl could take no more. I shall not listen to another word. I must go. She lowered her veil to cover her face once more. And so must you. She opened the door for Tory to leave.

'Alright, if that is your wish.' Tory stood.

It is. The young priestess sniffed, lowering her head. I cannot change what is predestined.

'A truer word was never said.'

Sibyl gasped at Tory's retort, but when she raised her head to ask what she meant, the daughter of Danuih had gone.

What to do? Tory paced up and down inside her palace quarters. Should she mind her own business? *Of course not!* she resolved; she never had before. Besides, she was the divine master of love and war; it was her duty to interfere.

As Xavier slept peacefully, Tory came to sit beside him. She observed him in silence a moment, fondly brushing the long strands of dark hair from his face; she did miss her son terribly.

'Sweet prince,' she whispered. 'I have found your lady fair.'

He roused himself from his dreams, and was somewhat hazy as he addressed her. 'Lamamu?' He squinted to make out her face. 'We have to stop meeting like this. People will talk.'

'I found her,' Tory repeated, rather impressed with herself.

'Dear gods! . . . Who is she?' He sat upright, eager to learn.

That's when Tory's enthusiasm waned. 'I fear you are not going to like it.'

'Why?' Xavier was wide awake now. 'Is she bound to someone else, deformed . . . what?' he appealed, grabbing Tory's shoulders.

'Much worse.' Tory released a heavy sigh. 'She is Nin Bau's novice.'

'Nin Sibyl!' He let go of his sister to grip his forehead. 'No. This cannot be!'

'Well, it is. And you'll never guess what else . . . she's got a crush on you.' Tory gave his shoulder a gentle nudge.

Xavier stared blankly at her, finding her words confusing. 'Is that good?'

'Let me put it this way.' Her impish grin grew.

'It would seem the Priestess has been a silent admirer of yours for some time.'

'Who told you this?' He smiled; he'd never had a secret admirer before.

'I got it straight from the horse's mouth.'

'Sorry?'

Tory rolled her eyes. 'Nin Sibyl told me herself, this very night.' She didn't feel she could put it any plainer. 'I did swear to her that I wouldn't tell another living soul, so I am afraid I'll have to kill you.'

'What?'

'Just kidding . . . but you didn't hear this from me, understand?' Tory moved to climb from the bed, but Xavier gripped her wrist to prevent it.

'You have seen her face?'

He inquired so meekly she felt compelled to respond. 'She appears exactly as I remember her . . . a bit taller, of course.'

'I know how tall she is, Lamamu! What I want to know is the colour of her eyes? Does she have strong features or fine? What is her nature?' The questions tumbled from him.

'Okay.' She held a finger to his lips to silence him. 'I get the picture.' She got herself comfortable. 'Exquisite was the word you used when you described her to me. The face of an angel, you said, and she has eyes like amber jewels.'

This was enough. Xavier appeared mind-blown as he lay back on his pillows. 'Wow.'

'Now, I don't know how you plan to get around the small obstacle of her vows . . .'

'Oh, I'll get around that alright.' He was determined. 'Have no fear of that.'

'Yes, well, you didn't hear any of this from me. I was not here.' She bowed her head and vanished from sight.

'Lamamu!' He sat erect, bemused by her disappearance. She'd not even given him the chance to say thank you.

In the early hours of the morning when Tory returned to Annunnaki, she was surprised to find that Jerram wasn't at all annoyed with her. In fact, he never mentioned the incident of the previous night, nor did he inquire as to where she'd disappeared to. He did, however, seem to be in particularly good spirits, so she didn't question him for fear of pushing her luck.

She considered it a great shame to be leaving the Annunnaki people before she'd really had the chance to learn more about their ways and culture. Tory promised herself that at some future time, when she found herself at leisure (if indeed she ever did), she would return to this fascinating period and investigate all the wonders that she'd not had the chance to explore this time around.

'I do believe that, one day, I shall write the memoirs of my travels,' Tory commented to Adelgar, as they stood on the bow of the ship watching Calisto and his men disappear into the mist from whence they'd come. 'It will be a definitive guide to history, and I shall thoroughly recommend this place as the ideal spiritual retreat.' She raised her face to absorb the warm rays of early morning sunshine.

'These islands are not always this tranquil.' Adelgar cocked an eye. 'I think you'd best wait for the outcome of this meeting with Zutar before you go drawing any conclusions like that.'

As the Annunnaki Islands were situated closer to Antillia than the Atlantean continent, it was shortly after noon when the coast of the great land mass was within sight.

'Are you ready for this?' Jerram didn't sound quite sure that he was.

'My dear Shar, I was born ready.' Tory grinned in a cocky fashion to boost his confidence.

The shoreline of Antillia was rocky and bordered by huge cliffs, making it too treacherous to approach at any random point. But down the coast a way, the huge cliffs parted to grant seagoing vessels access to the harbour of the main port.

As their ship sailed through the heads, horns sounded to either side of them alerting all on shore to the Atlanteans' pending arrival.

Once inside the large harbour, the land gradually sloped downward to meet with the sea and all around them the Antillian people began to pound upon drums as they observed the passage of the craft from their vantage point.

Holy shit. Tory cast her eyes along the ridges either side of them. 'There are a lot of them, aren't there?'

These people appeared much like the African traders Tory had encountered in Chailidocean, though they were taller and more primitive in appearance. This race, like the Annunnaki, painted their bodies and faces, and wore little besides the beaded jewellery and ornate headdress to distinguish rank and nobility.

Up ahead, long, thin canoes were guided into the water by the eight or so natives that manned each of them.

'Here they come.' Jerram turned to Tory with a look of warning. 'Stay close.'

When the smaller local craft reached the ship, the Antillian welcoming committee didn't wait politely to be invited aboard as the Annunnaki had. They scaled the ship using any means available, gibbering and howling in their frenzy to embark.

'They're just trying to unnerve us,' Jerram advised, staying perfectly still as he watched several of the Antillians clambering up the ship's rigging.

'Yeah, well, it's working,' Tory remarked, just before one of the natives dropped from the rigging above to land right in front of her. The two-and-a-half metres tall warrior gave her quite a start, but as Jerram quickly came to stand between them, he smiled and said, 'Do not be afraid, Lamamu. I am Rastus, son of Zutar. I bid you, and the youngest sons of Shu Sar Absalom, welcome.'

All three of the Shu Sar's representatives near fell over backwards.

'You speak English,' Tory noted. 'But how?'

'We have our ways.' Rastus' smile broadened, accentuating the dimples in his cheeks, and the dark features of his face beamed with the warmth of sunshine.

His dark hair fell in dreadlocks past his shoulders and Rastus' build, tall and slim, was nowhere near as solid as Jerram or Adelgar. His demeanour was so easy-going and friendly that Tory could scarce credit him to be one of the ferocious enemy she'd heard so much about. Her first impression of anyone was usually spot on and, in this case, she felt immediately relaxed and trusting in the presence of this stranger.

'Allow me to accompany you and your colleagues ashore.' Rastus addressed Tory directly, motioning her to the canoes gathered around the ship.

'Alright,' Tory replied in a diplomatic fashion. 'But I would ask that your men withdraw from this craft with us.' She didn't want to be so trusting as to leave the guard and crew to perhaps be murdered in their absence.

'As you wish.' The laughter in his voice made it sound as if she was being unduly cautious. Rastus turned and yelled instructions to his party in their tongue, whereby they all leapt from wherever they were into the warm, clear water of the harbour. He then looked back to Tory to seek her approval. 'Shall we go?'

'Yes,' Jerram intervened, not liking the way the son of his enemy was viewing her. 'Let's.' He led Tory to where they boarded the awaiting craft.

On shore, their party was adorned with beaded leis by the tall, dark women of the tribe.

'I feel like a midget.' Adelgar discussed his uneasiness with Tory quietly. 'They never seemed this big in battle.'

'I know what you mean,' she whispered, interlocking her arm in his. 'But remember — the taller one is, the greater the fall.'

'Good point.' The notion seemed to please him and he relaxed a little.

The village through which they were led featured primitive huts like those found in Portea — though they were not raised, as the area must not have been as prone to flooding. Off in the distance, however, there seemed to be some major construction going up, involving huge chucks of stone that were not characteristic of any other dwelling within eyeshot. Tory gave Jerram a nudge, referring him to it.

'Yes.' His raven eyes scanned from left to right, taking everything in. 'I noticed.'

At the end of the main thoroughfare, they came to a dwelling that was much larger and grander than the others.

'My father awaits us inside,' Rastus informed them. 'He has been very much looking forward to making your acquaintance.'

He spoke English very well, Tory considered, and his accent was delightful. 'If you don't mind me asking, Rastus . . .' she delayed him from his course, employing a little charm. 'How did you learn of me in the first place?'

'We have our ways.' He gave the exact same reply that he had to her last question, and went out of his way to accentuate the fact.

His smile was so genuine it seemed to her that he was hinting at something. Perhaps the source of his knowledge of English had been the same source that had advised Zutar of her presence?

'You didn't really expect him to answer that?' Jerram muttered, as they resumed their ascent of the stairs.

'But he did.' Tory informed, her eyes still intent on her likely ally. 'I suspect we'll hear that phrase quite often.' She followed Rastus inside.

Zutar was every bit as formidable in appearance as Tory envisaged he'd be, and he exhibited none of his son's genuine warmth. The Antillian leader's head was shaved to be completely bald, and an ornate headdress of brightly coloured feathers and beads sat high upon his crown. A large gold ring pierced his nose, and several strings of beads were strung from this to join the six gold rings through his left ear lobe. His eyes were like empty black pools that gave nothing away, and looking past his physical form with her etheric sight, Tory was amazed to find that not even the smallest dark patch could be seen in his aura.

After their introduction and some polite conversation, Tory attempted to get the peace talks underway, but Zutar wouldn't hear of it. He insisted that, as his guests, they must rest this day; the formalities could commence on the morrow. Tory found this most frustrating, wanting to complete her mission as quickly as possible so that she could go home. Still, as there wasn't a thing she could do about it, she sat back and enjoyed the entertainment provided for their benefit, all the while keeping a watchful eye on every movement their hosts made.

One thing she noted was that Rastus had not spoken a word of English whilst in his father's presence. He left Jerram and Adelgar to do the translating, even when he addressed Tory directly, and though this scenario did not go unnoticed by any of the three, none of them questioned this in front of the Chief. Something else that had piqued her curiosity was a pouch that hung from a piece of leather around Zutar's neck, which looked quite like a talisman. The reason it drew her attention was that no one else wore one, and it was unlike any of the other beaded chains Zutar wore.

The sun had yet to set and already they'd had their fill of food and drink, so Zutar summoned forth a young girl to sing for them.

This girl was not Antillian; she was tiny and red-skinned like the females of the Atlantean native races. Adelgar, though surprised, did not seem anywhere near as infuriated as Jerram did upon sighting her. This fragile little creature, whose voice was stronger and sweeter than any the Shar had heard, was obviously a prisoner of war. Her song, as beautifully sung as it was, seemed to Jerram to reflect the sadness and shame that was so prominent in her face.

A huge grin beset Zutar's lips as he shifted his dark sights to view both her brothers' reaction, and even though her etheric sight told her differently, Tory could see the evil intent behind Zutar's little presentation. After some contemplation, the leader aimed a question at Jerram, and as her brother appeared as if he might explode at any moment she demanded to know what the leader had said.

'Her name is Mahala, which means sweet singer. He considers her to be quite a catch, for she has brought them all much pleasure.' Jerram strained to control his anger, his jaw clenched. 'He wants to know if I, too, find her pleasing.'

This was an awkward situation, and Tory felt for him, but it was as plain as the nose on her face that Zutar was testing him, perhaps to see how short his fuse was. 'Be diplomatic,' she cautioned in a whisper.

The Shar forced a smile before confirming to their host that his treasure was most easy on the eye and the ear.

Zutar gave a hardy laugh, voicing his retort as he motioned to the girl in question. Jerram seemed somewhat stunned as he turned to Tory to fill her in. 'As a sign of goodwill he is returning her to me . . . she is a gift.'

'How very generous.' Tory's tone became rather dry, and her glare of disapproval bore into the evil source beyond the blackness in Zutar's eyes.

'Be diplomatic.' Jerram whispered a reminder, before graciously accepting the gift of their host.

Tory's patience was tested even further when Zutar had Mahala taken to Jerram's sleeping quarters for the night. The leader then motioned one of the local women to come before them, looking to Adelgar to seek his opinion of her.

Taller than Adelgar, the girl was an extraordinary beauty. Slender and graceful, her hair fell in long black curls to her waist. She knelt before the Shar to whom she was being offered and raised her large, deep brown eyes to his, offering him a flower as she stated her name was Lana.

I don't believe this. Tory *wanted to protest, but bit her tongue for the sake of the mission. She glanced to Rastus to see what he made of all this. He was still smiling broadly and as he caught her eye he winked at her. They're all bastards,* she resolved, maintaining her silence.

Adelgar told Zutar that his hospitality was far too generous and that he couldn't possibly accept. His host merely laughed at this, urging Adelgar to his feet so that Lana could show him to his quarters.

The Shar glanced back to Tory with a perplexed look on his face. 'We don't have to mention this to Nin Tabitha, do we?'

'That's for your own conscience to decide,' she told him; did none of these men have any scruples?

A couple of the native women encouraged Jerram to rise so they could escort him to his sleeping quarters. 'What about Lamamu?' he questioned Zutar in the leader's own language.

Rastus came forward to explain that he would show her around a little before seeing her safely to bed.

'Not without me.' Jerram wouldn't budge.

Though Tory did not understand a word that passed between them, she got the general gist of the conversation. The idea of getting Rastus alone so that they might talk freely appealed greatly to her. 'Jerram, I can take care of myself,' she assured him. 'Which is more than I can say for the poor girl who awaits you.'

He glared at her a moment, both insulted by her inference and jealous of her eagerness to be left alone with Rastus. 'I have never had to force myself upon any woman.'

This was true, he never had. 'Just checking.' She smiled. 'Go on then . . . and don't worry about me.'

'You watch yourself.' His cool glare shifted from Tory to Rastus, before he bowed to their host and was led away.

As proposed, Tory accompanied Rastus through the village and onto a path that wound its way up to the headland, overlooking the ocean.

'Alright.' Tory came to a standstill about halfway up. 'I think it's about time you told me what's going on.'

For the first time since they'd met, the smile slipped from the young warrior's face. 'I fear we are all in great danger, so I shall be brief.' He placed an arm about her shoulder and urged her to keep walking. 'Some time ago, when I was very young, a man came to these shores, a white man.'

'The one you call Engur.' Tory kept her voice low, and he seemed astounded that she knew of whom he spoke.

'Yes.'

'I know his history, so just tell me your woes.'

Rastus seemed suddenly flustered, at a loss as to what to tell her, for he wasn't too sure of the full story himself. 'I suspect so much, Lamamu, but Engur is very smart and hides his true intent well. When he first arrived here, the feats he could perform were so amazing to us that we thought him surely one of the gods . . . and for a time, he was a good friend of mine and served my father well.'

'So, that's when you learnt to speak English, yes?'

Rastus shook his head. 'Engur taught me the art of thought projection, so that I might understand and communicate in any language. But I think he is sorry he did now.'

'I see.' Tory raised her eyebrows. 'Well, back to your story, what happened to change your friendship?'

A frown beset his face. It was difficult for him to pinpoint the exact incident. 'Somewhere along the way everything got twisted around, and instead of serving us, we ended up serving him. We are a plentiful nation, and my father would never have declared war on our neighbouring lands had Engur not filled him with greed.'

'That little pouch your father wears on the piece of leather around his neck,' she inquired. 'Did Engur give it to him at about the same time as the situation here turned sour?'

'Yes! He did.' The coincidence only just occurred to Rastus. 'What does it mean?'

'I'm not sure.' She pondered on it, almost convinced that Mahaud was behind their dilemma. 'But it's my bet that if we removed it from his person, your father would return to his senses.' Then, recalling the spell that the witch had cast over Maelgwn and how it had left him ill, she added: 'But I cannot promise that if Zutar was separated from the charm, it would leave him unharmed. It may already be too late to save him.'

'Do you think he may have caught Engur's madness?'

'Engur's madness?' Tory frowned. 'What do you mean?'

'Lately, Engur has not been so well. He cannot keep his food down, and his head ails him with pain and dizziness, which leaves him very weak.'

Hmm. Sounds rather like radiation poisoning, Tory hypothesised to herself. 'I gather it was Engur's idea to lure me here.' She jumped straight to the heart of the matter. 'Do you know why?'

Rastus shook his head. 'I know only that he wanted to get you away from Chailidocean.'

To what end? Tory mused. They came to the end of the trail to behold the moonlit waters of the strait laid out before them. 'What is all that construction going on behind the village?'

Rastus turned to view it from their vantage point. 'Engur said he would build my father a palace, but much of the structure has been designed for Engur's own purposes.'

'Like the storage and study of rockets, perhaps?' she suggested.

'Indeed.' Rastus was again astonished by her foresight. 'But I have never seen any, as Engur does not trust me any more and has kept me well away from the building. He suspects that I resent the influence he now holds over my father; hence my safety is as doubtful as your own. It is only a matter of time before he finds me too much of a threat and I mysteriously die or disappear, as have so many of my father's trusted advisers.'

Now, a clearer picture was starting to take form. 'So why has Engur left you alone with me? Surely he realises we shall talk.'

Rastus shrugged. 'Who knows, for it was Engur who suggested that I get to know you. I do believe my father is under the impression that we should wed.'

Now she was really confused. What was Keeldar playing at? Perhaps he was trying to set Rastus up. 'I need to get inside that rocket base and take a look around.'

'I did anticipate this,' Rastus advised. 'You have been allocated quarters within the new structure at my father's request, so he can keep a close eye on you. However, I have arranged a diversion that will hopefully keep my father's guards occupied, so we can investigate the matter for ourselves.'

'Well done.' Her mind ticked over. As Keeldar wanted so desperately to keep her away from Chailidocean, she must check in with Taliesin at midnight and pass on a caution. She would also attempt an audience with Nin Bau again, to find out all she could about their foe. 'Let us make our move when the moon-star reaches this point in the sky.' She motioned to the position it would hold at about two o'clock in the morning, as this would give her time to get to Chailidocean and back.

'Agreed.' Rastus placed a hand on her shoulder, pleased to have an ally whose knowledge could aid him. 'But I warn you, this could be dangerous. Engur is no fool, and may be onto us already.'

'That's been the story of my life.' Tory did love a bit of adventure.

The smile return to grace Rastus' face. 'Then let me fill you in on what I have arranged.'

22

GENOCIDE

Only Tory had been allocated sleeping quarters in the new palace; Jerram and Adelgar were accommodated in separate huts in the village.

Adelgar, blissfully unaware that anything suspicious was going on, was more concerned with how he was going to decline this lovely young woman's favours without offending her, or his host.

Alone now, Lana extinguished the torches that lit the dwelling and lay down on the fur-covered bed on the floor, motioning the Shar to join her.

'I don't know how to say this . . .' Adelgar stalled. 'I mean, you are very lovely and all, but . . .'

'Shh.' She raised herself to take hold of his hand and guide him to a seat beside her. She gently kissed his neck, then whispered in his ear. 'I have a message for you from Rastus.' She slid her fingers along his jaw, encouraging him to look her in the eye before she kissed him passionately.

'Well, it's all in the delivery.' His head was awhirl, as she forced him to a horizontal position and climbed on top of him.

'You are in great danger.' She uttered so quietly that he wasn't sure he'd heard her right.

'What!' Adelgar moved to raise himself, but she thrust him back down to murmur an additional warning.

'We are being watched, so make it look good.' She smothered him with affection. 'I am under instruction to hide you. Under the furs you will find a trapdoor and some rope. You are to tie me up and then disappear down the tunnel that you will find beyond.' She giggled, slipping under the furs and motioning him after her.

Although stunned by the announcement, Adelgar put on a playful demeanour for the voyeurs and followed her underneath.

She groaned with pleasure as he bound her, uttering her instruction between breaths. 'Halfway along the passage you will find another trapdoor.

This leads to the hut where your brother has been taken. You must get him and Mahala out without being seen, then wait in the passage until Rastus sends word that it is safe.'

'What about my sister?'

'She is residing in the new palace.' She moaned, wriggling around to make her performance convincing. 'Rastus will use your disappearance to distract the guards and get her out.'

Adelgar slid his upper body under the trapdoor to briefly view the tunnel underneath.

'How did you arrange all this so quickly?'

'The tunnel has been in existence for years although it was never intended for this purpose. For you see, I am no one of great consequence . . . it was the only way Rastus and I could see each other.' Her tone was melancholy a moment. 'Now gag me and go, quickly.'

He did as he was instructed, taking her head between his hands before departing. 'I shall not forget this, Lana.' He kissed her forehead and disappeared.

As Tory followed Rastus inside the new palace, she felt comforted in the knowledge that her brothers would both be safe from whatever trouble she stirred up this night. Mind you, she was a little concerned about how Jerram would react to being hidden away, knowing how stubborn he could be at times.

Zutar obviously had no intention of resolving the trouble between their two nations, and as he'd insisted on starting the peace talks tomorrow it seemed reasonable to assume that whatever he was up to must be scheduled to take place tonight.

She entered her chamber behind Rastus, who wanted to make sure that nothing was amiss.

The first thing they noted was that, unlike any other room in the palace that Rastus had seen, the walls of this chamber were made of a grey material, that looked conspicuously like steel, or perhaps lead.

A bit worried about containing me, hey? she amused herself as she viewed the metal walls, knowing that no substance on earth could contain her. The chamber was square in shape, which also seemed rather strange, and looking up to the ceiling above the door there were windows that looked out to the night sky. How could that be? she wondered, sensing that they were being watched. She said nothing as she accompanied Rastus to the door. Only when they were both out of view from the windows did she say, 'I was under the impression that there was another floor above this.' She motioned to the windows above the door with her eyes.

She was right, there was. Rastus nodded silently to confirm that he would investigate. 'Goodnight, Lamamu. Sleep well.'

As she closed the door behind him, her heart began to pound in her chest. Something about this room didn't feel right — the sooner she got of out of here the better.

Tory climbed onto the bed of soft furs, but as she lay down to focus her energies on Taliesin she became aware of a great force bearing down upon her. *Concentrate*, she scolded herself, as she struggled to find her centre.

Tory, expecting to find herself in Turan's quarters, opened her eyes to discover she hadn't moved. *What's going on?* Even her eyes were constrained from movement.

Her sights were fixed on the ceiling directly above her where a panel was opening and a long metal arm, attached to the largest needle that Tory had ever seen, extended towards her.

Anything but this! Injections made her squeamish at the best of times.

The thin, red laser light, that guided the mechanism, zeroed in on her third eye area. The needle locked into position just above her brow, and seconds later the needle had penetrated her skull and thrust itself deep into her brain.

Is something the matter, Lamamu? The sinister voice was very clear in her mind, as was the laughter — both of which Tory presumed belonged to Keeldar. You weren't planning on leaving us so soon? He tormented her further: Because, I have to tell you, gravity is against you.

So that's what this great force was. It felt as if she were pinned underneath a great concrete slab and the pressure, combined with her nauseating predicament, was tempting her to pass out.

You see, gravity distorts all time and space in its vicinity. If the gravitational field is strong enough, time effectively stands still. In other words, my young warrioress, you are trapped in what is commonly referred to as a time warp. To try and resist is pointless, for even if you possess the concentration and willpower to transport yourself beyond these walls, the amount of time dilation that has already occurred within them means you would take infinitely longer to reach the world outside and manifest. Well, so much for the science lesson. His tone lightened in amusement. I bet you thought yourself infallible, didn't you? But I ask you to consider this paradox. What would become of you, if, say, your father was eliminated before he was even born, hmm? He chuckled maliciously. I fear, my dear Lamamu, you would cease to exist. He contained his delight. Now, before I put you into complete stasis, let us ponder upon where Darius has hidden this immortality potion of yours.

Rastus pressed himself into the annex of a doorway near to the room he guessed was located above Lamamu's, watching Engur exit and close the door. The scientist seemed rather bothered about something as he made haste down the stairs, and it was Rastus' guess that Engur was going to report to Zutar.

As soon as his foe was out of sight, Rastus crept towards the room in question and pressed the button on the control panel to grant him access.

Inside, he was confronted by a huge panel of buttons and levers that were far beyond his comprehension. Above the board of complex technology, windows awarded a view of the room below. There, frozen motionless, was Lamamu connected to a great steel device that extended from the roof and was attached to a thin steel rod that penetrated her forehead.

'Goddess, no,' he uttered desperately. His eyes rapidly scanned the panel before him, but he feared she was already dead.

Resting on a chair close by, he spied a small, unusual-looking metal headdress. Rastus lifted this and, after examining it, placed it on his head. The two padded pieces on either side of the curved metal band rested on his ears. The steel rod that extended from the headpiece was padded at the end. He positioned it in front of his mouth.

'Lamamu? Can you hear me?' There was no response. 'Please hear me,' he begged. He began to panic and took off the headdress to look at it again. On one of the earpieces was a switch, which he flicked to its opposite position, returning the device to his head. 'Lamamu?'

Rastus, is that you? If you can hear me, help me out of this, please!

He breathed a sigh of relief; she was still alive. 'I will, I promise . . . but I shall need help. Try and stay calm, I shall be back soon.'

Hurry, Rastus, she pleaded. We must stop Keeldar.

Halfway down the stairs, on his way to confront Engur in his father's chambers, Rastus came to a stop. *Hold on.* If there was an observation room above Lamamu's chamber, chances were there would also be one above his father's. A wide smile spread across his face as the young warrior turned and swiftly made his way back upstairs.

On the floor above, in the vicinity of his father's room, Rastus entered another room with large windows where one could observe the chamber below. This lacked most of the technology of the observation room above Lamamu's quarters; it must have been specifically designed for her. However, this chamber had the same headset, which Rastus placed upon his head after checking the switch was in the right position.

His father sat in a large chair before Engur, who was hypnotising him into a relaxed state.

'That's it.' Engur backed away from the Chief, who was now unconscious.

Rastus couldn't understand this. He'd felt so sure Engur wanted to convey some news to Zutar, so what was the point of putting him to sleep?

Zutar began to tremble as the features of his face contorted into a creature no longer resembling himself. When the beast's eyelids burst open, its eyes blazed with the colour of burning hot coals. 'You have restrained the girl?' he questioned Engur in a gruff, harsh voice that was not his own.

'It is done.' Engur bowed to the creature, holding his head as he did so — it was obviously ailing him again.

'And what did you learn?'

'She does not know where the potion is hidden.' Engur humbled himself to impart the bad news. 'Only Darius knows of its whereabouts.'

The apparition growled with annoyance. 'Never mind. When phase two of our plan has been set in place, we shall persuade Darius to lead us to it.'

'My very thought, O powerful one,' Engur agreed, still half-bowed over.

'Now, remember, you must ensure that all exits are blocked once the warhead has been placed inside the Great Temple . . . Nin Bau must not escape before it is detonated.' The creature rubbed its misshapen hands together, well pleased at the thought of ridding the universe of Myrddin. 'I have a few loose ends to tie up here, so when you report back to me that all is well, we shall take care of the other matter together. Set the timer for dawn. That should give us more than enough time.' As it paused to consider whether everything had been taken into account, the beast's breathing resounded like the purr of a wild cat, but with a tone far more ominous. 'I hope you have destroyed the manuals you found in that pile of twentieth century technological crap you fished out of the ocean? I wouldn't want that smart little student of yours figuring out how to disarm our surprise.'

'I have. Everything has been committed to memory. And you've no need to worry about Turan. He's in isolation.' Engur raised a quivering hand to his head as he forced a grin. 'It will all be over by the time he realises anything has happened.' He turned to more immediate matters. 'Now, what about Lamamu's companions, and Rastus?'

'I have already given the order to arrest them. They shall all be dead by the time you return.' The beast glowered with malign delight. 'Now, be about my bidding and do not disappoint me, Keeldar.'

'Have I ever.' He bowed and vanished.

Rastus threw down the headset and raced from the room. He had to get to Jerram and Adelgar before this creature did.

When Tory was two hours late to meet him, Taliesin became so concerned that he was obliged to disturb Shar Turan. The Shar was in meditation at the E-abzu Temple.

Not pausing to seek permission to enter, Taliesin found the Shar's free-floating form awaiting him. *My Shar! He was surprised to find that Turan had fully resumed his etheric form in only a few days. Your skill never ceases to amaze me.*

Turan raised his eyebrows. *Hopefully, our foe shall be just as unsuspecting. Our foe?*

Indeed. Lamamu has failed to meet you this night, has she not? Turan knew, for it was the only reason for which he was to be disturbed.

That is correct, but . . .

Then I must go to her, Turan announced in a tone that implied there was to be no argument. *Go to my father and advise him of what has happened. Tell him to be alert. I shall return with news as soon as I am able.*

The Shar faded into nothingness, leaving Taliesin a mite perplexed. *Advise him as to what has happened? He wondered what Turan meant. Be alert for what?*

'I don't like this one bit,' Jerram grumbled, pacing up and down the earthen tunnel. 'Our sister could be in real danger and we're hiding down here! How do we know this isn't a trap?'

Adelgar merely shrugged, tired of his brother's constant complaints. 'We don't. But I trust — '

'You'd trust any female who spread her legs for you.'

Adelgar rose to contest Jerram's inference, when Mahala intervened. 'I trust Rastus and Lana, too.' Her soft voice pacified the brothers. 'They have both been very good to me.'

Jerram backed off, turning to pace and ponder some more. 'Well, what if Rastus has — '

'Shh!' Adelgar hushed him to silence as a commotion erupted overhead, in the room that Jerram and Mahala had occupied. 'Quick.' Adelgar motioned his companions to follow as he hurried towards the trapdoor that led to the room where he'd left Lana.

A scuffle had erupted. When the guards had found Lana bound and gagged there was much shouting. It sounded as if they were turning the hut upside down as they sought the whereabouts of their prisoner, and finding no trace of him, their attentions again turned to Lana.

It was obvious they weren't believing her story, despite her convincing account of what had happened. Her cries of agony, as Zutar's men attempted to torture the truth out of her, tormented Adelgar till he could take no more. 'I have to help her.'

Jerram grabbed hold of his brother's belt and heaved him off the ladder. 'Are you insane?'

'Let her go.'

The voice of Rastus silenced the commotion above, at which time Adelgar breathed a sigh of relief. But the calm was short-lived. For the next thing they knew, Zutar's men were accusing Rastus of treason and a fight broke out as they attempted to apprehend him.

'If Zutar's men are accusing Rastus of treachery, wouldn't that seem to indicate that he's on our side?' Adelgar surmised.

'So what are we waiting for?' Jerram prompted, turning back to address Mahala. 'Stay here till I come for you.'

She nodded, reaching out to touch his arm a second. 'Do be careful.' Her soft, brown eyes besought him.

On impulse, Jerram chanced a kiss that met with no resistance from Mahala. 'I shall return.' He smiled a cheeky smile and followed his brother up the ladder.

Adelgar liberated the laser sword that was clipped to his belt, as Jerram did at his, and silently counting off three on their fingers, they thrust open the trapdoor with such force that all the furs on top were flung backwards.

The two Atlantean warriors charged from their hiding place, shooting bursts of coloured energy from the cylindrical objects in their hands. The local weaponry of the Antillian's proved no match for the lasers, and within seconds only Rastus, Lana, Jerram and Adelgar remained conscious in the hut.

'They'll come round by morning.' Adelgar waved off Rastus' fear that all his men had been killed.

'What took you so long?' Jerram asked, replacing his weapon on his belt.

'My father has been possessed by some sort of demon,' Rastus explained. 'And Lamamu has been imprisoned by a device of Engur's design. I am at a loss as to how to free her.'

'What did I tell you?' Jerram was enraged by the news; Lamamu was his responsibility. 'Where is she?'

They left Lana in hiding with Mahala. Rastus fronted up to the palace entrance with Jerram and Adelgar, their hands bound loosely behind their backs.

The two guards in attendance seemed confused by this development and crossed their spears to block his passage.

Rastus explained that he was bringing the two prisoners to Zutar to prove his innocence on the charge of treason. As the two guards were both good friends of his they moved aside, giving him the benefit of the doubt. They did insist on escorting Rastus to Zutar's chambers, however. As the guards followed the party inside, one of them locking the doors in their wake, Jerram and Adelgar turned and blasted them into an unconscious state.

'This way.' Rastus made for the large stone stairs that led to the next level.

The sad circumstance in which they found their sister brought tears to their eyes.

'Is she alive?' Adelgar's voice was hoarse, due to the lump that had welled in his throat.

'Yes, you can speak to her.' Rastus held the headset out to him.

'Lamamu?' Adelgar's voice was unsteady with the fear that she would not respond; she certainly looked dead from this perspective.

Adelgar? . . . Please say that's you.

'The one and only.' He nearly choked with relief.

'Is she alright?' Jerram demanded, and Adelgar nodded in the affirmative.

'We should never have left her alone!' Jerram got back on his high horse.

'We are so sorry about this,' Adelgar sniffled. The thought of being in the same predicament made him nauseous.

Don't be sorry . . . just figure out how to get me out of this. Nin Bau, Darius, and heaven knows who else, are in great danger.

Adelgar ripped off the headset, eyeing the control panel before him with complete disbelief. 'Any ideas?'

He looked to Jerram, who'd been examining the panel closely. 'None,' he confessed, wanting to punch something. 'Curse it! The person we need is Turan and I insisted he shouldn't come!'

So I was right and you were wrong. What's new? Turan's droll tones came from behind them.

Despite their differences, Jerram had never been so glad to see him in all his life. 'Indeed,' he agreed with a smile. 'And I do gladly admit it.'

Well, then, what seems to be the problem?

Once Tory was liberated from the time warp and had regained control of her limbs, Rastus told of all he had seen and heard during her incapacitation.

'It's Mahaud alright, no doubt about it. That explains Keeldar's interest in my family tree.' Tory held her forehead where Keeldar's device had penetrated her skull. The wound had already healed over without a trace. 'You see, Nin Bau is carrying a boy child, who shall one day be my father. If she perishes before she gives birth, then I shall never happen and will cease to exist!'

Now let's not get hysterical, Turan calmly advised. This situation is salvageable.

'You're right.' Tory quickly pulled herself together. 'We must get back to Chailidocean immediately.'

No, we shouldn't . . . not just yet anyway. We have no way of containing Keeldar there, only here. Turan motioned to the chamber they had just released Tory from, before looking to Rastus. Keeldar is going to report back to Zutar, you said.

'That is what they agreed.'

'But what about the warhead?' Tory asked in panic.

Well, it seems pointless to attempt to disarm it if Keeldar is still at liberty to rearm it. If it has been set to go off at dawn, that gives us some time. I say we contain those forces working against us, find out exactly what we are dealing with, then we can defuse the situation in Chailidocean unhindered.

Turan made good sense as always. Tory was now thankful that he'd resumed his etheric form, for he could view the situation logically without becoming emotionally involved. 'Aren't you forgetting about Mahaud? I know of no means to contain her . . . though I could probably make her flee with the help of one of those wooden flutes the musicians were playing on last night.'

Good enough, Turan grinned, a rare occurrence. Then this is what I propose.

'Where the hell have you been?' the creature in the guise of Zutar roared, as Keeldar's presence manifested before it.

The scientist trembled, perhaps from fear, perhaps exhaustion. 'Why, I was carrying out your — '

'Oh, shut up!' The beast had little patience left. 'Those pathetic excuses for soldiers have yet to bring me any corpses. Why?'

'Because I have freed the prisoners.' Rastus stood in the open doorway. 'They are long gone. You shall not find them now.' He marched into the room to confront the creature, projecting a dauntless countenance.

'My dear son.' The flaming red eyes of Zutar sized up his prey.

'You are not my father,' Rastus contested, and the creature gave a hearty laugh at this.

'You only just worked that out, did you?' Zutar's form swung quickly around to address Keeldar. 'Go and check on the girl!'

Keeldar humbled himself. 'He couldn't possibly have — '

'Go!' it demanded, almost blasting its subject out of the room with the order.

'Yes, at once.' The scientist raised himself and fled from the room.

'Now . . .' The beast's evil eyes came to rest on Rastus. 'How should one punish one's own flesh and blood for such treason?' It raised its misshapen hands and its fingertips began to glow red. 'I think . . . death.'

With a growl, the creature shot a ball of flame from its fingertips which engulfed the young warrior. Rastus fell to the floor in a blaze. The creature delighted in the sight of the burning carcass for a moment, before returning to Zutar's throne to ponder its next move.

'Think again, Mahaud.'

The creature turned to see Tory resume her usual form. It was stunned by a blast from the laser in Tory's hand.

'Piece of cake.' Tory raised herself and walked over to take a stand before her victim. 'It doesn't look like you'll be going anywhere in this body tonight.'

The pouch, strung on a piece of leather around his neck, dropped into the Chief's lap, and a mixture of red and black gas began to exude from Zutar's ears, nose and mouth. Freed from the influence of the evil entity, the Chief resumed his normal form and slept peacefully on his throne. The gaseous substance rose high above its previous host, continuing to boil and billow like an animated cloud that glowed like embers. This mass then contorted into the shape of a black, hooded figure with its arms folded. The apparition was completely featureless, except for its eyes of glowing red. 'No matter,' it said, 'there are others just as gullible.'

Tory pulled a small, wooden flute from her belt to discourage any thought of vengeance her foe may have had. As she lifted it to her lips, the dark figure hovering above waved her off.

'Don't waste your breath.' It spun into a whirlwind and vanished.

No! It's not possible. Keeldar held his thumping head between his quivering hands, viewing the empty chamber below him.

The communication mechanism was still engaged, as was the gravity function, so where was she?

It must be some sort of visual illusion, he reasoned, but the thunder in his head made it hard to concentrate. Yes, that must be it . . . she's trying to trick me.

Keeldar turned everything off and ran downstairs as fast as he was able. It would take her some time to recover her faculties; thus, if he felt her body present he could still re-trap her in the time warp before she could depart or retaliate.

Mindful of his captive's capabilities, Keeldar cautiously entered the chamber. The witch had been obliged to tell him a tale or two of Lamamu's cunning, so that he could design a cell that would contain the immortal warrioress.

As he passed his hand over the bed, it met with nothing. 'She's not here.' He was completely horrified by the realisation; Mahaud would fry him for this. 'But she must be.' He climbed onto the furs for one last desperate search, when the door to the chamber slammed closed and the force of his own creation began to bear down upon him. 'No!' He tried to will himself elsewhere, but his body collapsed flat onto the bed under the strain of the gravity field.

The steel tentacle from the communication device repositioned itself above its inventor's brow before entering his brain.

There was an old fool named Keeldar,
Whose intent was quite sinister.
His student, quite bright.
thus had the foresight,
to trap him in time warp, forever.

Many happy returns, friend. Turan goaded triumphantly, turning to Jerram who'd been manning the controls under his guidance. *Good job . . . we'll make a technologist of you yet.*

But whilst Turan, Jerram, and Adelgar were all still congratulating each other, Keeldar imploded. He splattered across every surface of the room below.

'Oh, gross!' Adelgar jumped back from the gut-splattered window.

Turan scratched his head in thought. *This would lead me to believe that only an immortal can withstand the pressure.*

Jerram looked at his older brother, exhibiting a similar complacency.

Damned shame we didn't consider that beforehand really.

'Did we get him?' Tory came rushing through the doorway with Rastus right behind her, but they both came to a grinding halt when they spotted the carnage dripping from the window.

'You could say that, yes,' Jerram informed her coolly. 'Though I think he'll have to pull himself together before he will be of any use to us.' He smothered a chuckle.

'What the hell happened?' She became annoyed with them; they were certainly not going to get any information out of Keeldar now.

He just couldn't take the pressure, Turan explained in all seriousness, but Jerram and Adelgar found the statement hilarious and doubled over with laughter.

'This is not funny.' She placed her hands on her hips. 'What do you suggest we do now?'

Let's go and have a look inside that rocket base, Turan proposed. *It may tell us a thing or two.*

They took a path along the observation level, venturing deeper into the palace.

Rastus had never seen the fabled rockets or the room Engur had built for their storage, but he had a fair idea where it was located, for there was an area that had been deemed out of bounds to all bar Engur and his father. Rastus led his new allies in that direction.

After knocking out the guards with lasers, the five of them entered an observation room that overlooked a huge containment area that had walls of solid lead. There, larger than life, was a twentieth century Soviet submarine.

'Holy smoke! Would you look at the size of that thing!' Adelgar could barely believe his eyes.

'The vessel is not our worry.' Tory's horrified gaze rested on the eight or so missiles lined up around the walls, which she pointed out for the benefit of her comrades. 'There is probably enough explosives in those cylinders to destroy the whole of the known world.'

'Whoa . . .' was all Jerram could say.

'Come on, Turan, let's have a closer look.' Tory motioned him after her.

'I am coming with you.' Jerram moved to follow them.

'No.' Tory opposed the idea strongly. 'I have reason to believe Keeldar might have been suffering from radiation poisoning. If the core of one of the reactors has been damaged and there is a leak, neither Turan nor I will be affected. But, to you, a dose of radiation would be lethal,' she explained. 'So please, stay here. We won't be long.' She smiled.

Jerram nodded reluctantly. 'Be careful.'

None of the missiles that lined the walls appeared to have been tampered with. Neither did the six warheads laid out on a large bench before them. Tory retrieved a solar torch from the scientist's work bench and motioned to the submarine. 'I'm going to take a look inside.'

As she climbed the ladder that gave access to the hatch on the top of the vessel, she noted a large pile of human bones in the far corner of the room.

'Well, at least I won't come across any nasty surprises.' She forced a grin, as she stepped inside the open hatch and began her descent into the belly of the sub.

'What is taking her so long?' Jerram stood with his forehead pressed against the window. 'She's been ages in there?'

'Look.' Rastus nudged the Shar as Tory appeared waving around some papers she held in her hand.

She climbed down from the vessel and bounded over to converse with Turan, before they both made haste from the room.

'What is it?' Jerram besought her as she entered the observation chamber. 'What did you find?'

'This is not as good as the manuals for the warheads, which Keeldar must have destroyed, but it's the next best thing.' She took a seat. 'At least this little piece of propaganda tells us what we are dealing with.' She opened a leaflet and asked Turan to translate.

'This is a Soviet Golf II Class Attack Submarine. It carries ballistic missiles, and nuclear warheads of eight hundred kiloton nominal yield, and seven MIRV warheads each of which has a one hundred kiloton nominal yield.'

'Holy shit, that's a phenomenal amount of explosive potential.' It blew Tory's mind.

'Each one of these MIRV warheads can be independently detonated,' Turan advised.

Tory cast her sights over the bench in the chamber below. 'There's one missing.' She looked at Turan, bewildered. 'So how the hell are we going to defuse something like this without any knowledge of its workings?'

We had best get to Chailidocean, he advised calmly. We'll worry about what to do after we've had a look at Keeldar's handiwork, hey?

Tory nodded, though the situation seemed hopeless.

Where there's a will, there's a way. Turan attempted to perk up her spirits.

'I hope you're right.' She stood to leave.

'Wait.' Adelgar rushed to her side. 'I have this awful feeling I shan't see you again.' He was probably right, for even if she did manage to salvage the situation in Chailidocean, she would be returning to Gwynedd immediately afterwards.

'My mission here is over.' She held a hand to his cheek. 'But I shall miss you, more than you could ever know.'

He embraced her suddenly, as if he would never let her go. 'I did love having a sister. I won't forget all you've done for us . . . for me.' After one last squeeze, he let her go and took a step away. 'May the Shining Ones guide and protect you, always.'

'Likewise.' She smiled through the tears that had begun to roll down her cheeks, then looked at Rastus. 'Thank you for being so forthright and courageous. We would surely have been doomed without your help.'

His sunny smile made his face beam. 'I could say the same of you, Lamamu.' He bowed his head to her. 'Antillia is forever in your debt.'

Lastly, she looked at Jerram, who was doing his best to look unaffected by her imminent departure. 'Goodbye, my friend,' she said, as she reached for his hand.

'I shall see you again,' he stated with certainty, taking hold of her around the back of her neck. 'So let us just say . . . see you later.' He kissed her as he'd wanted to ever since they'd first met.

Quite a few moments later, Turan was obliged to interrupt. *Dawn will wait for no one.*

'Of course.' She backed up reluctantly to view her pals one last time. 'I shall treasure every moment of the time we spent together . . . I am beholden to you all. She bowed deeply to them as she and Turan vanished.

'Kheit-Sin knows, I miss her already.' Adelgar slumped into a seat, all melancholy.

Jerram slapped his shoulder to reassure him. 'She'll be back.'

All in Chailidocean was quiet at this early hour. In fact nobody seemed to have been alerted to the impending disaster. Tory and Turan sought out Taliesin and found him in the palace's room of court in conference with the Shu Sar.

'Thank Helio!' Absalom exclaimed, as his children entered. 'At last. Now, would you mind telling us what the big emergency is?'

'The warhead Keeldar brought into the city . . .' Tory began, 'the one that is dismantled and in a safe place —'

'Yes, yes.' The Shu Sar grew impatient, having had very little sleep. 'What of it?'

'Keeldar has planted it in the Great Temple and it is set to go off at dawn,' she advised the Sar, handing Taliesin the papers she had taken from the sub.

'What!' Absalom didn't seem to believe her. 'Where did you —?'

'Father, it's a very long and twisted story, which we can explain later, but right now I think we had best address the problem.' She looked to Taliesin as he browsed over the information in his hand. 'I don't suppose you know how to deactivate a MIRV warhead?'

'I'm afraid not — '

'Shit!' She didn't even give him a chance to finish. 'Well, we can't just stand around here and wait for the damn thing to go off. Let's get to the temple and see what we can do.'

They did intend to take the conventional entrance leading to the dwellings below the great temple, but the doorway was blocked by a huge chunk of rock over a metre thick. Turan made an attempt at moving it psychokinetically, but the great boulder wouldn't budge.

'Keeldar must have changed its composition somehow,' the Shar surmised.

Instead, Taliesin, Turan and Tory teleported themselves inside to find the inhabitants in a state of complete dismay.

Thank heavens! Nin Sibyl approached them. We thought nobody knew we'd been trapped.

'Keep calm. Everything will be alright,' Tory instructed. 'Tell me . . . you haven't spied anything unusual hanging around?' She didn't want to panic the women any more than they already were.

Yes, indeed. Shu Micah and Shar Xavier are looking at it now. It's in Nin Bau's council chambers. She led them off in that direction.

Shar Xavier. What is he doing here? Tory wondered with a smile, as if she didn't know. 'What about the passage to Mount Dur-an-ki? Could we get these women out that way?'

I thought of that, Sibyl told her, but unfortunately, it too has been blocked.

'Turan, thank goodness you're here.' Xavier got to his feet as Nin Sibyl escorted the others into the room. 'I'm no expert, but I think we've got a real problem on our hands.' He motioned to the warhead.

Tory rushed to view the timer. 'We've got just a little over an hour remaining,' she informed them. Turan scrutinised the device. 'Can you defuse it?'

It would take time . . . probably more than we have. He analysed their situation calmly.

Tory was about to abuse him for being so nonchalant about the whole thing, when something else claimed her attention. 'Hold on. Where is Nin Bau?'

We do not know. Shu Micah answered sadly. Nobody has seen her for days.

'Holy smoke!' She gripped her head in both her hands. 'What if Mahaud has got her? I must find her. My life depends on it.'

Now you don't know that that beast has got her. Turan was firm with her. Why choose to think such a thing?

'He's right.' Xavier backed up his brother. 'Have I taught you nothing?'

'Well, help me out here, guys!' She felt as if she was losing her mind. The city of the Golden Gates was about to be destroyed three thousand years before its time, and it was all her fault. Not to mention the probability that she was going to be wiped from existence. 'Turan you're smart . . . can't you think of something.'

Turan pondered their options before speaking. *Lamamu, I feel it's time you told Taliesin what really happened back in Gwynedd.*

'What, now?' She felt the suggestion rather inappropriate.

Turan nodded in response. *There's no time like the present . . . create your own reality*, he added with a wink.

The revelation hit her like a brick. 'Yes, I see.' Her amazed look drifted to the Merlin.

'What?' Taliesin was wary. 'What are you talking about?'

'I lied to you, my friend.' Tory placed a hand upon his shoulder. 'You were in Gwynedd when everything went to hell . . . but now I realise why you left.'

'Pardon?' The Merlin drew in his brow. 'I don't follow.'

'Alright.' Tory drew a deep breath. 'Listen very carefully. The reason no one has seen Nin Bau for days is because you left Gwynedd in the chariot and came back here, say two days ago, to take her safely to fifth-century Britain. There is a nunnery in the town of Carmarthen, where she will be safe until she gives birth to my father, Myrddin.' That explained how Nin Bau had ended up in the Dark Age. 'From there, you must travel to the year nineteen-eighty and learn how to defuse this warhead, before returning here. The make and model is outlined in that paper in your hand.' She drew a deep breath in conclusion.

Very good. Turan was most impressed.

Poor Taliesin, on the other hand, was very perplexed. 'I shall do as you say, of course.' He gazed at the leaflet blankly, uneasy that the fate of the city now rested in his hands.

'But how can I be sure it will work?' Tory asked.

'I believe I can set your mind at ease in that department.'

Tory looked to the door. There stood the Merlin. 'Taliesin! My Taliesin!' She overpowered him with a hug. 'I knew you wouldn't abandon us. I knew it! Oh dear . . .' Taliesin's younger self had passed out cold.

'Nin Bau is safe, as is her babe . . . and you.' The older Taliesin smiled at the soul he treasured above all others.

'And the warhead?' Tory was simply beaming for joy now.

'I shall take care of it. But first, I want you to take the chariot and Maelgwn's cure, and get out of here . . . just in case.' He went on before she could protest: 'Turan, would you be so kind as to see Tory, or rather Lamamu, safely to her transport.'

It would be my pleasure.

'When Turan reports back to me to say you are safely away, I shall defuse the warhead.'

'But —'

'No buts,' he cautioned her. 'The procedure will take all of five minutes, thus we have plenty of time. I shall meet you back in Gwynedd presently, and we'll have a good laugh about this whole mess.'

'What of Mahaud?'

'She will follow you out of here, have no fear of that. We shall deal with her together upon my return to Degannwy.'

'Alright then.' Tory's expression was just short of a pout. 'If that's to be the way of it, I will go.'

'Wait!' Both Xavier and Sibyl cried at once.

'We just wanted to thank you for making us aware of each other.' Xavier took Sibyl's hand in his own. 'We have spoken to Shu Micah and we have his permission to court.'

'That's wonderful news. I am so happy for you both.' She kissed Xavier's cheek and raised Sibyl's veil to kiss her cheek.

'Tory?' Taliesin ushered her along.

'Alright, I'm going!' She was frustrated by the need for a hasty departure. There were so many people she wanted to thank and say goodbye to, but time would not permit it.

Lamamu. Shu Micah came forward. The evil ones will eventually succumb to the Shining Ones and the Chosen like yourself who are hiding within the circuits of time. This will bring about a new age of awareness, whereupon you will realise that your righteous acts, hard work, and suffering has not all been for naught.

She smiled at the extraordinary being that addressed her. 'I shall see you at the Gathering, then.'

He bowed his head to her. 'That you will, Lamamu, that you will.'

When Darius could not be found in his abode, Turan and Tory made straight for the Shi-im-ti to seek him there. However, much to their surprise and dismay, he was not in his laboratory either.

'Goddamn it!' Tory was working herself into a tizz. 'Where is he?'

Please, Lamamu, Turan besought her. There is a very simple answer to this problem.

'And what might that be?' The Shar's smug attitude was beginning to drive her nuts.

If we just close our eyes and concentrate on Darius, we shall go directly to him.

'Good call.' Tory's spirits lifted.

They found themselves on the lowest level underneath the Shi-im-ti Temple, and as Tory made to move she stumbled over Darius' unconscious form on the floor.

'Oh no . . . what's happened?' She crouched beside him to see if she could bring him round. 'Darius. Can you hear me?'

Turan spied Nin Melcah slouched against the wall. 'Mother?'

'Oh, Turan, what have I done?' She wept bitterly, too ashamed to look her son in the face.

'I don't know.' His voice was sympathetic. 'Why don't you tell me?'

She shook her head. 'I can't. I don't remember.' She raised the little pouch she had worn around her neck at Keeldar's request. 'The past few weeks are a complete blank.' She covered her face with her hands and sobbed.

'Lamamu.' Turan called her over, motioning to the pouch his mother was clutching.

'Oh shit.' Tory grabbed it from her. 'Where did you get this?' As Melcah was almost hysterical with grief, Tory had to shake a reply out of her. 'Answer me!'

'Keeldar.' She blurted out her confession. 'I wanted you away from my son. He said if I wore this charm, no one would suspect my deep-seated dislike of you.'

'Oh, Mother, you've done some low things in your time . . .' Tory was furious with her, 'but this takes the cake.' Melcah stopped her sobbing and stared at Tory, a look of horror on her face. 'That's right. Like it or lump it, in some distant future you shall give birth to me.'

Melcah gasped, unsure of how she felt about it, for her nerves and wits had been shot to pieces. 'Please, forgive me?' Her attentioned shifted from Tory to her son.

'That would be easier said than done.' Tory stared down at her, most displeased.

'What happened?' Darius mumbled as he began to come round.

'That's what I'd like to know.' Tory moved to give him a hand to sit up.

'Oh my god!' he cried suddenly, near startling Tory to death. 'Where is that creature?'

Mahaud was here. Tory wanted to kick herself. She should have known. 'The witch has fled. But I have a better question. Where's the potion?'

'It's in . . .' He raised his eyes to find the secret compartment in the wall was open. He raised himself quickly to search inside it. 'The potion has gone.'

'Did you see the creature take it?' Tory tried not to jump to any rash conclusions.

'No. It knocked me out as soon as I told it where the potion was.' He held his throbbing head, filled with remorse. 'I had no choice. It threatened to do horrible things to Anthea if I didn't.'

'It's alright.' Tory knew how persuasive the witch could be. 'Well, that's it then . . . it's all been for naught.' She looked to Turan, defeated, and gave a sigh. 'Maelgwn will surely die now, and if Mahaud has the means to become immortal, he's probably better off.'

'Please don't say that.' Darius felt terrible; he'd saved his own wife at the cost of Lamamu's husband. 'I could make another dose.'

Tory's eyes lit up. 'How long would it take?'

'Only a day or so.'

'No good.' Her hope dwindled again. 'I have to be out of here within the hour.'

No matter. Turan was encouraging. *There is another way.*

Back in the laboratory Turan supplied Tory with a metal detector that was set to detect orichalchum, the strongest material in Atlantis, unknown in future ages. The plan was to wrap the potion in a shell of orichalchum and bury it on the highest mountain in the Usiqua ranges that would one day be known as the Azores. All Tory had to do was find it and dig it up.

There was a possibility that the Azores were still submerged in the depths of the Atlantic Ocean in the sixth century. Also, in that time period, there was a lack of equipment and transport that would be required to complete such a quest, so Tory had a change of destination; she would now detour to the twentieth century before heading home to Gwynedd.

'I won't let you down,' Darius assured her in parting, and he went to work on synthesising the cure at once.

With her detector and map in hand, Tory accompanied Turan to his workstation in the Dur-nu-ga, where her chariot awaited. 'Let Taliesin know what has happened. Tell him I shall meet him as planned . . . with the chariot I shall be able to cheat time.'

'You may rely on it, Nin.' Turan pressed the button that granted entry to his lab.

'Well, partner, I guess this is goodbye.' Tory looked to him after taking her position behind the controls. 'How do I say thank you for all you've done?'

You can't, he shrugged, seemingly indifferent to the emotion of the moment.

Tory forced a grin. His etheric state made this goodbye much easier than expected. 'I know you don't remember anything that passed between us when you were in a physical form, but I just want you to know that I shall not forget any of it.' She blew him a kiss, and then smiled, turning her thoughts to her twentieth century home.

Turan did not lower his emotionless facade until he'd witnessed her gone. *Nor shall I . . . ever.*

PART THREE

AND
EVERYTHING

23

AN ECHO IN TIME

The last time Tory saw her true kin was at Dinas Emrys, near Beddgelert in Gwynedd. Here they'd uncovered the lost cave of Myrddin, where the Chariot of Arianrod and the other twelve treasures of Britain had been hidden for eons. Her family had made the trip from their home in Oxfordshire to see Tory and the chariot depart safely to the Dark Age. Though Tory had pledged she would return to the twentieth century, the time–space continuum permitting, it had been plain that none, bar her father, truly believed she would make it back.

This ought to blow their minds, Tory mused, as she traipsed through the forest at the base of the mountain.

She'd decided against manifesting inside the Merlin's cave, fearing an encounter with herself not yet departed.

But I didn't run into myself back then . . . therefore, I would not run into myself now, she reasoned, shivering from the chill of the breeze. 'I do wish I'd thought of that before.'

But the truth was that she wasn't really thinking straight, period. Time travel always wiped her out to some degree, much as an extreme case of jet lag would. Yet, by the same token, it was exhilarating to have made it home to her roots. She could hardly wait to see the look on everyone's faces when they saw her dressed as she was.

As Tory approached the clearing where one passed through an opening in the rock face into the Merlin's cave, she took cover in the bushes to view a disturbance beyond.

'But I half-suspected you were coming with me . . . what about your vow to Taliesin?' she heard herself say.

Professor Renford, or Myrddin as he was known by those of closer acquaintance, wrapped his arm around her shoulder as they strolled towards the mountain. 'Oh good heavens, no . . .' he exclaimed as they disappeared into the earthen mound, followed closely by Teo, Miles and Aunt Rose. Her brother, Brian, and his fiancee, Naomi, were the last to enter.

This is interesting. Tory sank slowly to take a seat on an upturned tree, feeling *suddenly rather faint. To think, all that time ago, I was here in the bushes waiting for myself to depart.*

A deep breath helped to relieve the anxiety that had welled within her and Tory took comfort in the knowledge that at least she knew she'd made it to the right place.

What are they doing in there? Tory paced, rubbing her arms briskly to dispel *the cold. I don't recall it taking this long to say goodbye.*

Brian and Miles had their eyes to the ground as they emerged from the cave and into the daylight. They were accompanied by Teo. Tory came to a standstill as her heart leapt into her throat upon sighting them.

'No way . . .!' Teo exclaimed, thumping his two companions on the shoulder. Brian and Miles looked up to find Tory smiling at them.

'Did you miss me?' She broke into laughter at the mystified expression on their faces.

Brian and Teo rushed to greet her at once. Miles appeared too stunned to move.

'Jesus! Tory, is that really you?' Brian looked highly amused by her clothing and hairstyle.

'It really is.'

'Your eyes . . .' He passed both hands over her brow, brushing the beaded braids aside to view her pupils clearly. 'They've changed colour!'

'Cool, hey.' She shrugged off the phenomena, and hugged both Brian and Teo at once. 'I missed you all so much.'

Teo took a step backward, cocking an eye. 'You don't really expect us to believe you went anywhere.'

He hadn't recalled most of what had occurred during Tory's last visit to the twentieth century, as Mahaud had gained conscious control of him before Tory even arrived. Tory and Brian had attempted to fill in the blanks in Teo's memory, once he had been freed from the crone's hold. However, most of their story had sounded way too absurd for him to readily believe.

'Excuse me.' Tory found his lack of faith disturbing. 'But I've been working on this body for twenty years! Don't tell me it doesn't show.'

Teo raised his eyebrows as he examined her, and was rather puzzled to note that her build had developed somewhat.

'Twenty years!' Brian burst into a grin, knowing she spoke the truth. 'So Rhun must be . . .'

'Twenty-one years old.' Tory confirmed.

Brian gripped his head in his hands as he slowly shook it. 'That's completely mad.'

'I told you she'd be right back.' Myrddin stole his daughter's attention with a chuckle.

'Father!' She launched herself into his arms. 'I'm so glad to see you're still here.' Tory squeezed him tight.

'Well, I wasn't planing on going anywhere.'

Tory pulled away to grip both his arms, near to bursting with excitement. 'I have been to Atlantis! I met our grandmother . . . your mother, when you were still in her womb.'

'It's a small cosmos.' Her father smiled.

'What are you talking about?' Brian burst into the middle of their conversation. 'That's impossible! Isn't it?'

He was suddenly unsure — having kept Tory's company these last two years, impossible seemed rather a redundant word.

'Nin Bau was her name.' Tory placed an arm around Brian's shoulders. 'High Priestess of Chailidocean . . . which is now better known as the City of the Golden Gates.'

'Plato's City of the Golden Gates?' Miles suddenly got a grip on the conversation.

'None other.' Tory looked to him. 'After all that's come to pass, Professor, you're not still a sceptic, I hope.'

His grin grew larger, half because he was overjoyed she'd come back to him and half because it was his nature to be sceptical. 'But I was under the impression that Myrddin was born in Carmarthen in the fifth century.'

'He was,' Tory grinned, 'because Nin Bau fled Chailidocean for the fifth century to save a run in with Mahaud. The witch intended to destroy the High Priestess' babe before he was even born, thus wiping me from existence in the bargain.'

'And me.' Brian was suddenly very alarmed. 'I thought we destroyed Mahaud.'

'She was one step ahead of us, I'm afraid. Before she followed me here to the future, she left the means by which to summon her back in the sixth century. She tricked Ossa, warlord of the Saxons, into freeing her. I have been fending her off ever since.'

'She's not coming back is she?' Naomi had a look of horror on her face as she moved closer to Brian. 'I couldn't go through that again.'

'Be calm,' Tory advised before anyone got too excited. 'I didn't even realise I was coming here until the last minute, so I doubt very much that she will find me here.'

Suddenly everyone had a million questions, but her aunt spared Tory an inquisition.

'Back off you lot,' Rose insisted. 'The poor girl must be exhausted . . . and cold.' She ripped the jacket from Brian's body to place it around her niece.

'How did you get back here? The chariot . . .' Myrddin guessed.

'Aye. I need your help, in both an advisory and financial capacity,' Tory beseeched her father with a look of desperation on her face.

'Fear not, child, I shall assist in any way I can. But first things first. Let us get the chariot returned to the safety of the cave and get you home, then we can talk.'

Miles accompanied Tory and Myrddin to retrieve the Atlantean transport from the bushes where Tory had hidden it.

When Myrddin disappeared to place the treasure alongside his others, Miles was rather gratified to find himself alone with his mysterious friend. 'I had hoped that this time you'd be staying for good.'

In the turmoil of the past few days, Tory hadn't really had time to consider how Miles might feel about her premature return. 'I wish it was as you expected, Miles, but . . .' An apology seemed rather inadequate after all she'd dragged him through. 'Believe it or not, I've discovered that there actually are some things beyond my control.'

Those large violet eyes of hers were completely captivating, and Miles felt himself more besotted than ever before. 'Are you still married to me, back there?'

She nodded. 'Twenty years now.'

He drew in a deep breath as he backed up a few paces, looking anywhere but at her. 'Goddamn it, Tory.' Miles paced to compose himself. 'What about us? When does our time begin?' He folded his arms across his chest, indignant.

Her expression turned sombre, as did her mood. 'He's dying, Miles.'

'Well, it's about bloody time.'

'How can you say that, when he is you?'

'Well, you don't regard me as such, so why the hell should I?'

Their eyes met, and the sudden animosity they felt towards each other forced them both to turn away in silence.

He's right, Tory resolved, brooding on his argument a moment. She suddenly turned and gave him a long, steamy kiss.

This took Miles totally off guard, for it was the first time in their year-long relationship that Tory had ever wooed him.

When their lips parted, Tory's eyes were still lulled closed; he even kissed as Maelgwn did. 'I have learnt a great many lessons in the past few years.' She smiled wholeheartedly, her eyes parting wide. 'I take life as it comes these days . . . no more procrastinating, I promise.'

'I suppose I could learn to live with that,' Miles decided with a smile.

'Are you still here?' Myrddin wandered out of the bushes and down the moist earthen track towards them. 'I have something for you.' He tossed his daughter a large, cut diamond. 'That ought to get you whatever you need.'

'I can't accept this.' She scrutinised the jewel in her hand, in awe of its beauty and size. 'It must be worth a fortune!'

Myrddin waved it off, continuing on his way. 'I have a hundred more just like it . . . they prove a good currency in practically any age.'

Tory sighed as she watched her father disappear down the forest trail ahead of them. 'You've just got to love my family.'

'Yes,' Miles gave her a squeeze, 'you do.'

24

THE HUNT

Everyone was accommodated on Mon that night. Miles invited Tory's entire entourage to his cottage, where he and Aunt Rose cooked up a feast.

Over the lavish roast dinner, Tory told of the events that had led her back to this century ahead of schedule. Miles was seeming a little discomfited by her tale, thus she didn't mention that the cure intended for Maelgwn was in fact an immortality potion. 'So, I headed here to retrieve it, safe in the knowledge that I was already acquainted with someone in the know.' Tory's gaze came to rest on Miles, and she smiled sweetly.

The professor slouched forward on the table, supporting his head in both hands. He felt she was taking an awful lot for granted, expecting him to come to her aid, as she'd be gone again as soon as they'd found her potion. 'Tell me, what is this orichalchum you mentioned? And where is the device you're to find it with?'

'Orichalchum is a pinkish metal, which is rather like gold, only much, much stronger,' Myrddin replied, as his daughter went to fetch the device from a pouch strapped to her belt. 'In fact, it's probably stronger than any metal we know today . . . it would survive anything.'

Miles leant back in his chair, still feeling rather miffed. 'If that is the case, then how come we have yet to dig up any of this amazing metal?'

Myrddin grinned. 'Perhaps you're digging in the wrong places. You know as well as I, that the deeper depths of the Atlantic Ocean have yet to be explored.'

'Ask and thou shalt receive.' Tory placed a rolled-up map and a long, rounded device in front of Miles on the table. Made of a shiny metallic substance, the instrument was flattened so that it was easy to hold. 'Don't ask me how you set it . . . En Darius programmed it before I left.'

'How does one switch it on?' Miles asked; all he could see were seven tiny circles embossed in the top of the object on one side. There were no switches, no buttons, no inlet for a cord or batteries — nothing.

'It's psychokinetic.' Tory suppressed a smile, knowing how absurd Miles would think her answer. 'You just will it on.'

'Oh please!' Miles placed it back on the table; now she was surely playing him for sport.

'You of all people should believe me,' Tory stated, amused, remembering that in some distant incarnation Miles had been Turan. 'The chariot functions in the same way. Nearly everything of Atlantean origin is operated by the power of the mind.' *A technology you perfected!* she wanted to say, but refrained.

As the professor was still hesitant to believe her, Teo thought he'd draw a little of Tory's attention his way. 'I'll give it a try.' He took the detector in hand. 'What do I have to do?'

'Just place it in your palm . . . so.' She positioned it correctly. 'And will away.'

On!

The seven tiny circles, arranged in an arc across the face of the instrument, flashed with one colour of the spectrum before settling so that only the first of the tiny light indicators shone red.

'Alright!' Teo was amazed by his feat.

'There you go!' Tory gave him a nudge, impressed. 'The closer you are to the substance you seek, the more colours in the spectrum that light up. When the last of the seven, purple, lights up, bingo! You're right on top of it.' She reclaimed the detector from him and switched it off before offering it to Miles, who waved it away.

'Tory . . . you do realise the mountain ranges you're talking about have probably changed dramatically in the last fourteen thousand years.' Miles spread her map out on the table before him, a frown of frustration on his face. But he soon changed his tune when he saw how intricate in detail it was. 'Maybe not . . .' He held up a finger as he paused to think, then made haste into his study.

At the invitation of a fellow archaeologist, who was testing the latest in deep salvage and surveying equipment for the Institute of Oceanography, Miles had visited the island of Faial in the Azores just a little over a year ago. The scientific researchers had discovered an old Spanish galleon, in the waters near the islands, completely intact. This had proven alluring enough to coax Miles out to the remote location in the Atlantic, a journey that turned out to have more legs than a centipede.

Miles returned unfolding a current map of the Azores to use as a reference. Aunt Rose and Naomi cleared the dinner dishes out of the way so that he could spread the charts alongside each other. The rest of the family gathered around.

'Alright, then.' Miles checked one against the other, mumbling calculations to himself. 'The way I see it . . .' he looked to Tory, 'the place you seek is above sea level . . . about one hundred and eighty metres above, actually.' He grinned, marking the spot on his map. 'Here, on the Isle of Pico.'

Tory planted a huge kiss on his cheek. 'Miles, you're a godsend.'

'If you say so.' He played down her adulation, looking back to the priceless information that had just been thrown in his lap. If this map was for real, he might well have the means to locate Plato's illusive city. Though he noted it was, at present, sitting at a depth of around three thousand metres somewhere off the coast of Spain, in the north-eastern Atlantic Ocean.

'Pico, hey?' Tory perused the map. 'Then that's where I have to go.'

'We,' Miles added, more disposed towards investigating her claim.

Tory smiled, pleased to have him on board; his expertise would not go astray.

'You can count me in.' Teo stated, not prepared to miss out on the adventure, or to leave Tory alone with another man.

'Us too.' Brian included Naomi and himself in the equation, though Naomi regretfully declined.

'No.' She placed a hand on her belly, yet to show any trace of her pregnancy. 'Not the way I feel at present. But you go,' she urged him. 'I don't mind, truly.'

'Look, I really don't think it's necessary for all of us to go.' Miles felt he deserved a little time alone with the woman he loved.

'Then you stay.' Teo was rather belligerent.

Great. Miles rolled his eyes. *I've just got through fending off her brother, and now I have to contend with the ex-boyfriend.* 'I know the area, and have contacts on the islands should we need any heavy equipment.'

'Actually Miles . . .' Tory intervened before it erupted into a full-blown argument. 'There is a chance Teo might be useful. Back in Atlantis he was the ruler in those parts.'

'No shit.' Teo was intrigued to learn. 'You met me back there?'

'Yes. You and Brian were brothers, the youngest set of sons of the Shu Sar.'

'Hey, bro!' Brian held out the palm of his hand, which Teo slapped in accord.

'Oh Tory, please!' Miles cringed. 'Not the Neptune myth . . . are you going to tell me that he really did have five sets of twin sons? You read too many fables.'

'His Atlantean name was Absalom, and he did have five sets of twin sons to five different wives.' There was a good deal of conviction behind her statement.

'You, my friend, being the second-born of the Shu Sar's first wife, Melcah.'

'Me!' Miles gave half a laugh. 'And where did I rule?'

'In the science lab.' She gained the professor's fullest consideration with her retort. 'You were head of the technologists at the Dur-na-ga Temple, in Chailidocean.'

It all sounded too wonderful, and Miles went to laugh it off.

'It was you who created this.' Tory waved the tracking device at him with a hint of irony in her tone. 'And the chariot!' *Bugger. She bit her tongue. I had no intention of going into this.*

'Tory . . .' Miles didn't know how to say it, 'I just can't comprehend all of this right now.'

'What's so hard to believe?' Teo challenged. 'Brian and I would be great rulers . . . Brian's already been a king!'

'That's right.' Brian seconded his friend's reasoning with zeal.

'Look.' Miles sucked in his cheeks to keep the condescending grin from his face. 'It's been a long day . . .'

'Quite right.' Myrddin helped the professor out. 'We can discuss the finer details of this expedition tomorrow.'

As the cottage was not equipped to accommodate so many, and Myrddin was already staying with Miles and Tory, Teo was finally persuaded to go with Naomi, Brian, and Aunt Rose to Naomi's father's house to sleep the night.

'Ah . . . alone at last.' Myrddin sighed, as he watched the car pull out of the driveway, looking to Miles and Tory with a grin. 'I'll see you both on the morrow then.' He turned and moved towards the back wall of the house and disappeared straight through it.

'I do adore that man.' Miles relaxed into a better mood, reaching out to draw Tory closer.

She couldn't help but grin at the prospect of spending the night alone with him, yet she shied from his advances. 'Miles, I know to you it was only this morning when last we met . . . but for me, it's been twenty years.'

'That didn't seem to bother you this afternoon.' He pursued her through the lounge room.

'Nor does it now really . . .' She was amused by his siren mood, as he swung her around and drew her body to his own. 'I just need a little time to adjust.'

'How much time?'

'Enough time to take a bath,' she proposed. 'Believe me, I have been to hell and back in the last forty-eight hours . . . it would be for the best.'

He smiled broadly at this, allowing her to slip from his grasp. 'If you need any help . . .'

'I'll let you know.' She withdrew graciously.

285

'Are you alright in there?' Miles inquired through the closed door.

Tory lay motionless in the steamy water, her head rested over the end of the large tub as her eyelids drooped. 'Oh . . . I can handle it.'

'I thought you must have drowned.' He turned and slouched against the doorway, in the hope of luring her out.

'I can't drown, Miles, I'm immortal.'

'So you are, silly me.' He raised his brows, pondering what to say next. 'Tell me something . . . did you think about me much in the last twenty years? Me meaning *me*, that is, not Maelgwn or the son of Neptune.'

'I did.' Tory raised herself from her watery haven and wrapped herself in a towel. 'Can I borrow this robe on the back of the door?'

'Be my guest,' Miles offered, happy to have succeeded in his purpose. 'Was I remembered fondly then?'

'Of course you were. So much so, in fact, that when I arrived in Atlantis the priests at the healing temple told me that I'd made myself sick pining over the issue.'

Miles was flattered. 'So, what did they advise?'

'They said . . .' She opened the door to lean opposite him in the doorway, lit only by the soft light from the candles burning in the bathroom, 'that in such situations, I'd do better to follow my instinct.'

'Excellent diagnosis.' He leant forward and lightly skimmed his mouth over hers.

Tory was aroused by the gentle caress, and seduced him into a kiss altogether deeper. She took hold of his hands, guiding them inside the robe she wore.

Miles revelled in the discovery of each perfectly rounded contour that met with his touch. The seed of his own desire was stirring in him now; thus his timid delving became more amorous and Tory's bathrobe fell open to expose her fully naked form. 'Oh, my . . .' Miles' voice went hoarse with longing. His sporadic breathing matched the panting motion of her chest. He reached down to trail his fingers over the subtle ridges of her stomach, across her hip, and down her taut thigh. He felt the firm muscles of her upper legs tense as his hand moved between them, and thus refrained from advancing further.

'Sorry . . . force of habit.' Tory reassured him with a kiss, parting her legs to grant him passage.

As his fingers resumed their ascent to meet with the warm moistness he'd induced, a soft sigh of yearning escaped her lips and Miles thought he would burst from the happiness he felt.

Her back arched to favour his kisses moving downward through her cleavage and towards her navel. 'I was wrong to have denied you this so long.' Her fingers began to massage his long dark head of hair, encouraging his descending lips.

Miles sank to his knees, stripping the shirt from his body and casting it aside. He drew her naked body against him, as he raised his deep brown eyes to vow: 'It will be my distinct pleasure to prove you right about that.'

In the wee hours of the morning, the fridge was raided and a bottle of red wine opened. Miles stoked the fire to its former raging glory, then sat back to quietly admire the object of his adoration.

She was wrapped up in his feather-down quilt, partaking of the fruity red as she gazed into the open flames.

'You look so lovely in this light,' he felt compelled to state, and was surprised when she appeared startled by the comment.

'Deja vu,' she clarified, wide-eyed.

'I've told you that before?'

'Twice.' Half her mouth curved in a wry smile as Turan came to mind. But the sweet memory was quickly swept aside as the last glimpse she'd had of her ailing husband filled her with sorrow.

'And I'll say it again, no doubt.' Miles dragged himself nearer to her, detecting the sudden swing in her mood. 'You look lovely in any light.'

Though Tory smiled in acceptance of his compliment, anguish consumed her. 'How soon can we leave for Pico?' She topped up her glass and took a long sip, in the hope of dulling the stress.

'I won't know until I make some phone calls. But I promise . . .' he hastened to add, already aware of her mind, 'I shall get us there as fast as I possibly can.' He smiled as he recalled all the trouble he'd had with connecting flights and boat services on his last visit to the Azores; with any luck, he thought, it could take them near a week to reach their said destination.

'Money is no object,' she emphasised, as he came and entwined his body around hers.

'I realise that, I did see the size of that rock your father gave you.'

Miles drew her face around to taste the red wine on her lips, when Tory was suddenly struck by a thought. 'Wait a minute!' She sprang to her feet, still clutching the quilt to her person. 'Do you have a picture of the isle of Pico?'

Miles was a little browned-off by her preoccupation with her quest. 'Well, I took some shots of it from Faial, which is about seven kilometres away.'

'Perfect.' Tory smiled sweetly. With a notable lack of enthusiasm, Miles rose to go look for the photos. 'Would you mind if I raided your wardrobe?'

'Be my guest.' He motioned towards the bedroom, not even wanting to know what she had in mind.

Tory rolled up Miles' jeans, which were way too long for her, and a bit large around the waist. She pulled them in to fit with the aid of a belt. The back pocket housed the detector rather nicely, and it was hidden from view by the jumper that she tied around her waist. She found a shirt that was pretty close to her size, but there was no chance on earth that any of his shoes were going to fit; bare feet would have to suffice for now.

She sat closely scrutinising one of the several photographs of the island Miles had dug out for her, whilst he watched in silence from the lounge opposite.

Why do this now? He gave a heavy sigh at the thought. *It's five o'clock in the morning. What could she possibly hope to accomplish at this hour?*

Tory closed her eyes, raising the picture to her brow, and within moments her physical form had faded from the room. 'Tory?' Miles stood to take a look around. 'Tory!' he called louder, running to check the other rooms in the house.

'Goddamn it, don't do this to me!'

'Do what?'

Her voice sent the professor rocketing back into the lounge room, where he found her returned. 'How did you do that? Where did you go?' He took hold of her, both amazed and angered by what she'd done.

'I went to Faial, the fastest possible way.' She grinned. 'Here, get dressed.' She threw the rest of his clothes at him, and waited whilst he got them on. 'Have you got your wallet?'

'Well . . . yes.' He pulled it from the pocket of his jacket. 'But I don't understand . . .'

She held a finger to his lips. 'A picture is worth a thousand words.' Tory took up both his hands.

'Oh no.' Miles went to back up.

'Shh.' She whispered. 'Just close your eyes and relax.'

Tory made her proposal sound so inviting that Miles decided to co-operate. But as he stood there, eyes closed in blind faith, he was having trouble taking to the suggestion of physical teleportation. *We are not going anywhere.* He resigned himself to the fact. Yet when he opened his eyes to tell Tory this, he found he was seriously mistaken.

The room was a blur of bright blue-white light, which gave the appearance of viewing it in the negative. *Sweet Jesus, Tory.* He squeezed his eyelids closed once more and tightened his hold on her.

Teo and Brian arrived at the cottage bright and early the next morning, keen to finalise the details of their trip. But when Myrddin informed them that Tory and Miles had already departed, the pair were ropeable.

'Well, let's go,' Teo urged, halfway to the door. 'Maybe we can catch them up at the airport.'

'That's not the way they went,' Myrddin announced, stopping both men in their tracks.

'What do you mean?' Brian cocked an eye, sporting a ferocious look as he approached his father.

'These photos are what gave their passage away.' Myrddin held the blank side of one up to view, which had the words *Pico Alto from Faial* scribbled on the back.

'So?' Teo grabbed the picture from the Merlin to take a look at their destination.

Myrddin raised his eyebrows to put forward his theory. 'I believe the extent of Tory's learning in the last twenty years goes way beyond how to wield a sword and ride a horse. For, according to my sources, she is already on the island from whence this photograph was taken.'

'What!' both his mystified listeners exclaimed at once.

'But that's impossible!' Brian sank into the lounge beside his father.

'Oh, do stop saying that,' Myrddin insisted. 'If one has mastered physical teleportation, it is very possible. I'll grant it is difficult if one has never been to one's desired destination, and has no idea of what it looks like.'

Brian grabbed the photos off the table, and noticed as he flicked through that they all featured the same place. 'So you think Tory used these to form an accurate picture?'

'It would seem so, yes.' Myrddin looked rather concerned. 'She was gone before I returned this morning.'

'Returned from where?' Teo demanded, outraged by the statement. 'You left her alone with him?'

'I needed to consult with the spirits about Tory's quest,' Myrddin advised calmly, as Teo had begun to pace.

'And what did they predict?' Brian chose to ignore his friend's tormented state.

'Much confusion and treachery.'

'It's Miles.' Teo ceased his striding around. 'I never did trust that guy.'

'Even though he helped save your life?' Myrddin raised his steely green eyes to the lad.

'Only at Tory's bidding,' Teo defended.

'I don't think Miles would ever consciously betray her.' Brian shook his head.

'Oh yeah,' Teo challenged. 'Sure about that, are you?'

Brian frowned and pondered; Miles had lied to her before. 'I would feel a whole lot surer if I were there.'

'I can arrange that,' Myrddin advised. 'But, as guardian of Britain, my place is here in the mother country, so once I get you to Faial you'll be on your own.'

'Fine with me. Where's that map.' Teo spotted it still spread out on the dining room table and folded it so it would fit neatly in his back pocket. 'Let's go.'

'I did take some pictures of the main port here in Faial. You could have asked me for one of those and saved us the hike,' Miles grumbled. He felt cheated as they'd nearly reached the Isle of Pico already, and at this rate their time together would be over by tomorrow night.

'Oh, stop complaining. It's good exercise and the scenery is magnificent.' She paused in her stride down the side of the road and drew a deep breath.

The sun had begun to rise over the ocean, igniting the colours of the fertile valley that descended from a large volcanic crater to a town by the seaside. It was little wonder Faial was sometimes referred to as the Blue Island, for an abundant amount of hydrangeas grew wild here and blanketed the slopes in places.

'I've seen it all before, remember.' Miles motioned around him . . . 'This valley is known as Falmengos. It peaks at the Caldeira Crater and runs down towards the town of Horta.' He pointed to the seaside port off in the distance. 'We should be able to catch a boat to Pico from there.'

Tory hadn't had a chance to view the ominous volcanic cone of Pico Alto as yet. For when they'd arrived at the spot near the top of the Caldeira Crater where Miles had taken most of the photos from, the sun had yet to rise, and the mount they now descended blocked their view of Pico off to the south-east.

They soon reached the upper town, where they came to an old church and a cemetery.

'There it is,' Miles announced, looking to the large triangular peak that was Pico Alto rising out of the sea.

But Tory's eyes had already been drawn to the magnificent mountain, shrouded in mist. 'It's beautiful,' she gasped, in awe of it.

Miles scoffed at this comment, continuing down the road towards Horta. 'Let's see if you still think so once you've climbed it.'

Although it was early morning when Tory and Miles arrived, Horta was already a hive of activity. For this was the finest harbour the islands of the Azores had to offer, protected by headlands to the north and south and a breakwater seven hundred and fifty metres long. This had been a major port of call between Europe, America and the Orient for as long as ships had been making such journeys; this explained why the place was so alluring to salvors and archaeologists. Horta was also a big fishing community and many trawlers were already returning with their early catch. Once famous for sperm whale fishing, which Tory was pleased to learn had been banned in recent times, the waters here gave host to rising numbers of the gentle giants; thus, Horta was home for many a marine biologist as well.

The town itself had a gay atmosphere about it; although Horta had no buildings of notable grandeur, the houses were brightly coloured and had large balconies where many in residence were taking breakfast.

'I'm starving,' Miles decided, as the smell of food wafted through the air. 'Before we do anything else, please let me buy us something to eat.'

'Fair enough.' Tory shrugged.

'Miles Thurlow?'

At the sound of his name, Miles and Tory did an about-face.

'Pearce!' Miles exclaimed, as he approached his colleague and shook his hand firmly. 'I was hoping I'd find you here.'

'Naturally. As long as I can manage to get my licence to explore these waters extended, here I shall stay,' he was pleased to explain. 'But what brings you back to this part of the world, Professor?'

'A friend of mine.' Miles turned to introduce Tory, who appeared rather taken with his friend. 'This is Tory Alexander . . . Tory, Doctor John Pearce, from the Institute of Oceanography.'

En Darius, she resolved on the quiet, coming forward to make his acquaintance. 'It's nice to meet you, Doctor Pearce.'

'John,' he insisted. 'And the pleasure is all mine. So, what's your field, Tory. Anything I can help with?' he inquired politely. Miles burst into a huge smile.

'Oh, it's more just an interest really . . . in Atlantis,' Tory put forward in all seriousness.

'Atlantis!' John repeated with a laugh. 'Well, I personally haven't found any evidence of that civilisation here, so I can't really help you I'm afraid.' He turned his attention back to Miles. 'I have, however, recovered something you might find interesting.' He opened up his folder and scribbled down some details, which he gave to Miles. 'If you get a moment, give me a call. I'd like to get your opinion.'

'I'll do that,' Miles assured his colleague.

'And, hey, good luck with your search.' The doctor gave half a laugh as he turned and headed dockside.

'Now I know where your cynicism stems from.' Tory folded her arms; she did hate being patronised.

'Well, you'll just have to be patient with us mere mortals,' Miles suggested, as he steered Tory towards a teahouse. 'We don't all have the wealth of your experience.'

Breakfast was being served on the upstairs balcony to make the most of the morning sunshine and the light sea breeze that blew in off the harbour. As everything seemed to move at a very leisurely pace here, Tory allowed herself to be charmed by the good cheer and hospitality of the local people.

The young woman waiting tables at the teahouse addressed Miles by name, as this was a favourite haunt for most of the island's visiting scholars and he'd frequented it often on his last visit.

'Muito prazer, Senhor Thurlow.'

The waitress smiled warmly, and for a split second Tory felt there was something altogether familiar about her. Though recognising people she'd never met was a common occurrence for Tory, in this instance, she was unable to place the face.

'Muito prazer, Donna,' Miles replied, and as he had a firm grasp of the local lingo, he ordered and translated for Tory. Whilst they waited for their meal, Miles took the liberty of teaching her some of the basic vocabulary. This she found a most enjoyable exercise. Tory had studied several languages in the past and did enjoy the challenge of a new one.

'Ask about the boat to Pico,' Tory urged, as the empty plates were being cleared from the table.

'Por favor, Donna . . .' Miles distracted her from her task. 'Informa me, pode indicar o caminho para Pico?'

Tory listened to the girl's detailed response, not following a word of it.

'Obrigado.' Miles thanked her as she departed to the kitchen.

'What did she say?'

'Well, she confirmed that there is a daily service to the island from here.' Miles sat back in his seat, finding it difficult to keep the smile from his face. 'Though unfortunately, it left about a half an hour ago.'

'Damn it.' Tory looked to the headlands, annoyed; they could have been halfway there by now.

Her sights drifted back to Miles and he was quick to flatten her unspoken accusation. 'I didn't know, I swear.'

Miles held a hand to his heart, but his confession was far too cheery for Tory's liking. 'You wouldn't lie to me, Miles?'

'Hardly.' His smile broadened. 'That would be a futile endeavour, wouldn't it?'

'Good morning all.' Brian pulled up a seat and sat down, obviously impressed to have stunned his sister for a change.

'No, I believe it's bom dia.' Teo played along, pulling up a chair and settling himself between Miles and Tory. 'Do go on . . . you were saying something about Miles lying to you?'

'No.' Miles' tone was rather cutting. 'We were saying that we'd just missed the boat to Pico.'

'I could have told you that.' Teo remained cheery. 'We've been waiting where it boards for the last twenty minutes, expecting you to show. But when you didn't . . .' He shrugged. 'We thought we'd better come find you.'

'Great.' Tory rolled her eyes, quietly thankful that her father had sent Teo and her brother to her aid; perhaps now she could stay on track.

As Donna approached to take an order from the new arrivals, Miles turned to Teo to ever-so-nicely enquire, 'Do you speak Portuguese?'

'No . . . but I'm beginning to wish I did. Bom dia, Senorita.' Teo sized up the local beauty with a smile, which Donna returned.

'Then allow me.' Miles gave Donna the order, and as he did she struggled to repress her amusement.

'I am sorry, Senhor Thurlow.' She was unable to keep up her front, and spoke in English for the benefit of the two young men for whom Miles was ordering. 'Flaming pig-balls are not on the menu.'

'What?' Teo became alarmed, but as all present were reduced to laughter, he smiled as he ordered. 'Just bacon, eggs, and juice, thanks.'

'Same again,' Brian added, turning to his sister, who'd once again begun to brood. 'So, as we've missed the one and only transport to Pico, what are we going to do for the rest of the day?'

As Donna departed, Tory voiced her mind. 'There must be a picture or a postcard around here somewhere that was taken on the face of Pico Alto?'

'Can't you just project yourself . . . I mean, it's only over there.' Brian waved a finger in the island's general direction.

'No, it doesn't work that way.' Tory sat back, disheartened by the query. 'I have to be able to visualise either the immediate landscape of my desired destination, or a person that I know will be there.'

'Tory. If you'd told us that before, Brian or I could have gone.' Teo shook his head.

'I know.' She realised her error. 'I'm sorry I left without you.'

Tory placed her hand on Teo's and Miles began to fume.

'What was I thinking, leaving without my team.' She reached out to take hold of her brother's hand also, furnishing him with a huge smile.

'Never mind. We're here now.' Teo patted her hand and rose, looking out to the harbour as he thought a moment. He looked back to Tory and Brian with a grin growing on his face. 'You know, I saw that stretch of water from the top of the town, and it couldn't be any more than seven kilometres wide . . . I reckon we could swim it easy.'

'Hey . . .' Tory's eyes lit up.

'Forget it!' Miles interjected. 'It may look like a peaceful stretch of water from here, but these islands are a major crossroads of currents and winds . . . you could end up anywhere from Africa to the Arctic Circle. Not to mention the marine life you'd have to contend with . . . try getting out of the way of a moving sperm whale.'

'Alright!' Tory frowned. 'Point taken. I'll have to go alone then.'

'No way.' All three of her male companions protested at once.

'Look, nothing can happen to me,' Tory insisted. Yet, recalling that the last time she'd thought thus, she'd wound up trapped in a time warp with a steel pin rammed through her brain, her decision altered dramatically. 'Okay, you're right . . . I'll be patient.'

'No more running off without us.' Teo made her promise, before Miles got the chance to.

'No more.' Her resolve was absolute, and she reclined to make herself comfortable where she was. 'If I missed the boat, it was meant to be. Perhaps this is the universe's way of telling me to go with the flow.'

25

CONFLICTING
INTERESTS

At the bottom of the four hundred metre crater looming over the town of Horta, was a lake bounded by lush green forest. When Brian was informed of this, he suggested taking a hike to the lake in preparation for the greater climb they had ahead of them tomorrow.

Teo and Tory were well disposed towards the idea, but Miles had already seen the sights and so declined. He said he'd arrange a couple of rooms at the hotel near the harbour whilst they were gone. As it was once the old fort of Santa Cruz, built in the sixteenth century, Miles assured them that the hotel would be easy to identify.

And so it was. With tired limbs and their lust for adventure satisfied, Teo, Brian and Tory trudged into the hotel. The reception desk had one room, with two single beds, reserved in Brian's name and Tory was given a separate key.

'That key wouldn't be to Professor Thurlow's room, now would it?' Teo inquired of Tory and the gentleman behind the desk.

'It is as Senhor Thurlow requested.' The man was polite.

'I see.' His raven eyes looked to Tory, who disappeared upstairs to avoid comment.

'This is not good.' Teo entered the room, too distracted to notice how charming it was. 'If Miles hurts her, he's a dead man.'

'Look, you promised,' Brian warned, not prepared to listen to his friend's jealous ravings for the duration of their trip. 'I've learnt better than to judge such situations, so take my advice and leave it alone.'

By the inflection in his tone, Teo knew exactly what Brian was thinking — but this time he was wrong. Teo had no delusions of winning Tory back; he'd accepted that she'd married another, and sincerely believed that he only wanted to protect her. 'I know you think I'm biased . . .'

'Think?' Brian scoffed, opening the shutters to check out the view. 'You are.'

'Okay, I am. But I still have a seriously bad feeling about the guy.'

As Brian found himself caught in the middle of this weird love triangle against his own better judgement, his predicament was awkward. 'There was a time when I had some pretty serious doubts about Miles myself. But I was proven wrong about him. So I'd proceed with caution, if I were you.'

How nonchalant Brian seemed about the whole situation. 'After what your father said, aren't you even mildly concerned that she's having an affair with . . .'

'An affair!' Brian gave half a laugh. 'Miles is the same guy she's married to, thus it could hardly be construed . . .'

'No! Not the same. Can you honestly say Miles has the same tendencies, the same line of reasoning, or the same interests Maelgwn does?' He put it to Brian, who fell silent. 'I think not. That's the mistake Tory's making. I have to talk to her.' Teo made for the corridor.

'Oi,' Brian cautioned. 'Go easy.'

Miles lingered in the shade of the palm trees that ran along the avenue by the sea. He'd spoken to his associate, Dr Pearce, and had arranged to meet him before dinner just across the road from where the project's offices were located.

He didn't much mind the wait, for it gave him a moment alone to just sit and think. The last time Miles had gazed out at the Atlantic from this shore, he'd entertained a very different viewpoint of life on earth. The events of the year that had passed since then were like a bizarre dream that he was not sure if he wanted to wake from or not. Tory wove an enchanting spell and it was hard to imagine what life would be like without a miracle a minute.

'Hope I haven't kept you waiting long.'

Miles was startled to find John standing beside him.

'Had a bit of engine trouble. You'd think with all this technology, we could at least get the damn boat to go.' He gave a laugh as the professor got to his feet. 'I must say I'm a bit disappointed — where's that exotic friend of yours?'

Miles smiled at the term, exotic, coming from a man who'd explored just about every place on earth that was humanly reachable. 'Tory's trekking the crater. She's rather keen on strenuous physical exercise, in case you didn't notice.'

'Lucky you,' John grinned, strolling off across the road.

'So. What have you dug up this time, Doctor?' Miles dared John to impress him.

'Actually, I was rather hoping you might tell me.' John swung open the door to his building, motioning Miles in after him.

'Now, do I have your strictest confidence on this?' John closed the office door behind them, looking to Miles for confirmation.

'I'm not even going to answer that.'

'Sorry, old man.' John rushed to his desk and began to search through the files strewn across it. 'You'll understand us wanting to keep this quiet, once you've seen it.'

'Seen what?'

'This.' John handed him a photograph taken soon after the find had been fished from the sea.

Miles began to laugh as he viewed the image. 'Let me guess. It's either an old helmet that's been at the bottom of the ocean for centuries, or it's an outstanding mass of sea fungus.'

'You know, we very nearly disregarded it as such.' The doctor took Miles' mocking with good cheer, and went over to punch a code into a wall panel. 'But, as you'll see, Professor . . . it polished up rather nicely.' The numerical sequence switched off the alarm and unlocked the door to the room where the find was being housed.

Miles' heart began to pound as he crept closer to the storage room. *Please don't let it be . . .* And there it was, encased in glass and surrounded by state-of-the-art security; a metallic ball, pinkish gold in colour.

'If you don't recognise the mineral, I'm not surprised, it's unknown.' John made a professional boast. 'We can only speculate as to its origin, but the inscription on top here, *Lamamu*, translates as 'divine master of love and war' in Sumerian, so that's a possibility. We're in the process of having it dated at present, so we should know more soon.'

Miles had to grin as he took Tory's line of reasoning for a change. 'The Atlantic Ocean seems an unusual place to be finding Sumerian artefacts, don't you think?'

John cocked an eye, seeming rather surprised. 'Your beautiful friend has had quite an influence on you, hasn't she?'

'Oh yes.' Miles certainly couldn't deny that. 'And it seems to me that this capsule is made of orichalchum, a metal fabled to have been prized in the Atlantean Empire because of its beauty, strength and durability.'

'Capsule you say?' John was curious to hear him refer to it thus. 'So you think it could contain . . .'

'Not as such . . . just a slip of the tongue, really.' Miles tried to erase the notion from his colleague's mind. 'What are you calling it?'

John gave a shrug, thinking the answer was obvious. 'Lamamu.'

'Tory?' Teo entered her room, finding most of her clothes discarded on the bed. The sound of running water was drowning out his call; he decided to enter anyway.

The bathroom door was ajar, and against his natural impulse he decided to avoid that area. Instead, he approached the bed, where the pouch containing the detector lay in clear view. Teo slipped the metal device from the pouch, holding it as Tory had shown him. *On.*

The seven colours of the spectrum flashed across the tiny light indicators. When the reading stabilised, five of the circles glowed the colour blue.

Jesus! We're real close, Teo observed, commanding the device off and putting it away as the sound of water was silenced. 'Tory?' he called out.

'Teo!' She sat bolt upright in the tub.

'Relax . . . I'm not seeking extra-marital favours or anything . . . I just need to have a word.'

'About Miles?' Tory submerged herself once more. 'No lectures, Teo, please!' She awaited his witty retort, but all was silent. 'Teo?'

'I wouldn't lecture you, Tory. I know I have no claim on you any more.'

He sounded rather exasperated and a little hurt as well; Tory could have hit herself for being so insensitive. 'Oh . . . don't say it like that.' She raised herself and reached for a towel, unable to continue the conversation through a wall.

'Sorry . . . but to me, it's only been a couple of years since we split up . . . most of which I don't remember.' He looked at her as she entered the room wearing Miles' shirt. 'I didn't end it because I didn't love you, Tory . . . the friendship was at risk. I was going to lose both you and Brian.'

'You did the right thing.' She came to sit beside him and took hold of his hand. 'You have to believe there is someone else you're meant to be with.'

The face of the sweet singer who'd had Jerram so enchanted at Zutar's court came to mind, and Tory suddenly recalled where she'd seen Donna before.

Teo didn't seem too sure about her suggestion; thus Tory took hold of his face in both her hands and stared deep into the black pools of his eyes. 'I know I'm right about this, my friend. I still love you. I miss times like today as much as you do . . . the three of us, off on some mad adventure. I wish it happened all the time, but . . . Brian's got a child on the way, and I'm here, there and everywhere trying to rearrange the universe.' Teo smiled at her joke, but Tory knew that underneath he was terrified of the idea of the three of them drifting apart. 'What I'm trying to say is this . . . you, me and Brian, we're a sometime thing, and I'll always be grateful for those sometimes. But you need to let go of the memory of us, so you can be free to find your all-time thing . . . do you understand?'

Teo only nodded in response, as the words wouldn't come, and he embraced her to endure the realisation that swept over him. 'It's just so hard to let go, to trust that it's all for the best.'

'I know it is.' She squeezed him tighter, a tear slipping from her eye in sympathy. 'But just remember — we are all of the same soul mind and can never be truly parted. Amidst time and space, we will invariably be drawn together, so there is always another adventure to look forward to.'

Teo pulled back to look in her eyes, brushing the long, braided strands from her face. 'I shall always be here for you, no matter what.'

'And I for you,' she vowed in return.

'I don't believe this.' Miles dropped his parcels in the doorway, turned abruptly and left.

'No, Miles, wait!' Tory chased him into the hallway.

'Just . . . save it,' he advised, making haste down the stairs, when suddenly he felt obliged to tell her what he knew. Miles paused from his sprint to contemplate this, but his anger compelled him not to. 'I want out of this equation. From now on, you're on your own.'

'But it's not what you think.' Tory's plea fell on deaf ears, as Miles gained speed and was gone.

Teo caught her up, and was as dumbfounded and bewildered as she by what had happened. 'I'm real sorry about this.'

'It's not your fault.' She waved his apology off. 'Unfortunately, jealous rages are the one thing Miles and Maelgwn do have in common.'

Tory picked up the parcels in the doorway and wandered back into the room, to discover that Miles had been shopping for her. In the bags she found new jeans, trekking boots, a waterproof, windproof jacket and a dress to wear to dinner. There was also a large bunch of flowers, complete with a very eloquent note.

'Oh damn it, Teo,' she sobbed, reading Miles' written words of devotion. 'Why do I keep hurting him? I don't mean to.'

'Hey, sunshine . . . don't cry.' Teo was almost too paranoid to hold her in case Miles walked in and got the wrong impression again. 'Why don't you get dressed for dinner, hey? Then we'll find Miles and sort out this mess.'

Teo could hardly believe what he was saying — an hour ago he'd wanted to thwart the relationship, and now here he was conspiring to save it. *Life really sucks, sometimes.*

The long, black halter-neck dress fitted Tory perfectly and lent itself well to bare feet.

The professor glimpsed her out of the corner of his eye as she made an appearance at the top of the stairs in the teahouse, looking every bit as splendid in his selection as he'd imagined she would. Spellbound by her presence, as were most who were dining in the restaurant, his heart sank as he spied Teo with her.

Donna led them to a table across the room from Miles, who was either completely ignoring them or oblivious to the fact that they'd entered. 'Maybe I should talk to him,' Tory suggested, before they were seated.

'No, no.' Teo sat her down, having hyped himself up for the task. 'Senorita.' He looked over to Donna, who was waiting to attend them. 'I'll have a double of the strongest spirit you have, por favor.' He left before another word could be said.

Tory didn't like the sound of this; be damned if Teo was going to drink himself into oblivion over her again. 'Cancel that order. He'll have a juice,' she corrected, as she watched him take a seat at Miles' table.

'And what would you like, Senorita Alexander?' Donna sensed the drama unfolding before her.

'A few less men in my life might be helpful.' Tory gave a heavy sigh, ahead of half a smile. 'Are you attached, perchance?' she enquired, noting Donna didn't wear a ring.

'That entirely depends on what's offering,' she grinned, turning her large, dark eyes to view the table where Teo and Miles sat conversing.

Teo returned before the drinks did. 'Off you go. All is forgiven.' He took a seat opposite Tory.

'What did you say to him?' She could barely believe the discussion hadn't ended in a punch-up.

'Never you mind.' He motioned her up as she seemed reluctant to leave him on his own. 'Go, go . . . I'll see you in the morning.'

'Thanks for this.' She moved to kiss him, but he reached out and shook her hand instead.

'Let's not push our luck.' He smiled, again motioning with his head for her to go.

He turned and watched her walk away from him, his heart growing heavier with every step she took. She waited for Miles to invite her to be seated and, with a kiss, she was reconciled with him. As he'd tortured himself enough, Teo looked back to the table where his elaborately decorated drink was being placed. 'Cheers.' He looked to Donna briefly, before whipping the straw from the glass and taking a long gulp.

'It would seem you're quite a matchmaker, senhor.' Donna noted how Tory and Miles were doting upon each other.

He appeared unimpressed with his achievement, as he raised his eyebrows to question: 'Is juice really the strongest thing you have?'

'The senorita changed your order,' Donna advised with an apologetic look.

'That figures,' he grumbled, reaching for the menu. 'Well, I'm changing it again, plus . . .'

'I'm sorry, senhor,' Donna interjected politely, as she removed her apron. 'The senora will take your order.' She motioned to a chubby woman, twice her age, who was across the room serving food. 'My shift should have finished an hour ago.'

'So what are you doing now?' Teo was quick to inquire before she'd had the chance to depart. 'Could I buy you dinner, perhaps?'

Donna smiled, slowly shaking her head. 'That's very kind of you, but . . . I've been in this place since daybreak.'

'I understand.' Teo sank back into his seat, accepting her refusal graciously. 'It would seem I am destined to dine alone tonight.'

'Well . . .' Donna stammered, to suggest with a shrug and a smile, 'I can cook.'

The evening's promise of being a rather sombre occasion was suddenly contested. 'What a coincidence, senorita. So can I.' Teo was straight to his feet, and at his charming best. 'Between the two of us, I'm sure we can create a connoisseur's delight.' He gestured for her to lead the way, his smile beaming with the sudden anticipation he felt.

'Don't tell me,' she playfully commented. 'You're great with dessert.'

'With dessert . . . as dessert,' he muttered under his breath, trailing her through the crowded restaurant and down the stairs.

Throughout the whole of dinner, Miles had been meaning to tell Tory that John Pearce had found her capsule, whereupon he expected she'd fly into action to retrieve it and vanish from his life. She might return, perhaps, in less time than it took to notice her missing, but how much would she have changed in her absence this time? How many more bizarre experiences would she have lived through?

Not yet ready to run the risk of her becoming lost in, or embittered by, time, Miles avoided the subject. Tory was so completely attentive — surely she would not be too furious if the information slipped his mind until morning. On second thought, he'd experienced her wrath if lied to. But, on the other hand, surely she would be so pleased that he'd found her treasure all would be forgiven? Then again, Tory had seemingly perfected many of her psychic talents since they'd last met; maybe she would perceive his deception before morning, which would certainly not reflect his true intention in a very good light.

Goddamn it, you'll just have to tell her. If she leaves, she leaves. Miles inwardly cursed this resolution as he unlocked the door to their room.

Tory entered ahead of him, switching on the lights only long enough to light the candles therein. 'I much prefer candlelight to any other.' She smiled, observing the room in the softer light.

As she approached him, sporting an ardent look, Miles' conscience won out. 'There's something I've got to tell you.'

The pending confession appeared to disturb him so much that Tory feared another argument was at hand. 'It can wait.' She drew his lips close to hers and took a long, loving taste.

'My, you do make things difficult at times.' Miles picked her up to lay her on the bed, yet wavered from his course halfway and placed her on her feet again. 'No, this can't wait.'

'Alright then, if you insist.' Tory thrust him back onto the bed. As he gazed up at her, stunned, she unfastened her dress and let it drop to the floor. 'Tell me, Professor . . . what's on your mind?'

God help me. Miles raised himself to welcome her naked body, as she strad-dled her legs to sit in his lap. I'll tell her first thing in the morning, I swear it.

As Miles hadn't closed his eyes in at least seventy-two hours, he proved rather impossible to wake. So, Tory left him a note and went to meet Brian at the reception desk.

'Where's Teo?' she wondered out loud, finding her brother alone.

'He didn't come back here last night. I presumed he was with you.' Brian was baffled to find he was mistaken. 'Where's Miles?'

Tory tried not to smile. 'He's exhausted, poor guy. I don't think he's slept for quite a few days. Oh, god . . .' Tory gripped her brother's hands, as her thoughts turned to Teo's mysterious absence and his woeful mood when last seen. 'You don't think Teo's done anything rash, do you?'

'Nah.' Brian tried to reassure her, not fully convinced himself. 'He's prob-ably waiting for us down at the boat.'

'Good call.' Tory gave him a slap on the shoulder, as they both bolted out of the hotel and down to the marina.

Ten minutes before their boat was due to depart, there was still no sign of him.

'I'll just have to delay this another day.' Tory resigned herself to the fact. 'I can't leave here without knowing he's alright.'

'No.' Brian put his foot down. 'You go. I'll stay and . . . wait a minute.' His eyes became fixed on the road leading down to the water. 'Here he comes. Ah-ha.'

Tory couldn't see the observation Brian had made at a glance. 'What?'

'I know that walk. That's Teo's "I just got laid" stride.'

'Really?' Tory was interested to learn this, and looked to Teo to note the added bounce in the way he moved.

'Sorry I'm late.' He bounded up the dock, doing a quick somersault and landing firmly on two feet before them. 'I didn't get much sleep.'

'It seems nobody did, except me.' Brian was rather miffed.

'I think I've found, what could possibly, eventually, turn out to be . . . an all-time thing.' Teo's cheeks flushed red as he burst into a huge smile. 'At least I hope so, anyway.'

'That's great news.' Tory went all teary-eyed suddenly. Now who was having trouble letting go? 'I'm sincerely happy for you.' She overwhelmed him with a hug.

'I'm sincerely happy for me, too . . .' He was surprised to realise how inwardly upset the announcement had made her. 'All this female attention, I can't cope.'

'That'll be the day.' Brian rolled his eyes and moved to board.

'Why don't you stay here, then?' Tory pulled away from Teo to suggest.

'No, I don't think so . . .'

'Brian and I can handle this,' she insisted, smiling. 'And as I've had to leave Miles asleep, he won't be half as annoyed to find I've gone without him if you've stayed behind too. Please?'

'Well . . .' He shrugged, a grin growing on his face. 'When you put it that way, it does seem to make sense.'

'It's settled then. We'll see you sometime tomorrow.' She moved to join Brian on board their transport, but Teo grabbed her arm.

'I am going to see you again, aren't I?'

'Cross my heart,' she motioned, and blew him a kiss in leaving.

Seated in the bow of the boat, Tory and Brian basked in the sunshine as they witnessed the stately green pyramid of Pico Alto growing nearer. A fresh breeze skimmed across the surface of the crystal clear water and kept the temperature down to a pleasant twenty-five degrees.

There was only one other person nearby and he sat, facing Tory and Brian, on one of the benches near the bow of the boat. This man radiated a lovely energy that was strong enough to inadvertently draw Tory's attention.

Of bronze complexion, as the local people were, he appeared much taller and leaner than most. The hat and sunglasses he was wearing, whilst reading a newspaper, made it difficult for Tory to get a good look at him.

She'd not been studying him long, when he looked up and held her gaze. Behind his dark glasses, his expression remained very cool.

Lamamu?

She heard the name so clearly, it made her jump.

'What?' Brian barked, annoyed that she'd startled him.

'Nothing . . . sorry,' she murmured, looking back to the man in question.

I told you we'd meet again. He smiled, lowering his glasses.

No. It couldn't be . . . Tory's eyes opened wide as his identity dawned on her. 'Thais?'

'Your memory serves you well, Nin.'

She rose, thrilled beyond reason to find a fellow immortal here in the twentieth century. 'But you've become . . .' she admired how fine he looked with two human legs, instead of four hooves, 'more compact since last we met.'

'And you, my dear Lamamu, have become even more beautiful.' He met her halfway, taking up her hand to kiss it.

'What's going on?' Brian was distrustful of this stranger showering affection on his sister. 'You know this guy?'

'Adelgar?' Thais laughed at seeing his old friend in the fair-skinned, blonde-haired, blue-eyed youth before him.

'Almost.' Tory was tickled by the observation. 'This is my brother, Brian.'

'Isn't life interesting,' Thais commented to Tory as he shook Brian's hand. 'I'm very pleased to make your acquaintance, Brian.'

'Thais, is it?' Brian queried, still not too sure how he felt about the tall foreigner.

'I go by the name of Thomas, or Tom, these days.' He spoke courteously, as they all seated themselves once more. 'So, what brings you back to my dominion, Lamamu?'

'Why do you . . .' Brian looked at Tom, then changed his mind and addressed Tory instead. 'Why does he keep calling you that?'

'Lamamu was the name the Atlantean's gave me. It means divine master of love and war.' Tory chuckled at how apt the name seemed when one considered all the romances and disputes she'd had a hand in of late.

Brian roused half a smile at this, his eyebrows poised high in disbelief. 'Are you saying, you two met in Atlantis?'

Tory and Thomas both nodded in the affirmative, at which point Brian seemed to go into a state of shock.

'To answer your question, Tom . . .' Tory regained control of the conversation. 'I've come in search of something En Darius and Shar Turan buried here for me.'

Thomas' eyes glazed over a second, and he smiled at a distant memory. 'Now there's a couple of names I haven't heard in a very long time.'

'You might be surprised to know that both the soul minds in question are presently on Faial.' Tory motioned back to the island from whence they'd come.

'So you've met Professor Thurlow and the illustrious Doctor Pearce?' Thomas was amused to hear this. 'I must say, I found both men more agreeable in the Age of Absalom.'

'That was an exceptional era for all mankind,' Tory conceded. 'So how do you know them, Thomas? And why are you headed for Pico?'

'I work for the IFAW . . . the International Fund for Animal Welfare,' he explained. 'I keep an eye on the wildlife here. I do feasibility studies, environmental impact reports, and so on.'

'Still!' Tory had to shake her head at his resilience. 'That's amazing.'

'But Doctor Pearce and I do not always see eye to eye on where the riches found through his salvaging should go: to scholars for scientific study, as he would have it, or sold to the antiquities markets and private collections, where the money can aid the Azorean economy and conservation work.'

'But then the treasure will be dispersed around the world, and the Azores shall lose it forever.' Tory could see the other side of the argument.

'Knowing the precise date of a jewel, where it came from and who made it, will not feed the people here or save the local wildlife.' He seemed rather passionate about his convictions. 'It's history.'

'I see your point,' Tory granted him.

Thomas turned and looked toward the misty mountain-top that lay ahead. 'I'm hiking up the crater to do a little whale watching . . . the heights of Pico Alto award a splendid view of the surrounding waters.'

'Was it you who got the harpooning banned?' Tory grinned, already knowing the answer.

'I had a small hand in it, yes. So tell me, Lamamu, do you plan to make the climb up Pico?'

'I believe that will be called for.' The thought became an increasingly daunting one, as the peak loomed higher with every minute that passed.

'Well . . .' Tom held out his palms and shrugged, as if it were a done deal, 'you are obliged to have a guide, and as you are already aware, I come highly recommended.'

'By whom, exactly?' Brian was most curious to learn. His sister and the stranger both looked his way.

'By yourself, in fact. Thais is the best scout on the island, you said . . . the smartest, too.' Tory and Thomas had a laugh at his expense, but she contained her amusement. 'So I thank you kindly for offering, Tom. We might just have to take you up on that.'

For the remainder of the crossing, Thomas graced his new travelling companions with a brief history of the islands. He told how the Azores had been devoid of human inhabitants since the great apocalypse, and had only been populated in the last four hundred years after being discovered by a Portuguese navigator. The first discoverers named the archipelago after the buzzards they saw soaring in the sky above the islands — Portuguese acores. However, the names of individual islands derived from a variety of sources. Santa Maria, Sao Miguel and Sao Jorge were named after saints. Terceira was so called because it was the third island to be discovered. Faial and Flores were named after their respective plant life, Corvo after its bird life and Graciosa and Pico from their ominous appearance.

Thomas spoke highly of their destination, claiming Pico was an island of bewitching charm. Its dark, lava landscapes, created by eruptions and covered in dense wood, were called Mysterios, or Mysteries. The island's haunting beauty was enhanced by the excellent local wine, a bottle of which Thomas would purchase to have with dinner. Once they'd reached the little rock-bound port of Madalena, they could catch a taxi for the first ten kilometres up the mountain — the rest of the hike was on foot. If they kept a good pace they could reach the summit, or thereabouts, by nightfall. There were mountain huts where one could spend the night, to save making the descent in the same day.

Miles rose in a fluster when he found Tory gone, and her note only served to intensify his panic. *She'll kill me. She's going to make that great hike for nothing! Shit!*

He raked on his clothes, of the mind to catch her up; perhaps Pearce could arrange passage across the strait.

Hold on . . . Miles pulled himself up. She doesn't know, I know what I know. If she returns empty-handed, she won't think it my fault. She will just assume the capsule has been lost over time.

This made him wonder what Tory planned to do in the event of never finding it? 'Don't even think it!' he scolded himself, but he couldn't block out the little voice in his head . . . *What if you didn't tell her? Maybe she'd find the capsule on her own . . . maybe she wouldn't.*

'I'm not listening.' Miles snapped himself out of his little daydream to get on with the task of finding her.

As he made haste across the Rua Conselheiro Medeiros, the main street of Horta, his inner voice persuaded him to stray from his course long enough to have a cup of coffee and think seriously about what he planned to do.

The next hour found Miles still seated in the sunshine of the teahouse balcony, mind-numbed from trying to reason with himself.

LA-MA-MU.

He'd written the name in large letters on a napkin, and pondered its meaning as he drank his third cup of coffee.

Divine master of love and war.

Did this refer to Tory? The ancients of Atlantis were obviously every bit as scientifically, technologically and spiritually advanced as the mystics claimed they were; had they, too, considered Tory to be a Goddess as the early Britons had?

I hardly revere her with the esteem a Goddess deserves. Miles was quite suddenly overawed by all the great feats he'd seen Tory accomplish; she truly was the essence of what gods and legends were made of. It seemed pure idiocy to doubt her when the enlightened all through the ages had seen fit to aid her, and hail her as divine.

But her touch kindled the marrow of life in his soul and making love to her was the closest the professor had ever come to a religious experience.

306

I should rather die than live without her. If there is a God, please don't let my hesitation cost me her love.

'What does it mean . . . Lamamu?' Teo startled Miles as he took a seat opposite him.

'Divine master of love and war.' Miles screwed up the napkin and tossed it on his empty breakfast plate.

Teo gave half a laugh at this. 'I assume you were thinking about Tory.'

'Why aren't you with her?'

Teo was confused to note that Miles sounded most annoyed. 'She didn't want you to go jumping to any more conclusions about us, so she asked that I stay behind.'

'Your coffee, senhor.' Donna placed the cup and saucer on the table before Teo, then gave him a short, but ardent kiss before going back to her duties.

'The service here is great, don't you think?'

'You don't waste any time, do you?' Miles couldn't help but be delighted by the development.

'For most of us, time is a precious commodity.' Teo shrugged. 'Why waste it on regrets.'

Miles pondered these words a moment, before rising. 'You know, you're absolutely right.'

'Well, I usually am,' Teo boasted, as he observed the professor, curious as to his mind.

'If I do something now, I may lose . . .' he murmured, not making any sense. 'But if I don't, I surely will.' Miles' expression turned grave as he hurried towards the stairs.

'Anything I can do?' Teo stood, alarmed by his strange behaviour. 'Miles?'

As the professor disappeared down the stairs, Teo rushed to the balcony and waited for him to exit out the front door.

'What's going on, Thurlow?' he demanded. Miles powered on, not even looking back.

Teo smelt a rat; perhaps he'd been right about Miles all along.

26

LOST AND FOUND ... OUT

While Thomas picked up supplies and equipment, Tory checked the detector to get a reading on how close they were to the canister. Four of the tiny light indicators shone yellow, so Tory figured they were on the right track.

As their taxi wound its way around the great mountain, the detector displayed five blue lights. By the time they reached the drop-off point, six of the lights were tending towards a shade of indigo.

Tory tried to appreciate the local fauna and flora that Thomas pointed out to her during their trek, but the thrill of the hunt was far too absorbing; she was so close and getting closer.

Her excitement drove her on, until all of the seven light indicators finally lit up with the colour purple.

'That's great,' Brian commented as he chanced a glance over the edge of the cliff before them, finding a sheer drop of about sixty metres.

'We must be right on top of it.' Tory became frustrated by her limitations. 'There must be an opening or a cave of some kind down there.' She strained to see, but the rock face jutted out to hinder her view.

'I'll investigate.' Thomas off-loaded the gear he was carrying and stripped off his hat, sunglasses, shirt and jacket. With his arms outstretched, he took a flying jump towards the edge of the great chasm.

'Thomas, no!' He near startled his two companions to death, but then a metamorphosis took place before their eyes.

His large muscular body transmuted into that of a fully grown hawk, his clothes falling to the ground in his wake. His arms became his wings, his legs became talons and tail and he took flight, soaring on the evening breeze.

'Jesus! That was amazing!' Brian couldn't believe his own eyes. 'Did you see that?'

'Yes, I saw it,' Tory confirmed with a smile of admiration, her eyes still

308

following the flight of her friend. 'It is known as shape-shifting. I have heard of such feats, but I have never before witnessed the practice.'

As the hawk flew in, alighting on the grassy outcrop beside them, his form began to expand, and Tory turned away to give Tom a chance to dress.

Brian, however, was far too intrigued to be so polite. He just stared in wonder as the man moved to retrieve his clothes.

'There is an opening, about three metres below us. I have gear that will get us down there.'

'Wow.' Brian's legs failed him, and he sank to a seat on the ground. 'Can you change into anything, or do you just do birds?'

'Anything that lives and breathes . . . and some objects.' Tom shrugged, as if it were commonplace, and fastened up his trousers. 'But nothing with mechanical moving parts, you understand.'

'Unbelievable!'

'Why so? Have you not seen your sister do the same?'

'You can do that?' Brian was shocked by the statement.

'Not with animals . . . as far as I'm aware, anyway.' She remained with her back to them.

Thomas gave a hearty laugh, turning Tory to face him. 'Still not very well informed, are you, little goddess? You have only to will it and the mental plane will comply . . . as is really true of most things. Mind you, in such states, one lives the reality of the animal form chosen, so I wouldn't go leaping off any cliffs until you've had a chance to test your wings.'

Tory contemplated the implications of what he'd said, as she moved to the edge to view the long drop down. 'Don't worry, I won't.'

As the power boat belonging to Dr Pearce sped them across the strait to Pico, Miles was feeling rather proud of himself. If Tory needed to complete this one last quest before they could settle down to a life of their own, so be it; he would do everything in his power to help her.

Yet, just as they'd reached the halfway mark of their voyage, the engine suddenly started to splutter, and smoke billowed out as it packed up and died.

'Jesus christ!' Pearce roared. 'Not again! I thought we'd fixed this?'

He looked to his skipper, who shrugged. 'I'm sorry, Doctor Pearce, but I'm going to have to wire Horta and get her towed back.'

'Back!' Miles protested, despairingly. 'But we need to go that way.' He motioned to Pico, so close and yet so far.

'I have no choice, Professor,' the skipper advised as delicately as he could, knowing the impromptu trip was a mercy errand of some kind. 'It's out of my hands.' He turned and took up the radio receiver to get Horta on the line.

Miles sank into his seat and, against his better judgement, was of half a mind to swim the rest of the way. He contemplated a moment what Tory would do in the same situation.

She would trust in the universe, he decided. If the boat has broken down, there is a reason. I must trust this is meant to be, for whatever unknown end.

Brian was the last to lower himself down to the mouth of the cave, and he was barely able to breathe for the exhilaration of executing the dangerous exercise.

'The things I do for you?' he grumbled, as his footing disappeared and Brian was forced to allow his legs to dangle, whilst his arms took his entire body weight as he clung to the rope with his hands.

'Aw . . . you love it.' Tory grabbed hold of his legs, and with help from Thomas guided Brian safely to the floor of the cavern.

As soon as he felt ground beneath his feet they ceased to tingle. 'It's alright for you two. You're both immortal.' He breathed through his fear until it passed.

'And you're not?' Thomas looked at him, rather amazed.

'Hardly.' Brian displayed the grazes on his hands that he'd sustained during his descent.

'It's not like you to make a mistake like that, Thomas.' Tory was intrigued. 'Don't you perceive information from a level of awareness beyond this earthly plane?'

'Yes.' Tom shrugged, unable to explain his misconception. 'My sincere apologies, Brian. If I'd realised this before, I certainly would've rigged you up to a proper harness.'

Brian forced a laugh, as the magnitude of the risk he'd just taken dawned on him. 'That's comforting, Thomas, thanks.'

'You're welcome.' Tom dug a torch from his pack and bounced the beam around the inside walls of the cavern, which were covered by hardened black lava.

'What's that?' Tory spied a sparkle in the darkness ahead, and moved to investigate.

The cave narrowed as they ventured deeper. They passed through a thin opening at the end, and entered what appeared to have once been an enclosed circular room. Part of the roof had caved in and lay in large chunks on the floor. Most of the chamber was lined with the dark lava coating, but the chunks of the domed ceiling on the ground divulged that the secret structure had once been entirely constructed of orichalchum.

'Looks like this place fell victim to an eruption, quite some time ago,' Thomas surmised, closely observing the solidified lava.

'But the capsule has to be here somewhere.' Tory searched frantically, praying to the Goddess it was not now encased under the hardened lava somewhere.

310

'Why is this mound here?' Brian circled the structure that rose out of the floor in the middle of the room.

Thomas had already considered this. 'It is my guess . . .' He squatted to chip away a piece of the congealed coating, to disclose the orichalchum underneath, 'that this was built to accommodate your capsule. But when the explosion blasted through the back wall, the capsule was most probably shot from its mount.' He cast his eyes towards the opening through which they'd entered.

'Shot where?' Tory urged, but he only shrugged.

'That would depend on the force of the blast . . . these islands have known eruptions that could fire such an object clear into the Atlantic.' Thomas looked to Tory, clearly not wanting to be the bearer of bad news. 'But if the metal walls could not withstand the explosion, the chances of finding the capsule still here and intact are minimal, I'm afraid.'

The news was devastating; Tory had to sit down. 'So what do I do now?' She raised her teary eyes to Thomas. 'This can't be the end, it can't be . . . I refuse to just let him die.'

This was a precarious situation; Thomas took a seat on the boulder beside Tory and placed an arm around her shoulder. 'Has it ever occurred to you, that maybe you're meant to let this man go?'

'No!' She stood and backed away from Tom, enraged by the suggestion. 'The divine mother herself helped to speed me on this quest. Do you think for a moment she would have done so, if he was not meant to live?'

He could feel Tory's pain, her confusion, yet Thomas could not bring himself to lie to her. 'Perhaps the quest was for your benefit, rather than . . .'

'Stop it!' she demanded. 'I've heard enough.' She approached Brian and took hold of his hand. 'I thank you kindly for your help and advice, Thomas, but I have to go now. Say goodbye, Brian.'

'See ya, Tom.' Brian complied, considering his sister's mood. 'It's been a real blast . . .' The pair faded from sight.

Thomas shook his head at being misunderstood, as he so often was these days. *Never listen, human beings.* He stood to make his leave. 'Still, I hope with all my heart that you prove me wrong, little goddess . . . though I believe that time shall prove me right.'

The sun set on the horizon in a blaze of colour.

Teo witnessed the spectacular vision from Donna's balcony, with a cool drink in his hand and his girl snuggled comfortably under his arm. In the stillness of the moment, Teo felt a sense of belonging and peace the like of which he'd never experienced before.

The identity of his parents was unknown to him; thus his ancestry had remained a mystery. A whole lifetime he'd spent wandering the earth in search of that instinctive feeling of origin, and though he'd only been on Faial a few days, this was the only place that had ever felt like home.

'Shall we go in?' Donna prompted, 'before the dinner is spoiled.'

'One moment longer.' He cuddled her, wanting to savour the extraordinary recognition he felt.

Although Donna could appreciate the beauty of the scene, she was starving. 'If you meant what you said last night,' she directed him to look her in the eye, 'you can watch the sunset from here, every night, for the rest of your life.'

'I meant it alright.' He smiled and reinforced his pledge with a kiss.

'Ah . . . hmm!' Tory cleared her throat to get their attention, startling the unsuspecting lovers out of their wits.

'Tory!' Teo swung round to find her and Brian.

'How . . .?' Donna drew in her brow as she tried to figure their sudden appearance.

'Sorry to intrude like this.' Tory spluttered out an apology. She hadn't realised, when she'd willed herself to Teo's location, that she would find herself in such an awkward predicament.

'Did you find it?' Teo wanted to know.

The question pained her. 'No. We found where it was once housed, but that place has long since been destroyed.'

'I'm so sorry.' He placed a hand on her shoulder, seeing how upset she was.

'What's going on?' Donna wasn't following a word of this. 'What is it you're looking for?'

'Hope.' Tory roused half a smile, before her features were again shadowed by grief. 'I suppose I should find Miles and tell him, though I don't believe he'll be too happy to hear that I intend to keep looking.'

'The good professor was behaving rather strangely when I saw him today,' Teo recalled. 'He was pondering some ancient word . . . something to do with the goddess of love and war.'

'The divine master of love and war?' Tory corrected, her spirits lifting.

'Yeah, that's it. La-ma-mu, I think it was.'

Please Goddess, don't let him know of this. Tory went ghostly white, as she looked to Brian to advise: 'I never told Miles my Atlantean name. So, how then, has he learnt of it?'

Brian was very perturbed, recalling his father's prophecy of confusion and treachery. 'There's something fishy going on here.'

'I'd second that hunch.' Teo's mood darkened, also recollecting the Merlin's caution. 'Have you still got the detector with you?'

'I do.' Tory pulled the device from her jacket pocket, and Teo took it from her.

'What colour did the lights indicate when you first set foot on Pico?'

he enquired. Donna observed the device over his shoulder, curious as to its purpose.

Tory thought this a rather peculiar query. 'Four of yellow, why?'

'That's interesting, isn't it?' Teo turned the device around to show his companions the current reading, that was five of blue.

'But, that would mean . . .' Tory's excitement mounted as she realised, 'we're closer to it here, on Faial.'

Teo winked at this, obviously rather impressed with himself. 'You got it, sister.'

Subsequent to an afternoon of hellish torment, Miles made it back to Horta just after sundown and joined Dr Pearce in his office for a much needed cup of coffee.

'I'm sorry I wasn't able to be of more help.' John felt awful about what had happened. He'd never seen his colleague so despondent.

Miles accepted the steaming mug from his friend, attempting to make light of the way he felt. 'Hey, we tried, right?'

'Miles!'

When he heard his name echoing down the corridor, Miles knew at once who sought him. 'Tory!' He placed the mug aside and rose to open the door, yet it was flung open before he reached it.

'Surprise, surprise.' Brian strolled through the door ahead of his sister, who had her head down marking the light indicators change from indigo to purple as she entered the room.

'What is the meaning of this?' Dr Pearce demanded, as Brian closed the door and took a firm hold of him.

'I'd say it's behind this door.' Tory looked to John. 'Open it.'

'Tory, please.' Miles softly beseeched her, but Tory turned abruptly and gripped his throat.

'Don't say a word.' She stared him down into a seat, before turning her attention back to the man held captive by her brother. 'What is the code, John?' She held his face between her hands, glaring deep into his eyes, and even though the doctor was determined to remain tight-lipped, Tory smiled as she stepped away from him. 'Thank you for playing.' She confidently approached the panel and punched a code in.

This pleased Pearce, because if one punched in an incorrect sequence it would set off the alarm. The doctor was left somewhat bemused as the door unlocked and opened. 'Who are you people? Do you work for the government?'

'Guess again,' Brian suggested. 'Let's go.' He motioned Miles in after Tory, then followed with his hostage.

As Tory viewed the treasure, the adrenalin began to surge through her veins. 'How long has he known about this?' She directed the question at

John, quickly covering Miles' mouth with her hand to prevent him from responding.

'Why, I . . .' John looked to Miles for the right answer, but Brian tightened his grip and he resolved to tell the truth, 'told him only yesterday afternoon.'

Tory gasped in horror as she drew away from Miles. 'You weren't going to tell me, were you?' She held up her hand in warning; she would not tolerate any more of his lies. 'No, don't answer . . . it was a rhetorical question,' she was saddened to admit. She backed up to the capsule, turned and placed both her hands on it.

'So you're nothing but common thieves.' Dr Pearce exaggerated his observation in a mocking fashion. 'Well, the two of you will never move that thing. It weighs a tonne.' He laughed at their folly.

'There is nothing common about me, Doctor,' Tory advised, as she vanished from the room, the capsule along with her.

John froze in horror. 'Who in hell's name are you people?'

'Look, Brian.' Miles had to make him see. 'I tried to reach you today and let you know, but the boat broke down halfway there.'

'Tell it to the judge.' Brian's cool glare conveyed his indifferent view perfectly. 'She'll be back, presently.'

Tory materialised back at Donna's place with the capsule, where Teo was waiting to assist her to retrieve the antidote from the metal casing.

'I've been told a thing or two about you during your absence.' Donna gave a shy smile as she watched Tory, down on her knees, positioning the large metallic ball. 'And I don't think I would've believed a word of it, if I hadn't seen this for myself.'

While politely listening to Donna, Tory turned the detector upside down and placed it on top of the capsule. *Retrieve*, she commanded.

Two long, thin metal prongs ejected from the device, startling all present as they penetrated the metal case with a thud, and split it down the centre. Inside was another orichalchum ball, much smaller than the first. This had a latch, which she opened to find the tiny crystal container housing the cure she sought.

'Wow!' Donna was thrilled, as she'd been told that this was what Tory had been in search of. 'It makes you want to run off on some crazy adventure, doesn't it?'

'Hey,' Teo cautioned in jest. 'Don't tempt fate. Tory here is renowned for dragging anyone who's willing to the ends of the earth on such quests.'

'Any time,' Donna assured her.

'Ignore that comment.' Teo overruled Donna's enthusiasm. 'We're settling down to the quiet life.'

Tory smiled as she observed the adoration that passed between Teo and the new love of his life; she'd never thought she would see him observe anyone else in such a way, and it wounded her a little more than expected. 'So you've decided to stay?'

'Yes, indeed.' He hugged his girl closer.

'Well, I must say I'm not really surprised. These islands were once your dominion, and so will they be again.' Tory stood to kiss his cheek, then Donna's. 'I'm overjoyed for you both. In the eyes of the universe you are meant to be together.' She looked back to the severed metal ball on the floor before her. 'Here, give me a hand with this.' Teo assisted her to push the two halves back together, whilst Tory held the device above them. *Seal*, she instructed, and so it was done.

'Well, then.' Teo leant back on his haunches, looking from their completed task to Tory. 'This is goodbye, isn't it?'

'Let's just say . . . Ate logo.' Which in Portuguese means goodbye, but for a short time only.

'Ate logo,' he echoed, his voice wavering from the sadness he felt. He gripped hold of Tory and gave her one of his big bear hugs. 'Thank you, for everything. I never would have found this place if not for you.'

When he pulled away, Teo was teary-eyed and Tory was fast becoming rather melancholy herself. So she placed her hands on the heavy orichalchum ball to avoid a drawn-out goodbye. 'Best wishes to you both. I shall not forget all you've done.'

'Don't be a stranger now, you hear?' Teo reached out to brush his fingers against her cheek, but before he could make contact she had vanished. He searched the empty space that was left in her wake, his hands clenching into fists as he realised the adventure was over and their last moment together had come and gone.

'Don't be sad.' Donna knelt beside him, gently smoothing the frown from his face. 'Where one door closes, another always opens.'

Her smile was as contagious as it was uplifting, and Teo's fear of loss subsided to that warm cosy feeling of coming home. 'I do like the sound of that.' Teo guided her to a seat on his lap, and as their lips met he realised that the adventure was only just beginning.

Dr Pearce was slowly driving Brian insane with his questions, and no threat seemed to subdue his curiosity.

'Look, we're not CIA, FBI, British secret service, thieves of any calibre, terrorists, or extra-terrestrials! Okay,' Brian impressed on the doctor, gripping hold of his shirt as he backed him up across the room.

John looked to Miles, who seemed completely oblivious to what was going on. 'Professor? This might be a good time for you to intervene.'

Miles turned and looked at Pearce blankly, not even flinching from where he stood.

'Wonderful,' John protested, despite Brian's fist poised in front of his face. 'You're part of all this, I suppose? You'll be held responsible for the loss of that piece, and mark my words, there will be hell to pay for betraying a professional confidence . . . ah!'

Brian slammed the doctor straight between the eyes, and lowered him to the ground unconscious.

'Thank you.' Miles drew a deep breath, grateful for the peace.

'My pleasure.'

Brian knelt to check his victim's vital signs as Tory's presence became manifest, returning the orichalchum jewel to its place of display.

'Thank god you're back.' Miles moved to greet her, but Tory avoided him and made straight for Brian.

'Yes. I've returned your precious relic.'

'That's not what I meant.' The tone of Miles' voice entreated her to hear him out. He took hold of her arm. 'And it's not what I hold precious. If you'd just grant me five minutes grace to explain . . .'

'You had ample chance to explain yesterday.'

As she turned and glared at him there were daggers in her eyes, and Miles' hopes of redeeming himself dwindled dramatically. 'I tried tell you yesterday — twice in fact.'

'Oh, and you were so insistent, weren't you?' She pushed him away from her, sickened by how gullible she was. 'Damn you to hell for this, Miles.' Her emotions burst forth to flood her eyes. 'If the situation had been reversed, Maelgwn would never have done this to you . . . he would have done everything within his power to help me save you.'

'I am not Maelgwn!' Miles was fed up with having to live up to her expectations of him.

'No, you're not.' She backed up a few paces. 'Not by a long shot. I loved you, Miles, I really did . . . but if you think that I could ever trust you again, you're even more misled than I thought.' She reached out her hand to her brother, who took hold. 'Adieu, Professor. We shan't meet again.'

'That's where you're wrong,' he pledged. 'If I have to go to hell and back to explain myself, I fully intend to do so!' The level of his voice raised as he watched Tory and her brother fade away. 'Goddamn it, woman!'

He wanted to scream and wail in the aftermath of his stupidity, but what good would it do him — by now she would be back in Britain. *Think.* He persuaded himself against having an emotional meltdown, given his present circumstances.

With the capsule returned to its place of storage, it appeared as if nothing at all had taken place. So Miles closed the door to the storage room, poured his cold cup of coffee all over himself, and dragged John to the lounge in his office before reviving him.

'Pearce? Are you alright?' Miles slapped him about the cheeks.

'Ouch!' Pearce came to, urging the professor away as he held his throbbing head in both hands.

'That was quite a knock.' Miles offered him a glass of water.

But as Pearce raised himself to accept it, he was seized by panic. 'Are they still here!' He sat bolt upright, scanning the room for the intruders.

'Sorry, John?' Miles frowned. 'To whom do you refer?'

'That wild friend of yours, and that gladiator she brought with her.' Pearce raised himself quickly and made for the storage facility. 'They came to steal Lamamu . . . just disappeared into thin air with it. Well, you know. You were there!'

'I was?' Miles gave a harsh laugh. 'You did hit the cabinet hard. Perhaps we should get you to a doctor, hey?'

'I am a doctor,' he insisted. 'And I know what I saw.' John punched the combination into the panel, but on attempting to open the door he found it locked. 'Damn, it's stuck.' He began to panic and punched in the code once more — whereby it opened.

As Pearce scanned the room, finding all as it should be, Miles just had to say it. 'I really think you need to lie down.'

'But it was so real.' Pearce sank as if he would pass out again, so Miles grabbed him up and escorted him back to the lounge.

'It was real for me, too. When your head collided with the filing cabinet, I copped my hot coffee in my lap.' Miles directed his friend's attention to the large wet stain on his shirt and trousers.

'Oh . . .' Pearce's eyes rolled around as he probed his brain trying to recall if it was as Thurlow said. After all, his own scenario did seem a bit far-fetched. 'I do apologise, Professor, this must seem an awful bother.'

'Not at all.' Miles assured him with a smile. 'You've put up with worse from me today.'

'We'll call it even then.' Pearce agreed.

Back at the cottage on Anglesey, Tory was gathering her things together. She left the large diamond her father had given her wrapped in a note on Miles' bed, to pay for any expenses he'd incurred on her behalf.

Brian watched his sister bustling about with growing concern. During the time that Tory was absent from Dr Pearce's offices, John had confirmed Miles' attempt to reach them on Pico. Brian, quite frankly, believed their story.

Stay out of it. He heeded his own advice.

Still, he'd become rather fond of Miles during the course of their association, and it did seem as if the professor was once again getting the blunt end of the stick.

'When you told Miles you wouldn't meet him again, do I take that to mean you don't plan on coming back here at all?'

'I don't know,' Tory snapped, then calmed herself when she realised she was expending her anger on the wrong person. 'I'm sorry, Brian . . . I just need some time to think.' She approached and gave him a hug. 'Surely you realise I could never be parted from you for any great length of time.'

'That's good.' He presumed this meant no. 'Because I'm naming you as my child's guardian.'

'I'll try and make it back before the birth then.' She flung the sports bag, containing all the trinkets she'd collected in her travels, including Maelgwn's sword, its hilt protruding from the end, over her shoulder.

'But the birth is over six months from now. Why stay away so long?' Brian inquired, as if he didn't know.

'I want to give Miles some time to think. I'm not so sure we're supposed to be lovers in every lifetime.'

'Now hold on.' Brian pulled her up as she made for the door. 'Why would it be true for everyone else you've ever known, but not for you two?'

Tory's eyes widened in horror. 'Oh, Brian.' She sounded disappointed in him. 'Don't tell me you actually believe Miles was going to tell me about the capsule? Please. Just spare me.' She made for the front door with greater haste, her hands over her ears.

'Well, if you'd just calm down for two seconds . . .' Brian raised his voice to combat her resistance, 'you'd see he only did it because he's crazy about you. And I don't think for a second that Maelgwn would have found it easy to aid you in the same predicament; not if he knew it meant losing you for an indeterminate duration.'

'Enough!' Tory's emotions welled up inside her, setting her tears flowing again. She thrust Brian away with both hands.

'Aw, Tory . . . I'm sorry, I thought . . .'

'Just . . . stop! . . . And back up.'

Brian stopped, at a loss for what else to do. *I distinctly remember telling me to stay out of this.*

'Forget the lift,' she sniffled, finally. 'I know the way.'

'Don't you dare disappear on me . . . . Tory!' She was gone before he'd finished the sentence. 'You're making a mistake!' he shouted into the void with all the conviction he could muster, before collapsing onto the lounge exhausted. 'Women!!!'

In the quiet solitude of the secret cavern at Dinas Emrys, Tory calmed herself to a rational state. *Perhaps I am being too harsh on Miles?* She shook her head to disagree with herself, spying her ride back to the sixth century just across the room. 'There are other more pressing matters to worry about.'

'No wonder the ancients named you Lamamu.' Tory stopped mid-stride, turning quickly to find Myrddin approaching.

'You seem to leave conflict and romance flourishing, wherever you go.' Her father gave a short laugh, though his inflection conveyed disappointment. Tory didn't understand this at all, what was wrong with everybody? 'I've caused no major wars here that I'm aware of. I just did what I came to do, and now I'm going.' She turned to do so.

'Yes, you got what you wanted alright, but at what price?' The sardonic strain of his voice taunted his daughter to a slow her pace. 'Never mind the lover you intend to leave in torment for the rest of his days, or the brother you didn't even bother to say goodbye or thank you to.'

It had been a long, long time since Tory had been lectured, and in her present mood she wasn't really finding it to her liking. 'Don't you start. I'm sure they'll both get over it. Besides, I'll be back soon enough.' She stepped into the chariot in the hope of departing before this debate got out of hand.

'If you choose to be so hard, Tory, you will be broken,' he warned.

'Miles lied to me. I'm not the bad guy in this scenario.'

'Then why, Tory, are you acting like you are?' He raised his dark, bushy eyebrows in question. 'If you want retribution for your betrayal, I'm telling you, you shall get it. Besides, there are certain things you haven't told Miles either. I know that's an immortality potion you've got in your hand. If Maelgwn is to be immortal, why on earth would you come back to Miles? Perhaps this little dispute is just one of convenience?'

Though it was a struggle for Tory to stay civil at this point, she thought it might be nice to depart with at least one person still talking to her. 'Dad, I love you dearly . . . but I think my love life is really my own affair. I can't even bear to think of that man at the moment, let alone discuss him with you. Give us all a little time to calm down, then we'll talk.' She looked to him for his blessing to leave.

'It's your choice, of course.' Myrddin took a step away, neither subscribing to, nor condemning her line of reasoning.

'Damn it, Dad. I have to go.' She begged his leave. 'I've come this close to ending this thing before, and I screwed it up. I won't run that risk again. I can't.' Not to be swayed or diverted from her task, she now placed her hands upon the chariot and envisaged the entrance room to Taliesin's labyrinth, as it had been on the day of her departure.

'Don't allow yourself to be guided by your emotions. Listen to your instincts. Consider the facts and . . .' Myrddin hastily conveyed these last words of advice, as he watched Tory and the chariot disappear once again, 'trust yourself.'

27

TRUSTING THE SELF

In the grand Romanesque entrance room, filled to capacity with Taliesin's favourite artefacts, Tory expected to find the Merlin awaiting her. Although she could not sense his presence, she called for him several times. When no response was forthcoming, she decided go on to Degannwy alone. She left the chariot in the safety of Taliesin's otherworldly abode; if Taliesin turned up it would announce her return to this time.

'Majesty?' Selwyn whispered in delight upon sighting Tory, conscious of not disturbing the ailing king. 'Could thou be back already?'

As Tory's body caught up to her spirit, she came to focus on the young bard. 'Selwyn.' She hugged him excitedly; it felt like an eternity had passed since they last spoke. 'Where hast thou been?' She held her dear friend at arm's length to view him.

Though Selwyn thought her a bit confused, he answered all the same. 'I have not left the king's side for the entire time thou hast been gone.'

That's strange? Then how could I have found Maelgwn alone when I came to collect the samples for En Darius? 'How long have I been gone?' She noted it was dark outside.

'The sun hast yet to rise on the day thou left.' When Selwyn saw how happy this made her, he added with glee: 'I thought thou must have forgotten something, but then I saw thy hair. And thine eyes . . .' He gasped as he realised her pupils had changed colour. 'I can hardly wait to hear the tales of thy quest, Highness, but . . .' he was a little shy in asking. 'Did thy efforts prove fruitful?'

Tory fished the orichalchum ball from the pocket of her jacket, smiling broadly as she opened it to disclose the crystal bottle. 'I would not have returned without it.' Her sights drifted to the bed where Maelgwn lay sleeping, and she was drawn to his side. 'You shall never know this suffering again, my love.' She pulled the stopper from the bottle and lowered it to rest on the side of the king's mouth.

The wails of a distraught woman, becoming ever louder in the corridor outside, forced Tory to refrain from administering the life-giving liquid. The woman howled out her grief amidst incoherent babble, as she pounded on the door of the king's chamber.

'No soul is to know I am here yet.'

'Of course.' Selwyn moved to discover the meaning of the disturbance, only opening the door far enough to converse with the culprit.

Though the woman's sobs could still be heard, Tory could not hear a word that passed between her and the bard.

When Selwyn finally closed the door, he leant his forehead against it. 'I don't understand,' he mumbled, disappointed in himself.

'What is it?' Tory replaced the stopper on the bottle, afraid she might spill some of the precious brew.

'Oh, Majesty, I have failed thee, miserably.' He turned to face her, his large, soulful eyes filling with tears. 'The prince is showing symptoms of the plague.' Selwyn bowed his head in shame; his amulet had not protected him.

The news swept through Tory's body like a shock wave from hell; every inch of her being screamed in pain. 'Nay!' she cried, racing for the door, but she staggered and fell short of it. 'You can't do this. Not my son.' She cast her eyes to the heavens as she got back to her feet. 'He will not be one of Mahaud's casualties,' she announced, as if warning the powers that be against defying her will. 'Come Selwyn, I need thee to be strong for me now.' Tory held out her hand to him, and the bard clasped it firmly as they hurried towards the room where the prince had been quarantined.

The fever had firm hold of Rhun and the young prince was well aware of the suffering that lay in store. Yet the worst was not that he would die, but that he had failed Gwynedd. That was far more agonising than the swelling in his loins or the heat that pulsed through his body.

'Oh, sweet prince.' Tory cradled him in her arms as she used to do when he was little. His head rested gently against her breast as she wiped his brow with a cool, damp cloth. She forced herself not to think of the implications of this development, for even in his weakened state Rhun would pick up on anything she thought or felt. 'Do not fear. Thou art well aware what a clever mother thou hast. I shall resolve this dilemma just as I have those before it. You shall not suffer long, I promise thee.'

'I deserve to suffer . . . this ailment be the result of my own stupidity.' Rhun looked to Selwyn, who was seated beside the bed where he and his mother lay. 'Forgive me, wise Merlin, I did not heed thy word. I assumed to think I knew better than thee, and gave my talisman to the Lady Bridgit.'

So, it had not been his own failing after all; Selwyn didn't know whether to laugh or cry. 'But my dear prince, the Lady Bridgit be in no danger. I would have seen to her protection if this had been the case.'

Tory's heart was too heavy to be angry with her boy, and she knew a scolding wouldn't help. 'These things were sent to try us.' She lowered Rhun's head back onto the pillow.

'Please do not leave me, Mother. I know thou art angered and disappointed, but . . .' Tears of disgrace streamed down the drawn features of Rhun's yellow-tinged face, 'I have never felt so afraid in all my born days.'

'Shhh.' She placed her fingers over his lips. 'Just believe and trust in me, as thou always hast. I shan't be defeated unless thou art.'

'Never.' He forced a smile.

'I am warning thee, Rhun,' Tory cautioned, sensing doubt. 'Do not assume to know better than I. One negative suggestion from that brain of thine and I shall kill thee myself. Clear?' She smiled, sensing he was now more disposed towards her plea. 'Now, I have to go. I do not wish to leave thy father alone too long . . . alone!' She looked at Selwyn, stunned by a revelation. 'He be alone, so I must be with him now! Quick, we have to catch me before I go back.' Tory leapt for the door, leaving Selwyn none the wiser as to why his Queen was so excited.

Tory raced down the corridor at a deadly pace. If she could get to the king's chamber before she returned to Atlantis, she could tell herself she needed two doses of the antidote and the problem would be solved.

'Wait!' she yelled before she'd even reached the door, but upon bursting it open she found no one but the sleeping king in the room. *I could be wrong, of course*, but as she approached Maelgwn, she spied the large amethyst wand in his hands. 'Goddamn it!' she cursed in a whisper.

'Majesty?' Selwyn slipped into the room in a timid fashion, afraid his poor Queen was losing her mind. 'Something else ails thee?'

'Oh, Selwyn. I am sorry.' She drew a deep breath. 'I suppose I'm not making much sense.' Her gaze shifted to Maelgwn, her thoughts on their son. *So the choice is mine. To one I can give immortal life, and the other . . .*

'Where art thou going, Majesty?' Selwyn watched her wander past him on her way to the door.

'I need a moment alone to ponder my next move. I shall be in the room of court, if I am required for any reason.'

'Yes, Majesty.' He bowed and stood tall to watch her depart. *How could the Goddess be so cruel to one so loyal?* He shed a tear for her, and the choice she was being forced to make.

It is impossible to be calm and reason with oneself when, with every second that passes, the two people you care about most are being tortured to death.

'Oh, great Mother. I know thou said thou would aid me no further, but I beseech thee . . .' Tory fell to her knees before the throne of Gwynedd, 'I do not have the strength for this. Please, tell me what I should do?'

The trials she now faced were too great and too many to combat on her own. Where was Taliesin? Where was Sorcha, Keridwen, Don?

'Somebody?' she cried. 'Anybody? Please, help me.' Tory lowered her head and began to weep bitterly.

'God helps those who help themselves.'

That voice, Tory gulped, her crying subsiding into spasmodic breaths.

'Come on, don't be chicken . . . you can look at me.'

Tory raised her eyes to view the throne. There sat a woman who was the very image of herself, although it was definitely not Sorcha who addressed her this time.

Her eyes were like ice, though her skin was of a dark copper colour. Her snowy white hair, as long as Tory's own, was shaved on both sides of her head in a Mohican style, and was laced with feathers, beads and braids. She wore jeans with black leather chaps, much like a cowboy. Her singlet, fringed vest and steel-capped boots were all black. Curiously enough, the gold, silver and orichalchum headband was upon her brow. She also wore the silver armbands and the gold waistband.

'G'day, mate.' She winked at Tory, throwing a leg over the armrest of the king's throne and reclining to a more comfortable position.

'Who . . . are you?' Tory managed to stammer a query.

'I'll give you one guess.' She grinned, raising her brows as she awaited a response.

'No, you couldn't mean . . .' The woman nodded as Tory slowly got to her feet. 'But you can't be me, I promised myself I'd never do this.'

'Hey, shit happens.' She shrugged. 'I had to come, for two reasons. One, because I was told to. And two, because I remember being in your predicament and me showing up to advise you. I know it's a little awkward, but when you're me you'll do the same for you.'

This scenario seemed somewhat suspicious to Tory; what if this was Mahaud? Still, she had to admit she could not sense nor espy any evil presence. 'But how did you get here? Where's the chariot?'

The outrageous character before her began to roar with laughter. 'I do not require that cumbersome man-made nightmare to time travel any more! I traded it in eons ago for a more ideal and reliable means of transport.' She motioned to her brain.

'What year did you come from then?' Tory was most curious about her attire.

'These are not the questions I came to answer.' Her future self sat upright in the chair, more serious now. 'You are wanting to know whether you should give the potion to Maelgwn or Rhun?'

'Yes.' Tory became anxious once again, not really wanting to hear the response.

'The answer is . . .' Her other self smiled, 'neither.'

'What?!' Tory backed up, disenchanted.

'Hear me out.' She remained so calm that Tory felt compelled to listen. 'Maelgwn is one of the Chosen. You know that. Right?'

Tory nodded, still fearful.

'As such, he is destined to be present at the Gathering, as indeed you are. Yet, as two perfect halves of the whole, you have different roles to fulfil as far as the Gathering is concerned.'

'Tell me about the Gathering.' Tory was intrigued.

'Don't interrupt . . . I am not telling you any more than you need to know.' She took a deep breath to recall what she still needed to explain. 'As a guardian and a leader of men, you are pretty much bound to this earth. Though you are, of course, free to explore the etheric realms, and fairly soon you shall do so. Ah!' She held a warning finger up, not giving Tory the chance to enquire further. 'Now Maelgwn, on the other hand, has done all he can here. It is time for him to move on to a place where he shall benefit from new learning experiences.'

'Don't tell me I must let him die.' Tory began to fret.

'Come on . . . do you really think that I would let that gorgeous hunk of a man of ours be fed to the worms, or the flame? I think not.'

'Well, what then? I don't understand.'

'You will.' She stood and descended the stairs to confront herself head on. 'Take Maelgwn and lay him on the alter stone at Lynn Cerrig Bach. All shall be made clear thereupon.'

Tory wasn't liking the answers too much. *It could be a trick, to delay me saving Maelgwn until it's too late.* 'You said you were sent here. By whom, may I ask?'

Her future self placed her hands on her hips and wore a cool smile. 'Maelgwn sent me.' She nodded firmly, Tory being struck speechless. 'And the man I spoke with was much enlightened for his experience. He told me to tell you that you're doing the right thing.'

Tory raised a hand to support her brain as it exploded with possibilities, questions and doubts. 'So, why then, do I not give the cure to Rhun?'

'Because you don't have to. Rhun inherited his immortality from you.'

'But, he injures and heals like a mortal does,' Tory argued, despite wanting to believe the claim. 'He's ailing as we speak . . .'

'I know that!' The future Tory raised both hands to her mouth to calmly consider how she might convey this most aptly. 'Listen to me, Tory. I am going to ask you to do something now, and if you refuse, Rhun will suffer, as will many others.'

'Go on.' Tory agreed to keep an open mind.

'Like you, Rhun, too, must experience physical death before his immortality kicks in. So, you have three choices here, and I'm warning you, the last time round you chose wrong.'

'You want me to kill him?' Tory was mortified by the suggestion. She did not recall her alleged death, so how could she trust that the process was as she was being told.

'Either that, or he suffers through the course of the virus, whereby its lingering presence will cause an epidemic. But, end it quickly, and Gwynedd will be spared much death and suffering.'

'Or I could just give him the potion.' Tory was both cynical and determined in her retort.

'That would be a complete waste of a precious resource,' she was firmly advised. 'In the future you shall be very grateful if you heed this warning and conserve it . . . for it is meant for somebody else.'

'Who?' Tory couldn't think of anyone she'd risk Rhun's life for.

'Look, I'm not getting into this with you.' She held up the palms of her hands as she retraced her steps to the throne.

'Prove to me that you're me!' Tory challenged, as she watched this wilder version of herself take a seat once again.

'I don't have to.' She was very casual about it. 'This time round I have a back-up plan to ensure you do the right thing.' She held up two fingers to make the peace sign, and vanished.

'No, don't go!' Tory's nerves were in tatters as she made off up the stairs after herself. 'I wouldn't leave me this unsure!' The large double doors at the opposite end of the room opened, and Tory swung round to witness Taliesin breeze in with Selwyn hot on his heels. *Praise the universe.* She collapsed into the vacated throne. 'Where have you been? You won't believe what's just taken place in here.'

'So, you've received your instruction? Splendid! We thought it would sound better coming from yourself.' He stopped at the bottom of the stairs and bowed to her.

Tory shook her head vigorously, completely floored by his remark. 'You know about it then?'

'Indeed . . .'

'And who is we?' She sat up straight.

'Why, myself, you and Maelgwn, of course. I've been to the future, that's why I'm late,' Taliesin stated, as if making perfect sense. 'There are some serious strategies being formulated there, part of which was your visit to yourself. I am now here to second what you told yourself, in case you're still unsure.'

Either Mahaud is very clever, or I am, she mused on the quiet.

'You did die at Arwystli,' the Merlin announced. 'Ask Sir Tiernan if you don't believe me, for you died in his arms after I'd given you the potion. Now, I know for a fact that the potion you are holding will one day be needed to save another who is very dear to you, so please don't waste it unnecessarily.'

'But Taliesin, what of Mahaud? How can I be sure she's not behind this? The original cure Darius made for Maelgwn was stolen from his lab, before I — '

'I know, I know,' the Merlin confessed. 'I stole it.'

'You stole it!' She was incensed when she thought of what she'd been through as a result.

'Well, not exactly, no. En Razu, my younger self, did. See, when you told me it was I who had made you immortal, I couldn't think of where else I'd acquire such a potion. Thus I stole it, in the knowledge that Darius could make you another. Mind you, I had no idea you would be forced to leave in such a hurry.'

'So it was already missing when Mahaud took Darius to fetch it.' Tory held up to view the bottle containing the brew that had caused so much trouble. 'Well, that's kind of a blessing, I suppose.'

'Indeed.' Taliesin was glad she chose to see the upside.

'And that answers the question of where you got it.'

'Exactly. Now, as much as I would love to stand around and reminisce, we have much to do . . . starting with young Rhun.'

'Now just wait a goddamn minute!' Tory planted both feet firmly on the ground and took a stand. 'I refuse to be bamboozled into murdering my son. Can't you see how this looks from my point of view?'

Taliesin made up the stairs to take hold of her. 'I know you fear Mahaud, Tory, but we're back on Gwynedd time now. With every second that passes our chances of avoiding a disaster grow less and less. Look into my eyes, my soul, and tell me if you see the crone there?'

With a deep breath, Tory took a step away and focused her sight upon him.

Beyond his physical being the whirling, coloured vortexes of his chakras empowered his aura with energy and lustre, without so much as a hint of a shadow to blemish the clarity and brilliance of it.

'I see nothing that would suggest the influence of such a presence,' she announced. 'You look like an angel.'

'Then please, believe it is I, Taliesin Pen Beirdd, who appeals to you now. We must do this, Tory, and can waste no more time procrastinating. Are you with me, or not?'

Tory looked to Selwyn, who gave a slight nod in encouragement. 'Goddess forgive me if I am wrong about this,' she consented finally. 'But, we must let Rhun decide how it will be done.'

'Agreed.' Taliesin didn't like it any more than she did, but it was high time to make amends for this mess.

Considering the severity of his circumstance, Rhun handled the news of his imminent murder with apparent ease; instant deliverance would be a blessing compared with the agonising and drawn-out death he would suffer at the hands of this plague.

'Well then . . . I have always thought I should like to die by the sword,' he told them plainly.

'Oh, Rhun, why not poison or something?' Tory implored, as she sat on the bed beside him wiping his brow. 'There be not a swordsman in the whole of Gwynedd who could find it in his heart to run thee through.'

'Nay, Mother. I want thee to do it.' He gripped Tory's hand to stop her fussing. 'Thou art strong, and thy aim be true . . . I trust thee.'

Both her hands went to her mouth to hide her dismay. She so wanted to say that she could never . . . yet propriety prevented it; she could not deny her son his last mortal request. 'So be it then.' She summoned what strength she had left, determined to believe with all her heart, mind, and soul that Rhun's resurrection was only a matter of course. She held out both her hands, willing Maelgwn's sword to manifest there, which it did.

Impressive. Taliesin raised an eyebrow. Her travels have worked wonders. He looked on in silence as she drew the sword from its scabbard.

'Be brave, my prince,' she gasped to hold back the tears. If she didn't think about it, the deed would be done before she lost face. 'I shall see thee on the other side, where there is no pain.'

'I look forward to it.' He relaxed to make himself comfortable. 'No fear; promise me?'

'I do.' She reached down and gently drew his eyelids closed. *I must not waver.* She stood, gripping the sword firmly with both hands, and closed her eyes to centre herself. She raised the weapon and poised its razor-sharp tip above Rhun's heart.

'Stop!' Sir Tiernan froze in the doorway, shaken by the scene he was witnessing.

'Damn it.' Taliesin cursed the interruption and waved a finger in the general direction of the door, whereby it slammed shut in the knight's face, locking him out. 'Be done with it!' He encouraged, shouting over Tiernan's pounding and yells of protest.

Tory repositioned herself and drew a deep breath. 'I . . . love . . . you.' Her voice went hoarse as she plunged the sword right through his body. 'No!' she cried out, as if the blade had penetrated her heart instead of his. There was not so much as a murmur from her boy, however, even as she withdrew the blade. 'Forgive me.' She threw the weapon aside, falling to her knees and holding him fast.

'Thy aim be true,' he whispered as the last breath of air slipped from his body.

'Taliesin?' Tory stared into her boy's lifeless face.

'Give it a moment.' He encouraged her to be patient.

'I command thee, in the name of King Maelgwn, to open this door!' Tiernan roared, kicking it repeatedly and damn near breaking the bolt with every thud. 'Open it!'

'Taliesin?' Tory began to despair, her forlorn expression near breaking the Merlin's heart.

'I am right about this, Tory.'

The Merlin's sweet smile reassured her and she looked back to her son with renewed hope, noting the wound in his chest was closing. 'Come on, Rhun.' She slapped him lightly around the cheeks. 'Come on back to us.' As the prince's empty carcass suddenly filled with the breath of life, Tory burst into laughter and tears; this seemed the only sound decision she'd made in the last twenty-four hours. 'How do you feel?' She gently stroked the feeling back into his face.

'Much better.' He lowered his groggy eyes to view where the sword had passed through him, to find no trace of the wound, bar the stain on his shirt. 'What, not even a scar for my troubles?' he whinged, reaching between his thighs to find the swelling gone.

Tory giggled, overwhelmed with happiness to see him alive and well. 'That's exactly what I said.'

'From whence comes that pounding?' Rhun cringed, thinking it might be in his brain.

'Let me . . .' The hinges and bolt finally gave way and the door fell flat on the floor with Sir Tiernan on top of it, '. . . in!'

'Be there a problem, Tiernan?' Tory made light of his exhausted state. 'I distinctly recall confining thee to quarantine.'

'I do not have any symptoms,' he grumbled as he got to his feet. 'But when I heard that the prince did, I . . .'

'Thou thought thou might come and get it from him,' Tory concluded. 'I see.'

'Sorry, Majesty.' Tiernan acknowledged his mistake as he witnessed the prince rise to a seated position, appearing perfectly well.

'Well, as it turns out,' Tory looked to her son, well pleased, 'he doesn't have the plague after all, so there's nothing for thee to fret about.'

'Very good, Highness.' Tiernan backed out of the room, confused and unsure about what he thought he'd seen. 'Be the emergency over then?'

'Almost.' Tory's heart lost its buoyancy. 'Dress thyself, quickly.' She instructed Rhun. 'It be high time we put an end to thy father's suffering.'

Taliesin, Rhun, and Tory gathered in the king's chamber, and transported Maelgwn to the altar stone at Llyn Cerrig Bach.

'It shall be over before daybreak, I promise thee.' Taliesin endeavoured to put Tory's fears to rest. Her energy levels were greatly diminished, and she needed this burden to be lifted from her shoulders before they could even attempt to tackle the crone.

'Maelgwn.' She gripped his hands, which were crossed over his chest, staring at his face that was near unrecognisable from the bloating and discolouring effects of the disease. 'Thou art going to be fine . . . thou told me so. I love thee, more than life . . .' She wiped her tears away quickly. 'If we could trade places, I would . . . in a second.'

'Tory.' Taliesin encouraged her to back away, looking to the darkened sky beyond the roofless temple.

A large, dark cloud unfolded there, ablaze with light and brilliant colour. Tory had seen many a strange light phenomena before, but this one was a mystery. 'What is it?' she asked over the booming sound it emitted and the turbulent winds it stirred up.

'One could say it's Maelgwn's connecting flight.' The Merlin grinned, his eyes never leaving the spectacular display.

A single beam of light, blue-white in colour, burst through the glittering cloud cover to where lay the dying king.

'I don't know about this.' Tory took a step closer, but Taliesin clutched her arm.

'It be time to let go,' he told her, as Maelgwn sat upright and beckoned Rhun to him.

'Father?' The prince ran straight into the light, jumping up onto the altar stone to embrace Maelgwn.

Tory held back so that they might have a moment alone together. How sad it was that their son would inherit the huge responsibility of king at the tender age of twenty-one.

Once Maelgwn had passed on his last words of advice, Rhun confirmed his understanding with a nod, and with one long last gaze at each other Rhun slid from the altar and motioned Tory to approach.

Maelgwn stood as she ran to join him on top of the stone platform, and he held her fast as they rocked to and fro in a long embrace.

'We strangely met, like not so many, yet still my love be true as any. In the Old One's choice, my soul dost rejoice, and no gift could express the love for thee, I do possess.' Maelgwn recited the poem he'd written for her on the day of their wedding, and Tory sniffled as she recalled the rest.

'So love her in thy heart, whose forever joy thou art. And our love will know no end, my dear and sweetest friend.' She kissed him for all she was worth. When they parted and she gazed into those large, dark eyes of his, he was calm and accepting of his situation, not at all apprehensive about the journey he was about to embark upon. 'Dost thou know where thou art going?'

'Aye. All through my fever I have seen visions of what lay ahead.' He smiled at having foreseen this very moment. 'You look so lovely in this light.'

She melted to a smile, though she'd never felt more miserable.

Maelgwn looked to the explosion of colour in the sky above them, lured by the promise of the unknown. 'I shall miss thee, Tory Alexander.' He wished he could find the words that would reassure her, though he knew he never could. 'We shall meet again.' He wiped the tears from her cheeks.

'I know it.' She stole one last fleeting kiss before he ascended into the heavens. *Goddess protect him.* Her knees went weak and Tory sank to the ground to witness both her love and the disturbance vanish.

28

FUN AND GAMES

As day gradually shed light upon the vast expanse of sky, Tory stirred from her long trance. She'd passed beyond hysteria to a drained state of feeling absolutely nothing. 'In what year will I find him again?' She directed the question at Taliesin, who was seated on the crumbled stairs of the ruin, absorbing the early morning rays that filtered down through the forest.

'Only time will tell for it be not my place to say. Besides,' he opened his eyes and looked at her, 'you have much to do and learn before that time.'

'But what is there for me without him here?' She gave a heavy sigh. 'All the plans we've made for Gwynedd and Britain. They have no meaning without Maelgwn at my side.'

'That be why we must see to Rhun's inauguration and wedding. Once things have settled under his rule, thou art free to go.'

'Go where, High Merlin?' Tory beseeched him, jumping from the altar stone as Taliesin stood and brushed his hands over his robes to straighten them.

'Wherever life leads thee.'

'Name the year.' She thought she deserved to know that much.

'Nineteen ninety-six,' Taliesin announced with glee.

'But that be the year I just came from?'

'Funny about that.' He raised both eyebrows in a cocky fashion. 'But I have the strangest premonition you'll be wanting to go back there . . . though Maelgwn, as such, be not the reason.'

'Did I hear my name and the word "wedding" mentioned in the same sentence?' Rhun barged into the middle of the moderately heated conversation, having returned from answering nature's call in the woods.

'Shush!' Tory scolded him, determined to get to the bottom of Taliesin's smugness; it seemed as if he knew something she did not. 'If Maelgwn shall not be in the twentieth century, then why on earth would I be in any drastic hurry to go back there?'

'Because . . .' He smiled broadly as he placed a hand upon her shoulder and shook his head, 'thou really hast no idea, hast thou?' The Merlin couldn't refrain from being amused by her blissful ignorance. 'Well, I suppose it be a bit soon for it to have come to thy attention?'

'Taliesin!' She was going to throttle him . . .

'Thou art with child.' The Merlin watched as Tory's rage lost all momentum.

'That be fantastic,' Rhun cheered.

'Please, Taliesin, thou art joking?' Tory ignored her boy's excitement, feeling rather faint.

The Merlin only winked, delighted by the notion.

'But surely I am too old,' she protested.

He shook his head. 'Never too old, Tory. Not thee.'

'Well, that hardly be fair.' She began to pace, throwing her arms up in the air. 'What am I . . . some kind of inter-continuum incubator?'

'I am finally going to get a little brother,' Rhun chanted, rubbing the palms of his hands together briskly, absolutely ecstatic about the news.

'A little sister, actually.' Taliesin corrected, to draw both Tory's and Rhun's fullest attention.

'Thou art already aware of the sex?' The way Tory saw it, the conception couldn't have taken place more than a few days ago.

'Of course.' The Merlin beamed with satisfaction, observing how Tory's energy levels had already begun to increase. 'I've been to the future, remember? I could even tell thee her name, if thou desires?'

'Please.' Tory waved off the offer. 'I would like to think I have some say in that.' She really didn't know how to feel, but despite all she'd been put through since Lughnasa, Tory couldn't keep the smile from spreading across her face. Like the mythical phoenix that consumes itself in fire to arise from its own ashes, something wonderful had been born amidst all the loss and destruction.

'Will she be like Rhun . . . immortal, I mean?'

'Of course she will.' Rhun had snuck up from behind to give his mother a squeeze. 'We have the same parents, after all.'

Well, almost, she thought, before she could stop herself.

'What dost thou mean, almost?' Rhun turned his mother around to answer him. 'Please tell me that thou hast not been unfaithful to my father.'

'Oh, do calm down.' Taliesin grabbed the prince by the scruff of the neck, and guided him to a seat on a fallen column. 'The man in question thou called father for the first year of thy life.'

'So he did.' Tory smiled as she recalled the sweet isolation and anonymity the three of them had known that year.

'Professor Miles Thurlow be thy father's twentieth century incarnation,' the Merlin advised, 'although he be not as genetically or metaphysically advanced as thy father was. Even so, this child be as important in the great scheme of things as thou art, Rhun. A warrior, like her mother before her, this girl be destined for greatness. I expect thee to guide and protect her.'

'But once I am king, Mother plans to leave. I heard thou say so, just now . . . I shall never even know her,' Rhun said indignantly, disappointed by the hand he'd been dealt.

'Hello?' Taliesin tapped on his brain. 'Thou art immortal. In the fullness of time thy rule here shall come to an end and thou shall be free to seek out the others, who like thyself, are everlasting and have been strewn throughout history. Thy sister will be one of the greatest of these immortal activists and I know for a fact that one of her greatest influences was thy good self.'

The prince very much liked the picture the Merlin painted, but it all seemed so far away. Even if Rhun could catch up with his mother and sister sometime in the future, right now he was to be king. His mother was, and always had been, the only person on this planet that he truly related to. Thus Rhun was none too eager to grant her right to leave. 'Thou must stay until the birth then,' he demanded. 'Please allow me to see my sister before we art separated.'

'Oh Rhun . . .' Tory took up both his hands, knowing that in reality it was the idea of being abandoned that bothered him most. 'I shall not leave Gwynedd until such time as thou art well established in thy own right . . . however long it takes. Once thou art married and all hast settled — '

'Whoa there!' He stood and backed away, palms raised in defense. 'What if I do not want to get married yet?'

Tory rolled her eyes at this, thinking it comical. 'Art thou saying that thou risked thy life for a girl thou art not even in love with?'

'Love be a very strong word, Mother. I was just trying to be gallant. I hardly know the girl.'

'I see.' Tory glanced at Taliesin, and replied tongue-in-cheek. 'Well, Bridgit be of too fine a stock to risk losing her to some impropriety, so I guess we shall just have to marry her off to Blain.'

'Splendid idea, Majesty!' Taliesin played along. 'Her father shall probably prefer it thus, anyway.'

'Thou would not,' Rhun appealed, most unwilling to forfeit his bachelor ways to prevent the match.

'Try me,' Tory challenged, before melting into a smile that was more reassuring. 'Oh, come on, Rhun. Thou cannot hide thy true feelings from me.' She placed an arm around his waist. 'Marriage be like a partnership, and thou shall need all the support thou can get when thou art king. It won't be so bad, thou shall see.'

'That be easy for thou to say. Thou dost not have to ask Vortipor for her hand.'

'Just leave everything to me.' She kissed his forehead. 'I have a real knack for this sort of thing.'

An impromptu meeting of the alliance was called at Degannwy to inform all the respective leaders of the High King's passing, and to nominate a replacement to head the council in his stead.

Though the peculiar details of his departure from this earth were not discussed, everyone present knew Maelgwn had been marked as one of the Chosen at his inauguration. Thus, the mysterious absence of his body was easily explained as having been taken to the Otherworld — as the Druids foretold would happen to all the Chosen.

As the soon-to-be monarchs of Powys and Gwynedd, Blain and Rhun were permitted to attend the meeting and vote for the new head of the council of Britain. Old King Catulus sent his right-hand man, Sir Guillym, to place his ballot. Vortipor cast a vote for Dyfed, and also for Gwent Is Coed, for the young grandson of the late Aurelius Caninus was not yet old enough to be entrusted with such decisions. Fergus MacErc of Dalriada was the only other person to have a say in the decision. As the Saxons had yet to sign the pact they were not allowed a vote, but Eormenric was invited to sit in on the proceedings — as were all the current members of the circle of twelve, and Queen Katren of Powys.

Once all the secret ballots had been received and noted, it was Tory's distinct pleasure to announce Vortipor as the new Head of the British alliance.

Vortipor humbly accepted, though he still mourned his departed colleagues far too deeply to be excited by the appointment. The first suggestion he put to the council, as their leader, was that a memorial service should be held at Degannwy the following day. This was to pay tribute to all those souls who had been so abruptly stolen from them: King Maelgwn, King Brockwell and Sir Rhys amongst them. This motion was seconded by every person in the room.

It was Taliesin who addressed the gathering next, advising that the inauguration ceremonies of both Prince Rhun and Prince Blain would take place two days hence. Rhun's initiation would be held at Llyn Cerrig Bach in Gwynedd, according to the tradition of his forefathers, and Taliesin would preside over these proceedings. Blain would be inaugurated at Maen Llia in Powys, in accordance with the sacred rites of his kingdom, where Selwyn would preside as Master of Ceremonies. When each had executed the task set for them by the Goddess, they would be crowned in their respective kingdoms the day following their return.

'So be it!' replied all in court. The Merlin took his seat, and Tory rose to conclude the conference.

'In closing, I have a couple of announcements to make. Firstly, with the departure of King Maelgwn from this world, I have appointed the son of Sir Tiernan and the Lady Ione, Sir Gareth, to take his place in the circle of twelve.' A brief round of applause broke out in approval. 'As my partner in the circle be no longer with us . . .' She spoke up over the din, 'I bequeath my position to Sir Bryce's prize student, Sir Lucus.' Her audience seemed to change their tune somewhat, voicing strong protest at her announcement.

'Thou cannot resign.' Vortipor stood outraged.

'I shall still be overseeing the training of the Masters,' she stated calmly, 'but I need more teachers, and Sir Lucus shall be a far better match for Sir Gareth than I.'

'Thou art right, Mother . . . Sir Gareth would be lucky to last a week with thee,' Rhun exaggerated, to the amusement of everyone present.

'Now to the last thing on the agenda. Two weeks hence, Bryce, Prince of Powys and Duke of Penmon, shall wed the Lady Aella at Arwystli. And to double the celebration value, Eormenric, Son of Ossa, and Vanora, Princess of Powys, will wed on this day also.'

'Oh . . .' Another round of applause was forthcoming.

'There could be a few more couples to add to that list before then.' Her gaze drifted towards Blain and Rhun, who both shrank from the suggestion. 'We shall keep ye all informed.'

'So be it!'

The arrangements for a multiple wedding were just what Katren needed to put Calin's death to the back of her mind — she enjoyed pomp and pageantry, and playing hostess was her forte. Tory had other things to worry about, like keeping Mahaud at bay long enough to get the two young princes betrothed and crowned.

Directly following the conference, when everyone else headed to the great dining room and the feast that awaited there, Tory and Katren slipped away to the library to discuss who should wed young Blain.

Food and mead awaited them by the fire, where they kicked off their shoes and relaxed. As they both understood the other's recent widowhood, they did not speak about the loss of their husbands. Tomorrow was the memorial service, where such grief could be expressed. Today was for planning a brighter future.

'The last time we saw such upheaval, it was the two of us who got wed.' Katren gazed into the fire, her lips poised upon the rim of her goblet as she marvelled at a string of memories. Then she smiled. 'How bold we were, how passionate.'

'I think Javotte,' Tory stated firmly.

'Alma's daughter?' Katren didn't sound as convinced. 'She was rather a wild one when last I saw her. I think Blain needs someone more sensitive,' she appealed, finally taking a sip of her drink.

'Rubbish,' Tory scoffed. 'Blain needs someone who will be strong for him. Javotte is smart, attractive, and . . . she be his sparring partner.'

'Say no more.' Katren waved a hand, realising it was fate; there wasn't a male-female match made in the Dragon's circle that hadn't ended up in marriage. 'How does Blain feel about her?'

'Oh, Blain be not the problem,' Tory reckoned. 'It be more how Javotte will react that concerns me.'

There was a knock on the door and Vortipor entered. 'Alright, you two. I know what this be about.' He observed the pair huddled in a mischievous fashion on the lounge, and closed the door behind him. 'Which prince does thou propose to marry my daughter off to?'

'Why, the one she be in love with, of course.' Tory stood to offer him a goblet of mead.

'All well and good.' He accepted her hospitality and took a seat opposite them. 'Until my girl discovers her husband be not in love with her.'

'I believe thou art much mistaken there.' Tory took a seat beside her old friend. 'Thou knows my son and I art connected emotionally, and he hast never felt for any woman as he does for Bridgit.'

'Thou sees what thou wishes to see, as the boy's mother. Do not get me wrong, Highness, I loved his father dearly, and nothing would make me happier than to link our clans thus. But thou would be horrified to know how many women he hast ravished in his relatively short career.' He shook his head at the stories he'd heard.

'How many women had thou known at the same age, Vortipor?' Katren was most interested to know. 'Was Calin, Tiernan or Maelgwn any more notorious when single than young Rhun be today?'

'That was different!' he objected, evading the question. 'We had no special powers to manipulate the minds and hearts of the women we wooed.'

'Huh?' Katren nearly choked in her drink. 'That be news to me.'

'Look.' Tory stood. 'My son more than loves thy daughter. He reveres her,' she stressed, to get the point across, as Vortipor rolled his eyes preparing to differ. 'If he did not, her virtue would already be his. Bridgit hast vowed her pleasures to him, married or no . . . I know this for a fact.'

'So,' Katren summed up their argument, 'if we do not pair them off, we shall have a scandal on our hands.'

The leader conceded defeat, looking from one Queen to the other. 'I never had a hope, did I?' He smiled, consoled by a thought. 'Once Rhun hast been crowned, he may ask me for the hand of my daughter.' He chuckled to himself. 'How does that sound?'

'Precarious.' Tory voiced what she knew would be her son's view, as she turned to a knock at the door.

'Ah, Sir Angus.' Katren greeted him warmly. 'Just the man we wanted to see.'

'Thou art in for it now,' Vortipor warned the knight in jest, as he rose to escape. 'Prince Rhun sent me to see what was detaining ye all.' Angus couldn't understand why he was in trouble.

'Little bugger,' Tory mumbled under her breath. *He's been listening in the whole time.*

'Thanks for doing this,' Blain whispered, not wanting to disturb Rhun's concentration. 'What art they saying now?'

'Shhh! Mother knows we art listening.' Rhun clenched his skull tighter to maintain concentration. 'I told thee sending Javotte's father up there would be a dead giveaway.'

Rhun's bedroom door opened, and to Blain's horror Javotte entered. 'What art thou doing here?' He rushed across the room to escort her out.

'Ye art both wanted downstairs?' Javotte informed them, more interested in Rhun's curious conduct. 'Dost he have a headache?'

'Ah . . . aye.' Blain attempted to turn her around and get her out of there.

'What art thou up to?'

'Thou hast to leave,' Blain implored.

She dug her heels in. 'Be that an order, Highness.' She stared him down.

'Aye,' Blain ventured.

'Thou art not king yet.' She shoved him away and walked around him. 'Thou shalt have to make me.'

'I cannot concentrate!' Rhun stood to roar. 'If thou wants to play with her, for Goddess' sakes, take her in the next room.' He immediately sat to resume their mission.

'Play with me!' Javotte protested, outraged, but Blain had her over his shoulder and out the door before she had a chance to retaliate.

'Put me down!' She gave his kidneys a good punch for the third time.

'Ouch!' Blain gladly offloaded her onto his bed, exhausted. He backed up to close the door.

'I want to know what be going on?' she demanded, flinging her shoulder-length blonde curls back off her face as she got to her knees.

'Shhh!' Blain urged, leaning against the door as he caught his breath. 'I do not think we art supposed to know anything yet.'

'What? About how they plan to marry us off?' She gave him a wink, her eyes of pale blue twinkling with amusement.

'How could thou know? My mother only conceived of it moments ago.'

He moved to sit on the edge of the bed, where Javotte was more than an arm's length away.

'I realised days ago,' she boasted. 'Did thou not even suspect it when our sensei made us sparring partners?'

'Nay.' Blain hadn't a clue what she was on about. 'I cannot say that I did.'

'Whenever the opposite sex be paired in the Dragon's Circle, they art paired for life. Hast thou not noticed?' She giggled at his naivety.

'Thou art right,' he admitted, having thought about it. 'And this dost not bother thee?!'

She shrugged in a casual fashion. 'My marriage options art limited. Thou art the pick of a bad bunch . . . and thou shalt make me a Queen — which be to thy favour, of course.'

'That be very flattering.' He couldn't believe she was actually for the idea. 'Thy passion overwhelms me.'

'Oh . . . there's nothing to worry about in that regard for at least another year.' She leant back on her elbows, assuming a provocative pose. 'My father won't allow them to wed us off until I come of age.'

'Really?' Blain questioned, unsure if this was good news or bad.

'Well, it be official.' Rhun entered to inform the lucky couple. 'They have agreed to the match.'

'What?' Javotte got to her feet. 'No conditions?' She couldn't understand it.

'Ah well, there was one. If ye both agree, they intend to marry ye at the same time as Bryce and Eormenric, but . . . they do not intend to let ye consummate the marriage until Javotte hast turned eight and ten.' Rhun grinned at his young friend's misfortune.

'What!' Blain objected; this was far worse than postponing the wedding a year. He could have no lover at all.

'I told thee.' Javotte suppressed her amusement as she slipped from the room. 'Happy hunting, chaps.'

'I shall not agree!' Blain protested more adamantly once they were alone. 'Where be my father when I need him. He would never have stood for this!'

'Calm down,' Rhun advised. 'Once thou art married to Javotte and crowned King of Powys, what can they do?' He gave Blain a whack on the back, and a wink of encouragement.

'Indeed.' Blain was appeased somewhat.

'Now thou hast only to worry about what Javotte will do to thee.' Rhun could only just beat her in hand-to-hand combat, and he was years more experienced than his young friend.

'Aye,' Blain whined, already pondering how he might get around her. 'I shall just have to provoke her.'

'Have I taught thee nothing? Thou means persuade.' Rhun corrected.

'Nay.' Blain smiled. 'I mean, provoke.'

The memorial service was held at dawn and although Taliesin gave a beautiful liturgy, Tory could not bring herself to mourn. Maelgwn was not dead. He was off on an incredible adventure, and in fact, she couldn't help but be envious. Tory was just beginning to put the deaths of Brockwell, Alma, Rhys and Jenovefa behind her, having lived with their other incarnations for months. She'd seen Brockwell in Adelgar and Brian; she'd seen Rhys in Darius and John Pearce. No one really died. Death was one phase of the journey, a graceful pause; a chance for a new start in an entirely different time and circumstance.

Fortunately, by the end of the service, Taliesin had urged everyone to the same mind:

'So if I should go before thee
break not a flower, nor engrave a stone.
Do not speak in reserved voices,
but be the good selves I have known.
For I preside in the Otherworld,
where the sun dost not rise nor set,
So if thou wilt, remember,
and if thou wilt, forget.'

Tory looked across to Katren with her four boys standing dutifully beside her, each one so like Calin in different respects. *I do miss him.* She gave a sigh, and sniffled back a tear.

The younger folk seemed to be coping with their losses rather well. Although they had been most reverent during the service, once the memorial was over and the wake was well under way they begged their parents leave, having made plans of their own.

Tomorrow Rhun and Blain would face inauguration; they would not see too many more carefree days such as this again, so Tory let them have their way.

'We won't go far,' Rhun vowed as he kissed his mother's cheek, and headed for the stables after the others.

'Should we send Selwyn with them?' Katren could just imagine what they might get up to unsupervised.

'Nay, let them go.' Tory took her friend's hand and patted it. 'We have to start trusting them sooner or later. They shall be running the country before long.' She was confident and trusting on the outside, but as Rhun could spy on her movements so could she spy on his.

Javotte pursued the gaggle of boys out into the hallway. 'Where art thou going?'

'For a ride,' Blain answered.

'Can I come?'

'Nay,' young Cai yelled back, pacing along beside Rhun. 'Girls have to stay here. Be that not right?' He gazed up at his hero, who patted his head.

'That's right!' Rhun seconded, as all disappeared out the door.

Javotte had grown up with many of these boys, and they'd never excluded her before. 'Thou cannot stop me! It be a free kingdom!' she yelled after them.

Javotte caught up with them at the stables, where Gareth, Gawain, Eormenric, Rhun and the four princes of Powys had mounted their horses.

'Why won't thou let me come? Where art thou going?' She questioned Blain in what he construed to be a rather stubborn and unbecoming fashion. 'Thou dost not want to know, little girl,' he teased her with a cavalier smile, much to his comrades amusement.

'Get down off that horse. I shall show thee who be the little girl.' She challenged, feeling awkward and left out.

'Oooh!' They all jeered at her proposal.

'Be that a promise?' Blain raised both eyebrows in a suggestive fashion.

'It be a threat.' Her hands clenched into fists.

'Not the answer we were looking for.' Blain made light of her vexation. 'Better luck next time.' He took off on his steed, the others right behind him.

'This not be fair,' she yelled once they'd gone. 'Curse womanhood, curse it!' She spun round in circles a moment, at a loss for what to do. 'They art not kings yet.' She collected her riding gear and headed off down through the stables to where her horse was housed.

Rhun led the party a small way into the mountains, to where a large, grassy field overlooked the citadel and the river below. Here, in this idyllic, isolated setting, they found seven lovely maidens on a large blanket, laying out a picnic fit for a king.

'Surprise.' Rhun sprang to the ground. 'Please meet Eva, Gwendaline, Andrea, Lily, Rebecca, Catalina and Margarette.' He grinned at the delighted confusion his companions' could not hide as they dismounted. 'This be my way of ensuring that we see out our bachelorhood with a bang.'

'How very thoughtful. And though I have no intention of getting wed,' Gareth thumped Rhun on the shoulder in appreciation, 'I shall accept all the same.'

'Where did thou find such divine creatures.' Blain wandered aimlessly towards the splendid vision of paradise.

Gawain placed an arm over Rhun's shoulder. 'This be awfully sporting of thee, I must say. It appears thou hast completely outdone thyself this time, my lad.' He staggered to the closest female and fell to the ground, his head landing comfortably in her lap. 'Ah, much better.'

'Rhun . . . thou art going to get us all in strife.' Bryce hated to be the voice of reason.

'It be only a picnic,' Rhun countered, playing innocent.

'And what a feast.' Owen made a move to dive right in, when Bryce caught him up by the collar.

'Thou art not old enough for this.'

'I beg to differ,' Owen appealed. 'Father wast my age when thou wast conceived.' He reclaimed his person from his older brother and moved to find himself a willing maid.

'Thou said no girls,' Cai protested; this wasn't going to be any fun at all.

'Nay, I said no girls were coming with us,' Rhun corrected. 'These girls were already here.'

'Cai most certainly be underage.' Bryce felt he had to draw the line somewhere.

'Yeah . . . what am I going to do?'

Rhun gave them both a knowing smile as he reached into his saddlebag and pulled out a silk-wrapped package, which he handed to Cai. 'The complete works of Aristotle, from my father's private collection.'

'No kidding?' Cai peeled back the silken cloth to view the priceless work. 'Wow, this be amazing.' He wandered off to find a quiet spot to read, his eyes already glued to the text.

'There. Everybody's happy,' Rhun exclaimed, noting Bryce didn't seem any more appreciative. 'Oh, come on. Indulge while you still can,' the prince urged his friend. 'There be nothing wrong with a good orgy . . . thou taught me that.' He gave Bryce a nudge as he moved to join the party.

'Worst mistake I ever made, introducing thee to women.' Bryce resigned himself to humouring his friend — but only to a point.

A bonfire was stacked and set alight to combat the evening chill; thus all the lads and lasses took time to watch the stars come out.

'Surely, not even in the Otherworld, do things get better than this.' Owen snuggled between the exposed breasts of the maid beneath him; her skin felt softer than down against his cheek.

'Ah . . . the Otherworld.' Rhun stared up at the huge, dark expanse overhead, trying to imagine what his father was doing at this instant. 'I propose a toast.' He sat upright, working around the girl still straddled over his lap to pour a drink. 'To the warriors of the Goddess, past and future. May the Otherworld ever grant them glory.'

'To the warriors!' all voiced with conviction, and drank.

'No offence, Rhun.' Blain sat up. 'But although the High King wast a great warrior, I believe my father wast greater still.'

'Nay,' Bryce corrected, throwing on his shirt in the wake of a long shoulder massage; he didn't feel he could be chastised for that. 'Calin Brockwell was the greatest warrior that ever was, or ever will be.'

Rhun refilled his goblet quickly, accidentally spilling mead down Catalina's cleavage and sipping it away. 'To King Brockwell, a warrior beyond compare.'

'To King Brockwell!' they cried, and drank again.

'What was the greatest thing thy father ever did, Eormenric?' Rhun enquired of him, refilling both their glasses.

Eormenric laughed at this. 'I think, fighting Britons and living to tell of it.' Rhun translated his response for those who didn't speak Saxon, whereby they all fell about laughing. 'What about thee, Gawain? Do tell us; What was Sir Rhys' finest achievement?'

'My father's finest achievement?' Gawain propped his head up on his hand and grinned. 'Well, quite obviously, that must have been me.'

'Obviously!' The maid at his back gave him a squeeze and a kiss.

'And thou, my prince,' Catalina quizzed Rhun in her exotic foreign accent, still entertaining his fully erect member underneath her skirts. 'What wast the greatest thing thy father ever did?' Her hips thrust forward to distract him.

'Oh.' Rhun considered the question, then his expression lost all its frivolity. 'Wedding my mother wast the best thing my father ever did.' The prince gave a thought to his intended, feeling a twinge of guilt. He withdrew from Catalina abruptly, doing up his trousers and lifting her from his lap.

'I would marry thy mother,' said Cai, having wandered back from his secluded reading nook to be by the fire.

'In a heartbeat,' Bryce agreed, taking Cai under his arm as he came to sit beside him. Bryce watched Rhun get to his feet, seemingly perplexed. 'Art thou going somewhere?'

'Indeed.' Rhun took up both of Catalina's hands, kissing them in turn. 'I must pay my betrothed a visit . . . but I do urge thou all to stay and enjoy.' He took one last swig of mead, and with a hiccup, vanished.

'Holy mother! Where did he go?' Blain staggered to his feet to look for him, as did most of the others.

'What a show-off.' Bryce rolled his eyes, grinning broadly. But his amusement dwindled as he noted the sound of a horse approaching, and turned to espy the rider. 'Sir Tiernan!' Bryce announced in a loud voice to alert the others. 'What art thou doing here?'

Everybody froze as the warrior dismounted and approached. He wore a look upon his face that spelt ruination for those before him, as he cast his sights over the scene.

'Well, I hope ye all enjoyed thyselves.' His tone hinted at their doom. 'This little stunt could cost the alliance dearly.'

Bryce's eyes narrowed. 'What dost thou mean?'

'Javotte saw ye all!' Tiernan scolded them for their stupidity. 'She told the other maidens, and now all marriages are off!'

'All marriages?' Bryce near died from the shock of it.

'All!' Tiernan repeated harshly. 'Where be Prince Rhun?'

'He disappeared,' Blain advised, with a good serve of accusation behind the statement.

'Gawain, Gareth. See these women safely back to the village. The rest of ye — mount up . . . . now!' Tiernan shouted to snap them to action. 'Ladies.' The knight bowed to the stunned females, and took his leave with the disgraced princes of Prydyn.

29

THE DRAGON'S SEED

Prince Rhun stirred to an annoying stabbing pain in his side, which he tried to prevent with a wave of his a hand.

'Rhun.' Tory poked him harder. 'Some friend thou art. And look at thee!' She stood to get an overall view.

'Mother?' he croaked, shielding his eyes from the light to get a look at her. She smiled in a mocking fashion, crouching beside him to whisper her wrath that built to a deafening crescendo. 'Wake up and smell the roses, sweetheart. Thou art in deep shit!' She stood and began to pace.

Rhun held onto his head as her voice vibrated through it, managing to get to a seated position. He was in a forest by a stream, though he did not recognise the place. 'Where am I?' he dared to ask.

'We art in Powys, somewhere,' Tory stopped still long enough to tell him. 'Apparently, thou vanished from the orgy last night to see Bridgit in Dyfed. Luckily thou never made it that far.'

'Thou dost know about the picnic then?' He cringed.

'If thou can see into my private affairs, art thou so bold as to think I could not do the same? Of course I know! Everybody knows!' Tory could barely constrain her urge to wring his neck, and so returned to pacing out her frustration.

Rhun stood up to vent his annoyance, but had to fall back on the support of a tree. 'Thou betrayed us to everyone?'

Tory stopped still and glared at him. 'Javotte saw thee. She saw her husband-to-be ravishing another on the eve of their engagement. How dost thou think she feels right now?'

Rhun looked away, unable to answer. His mind was foggy and it throbbed with a vengeance.

'Aella be not speaking with Bryce, nor Vanora with Eormenric. And need I tell thee what Vortipor thinks of thee marrying his daughter?' Tory was almost enjoying rubbing salt into his wounds. 'What it hast taken us twenty years to build, my son, thou hast destroyed in one day.'

'I did not mean for this to happen.'

He sounded very sorry for himself, so Tory decided that a bit of understanding might be of more help at this stage. 'What wast thou thinking? I cannot believe thou really thought I would not know. Thou art just not that stupid.'

'I knew thee would find out. I thought it might prove me too irresponsible to be left to rule a kingdom . . . which, I guess, I have pretty much established.' He paused, having a bitter taste in his mouth. 'But I knew thee would not tell anyone else about it. Thus it just seemed like a bit of fun with the lads before we all settle down. I truly did not intend to get anyone into trouble, bar myself.'

Her heart broke upon hearing his explanation, yet her exterior appearance remained unaffected. 'And what wast thy intent in visiting Bridgit, still reeking of another woman?'

'I wast not even going to wake her,' he swore. 'I just wanted to watch her sleep.'

'Well, unless a miracle happens, thou can kiss goodbye any hope of ever doing that.'

'I have to get back to Degannwy.' The prince knelt by the river to splash water on his face.

'Thou shall find all concerned in the room of court, being rebuked by Sir Tiernan,' Tory forewarned him. 'This would have taken place last night, but they were all too drunk to stand.'

Rhun nodded, accepting the fact that he was not going to be well received upon arrival.

'Boy . . .' Tory neared him. 'Thou could never convince me that thou art unfit to be a king. For I know otherwise.'

'Then it must be so.' He smiled, grimly. 'I shall justify thy faith.' He kissed her forehead and thought of his friends.

'Well, thank thee so much for joining us. Majesty!'

Bryce had a hold of Rhun before he'd even realised he was there. 'My lady refuses to see me.' He belted his king-to-be clear across the room.

Holy smoke. Rhun shook his head as he recovered. It be a good thing I am immortal. Gawain and Eormenric restrained the Prince of Powys, whilst the Prince of Gwynedd dragged himself back to his feet to assure Bryce: 'I have an eyewitness who can testify thou got no more than a back rub and a free feed.'

'Who? Javotte!' Bryce seethed, unable to break free from his fellow masters. 'She be so distraught, she would swear Cai had been involved!'

'Nay, my mother,' Rhun shot back at him. 'She saw the whole thing through my eyes.' His tone weakened as he confessed.

'The whole thing!' Owen turned white.

'And what about Javotte?' Blain came forward with his gripe.

'Look, I shall talk to her . . .' Rhun put forward.

'Talk to her!' Blain grabbed hold of Rhun by the shirt. 'She saw me making love to another woman. No amount of talk be going to wipe that image from her mind.'

The two princes glared at each other a moment, but it was Rhun who broke the silence. 'I did not force thee to take pleasure with another, Blain. That wast thine own choice.'

'Damn thee!' Blain threw a punch, which Rhun managed to avoid.

'Enough!' Tiernan couldn't take any more of this infantile display. 'Sit down . . . the lot of ye!' He shoved those still standing into chairs. 'If you think it will be so easy to fill the shoes of thy fathers . . . think again! The goddess herself shall sit in judgement on thee this night.' He looked from Rhun to Blain. 'And so help me . . . thou had better have thy wits about thee by then.'

Taliesin and Selwyn came forward from where they'd been quietly observing the goings-on. 'Rhun, come with me.' Taliesin spoke briskly. 'It would seem we have much work to do before nightfall. Tiernan, I shall met thee and the rest of the initiation party at Llyn Cerrig Bach this evening.'

Tiernan bowed his head.

'Blain, thou shall go with Selwyn. The rest of thy party shall catch thee up by dusk.' As the two Princes moved silently to obey, Taliesin advised: 'We shall resolve the rest of this matter upon thy return to thy respective cities for inauguration.'

The High Merlin was concerned, to say the very least.

When Maelgwn had faced the Goddess before his inauguration, he'd fasted and meditated for two whole days and nights beforehand. Here Rhun was, less than half a day away from the test, hung-over, emotionally stressed and physically exhausted. Taliesin was of half a mind to postpone the initiation, but he felt this course of action would be too risky. Mahaud would be gestating somewhere, on the lookout for a negative soul to latch onto. Everyone who had any power in Britain was protected from her at present, so her chances of thwarting them in the near future were considerably lessened. Still, he wasn't prepared to take any risks. They needed a ruler on the throne of Gwynedd and Powys just in case all hell broke loose again.

The prince trailed Taliesin through his labyrinth, wondering what kind of gruelling preparation the Merlin had planned for him. He wanted to live up to the legend that his father had begun, though he couldn't imagine how he would. It was hard to feel like a great hero when you'd just placed your homeland's future in jeopardy, and all your friends and subjects despised you for it. He eyed over the battledress of past and future warriors that seemed to be looming over him in judgement as he passed them by in the corridor. He knew these different characters were the key to finding the way around the Merlin's labyrinth. However, he had been here many times before and every time he thought he'd seen it all, he would discover another doorway, corridor or stairwell that he'd never seen before — like the passageway they proceeded down at present.

Although the doors in the corridor appeared to be no more than two horse lengths apart, the Merlin led him into a room that was the size of a large cathedral.

Rhun was intrigued to find that this held a huge sandstone pool of steamy water. Large, white marble columns towered upwards to meet ornately carved arches, depicting heroes, lovers, gods and goddesses. 'Space be an illusion.' Rhun came to a stop beside the Merlin at the pool's edge.

'Indeed.' Taliesin turned to his pupil and thrust him, clothes and all, into the water. 'Now bathe.'

Rhun stiffened, having been caught off-guard, but as he plunged downward through the warm, aerated pool he relaxed to enjoy the sensation. He surfaced, ripping the soiled clothes from his body, so as to float on his back in unrestricted bliss. 'Ah . . .'

Clear thy mind.

Taliesin's voice echoed through his brain.

Nothing external matters here . . . for the battle of the spiritual warrior be always with the self. The ability to rise above setbacks in life be one of the three main prerequisites of a king. Forget the insignificant details of ordinary life and embrace a broader vision . . .

The Merlin spoke of the great leaders who'd gone before him, of their fears and doubts before inauguration and of the legendary feats they'd gone on to achieve. He told of the Dragon of Keridwen, who had been his father's Otherworld affiliate. The descendant of this animal had been spawned at about the same time Rhun himself had been conceived.

Rhun would have to summon forth a beast to guard the gateway to the Otherworld, so that his spirit might travel through it unharmed. If the Otherworld still favoured the young prince the offspring of the Dragon of Keridwen was the creature the Goddess would send to his aid.

The Merlin reviewed the nine metaphysical laws, especially the laws of Rebound, Challenge and Equality, for if the crone should try to obstruct the prince in his quest, these were the laws that needed to be foremost in his mind.

Though Rhun knew the attributes and functions of all the gods and goddesses of the Otherworld backwards, Taliesin defined those that were involved in the initiation process. Gwydion, the deity of science, light, and music would set the task required of the prince. But as the dispenser of the old truths, it was the crone, Keridwen, who would announce it. Taliesin's role was to record what took place during Rhun's flight into the Otherworld, so that his story could be imparted to future inaugurates.

Once he'd crammed the prince's brain with more information and words of wisdom than he could barely ingest in one sitting, Taliesin supplied Rhun with a clean pair of trousers and led him to a meditation chamber.

As the prince entered the room, which was round and of a moderate size, he was confronted by an image of himself in a large mirror situated on the wall directly opposite the door. The floor beneath his feet was of padded white leather which sank into a pit filled with pillows. The timber-lined walls scented the interior with the pleasant smell of cedarwood; combined with the dim lighting, this was most soothing to the senses.

Taliesin motioned the prince to the pit in the centre of the room, and once Rhun was seated comfortably therein the Merlin conjured up a golden goblet and offered it to his initiate. 'Drink.'

As Rhun accepted the chalice and raised it to his lips, he caught a whiff of the brew and hesitated. 'Must I?' Taliesin, who'd been regarding him with the same austere gaze all day, nodded.

'It be the elixir of Kings.' The High Merlin couldn't help but smile as he recalled Maelgwyn's impression of the mild hallucinogen. 'Thy father highly recommends it.' Upon hearing this, the young prince gave a shrug and gulped down the brew. 'From the cauldron of inspiration, it shall heighten the senses and aid the ease of separation of the spirit from thy body.'

'Whoo . . .' Rhun thumped his chest with his fist to endure the tingling, burning sensation of the potent mixture as passed down into his innards. ''Tis as harsh as it smells.' He handed the goblet back, whereby it vanished and the Merlin made for the door.

'I shall return for thee when thy time hast come.' He paused before exiting. 'Until then, I suggest thou be still and let the elixir take effect. Block out everything external, and no matter what thy seven senses tell thee, do not break from thy meditation to heed them . . . understood?'

Rhun nodded, assuming the lotus position. He closed his eyes to seek the muse.

Most of the men had departed to attend one initiation or the other, when Katren came to visit Tory in her chambers. As she'd had no success in reasoning with the no longer brides-to-be, the Queen of Powys was a complete nervous wreck.

'If those boys were hares on the mountainside, I swear those girls would grab a bow and go a-hunting,' she mumbled through her tears, wiping them away with a handkerchief. 'Powys shall be without a Queen, and therefore

infertile and barren . . . that will be how the general populace shall see it.'
Katren collapsed into tears again.

'Right.' Tory had had enough of the fun and games; time to put a stop to this nonsense before it got out of hand.

'What art thou going to do?' Katren was relieved to see her friend looking so determined, and hurried after her to bear witness to the proceedings.

The girls in question were gathered in the sewing room, where all work had ceased on the bridal gowns. Aella and Vanora were still consoling young Javotte, cursing men for their thoughtless acts and absence of heart.

'Sensei.' Javotte spotted Tory poised in the doorway, whereby all three girls rose and bowed their heads dutifully.

'Be at ease, ladies.' She motioned them all to take a seat, a little annoyed by their harsh view of the opposite sex. 'Javotte, I want thee to forget everything Aella and Vanora just said to thee . . . men art wonderful creatures when understood and handled properly. Lest we forget,' Tory's voice rose upon sensing their resistance, 'if not for the brave deeds of these men, who thou art so quick to condemn and dismiss, we would all be living a nightmare right now.' Katren repeated the conversation for the Saxon lass's benefit. When Tory turned to address Aella, she and Katren switched languages. 'After all young Prince Bryce went through for thee . . .' She shook her head, as if disappointed with the girl. 'Thou would throw away such a treasure, because he wast massaged by another woman?'

'What?' Aella's eyes opened wide.

'That was the extent of his involvement. Prince Rhun and I have a mental link. As he can perceive my affairs through my eyes, so can I view his.'

''Tis true,' Katren confirmed.

'Make no mistake, Aella, Bryce loves thee, and hast done nothing to warrant thy disfavour. I am sure if Javotte thinks hard enough, she shall recall it was as I say.'

Although the recollection of the scene filled Javotte's eyes with tears, after a moment the girl nodded to confirm her sensei spoke the truth.

'There,' Tory put to Aella, who still seemed a little hesitant to reconsider. 'So be warned. If thou art foolish enough to relinquish a lover so true, I might just have to wed him myself.'

The girl was rather taken aback by the suggestion, knowing her intended did hold deep feelings for the once High Queen — despite the age difference. 'I am no fool, Highness.' The girl resolved, much to Katren's relief. 'I shall wed as planned.'

'Thy faith shall be rewarded, I promise thee,' the Queen assured. Looking to the next on her hit list she again changed her dialect. 'Now Vanora . . . I know what Eormenric did wast wrong. But, in asking that thou find it in thy heart to forgive him, I request no more than he did for thee. After all, thine own conduct hast not always been exemplary, and he did risk much to save thee from Mahaud. My son can be very persuasive at times, and Eormenric, being the outsider, wants so desperately to be accepted by his new companions that . . .' Tory shrugged, hoping she'd understand.

Vanora inhaled deeply as her feelings and emotions did battle. 'Perhaps I am being a little harsh on him . . . but that be not to say that I won't make him suffer for his thoughtless act.'

'By all means do,' Tory agreed. 'But to walk away from him now, I truly believe, would be a mistake . . . everybody deserves at least one chance.'

'Well, as thou hast given me two such opportunities in the past . . .' She felt strangely warmed by the notion of forgiving her love instead of chastising him. 'I too shall wed as planned.' Vanora melted to a smile, inwardly elated by her decision.

'Thou shall not regret it,' Tory pledged, well pleased.

As her sensei's sights drifted her way, Javotte stood to protest. 'Please do not say I must still marry him, sensei . . . I could not!'

'I would never make thee do anything thee did not want to, Javotte.' Tory neared her, and took hold of her hands to urge her to a calmer state. 'But, if thou shalt not wed him, I ask that thou tell Blain so, to his face.'

'Nay, I beg thee.' Javotte was aghast. 'I could not.'

'And why not?' Tory ruthlessly pursued the issue. 'Because thou still carries a torch for him, perhaps? As thou hast done for years?'

'Alright! Aye, I admit it!'

The girl began to weep and Katren moved to comfort her, yet Tory motioned her friend to stay where she was. 'I never thought I would see the day when thou gave up anything thee desired without a fight, Javotte.'

'He doth not love me!' the young warrioress snapped at her superior, having reached her wits' end.

'I suspected thee thought as much.' Tory eased off on her interrogation. 'But what if thou wast to discover that exactly the opposite was true?'

'Nothing could convince me of that now, sensei.' Javotte calmed a little, drained of emotion.

Tory approached to hold her, and the girl did not resist. 'What if I was to tell thee that, at present, Prince Blain be under the influence of the elixir of kings, which be a brew of inspiration, and . . . a truth serum of sorts.' The girl looked up at her, obviously curious to hear more. 'If I were to take thee to him now, thou could ask Prince Blain any question, and he could not lie to thee. Art thou up to it?' Tory raised her brow to await an answer, whereby Javotte agreed.

Katren looked to Tory amazed, and mouthed the words, 'Bless thee.'

Selwyn was tutoring the young king-to-be in a forest glen by the edge of a lake, not too far from Maen Llia. Blain, too, had been swimming to get his wits about him, and having taken some of the elixir was absorbing nature's elements from a rock in the sunshine.

While he listened to the holy man's counsel, the prince's attention wandered up the hillside where he spied the Queen of Gwynedd descending with Javotte. 'Merlin, I think I am hallucinating.' He motioned to their visitors.

Selwyn laughed once he'd viewed their company. 'Nay, I think not.'

'She be really here?' Blain rose, in a rush to get to her, before reseating himself in an anxious fashion. 'May I be excused?'

'That thee may.' Selwyn was more than happy to grant him leave.

'Greetings, sensei.' Blain bowed as he raced past, heading up the hill to where Javotte awaited him.

'I am so glad thou got her here,' Selwyn said as he reached Tory. 'It has been near impossible to get him to focus on anything else.'

'I thought that might be the case.' She took her friend's arm to stroll a way with him.

'Javotte.' Blain scampered up the steep incline on all fours. 'I am so thankful thou art here. I have not been able to think of anyone else all day.'

The prince came to a stop before her, dressed only in a pair of trousers. His long, dark curls were still damp from his dip, and they dripped water down over the well developed muscles of his smooth upper body.

'Pity that wast not the case yesterday.' Her voice projected disbelief.

'But I wast thinking of thee.' He spoke with passion. 'I wast thinking of thee the whole time.'

'Blain Brockwell!' She placed her hands on her hips, furious with him. 'Thou art coming very close to a beating.'

'I know I am . . . but it be the truth.' His words were full of fire. 'She rather looked like thee,' he said guilelessly. 'Though her body hardly did thine justice.'

'Blain!' Javotte fought off his advances, unsure as to whether she should be flattered or horrified. 'What art thou saying to me?'

'I am saying that I worship thee.' Blain clutched hold of her wrists. 'Thou art a goddess in thine own right. I never told thee so before, because I wast too afraid thou would belt me. Maybe it be the elixir, but I . . . I . . . I love thee, Javotte.' His eyes, bluer than the sky above, were alive with vigour as he confessed his ardour. 'So do what thou wilt, but my feelings shall remain unchanged.'

He could not be fibbing, sensei said so. She stared back at him blankly a moment, then grabbed his head between her hands and kissed him long and hard.

'That be because I love thee, too.' She held her dazed victim at arm's length before landing a spirited punch to his abdomen and watching with great pleasure as he keeled over on his knees. 'And that be for not telling me sooner.'

He gasped under his breath, winded from the blow. 'So dost this mean thou will marry me?' He wobbled back to his feet. 'Even if I must wait a year to claim thee, I still want to . . . if thou will have me.'

'No fear!' she protested strongly. 'That would just be asking for trouble.' She placed both her arms around his neck. 'I shall be thine on our wedding night, or there shall be no wedding.' She revelled in the look of relief on his face, before grabbing hold of a clump of his hair and pulling it taut. 'But, I tell thee this — if thou dost ever so much as look at another woman thou will not live to make the same mistake again.'

'Ah, ah . . . I understand,' he conceded, gently freeing her fingers from his hair. 'Thou art more than gracious.'

'Just thou remember it,' she warned with a kiss, thrusting him backwards as she headed off down the hillside to rendezvous with her lift home. 'Long live the king!' Javotte turned back to him briefly to shout, raising her powerful arms into the air as she did.

Blain smiled, holding up a hand in response, the joyous expression upon the face of his betrothed filling him with renewed hope and determination.

Hours later, Taliesin entered the meditation chamber fully expecting to find the prince painted from head to toe with the artwork of the Otherworldly folk. Rhun's father had been blessed thus by the Tylwyth Teg before initiation; there had scarce been a bare patch of skin on his body that had not been adorned by their artwork.

But, to the Merlin's profound horror, Rhun appeared exactly as he'd left him, his ivory skin clean. *I do not understand. I know he be one of the Chosen. He stared at the lad, still cross-legged in the pit before him. The Tylwyth Teg grant him ease of mobility through their realms, so why then have they not claimed him?*

'Be something the matter, High Merlin?' Rhun was bemused by the Merlin's perplexed stance.

'Not at all.' Taliesin motioned him to his feet. Maybe the boy's foolish stunt had cost them more dearly than he'd expected; the support of the folk meant the difference between a prosperous reign and famine. The men that had been at Maelgwn's inauguration would notice the absence of the markings at once. *Surely the folk would not judge him so harshly for one simple mistake. On the whole, Rhun's behaviour and ability has always proven exemplary.* The Merlin moved to follow the prince from the room, beholding on Rhun's back that which he thought was missing.

'Caduceus!' The Merlin announced, both shocked and excited. 'I have never seen this depicted on any initiate before.'

'Pardon?' Rhun frowned, as the Merlin dragged him over to the mirror to see for himself. 'Unbelievable! I did not feel a thing.' He marvelled at the picture of the winged rod, extending all the way up his spine with serpents entwining it. 'What doth it mean?'

'This be the age-old emblem of the Lord of Time and Space. In ancient times it was worn by those who had earnt the right to hold a royal office. The serpents represent polarity, good and evil, order and chaos, that are brought into balance under the wings of transpersonal consciousness.' The Merlin was simply delighted by the implications of this. 'It would seem the Goddess' folk have high expectations of thee. This be a very good sign for thy rule.'

'Art thou saying the Tylwyth Teg put this here?' Rhun sounded a little sceptical, having never met with any evidence of the fabled folk of the mists.

'Ha-ha!' The Merlin chuckled. 'Thou art in for an eye-opening experience this evening.' Then, placing his hands on Rhun's shoulders, he told him in earnest: 'But no matter what transpires, remember all who gather here tonight, do so in thy honour and support. There be nothing, and no one, for thou to fear here.'

'I am not afraid, High Merlin,' Rhun advised, raring to go.

Taliesin's brow raised at this boast and his smile broadened. 'Nay, but thou might well be.'

Back in the real world, the turbulent clouds in the night sky were alive with electrical activity. Torches encircled the perimeter of the initiation site, and despite the spectacular commotion overhead, the atmosphere in the valley was still and calm.

The nobles of Gwynedd, and their guests, were gathered in a circle in the clearing outside the temple — Sir Tiernan, Vortipor, Fergus MacErc, Sir Guillym, Sir Gawain and Sir Gareth amongst them. All were decorated with body paint in accordance with the old tradition, and seated around a cauldron that simmered away furiously over an open fire.

The drums pounded and the thunder boomed as Taliesin led Rhun from the temple to his place before his subjects, who all appeared a mite baffled by his spotless appearance.

The young prince bowed to them all, raising his arms to flex the well rounded muscles of his upper body as he turned to display the symbolic caduceus that ran the length of his spine — its wings extending across his broad shoulders.

Praise the Goddess, Sir Tiernan thought, most relieved to see the blessing of the folk.

As the High Merlin began the ceremony, a goblet was dipped into the elixir that brewed inside the cauldron and each of the men present took a sip.

As Rhun consumed another whole cup of the liquid, the sensation of separation between his body and his spirit increased. The pounding drums numbed his physical form, so that it felt weighted to the ground, yet Rhun's subtle body seemed to be hovering just slightly out of alignment with his earthy presence as it prepared to take flight.

'I am the one who heartens the soul,
to the glory of the spirits.
It is mine to exalt the hero;
to persuade the unadvised;
to awaken the silent beholder . . .
the bold illuminator of Kings!'

At the Merlin's words, the storm above became more agitated. The dulcet tones of the ancient's bell tolled, whipping up a wind that began to howl around the peaceful glen. In the distance, behind the temple ruins where the valley rose to its greatest height, there was a great burst of light. After the initial blinding flash, this settled to a seething lustrous ball that spewed mist into the valley below.

The haze rolled over the assembly, bringing with it all the aroma of a spring day, as voices, sweeter than any the prince had ever heard, raised in song. *The Tylwyth Teg?* He could scarce believe it.

'The Otherworldly realm hast opened to the initiate. Summon forth the beast who shall guard the gateway,' Taliesin intoned, and silently prayed as he watched the young prince close his eyes to focus.

After a moment or two, a great rumbling sound was heard. The men who'd not borne witness to King Maelgwn's rites, looked to each other fearfully.

A deafening screech followed, as a great winged beast burst forth from the blazing vortex of light on the mountain peak.

Not weighty and cumbersome as King Maelgwn's Otherworld affiliate had been, this beast was slender, agile and far more ferocious in appearance.

'It be the legend!' Tiernan stood and looked to the red creature as it hovered above, spewing flames into the stormy night sky between screeches. 'It be the pet of the goddess Keridwen herself.' He laughed in exultation. There was a time when the knight would have been as fearful of this phenomena as the rest of those present were, but experience had taught him better.

The dragon alighted behind the young prince, looking down upon the earthling he'd been assigned to protect. *The Goddess awaits thee. Go to her, knowing thy return to the Middle Kingdom be assured by Archimedes, spawn of Rufus, the new guardian of this land.*

Rhun opened his eyes to behold a miraculous sight before him — himself! He sat informing his men that he'd taken leave of his physical form. *Now what?* he wondered.

'Son.'

A familiar voice sought his attention from behind, and the prince turned to find Maelgwn awaiting him. 'Father! Praise the Goddess thou art here! But how art thou here?'

'The Otherworld be a universal place,' his father informed with a smile. 'But it be not just I who have come to greet thee.' Maelgwn motioned to the surrounding forest emanating brilliant colour.

Hundreds of tiny beings of light twirled their way through the air; others hovered in and around the foliage of the forest. Strange hairless beings, of all sizes, with heads and bodies much larger than their skinny little limbs, watched him through large, black, slanted eyes. Dwarfed men and breathtaking nymphs emerged from trees, rocks, and flowerbeds. Strange, indescribable creatures crawled, slithered, flew and burrowed around him everywhere.

'The . . . folk?' He gaped at the wild array.

'Indeed.' Maelgwn motioned to his son to close his dropping jaw. 'But it be not polite to stare.'

Rhun followed his father to the temple, that now appeared as if it had just been erected. Inside he found that the large altar stone had been moved aside, to reveal what appeared to be a bottomless pit.

'Come.' Maelgwn urged him to follow, as he jumped into the void and disappeared into the darkened depths.

'Father?' Rhun called for reassurance, but when there came no response he closed his eyes and leapt into the void.

He fell — no, he floated, or perhaps he wasn't moving at all.

'Rhun?' Maelgwn urged him to open his eyes.

The young prince complied to behold a landscape so fair that no earthly place could possibly compare to it.

The earth was greener than the Snowdon ranges in spring, the flowers more beauteous and abundant than those that had once grown in the inner bailey gardens at Aberffraw. Stately fountains spouted water in the middle of large pools that glistened like crystal jewels. In the sky above not a cloud could been seen, and astonishingly enough, that source of earthly light and warmth, the sun, was not present either — for everything here emitted its own light.

Not far across the grounds in front of them was a small round marble gazebo, with stairs that led up to the central platform. As Rhun approached alongside his father, he couldn't help but notice the two lovely maidens that lazed against a pillar to each side of the stairs, watching his approach.

The dainty, dark-haired woman was dressed all in white. But the other, who had fiery auburn locks and a physique that could only compare with his mother's, was attired entirely in red.

Maelgwn came to a stop at the bottom of the stairs. 'This be as far as I may go. I wish thee success in thy quest, though I know thou will not fail.' He bowed his head and faded from sight.

'Father!' Rhun had not expected him to leave so abruptly.

'Thou art the Dragon of the Island now.' The petite maiden in white came down the stairs and took hold of his hands. 'Thus we call on thee to defend the Chair.' Branwen backed up, leading him up the stairs. 'All the pleasures of this world shall be thine, if thou succeeds.' She stopped halfway to run her hands over the well defined ridges of his stomach, up over his pectorals and across his broad shoulders, admiring every inch of the journey. 'Passion and desire beyond thy wildest aspirations.'

Rhun was so captivated by her sultry promises, he had not even noticed the warrioress come to stand at his other side.

'There be a menace in our midst.' Rhiannon directed his attention to herself, pressing her body against his. 'The elements of its nature, drawn from the darkest depths of creation.'

'Mahaud?' Rhun guessed at her meaning.

'Ahh . . .' She smiled, slinking away from him, as she backed up with the other maiden to the plateau, where a third woman, dressed all in black, stood with her back to him.

'Correct.' The tiny, silver-haired crone turned her huge green-grey eyes to view him.

Keridwen. Rhun scaled the stairs to kneel before her.

The three women merged to become the one glowing green being, known as Don. The divine mother spoke with the voices of the maiden, the warrioress and the crone. 'As we draw our power from the realms above the earthly plane, the said abomination draws its power from those below it. The earth, as a polarised entity, hast places where positive or negative power might be drawn from it, depending upon thy intent. Find the select location from whence Mahaud draws her life force, when not doing so from human beings, and destroy it . . . then she shall plague thy nation no more.'

'I understand.' Rhun bowed his head in reverence, as the three women separated.

'Gwydion hast decreed that thou must go as thou art to Ongen, son of Ossa, in Londinium.' Keridwen advised. 'In the dungeon of the Saxon stronghold, thou shall find the four implements belonging to Mahaud, by which she was summoned back from the lower etheric realms. Her wand of Fire thou must take to the southern-most tip of Britain, where the land of Lyonesse once stood. Here the wand must be broken and burnt, until nothing but ash remains. The sword of the archtraitor, Vortigern, must be taken to the eastern-most tip of Anglia, where thou shall find a tiny seaside town and a blind smithy, who answers to the name of Morda. Take him this sword, and he shall melt it down to use as scrap metal. Both the large and small cauldrons of the witch must be taken beyond the western shore of Britain, over the sea, to where thou shall find an island with a mountain of fire. Drop the cauldrons into this and they shall be lost forever. Lastly, take the black crystal to the Isle of Orkney, off the northern tip of Alban, and there thou shall find a large ring of stones. Place the black crystal in the ground in the middle of the site; the positive energies there will shatter the evil stone into a thousand pieces. Archimedes knows thy designated voyage, and shall accompany thee throughout. For this be the will of the Great House of Don and Llyr.'

'So be it,' his subjects cried in unison.

Thus it was that Rhun opened his eyes to find himself returned to their company.

30

OPPOSING ELEMENTS

Ongen was roused from his bed, somewhat sceptical of his soldiers' claim that a dragon had landed in the courtyard of his stronghold.

'Heaven forbid.' The leader grabbed the closest sword upon confronting the creature.

'Fear not.' Rhun slid from his flight position near the neck of the beast, thoroughly impressed by his own entrance. 'It be only I.'

'Prince Rhun of Gwynedd?!' Ongen was most relieved to see him, motioning to his men to lower their weapons. 'Doth this creature belong to thee?'

'Nay. Archimedes be here of his own accord. We art on a mission from the Goddess, and require assistance.'

'Well, anything I can do to help. I am more than happy to oblige.' The Saxon warlord motioned him inside, with his eyes still fixed on the wondrous beast.'

'Oh . . . and I would advise thy men not to taunt my transport,' Rhun told him as he accompanied Ongen into his fortress. 'Archimedes hast a very short temper.'

The warlord raised both brows at this. 'I can well imagine.'

When Ongen heard the prince's plan to rid them of the witch's implements, he was overjoyed.

He showed Rhun to the dungeon where the implements were being stored. They radiated the foulest energy and odour.

'Thou can see why I desire to have them removed.' Ongen held his nose to stop himself from feeling nauseous.

'Aye.' Rhun eyed over the pieces for disposal, bearing in mind what the triple Goddess had told him. This could not be where the witch was energising herself — it being a man-made structure. 'Tell me, where did Ossa find these?' The prince leant over the lid of the larger cauldron, wondering about the two bulging circular features upon it. When they opened to reveal two living eyeballs underneath, glowing red like the witch's own, Rhun jumped back.

'I am watching thee, little Dragon.'

Her laughter echoed around the chilly chamber.

'Oh yeah?' Rhun grabbed up her evil sword. 'Not for long.' He thrust the blade into one of the exposed pupils, whereby it excreted copious amounts of a pus-like substance, and with a shrill shriek the iron lid of the other eye closed.

'Good heavens!' Ongen's stomach turned. 'Hast thou no fear?'

'Fear be the air this foul hag breathes.' Rhun emphasised his disgust. 'Mahaud shall get no such satisfaction from me.'

'But I know what drives thee, boy.' The cauldron's one good eye opened again. 'Destroy that which I hold dear, and I shall show thee the same courtesy.'

Rhun forced a smile, knowing better than to believe anything the witch said. 'Eat me.' He grabbed his private parts in one hand, and with the other thrust the point of Vortigern's sword into the remaining pupil.

'Oh god.' Ongen saw all the festering ooze that resulted, and exited from the room to throw up.

'Ongen?' Rhun went after him. 'Could thou instruct thy men to move these to the inner bailey?' He patted the warlord's back, as the man's stomach rejected everything in it.

The Saxon nodded at this, too preoccupied to verbally respond.

'Meanwhile, when thou art ready,' the prince commented, unable to believe any man could hold so much liquid, 'thou can fill me in on where thy father dug this up, ay?'

'One moment,' Ongen mumbled, waving him away.

Once enlightened as to the original burial place of the implements, Rhun hit himself in the head.

'Of course! How could I not have thought of it before! It be the elder tree that be her source.'

The prince couldn't count the amount of times he'd been told the story of his twentieth century birth. Of how his father had been forced to leave his mother during labour to rendezvous with the doorway created by Taliesin at the stones, on the night of the summer solstice. His father had seen the witch festering in the tree, just prior to his departure from the future, and in Rhun's mind, this was confirmation enough.

'But first, the implements.' The prince resolved.

It was no use destroying the witch, if the means by which to summon her back were still intact.

Flight on the dragon was an exhilarating experience, and proved a much faster mode of transport than the prince had first imagined.

Archimedes climbed through the clouds to soar above them. The air was freezing cold and thin at this altitude, but as these conditions were hardly going to kill him, Rhun focused on the other more thrilling aspects of the adventure. Like the full moon, out in front, which was so large and so bright, it seemed he could almost reach out and touch it. As they approached their destination, the dragon went into a death dive and Rhun clung on to endure the adrenalin rush as they plummeted downwards through the haze. Then, wings flapping in the opposite direction, Archimedes swung his huge lower body forward, and his large, clawed feet made contact with the ground to set them down to a perfect landing.

It was still dark at land's end in the south. Very little light penetrated the cloud cover and despite a mild sea-breeze the cliff face was shrouded by a heavy mist.

Rhun approached the ledge cautiously, all the while suspecting the witch was looming in the shadows to ambush his quest at the first opportunity. He held her wand out before him in both hands, every sound, every movement being noted. 'Denizens of fire, the bringers of love and elders of life, rejoice! I free thee from the selfish influence of this darkness, in the name of the Goddess and all those who serve her in pursuit of truth, wisdom, and love.'

So be it, Archimedes snorted, hoping to move the proceedings along.

Without further ado, Rhun snapped the wand over his knee and cast it to the ground. Archimedes finished the job, reducing the evil twig to ash with one exhale. Sparks flew from beneath, as the dragon pounded the fire to dust underfoot. The embers that escaped rose, their orange lustre intensifying as they swirled and danced upwards through the mist.

Dawn broke over the sea, as the cloud cover beneath them thinned to reveal the tiny seaside town that marked the eastern-most tip of the land.

The blind smithy proved easy enough to find, as he was the only soul lurking in the nameless place. Morda had been expecting the prince, and led him straight to his forge. The huge, rotund craftsman, with eyelids permanently sealed closed, had been keeping his furnace blazing at full heat so they could carry out the instruction of the Goddess without delay.

'Beings of the Air, givers of knowledge, mobility, and birth, take heart!' Rhun placed the sword of the archtraitor Vortigern into the vat of molten metal. 'I liberate thee from this instrument of destruction, in the name of the Goddess, from whence all life comes.' The weapon burst into flame and bubbled as it slid into the glowing orange-yellow mixture.

A steady stream of air seeped from the centre of the large, glowing pot. It swept past them in the form of a warm breeze, as it rushed once around the room and was gone out the door.

Morda grinned at this, exposing his near-toothless gums. 'Thy job here be done, young master.'

The prince was far more confident of success now, having reached the halfway mark of his journey — and still no sign of the witch. Not that he was even too sure what form Mahaud would take, for Rhun had never dealt with the evil crone directly. With no human soul to milk, maybe Mahaud was weaker then he'd imagined? Perhaps she'd been forced to fake her threat to him, in the hope that he would lose his focus and deviate from his purpose? For surely, if she was at all able, the witch would be doing everything within her power to save her life-giving paraphernalia.

With three of the marriages back on, Katren and all the brides had departed Degannwy to await the return of Prince Blain at Arwystli.

Thus, peace reigned supreme for all of one morning, until Rhun's initiation party arrived back from Llyn Cerrig Bach to await his return and crowning.

'Vortipor?' Tory stuck her head around the door of his quarters and gave a knock as she entered. 'May I speak with thee?'

'If it be about this damn wedding, there be nothing to discuss.' He motioned her in, all the same. He knew young Prince Rhun was an exceptional man, and would make a fine ruler. But a fine husband? That was quite a different matter. 'However.' Vortipor motioned her to be seated. 'Thy son did his father proud last night.'

'I knew he would,' she stated, not mentioning the fact that she'd been watching the whole time. Initiation was a male affair, thus Tory didn't feel her spying would be appreciated. 'But I am not here to pry into last night's goings on. The mist hast settled over the land, thus I presume all went well. What I really came to do was apologise . . . what resulted the day of the memorial service was largely my fault.'

'Thy fault!' Vortipor scowled. 'I can hardly see . . .'

'Please, let me finish.' She stood, and began to pace slowly as she chose her words. 'Rhun did what he did in an attempt to keep me here.'

'Art thou planning on taking up residence in another city, Majesty?' Vortipor enquired lightheartedly.

'Nay . . . in another time zone,' she confessed, looking at Vortipor to catch a look of horror. Before he could dispute this, she added: 'I am with child, conceived of a future incarnation of Maelgwn, whom, as thou might recall, I met in the twentieth century.'

Vortipor had been present at the stones, some twenty years past, when Maelgwn and herself had made their first journey to the future. He knew of the man to whom she referred.

She bowed her head slightly, hoping he would not look poorly on the indiscretion. 'The father be unaware of this, as I only just learnt of it myself. But I could no sooner raise this child in this century, any more than I could have raised Rhun in the future . . . she be not of this time. It wast not meant.'

'And Rhun knows of this?' Vortipor was getting a clearer picture.

362

'Aye.' She sat once again. 'Rhun hoped that I would think him too irresponsible to entrust with Gwynedd, and expected no one but I would learn of the picnic incident.'

'Whereby, he hoped thou would postpone thy departure,' Vortipor concluded on her behalf.

'Please do not hold this silly act against him.' She placed a hand upon his to seek his understanding. 'I know in my heart Rhun loves Bridgit, though foremost be his love for me . . . that be why he took such a stupid risk, and for no other reason.'

'When dost thou plan to leave?' he questioned, feeling a little twinge of remorse at his acceptance of the situation.

'Soon after the birth. I promised Rhun he could see his sister before I return her to her father.'

This was sad news, indeed. 'The united kingdoms will greatly mourn thee, Goddess . . . my daughter shall prove no substitute.'

'I think thou art selling her short.' Tory smiled, as she recalled Nin Sybil. 'I have met Bridgit in another age, where she wast a truth-seer of the Goddess of very high repute. Oh, I know right now she be young and in love . . . but given time, and Taliesin's instruction, Bridgit shall be every bit as good a Queen as I. And when one thinks about it, she be much better qualified than I ever was.'

Vortipor gave half a laugh as he considered her statement. 'Well, I suppose if the Goddess' quest doth not kill him first . . .'

'Which it will not.' Tory was quite sure about that.

'We might reappraise the situation.' Vortipor gave in at last.

'Oh, bless thee.' Tory threw herself into his lap, giving him a hug.

'Whoa there.' The leader delighted in her affection. 'Art thou not already in enough trouble?'

Tory laughed. 'Aye. But thou must promise to keep it our little secret for now.'

'I will. On the condition that thou must say goodbye to me before departing. Agreed?'

This seemed a reasonable enough bargain. 'Agreed.'

With the sun at their back for this leg, Archimedes made for the western coast and beyond. Once over the ocean, where they were safe from human sight, they dropped below the cloud, and the great body of water thereunder just seemed to go on and on forevermore.

However, just as the prince was losing hope of ever seeing the fabled fiery mountain, the overcast conditions cleared to a sunny day. The green-grey sea below turned bright blue against the sky, and billowing black smoke was spotted on the horizon.

This huge rocky crater, that rose only a small way above sea level, was host to an exploding pool of liquid fire, the magnitude of which the prince had never seen.

The dragon made a pass at their target from a good height above it, for the smoking mound spat flaming chunks towards the sky and into the ocean that pounded at its cliffs.

'Spirits of water, granters of depth and quiet age, give praise!' The prince untied the rope that bound the two cauldrons to the neck of his beast. 'I offer thee liberty from the negative forces of creation that have been brewed within these vessels, in the name of the Goddess, for whom all good deeds art done.'

As their offering dropped into the fiery pit below, a great rumbling was heard deep within the mountain. The dragon didn't stop to hover until they were some distance away.

In a burst of fire and smoke, the walls of the crater began to collapse inward on themselves. The earthen mound, bombarded by the surrounding sea, disappeared beneath the waves that spouted water high into the air as they claimed the small land mass.

One more to go.

By afternoon they'd found the Isle of Orkney. In the centre of the ring of stones he found there, Rhun gouged a hole in which to place his offering. 'Dwellers of the Earth, dispensers of prosperity and eternal peace, unite!' Rhun secured the crystal, pinnacle upright, in the hole and backed beyond the circle's perimeters. 'I release thee from the opposing duress of this stone to embrace thy true mother, the guardian of this land.'

The crystal began to tremble as it turned from black to red, and shattered to the four winds in a fountain-like spray of sparks.

The prince awaited a sign of success, as had been forthcoming when the previous three pieces had been destroyed. Where the crystal splinters had fallen in the field inside the ring, new green shoots reached for the sky. These budded and bloomed whilst he watched, into flowers of every colour imaginable.

The prince picked a large bunch of these, binding them together with the stem of another. 'These ought to impress the little woman.' He had a whiff of their aroma, which sent his senses swimming. 'Very good!'

Thou art counting thy dragons before they art hatched, Archimedes warned. *We still have one last duty to perform before thou contemplates the seduction of thy intended.*

'I am aware of that.' Rhun was reluctant to part with the first pleasurable thought he'd had all day, but did so in the hope it would become a reality all the sooner.

Dusk approached as they arrived at the ring of stones standing beside the tree suspected to be Mahaud's haven. The overcast conditions caused a light mist to drift over the site, and although visibility was not the best the witch was nowhere within eye-shot.

'Alright, Archimedes.' Rhun observed the elder tree. 'Torch this thing, so we can go home.'

At the prince's word, the dragon reared up to comply.

'Not so fast.'

Rhun recognised the sinister voice. When he turned to confront the hag, he was horrified to find she had Bridgit in her clutches.

'If that tree burns, so dost thy bride,' she threatened, hidden behind her large, black hood.

But this be impossible. What happened to the talisman? The prince backed into the stone circle to fortify it with his own positive energy; thus all her negativity could not penetrate to read or manipulate his thoughts.

Good lad.

Tory's voice came to him, clear as a bell. *Mother? I knew thee would be watching. What should I do?.*

I think she be bluffing. Just stall her a moment, and I shall prove it.

Hence, with a shrug, Rhun attempted to strike up a conversation. 'Look Mahaud, thou knows as well as I that thy days art numbered, so why not — '

'It be thy kingdom's days that art numbered, pretty boy.' The tone of her voice was so cutting, it made the hairs on the back of his neck stand on end. 'I, too, have access to a dimension of timelessness, far below this earthly plane. I can retrieve those implements faster than thou disposed of them. Thou shall never be rid of me!' She laughed at his futile attempt. 'Thy effort this day hast been naught but a waste of energy.' She raised her glowing red fingertips to scorch the skin on Bridgit's neck.

'Ahhh . . .!' The maiden shrank away. 'Rhun, please!'

'Alright, alright!' He urged everyone to keep their cool. 'I am sure we can work something out here.' *Mother! What art thou doing?* he bethought.

Rhun, I am in Dyfed. Tory enlightened him. *Bridgit be here in front of me, perfectly safe. I told thee she was bluffing . . . fry the bitch.*

The prince smiled as he was granted the upper hand. 'Archimedes.' He looked from the dragon to the crone. 'Proceed.' He casually motioned to the elder tree, whereby the creature ignited it with its fiery breath.

'Curse on thee, Rhun of Gwynedd, and all thy kin,' the witch screeched, as the image of Bridgit faded from view, and Mahaud began to chant out phrases in a language the prince did not recognise.

The sky rumbled and flashed in fury, bringing a sudden downpour of rain that smothered the fire the beast had started.

Two can play at that game. The prince felt he'd earnt a bit of support from the elements this day, and so turned to the south to seek their support. 'Come to my aid ye of Fire, the fire that first gave me life.' He turned to the east, raising his voice to be heard over the crone's shrieking. 'Hear my plea ye of Air, the breath of life that set me free.' He faced west. 'I seek thy comfort ye of Water, purge me and bring me clarity.' And lastly, he revolved to face north. 'Be my support ye of Earth, the mother that hast always nurtured me.'

He raised his sights to witness the storm clouds parting, to see the stars in the night sky beyond. Yet, as the witch continued her chanting, the hole began to close just as quickly.

'Nay.' Rhun focused harder on his summons.

'I am the voice of this land,
the devoted servant of the Goddess,
and eyes of the dragon on this earthly plane.'

Rhun turned his back on the crone, holding his arms outstretched to taunt her with the mark of the folk upon his back.

'I am the master of my reality.
and no will be stronger than my own.
I alone advise the four winds
and their elements,
that were the source of my creation.
Disperse this storm
that threatens the great mother,
in the name of my illustrious
forefathers and the great houses
Don and Llyr!'

The clouds were forced apart in all four directions, forming a large expanding diamond filled with stars. Tiny, red glowing beings, like the embers the prince had freed at land's end, came rushing down through the opening overhead on the back of a warm breeze. This dazzling dance of light began circling the elder tree, drying its bark and leaves in a matter of moments.

The witch began to shrill as the rain stopped and the young prince looked to her, empowered by his victory and his new-found allies.

'Time to meet thy maker,' Rhun cued the beast, who bombarded the tree with a constant stream of flame.

The witch began to wither, transmuting into one hideous form after another, mumbling curses through her cries of agony.

Archimedes, impatient to be done with it, ripped the burning tree from the ground, roots and all, then pounded it to ashes.

With this the crone shrivelled into nothingness, and her black hooded robe fell to the ground.

As the prince retrieved it, tossing it onto what was left of the smouldering tree, he couldn't help but feel sorry for the witch. 'Misled fool. All that power and knowledge wasted.' He shook his head slowly, watching the last remnant of the hag disintegrate.

Well, don't just stand there philosophising, Archimedes chided, *when thou hast a woman waiting to be wooed.*

'Indeed.' Rhun snapped to it. 'To Dyfed then.' He climbed upon the dragon's shoulders. 'And do not spare the horses.'

From the balcony of her room, Bridgit watched the wall of cloud roll back to disclose a universe full of stars. *This be his doing,* she smiled with a sigh.

The Queen of Gwynedd had left her to await Prince Rhun. He was safe and would be king, that was all his mother would tell her.

'He be going to ask for my hand.' Bridgit clutched her maid's hands tightly. 'I just know it!' The mischievous smile on the High Queen's face had said it all. 'The Dragon of the Isle be coming for me.' Bridgit strolled back inside to peruse her appearance in the mirror, elevated to a dreamlike state by the romance of it all.

'I think thou art right, lady.' Her maid, who was still on the balcony, stared at the clear night sky, frozen with fear.

Bridgit bundled up her skirts as she ran to see the dragon come to land in the courtyard. This was not the first time such a creature had alighted there — the last Prince of Gwynedd to be inaugurated had also visited Dyfed thus. 'Be he not the most audacious and wondrous man alive?'

'Aye, lady, that he be.' The maid was still spellbound, yet Bridgit was rushing around her room in a fluster.

'Do I look beautiful?' She tugged down her dress to give her cleavage maximum exposure, and toyed with the ringlets around her face.

'Like a Queen, my lady,' the maid assured, preparing to take her leave so that the young lovers could speak alone. 'Behave thyself now, or thy father shall have my head for this.'

'Have no fear.' Bridgit thought her concern a bore. 'My prince seems to insist on it.'

'Well, such a fine catch should not be allowed to slip through thy net before thou hast well and truly got him on board.' The maid gave her a wink on the way out the door.

'Many thanks, my friend.'

Bridgit heard Rhun's voice coming from her balcony, and approached the open doors to be confronted by the half-naked warrior's back. The artwork depicted there sent chills through her body. This symbol was a very sacred one, yet she could not understand how she knew this. 'Caduceus.'

He swung round abruptly to see her looking every bit the fairytale Princess in her silken gown of palest pink. 'Quite correct. How did thou know?' But the girl just stared blankly at him, appearing dazed.

'What?' she uttered.

Once she'd mistaken Rhun for an angel, but at this moment he looked more like a god. His strong, muscular torso held her gaze; how she longed to take that body to her bed.

'Thou shalt have to marry me first,' Rhun grinned, knowing her mind.

The lady was embarrassed and inclined to be angry with him, but as the prince presented her with a large bunch of the most exquisite flowers all was forgiven. 'Name the year?' She doubted the sincerity of his proposal, luring him further inside to where she could get a better look at him.

'Four days from now,' he suggested, delighted by the stunned look on her face. 'At Arwystli, along with Bryce and Aella, Eormenric and Vanora, and Blain and Javotte.'

'Thou art serious!' She was bursting with joy as she rushed to embrace him and smother him with kisses.

'I presume this means thou art in favour,' he managed to say, between her bursts of affection.

'Oh, aye!' She beamed. 'If thou dost love me truly, I do agree.' The prince seemed bothered suddenly, and put her at arm's length. 'What be wrong?' This unnerved her; maybe he was only wedding her because it was what the High Council wanted.

'It be my past, Bridgit.' He prepared to do a lot of confessing. 'People art going to have horrible stories to tell of my escapades and, unfortunately, most of them will be true.'

'I certainly hope so.' She stated enthusiastically. 'Thy romantic exploits art the reason I sought thee out in the first place . . . I too want to know such pleasure.' She drew him into a long and tender kiss.

'But a recent incident . . .' He attempted to enlighten her, when her fingers on his lips put a stop to it.

'Shhh . . . It matters not. All that will change once we art wed,' Bridgit explained in a voice that brooked no contradiction. 'I intend to keep thee so occupied, even thy Kingdom shall scarce get a look in.'

Her demeanour became all amiable again, and Rhun thought he'd best get out of there before he did something he'd regret. 'I shall see thee at Arwystli in four days then.' He claimed one more kiss for the road, and stepped away. 'I do love thee, Bridgit. Thou art my joy, my passion and my treasure. My peace, my dreams, my hope and my pleasure art all embodied in thee.'

Bridgit stood speechless long after the prince had faded from sight. His words lingering in her mind were more eloquent than any she'd imagined he'd say. How did he just come and go as he pleased, like a Merlin would, and enchant otherworldly creatures to his aid?

I must learn the ways of the Otherworld, if I am to keep him intrigued, she decided. I want to be the only Goddess in his eyes.

31

LOVE, BIRTH, LIFE AND DEATH

A wedding celebration the like of that being staged at Arwystli was unprec-edented in Britain. Leaders from all four corners of the land would be attending.

For it had been young Prince Blain's quest to invite the leader of the Pictish to take up a place on the High Council. An honour Cailtram, their leader, was a little wary to accept. The High Council's influence extended the whole breadth and length of the land, and a position therein made more sense than trying to oppose them. But after centuries of bloodshed between his people and the Scots, Cailtram was not too sure how he and Fergus MacErc would exist together in an alliance. However, as Ongen and Eormenric of Mercia had signed the treaty after centuries of warring with the Britons, Cailtram agreed to attend the celebration and discuss the issue.

Both Rhun and Blain were crowned in their respective capital cities the day after their return. The people who had attended Rhun's ceremony left Degannwy the day after it to attend the wedding of the century in Arwystli.

Any ill-will the lads had borne one another faded in the midst of an excited exchange of stories and pats on the back. Rhun disappeared to the dining hall to feast with his friends the moment they arrived in the host city.

Katren had accommodated all the brides in the large tower room for the night. This resulted in their husbands-to-be, who were a little worse for mead, serenading them with sonnets and songs from the courtyard in the middle of the night. Which, in the end, was broken up by Sir Tiernan and Sir Angus, in the hope that those staying at the household might get some sleep prior to the four days of celebration that were to follow.

The morning of the wedding was as fresh, clear, and warm as any could have hoped.

Tory was up at the crack of dawn, assisting Katren to prepare the girls, the banquet room, and the courtyard where the wedding was taking place.

The mingling smells of all the food cooking in the kitchen made Tory's stomach turn, and she had to pause a moment to control the nausea. *And so it begins.* She breathed the fresh air wafting through the servants' door that led to the herb and vegetable garden.

'Art thou alright?' Katren backed up a few paces to check on her friend.

'I am fine.' Tory forced a smile. She'd not experienced any morning sickness last time round, and on today of all days this was most inconvenient.

The Queen of Gwynedd's face had gone as white as a sheet. As Katren had given birth to three children herself, this was a look she recognised all too well. 'Thou art pregnant,' she gasped, holding a hand over her mouth.

Everyone was bound to find out sometime, so Tory nodded to confess that this was indeed true.

'Oh Tory, thou must be overjoyed!' Katren was excited for her, though she kept her voice to a discreet level.

'Oh, I am thrilled.' The unrest in her stomach subsided; thus Tory moved out of the draught from the open door.

'And where dost thou think thou art going?' Katren demanded to know in a concerned fashion.

'To get on with . . .'

'Oh no, thou will not . . . thou should be resting.' Katren pulled her up.

'Do not start with me,' Tory warned.

Katren kissed her cheek and gave her a squeeze to subdue her. 'If thou wants to do something useful, go and see how our boys art faring. I shall take care of everything else.'

As this task was well away from the food, Tory was persuaded to comply with Katren's wish.

Tory had thought the four brides, all in their different gowns of pure white, a sight to behold. But viewing the four grooms, clean-shaven and dressed in their best, was even more of a novelty. Here they stood, Britain's finest, at their finest; she was so very proud of them all. As the four lads had each other to lean on for support, last-minute marriage jitters were kept to a minimum and all were keen to proceed.

Tory accompanied her four masters to the flower-adorned altar, where Taliesin awaited to perform the ceremony. All the guests had gathered in the courtyard, creating a great gaggle of rowdy goodwill. The Queen of Gwynedd, after kissing all her lads for good luck, took up her place behind them.

Rhun had asked Blain to be his best man, and vice-versa. So, too, were Bryce and Eormenric fulfilling this role for each other. Hence they all stood about reassuring one another, until the crowd hushed and all eyes turned to the huge entrance doors.

Katren sneaked up beside Tory, gripping hold of her hand, as Selwyn and Cai began to strum at their harp strings and the doors parted wide.

Vortipor led his daughter down the aisle first, followed by Angus and Javotte, then Ongen and Aella. But it was young Prince Owen who led Vanora to her betrothed, being her oldest living male relative who was not getting wed. One by one they kissed the girls goodbye, handing them over to their intended.

Vortipor, the first in line, gave Rhun a stern glare as he did so, whereas Owen, the last, was happy just to score a free kiss.

Selwyn and Cai assisted Taliesin during the service, which had been written by the High Merlin especially for the occasion. Katren was reduced to tears, of course. She clung to Owen whom she knew she would also lose thus before too long. As Vortipor and Angus were also a mite teary-eyed at parting with their only daughters, Tory stood between them gripping their hands in her own.

Only half of the original masters still dwelt in the land of the living, but a whole new generation of leaders and warriors had been born.

As Tory cast her sights over the gathering, Pict beside Scot, Saxon beside Briton, she realised this was what they'd all fought so hard for. This had been the vision of that first circle of twelve, and today that dream had become a reality.

Once the hullabaloo of the wedding had died down, and all had returned to their respective kingdoms and estates, the isle of Britain resumed some normality.

Eormenric and Vanora returned with Ongen to Londinium with abundant supplies to see them through the cold seasons. Cailtram, having signed the pact, left in the company of his sworn enemy, Fergus MacErc, whose troops were helping to lug and herd the Pict's winter stores the great distance back to Alban. Sir Angus and Sir Lucus remained at Arwystli, in the service of King Blain and his Queen, Javotte. As Sir Bryce had won the quest for Gwynedd's champion at the wedding, he and his bride settled at Degannwy. Here Bryce finally assumed his father's old position at the side of Gwynedd's King, Rhun. In addition, as Prince Bryce was clearly the finest warrior in Britain, and who in all probability would never be king, Tory nominated him to assume her role of sensei to the circle of twelve, once she had departed for the twentieth century.

Come winter, all of the twelve masters gathered at Degannwy to perfect their art, as they did every year. This was the last time this assembly would be overseen by the sensei who had begun the circle of twelve. Thus they worked hard and played little; still, a good time was had by all.

Tory's belly expanded with every passing month, but she was not alone. By the time the masters disbanded to resume their normal duties, all four of the newly wed women were with child. And, not to be outdone, Rhun and Bridgit's babe was the first due.

Hence, even after the birth of her own child, Rhun managed to keep Tory around a while longer to see her first grandchild into the world.

Her daughter, whom Tory had aptly named Rhiannon, after the War Goddess, was not at all the placid, obliging baby Rhun had been; she was full of fire and energy. But, by the same token, she was a happy soul, and everyone, especially Rhun, adored her. Rhiannon was dark-haired and darker-eyed, like her brother, with beautiful ivory skin. She had her mother's looks, however, and was just as sensitive to Tory's moods as Rhun was.

A month rolled by before they greeted a new heir to the throne of Gwynedd, whom Rhun named Cadwell, meaning war-defense. He was of fairer hair than his father, and his eyes a pale shade of golden brown.

Tory wished, in retrospect, that she'd left before the new prince had been born. It broke her heart to think she'd miss him growing up — and all the other babes not yet born. Still, all the affairs of state had been seen to, Mahaud had been destroyed, and the leaders of the land were united and at peace. The time when Tory must leave the Dark Age for good, drew ever nearer.

It was clearly understood by one and all that Tory would not be making a dramatic exit. In fact she'd already said most of her goodbyes.

Katren had been up to visit as soon as Rhiannon had been born, but had returned to Arwystli to await the birth of Javotte's child soon after. This farewell had not been an easy one; their friendship spanned two decades and had seen some phenomenal events. Yet the Queen Mother of Powys had two grandchildren on the way. Tory felt sure she would barely have time to notice her missing. Katren had sworn blind, through her tears, that this would never be the case.

All Tory's masters had been prepared for her departure for months. She would just slip into the shadows, as Maelgwn had, no sad farewells, no tears.

Tory did pop down to see Vortipor, as promised, to drink one last toast of fine Roman wine in honour of their grandson and old times. She decided she was leaving the alliance in good hands; they didn't call him the Protector for no reason.

Bryce had threatened suicide if Tory didn't see him before she left. Thus it was that late on the day of her departure, before she confronted her son, Tory sent Sir Tiernan to fetch Bryce to her chambers.

'It be time.' Bryce knew it before he'd even looked at her. 'Nay, please tell me I am wrong.'

Tory had never seen Bryce weep before, not even at his father's funeral. Yet he did so now, down before her on one knee, begging her not to go.

'Bryce . . . Bryce, listen to me.' She encouraged him to look her in the eye. 'This be thy destiny, my friend . . . thou hast sought it, and thou hast found it.'

'Nay,' he pleaded. 'I cannot stand that I shall not see thee again.'

'But Bryce, thou will.' She crouched beside him. 'I shall go on and on, and thou shall reincarnate. And even though thou may not recognise me, I shall know thee . . . and I will find thee again, I swear it.' Tory crossed her heart and held up her hand in promise.

As the knight calmed, he startled Tory with a kiss.

'What was that for?' she laughed in the after-shock.

'I have wanted to do that since the day I met thee.' He shrugged coyly. 'I figured it was now or never.'

'Oh Bryce!' She smothered him with a huge hug. 'Thou art good for my ego.'

'Thou art not going yet, surely!' Rhun stormed into the room, slamming the door closed. 'Rhiannon be not old enough for time travel.'

'Really, Rhun.' She brushed off his argument with a steely gaze. 'It will not hurt her.'

'But I am not —'

'Oh, hush up, and come here.' Tory was determined there was not going to be a scene. 'I have something for thee.' She wandered over to the bed to retrieve Maelgwn's sword and scabbard. 'I think thy father would have wanted thee to have this.'

'Nay!' Rhun protested. 'Father wanted thee to have it, for protection.'

'Well, then.' She smiled, handing it to him all the same. 'Thou can bring it to me when thou comes.'

He admired the mighty weapon, as he had many times when it had hung at his father's side. 'Oh, Mother.' He embraced her suddenly. 'I long for that time so much . . . promise me I shall find thee. Promise me Rhiannon and thee will wait.'

'I promise, thee . . . sweet prince.' She kissed his forehead, her voice faltering as she suppressed tears. 'But thou art a king now,' she sniffled, holding him at arm's length and forcing a smile. 'And what a fine king thou dost make.' She moved to collect the basket in which Rhiannon lay, that had once served as Rhun's time capsule many years ago. 'Be wise, my beloved. Be safe, be strong, be truthful and be just. But most of all . . . be happy.' Tory blew them both a kiss and vanished in a flood of tears.

She materialised in the entrance foyer of Taliesin's labyrinth, where her chariot awaited, to find Taliesin and Selwyn in attendance.

'Damn it!' Tory cursed out loud. 'Why did thou have to be here! I cannot say goodbye to thee!' She was on the verge of collapsing into an emotional mess.

'Then let us just say . . . ate logo,' Taliesin suggested with a huge beaming smile, that made Tory catch her breath. 'After all, where dost goodbye end and hello begin? It be all just an illusion anyway.'

She set down the basket beside her and ran to embrace him. 'I do love thee, Taliesin. Only the Goddess knows how I shall miss thee. Catch us up quickly.' She closed her eyes as she squeezed him, absorbing his lovely energy for the last time in a long time.

'Majesty?' Selwyn politely called for her attention. 'This be a little something I wrote for thee.' He presented her with a scrolled parchment, sealed with wax. 'I would like thee to read it, once thou art settled in thy new home.' The lump in Selwyn's throat was near choking him, and the tears were streaming down his face. 'I owe thee more than . . .' The rest wouldn't come, and he was thankful when Tory held him and put an end to his fruitless search for words.

'It be I who owes thee, Selwyn. What would I have done without thee?' She rocked him in her arms a moment; she was the only one who'd ever comforted him thus. 'Cry if thou must for parting is hell. But life still goes on, so party as well.' She let him go, and gave him a nudge and a wink of encouragement.

'Aye, Majesty, I will.' He melted to a smile, chin up.

Tory took a deep breath, finding herself at a poignant moment.

'Now then. I took the liberty of giving thy transport the once-over,' Taliesin advised as he walked her to the chariot. It was parked right beside its future self which he'd brought back with him from his travels. 'And I note that the crystal that operates the thought amplification drive be cracked. Thou really should not try to operate complex machinery when thou art emotionally distraught.'

Tory rolled her eyes at this; when wasn't she emotionally distraught lately? 'Well . . .' She placed Rhiannon's basket inside their vehicle. 'As far as I am concerned, it only need make one more trip.'

'Indeed.' The High Merlin smiled a peculiar smile. 'Best get Myrddin to take a closer look at the other end, ay? Just to be safe.' He winked. 'Nothing must happen to this treasure, or all that I have just done will not be possible. Thou and Rhun will be trapped in the twentieth century, and Maelgwn and myself shall fall into a bitter feud.'

Tory motioned him to hush; she got the picture. 'It sounds as if thou hast lived it all before.'

'Another time, another place, another dimension.' He was rather pleased about that. 'So, will thou be heading for the day thou left?'

'Heavens no!' Tory had to laugh. 'I think that meeting his babe two days after conception, might be a bit much for Miles to cope with.' She jumped into the pilot's seat, making sure Rhiannon was comfortable and secure. 'I shall aim for the birth of Brian's child, and see how we go from there.'

'Well, it be thy choice, of course.'

As the Merlin took a step backwards, there was that odd smile again. Tory was tempted to enquire after its meaning, but she knew that would only prove a waste of time. 'I leave the kindred in thy very capable hands, gentlemen.' Tory's mind focused on the future, yet her eyes remained fixed on the two merlins until their forms became obscured by the ethers of her flight.

Tory arrived in Myrddin's cave at Dinas Emrys in a shower of sparks. She was quick to get Rhiannon to a safe distance, as the short-circuiting drive mechanism shot electrical currents over the nose cone of the vehicle.

When all the activity had died down, leaving smoke billowing from the transport's casing, Tory opened up the hatch of the chariot to take a closer look. On this trip, the emotional stress had proved too much; the crystal that was the nucleus of the drive system had been completely shattered. 'Dad is going to be pissed.' She gave a heavy sigh.

Actually, she was rather surprised that Myrddin was not here to meet them. But, no matter, she would find him soon enough.

'Come on.' She retrieved the basket containing her sleeping babe. 'Let us first find thy father.'

No sooner had Tory conjured up a picture of the cottage that stood where the house at Aberffraw once had, than she was standing before it.

'What?' She couldn't believe what she was seeing; the cottage was up for sale. 'Miles would never sell this place . . .' Tory strode towards the front door in a daze. 'It's belonged to his family for centuries.'

After knocking several times at both the front and back doors, Tory accepted the fact that the place was deserted. 'We'd best find thy uncle,' she commented to Rhiannon. 'Maybe he can shed some light on this.'

Naomi answered the door, bearing a tiny bundle perched over her shoulder. 'Tory! You . . . you're back.' She gaped at her sister-in-law, overawed to see her.

The tiny bundle in Naomi's arms held Tory's gaze, and she moved closer to get a better look. 'My god, is this . . .'

'Daniel Alexander.' Naomi relaxed a little as she showed off her prize, who was not yet four days old.

'Look at you.' The little dimple on his chin brought tears to her eyes. He was as fair as his father, this one, and as his eyelids ventured to part they revealed pupils of piercing blue. 'He looks so much like Brian,' Tory mumbled, in tears again; Daniel was, in fact, the splitting image of Cai.

Naomi nodded, reduced to tears also. 'Where are my manners?' she sniffled, pulling herself together and assuming a more light-hearted approach. 'Come in, sit down. Brian should be back any minute, he's just popped down to the shop.' Naomi guided her inside to the lounge room. She so desperately wanted to ask about the child Tory had with her, but hesitated to do so in case the subject of Miles came up. 'I shall make us a cup of tea.' She forced a smile, escaping into the kitchen.

Tory sat gazing about the room, not really taking in the decor. Naomi's behaviour seemed somewhat odd, and something told her that there was more to her sister-in-law's emotional state than a case of post-natal depression.

'Honey, I'm home!' Brian's chirpy self cruised through the front door, his arms loaded with bags of groceries.

Tory stood as her brother wandered past the lounge room door, en route to the kitchen. She presumed he'd not spotted her, but then he backed up to take a second look. 'Hello,' she said softly, uncertain whether to approach him, for he too looked sadly stunned by her presence.

'So, you finally decided to come back, did you?' His chirpy mood turned icy, as he offloaded the groceries onto the closest chair.

'Well, yes . . . things were kind of hectic.'

'What happened to six months?' He demanded an answer. 'Before the baby was born, that's what you said!'

'Brian?' Her tears were welling again. 'What is the matter with you?'

'What is the matter with me!' he roared, completely and utterly enraged. 'I'll tell you what the matter with me is . . . I had faith in you, that's what! Six months I told him, tops! But, oh no, you had to make him suffer.'

'Who suffer? What are you talking about?'

'Miles, Tory, I'm talking about Miles!' Brian observed the dismay spread across her face. 'I watched him wither away, month by month by month.'

Tory felt his words clutch hold of her heart and wrench it out. 'Are you saying Miles is . . . dead?' She sank to a seat.

Brian leant closer to taunt her. 'If he could not be with you in this life, he said he'd find you in the next. Miles went to his grave, every bit as heartbroken and remorseful as you could have wanted him to be.'

'How can you stand there and torture me this way? I loved him, Brian.'

'Yeah?' He backed up. 'Well, you have a real shitty way of showing it.'

'That's enough!' Naomi stood in the doorway, tea-tray in hand, appalled by her husband's relentless and heartless attack.

'No, Naomi. I fear it's not nearly enough. All this goddess rubbish has gone to her head! You are not god, Tory! And despite what you may believe, mankind was not put on this earth to live up to your expectations!'

The sound of a child crying broke Brian's train of thought. Curious, he pursued the source to find the basket tucked up beside the lounge. He gulped. 'Miles?'

Tory nodded. 'That's why I waited so long . . . I thought the shock would kill . . .' She stopped before she said it, covering her mouth with her hands as if she would be sick.

'Aw, sis. I'm sorry.' Brian joined her on the lounge, wishing he could take back every word. 'I was way off the mark . . .'

'No, you were right.' She stood and backed away. 'At the time I left, I did want to hurt him. Father advised me to stay and resolve the situation, but I wouldn't listen. I just used him for my own selfish purposes and left him for dead.'

'No, you didn't.' Brian insisted, standing to attempt an embrace. 'Don't listen to me, what do I know?'

Tory submitted wholeheartedly, thankful for the support. 'What will I do now?' she mumbled into his shirt, as she gripped it tight.

'Well,' Brian searched for a constructive solution. 'You could always go back and change it?'

Tory shook her head, recalling the mess she'd left the chariot in. 'That's impossible now,' she sobbed, trying to breathe normally and regain her composure.

'Pardon?' Brian held her at arm's length. 'I didn't think that word was in your vocabulary.'

With her head bowed low, Tory could not even bring herself to explain; it all seemed so hopeless.

I don't require that cumbersome man-made nightmare to time travel any more! I traded it in eons ago for a more ideal and reliable means of transport.

The image of her future self motioning to her brain brought a smile to her face, and Tory's head shot up. 'Where is Dad?'

Brian shrugged. 'Hanging around somewhere? You know what he's like.'

'I have to find him!' Tory kissed Brian's cheek in gratitude. 'I'll see you six months ago.' She collected her child and was gone in the blink of an eye.

'She really is weird, isn't she?' Brian looked to Naomi, who nodded, giving a sigh of relief.

'Praise the universe for that.'

With the thought of her father, Tory found herself back in his cavern of treasures. The Merlin was attempting to get all the crystal splinters out of the chariot's body with the aid of a mini-vac, and seemed none too pleased about the state she'd left it in.

'Can you fix it?' Tory hesitated to ask.

The Merlin was startled to a standing position, plunging one hand into the large pocket of his robe. 'There you are?' His demeanour was now as cool as a cucumber. 'You have made a fine mess of it, I fear.'

Tory sighed at this, though she had known the answer before she'd even asked the question. This was her punishment for being so cruel; now she must make it back to Miles of her own accord. 'Have you ever time travelled using only the power of the mind?'

'No, not I.' Myrddin raised his brow. 'But then I have never really had just cause to try.'

'So you think it might be possible, then?'

The Merlin smiled broadly. 'Anything is possible.'

'But do you think I could do it?' She hounded him for some positive reinforcement.

Myrddin shrugged casually. 'The question is more, do you believe you can do it?'

'Oh!' she whined, wanting to feel strong and confident; where was all her faith when she needed it for herself?

'Tory, dearest . . . let me put it to you this way.' He took her under his arm to muse: 'This machine does naught but amplify thy will, and therefore, it is my theory . . . that, if your desire be strong enough, the universe must comply.'

'Will you help me?' She gripped hold of both his hands, inspired by his reasoning.

'I can point you in the right direction, if that's what you mean?'

'Yes, yes . . . do.' She urged, seating herself on the ground and placing Rhiannon's basket in her lap.

The Merlin crouched to view his granddaughter, tickling her under the chin.

'Yes, I know my dear Rhiannon. Your mummy is a very silly girl, isn't she, yes. But I think she has learnt her lesson now.' He smiled at Tory. 'Am I always right, or am I always right?'

'You're always right.' She humoured her father with a kiss.

'Absolutely correct . . . and I say you are going to make it.' He gave her a wink of encouragement. 'Now, there is only one way to truly pinpoint where you are in relation to the time and space of this third dimensional reality. Can you guess what that might be?'

Tory stared back at her father blankly, not even understanding the question. 'Is this a test?'

'Astronomy, my darling.' His tone became patronising. 'Did they teach you nothing back in the Old Land?'

Myrddin rolled his eyes, then directed her to the earthen floor where he began mapping out the solar system in the dirt with his finger.

'It takes two hundred million years for our solar system to make the trip around the galactic centre of the Milky Way. This gives us much scope in which to place ourselves. This is how the planets were placed around the time you seek.' Off to the side of his solar system the Merlin drew the spiralling arms of the Milky Way. 'At present the solar system is located here, at the edge of the Orion spiral arm.'

Tory's eyes ran over the composition, considering how it looked rather like a crop-circle formation.

'Have you committed the coordinates to memory.' Her father emptied the crystal splinters from his mini-vac into a little pouch, and then placed the pouch in her hand.

'I think so.'

'Good. Close your eyes.' He urged them shut with his fingers. 'See it still?'

She nodded.

'Then let it form.' The Merlin began lugging large quartz crystals from his piles of treasure, which he placed in a circle around his daughter, to contain the vortex they were conjuring.

'Float out into the cosmos and see its vast body stretched out before you. The planets and their moons, the stars and the sun . . . asteroids, meteorites, heavenly bodies, all twirling round the spiralling arms of the galaxy!' He let loose a laugh, inspired by the splendour of the mighty vision. 'That's it . . .' The Merlin looked to Tory, noting that the pouch in her hand was glowing and she had begun to fade. 'Ah-ha!' He clapped his hands, proud of her. 'What do you know, it does work.'

Once she had gone he pulled a crystal from his pocket, just like the one his daughter had demolished in the chariot, and kissed it. 'Finally! I was wondering when I was going to get it back.' He looked at the chariot, impressed with himself.

When Tory's vision of the galaxy was exactly as her father had drawn it, she found herself speeding towards the earth. She soared past the moon, down through the coloured ethers of the atmosphere, the cloud cover and over a large body of land. An ocean appeared on the horizon, when suddenly everything came to a standstill.

Her eyes came to focus on a man standing some distance away, hands sunk deep in pockets as he gazed out to sea. After checking on Rhiannon, who'd obviously slept through the whole thing, Tory came to realise she was standing out the back of the cottage at Aberffraw, and that the man before her was Miles.

'What are you thinking about?'

Her voice sent shivers down his spine, but he did not bother with a response; his imagination played him for the fool quite often these days.

'The strong, silent type, hey?' She laughed as he spun round to face her.

'I'm so sorry.' He realised his mistake, and was so completely stupefied to see her that he didn't know what to say first. 'In fact, I'm sorry about everything. I was a fool . . .'

'Please, Miles, forget it.' Tory waved it off with her free hand. 'I have.'

'Hello?' His voice landed on a low note, as he realised what she was holding. 'Maelgwn's?' he questioned timidly.

'Nope,' she teased. 'Guess again?'

Miles staggered back a few paces, a smile threatening to form on his lips. 'No.'

'Yes . . .!' Tory mocked him, setting down the basket and lifting Rhiannon from it. 'Miles, I'd like you to meet your daughter.'

'Daughter!' He took a giant step forward, drawn in by the strange excitement of sudden fatherhood.

'I hope you don't mind . . .' Tory bundled the babe into his arms. 'But I took the liberty of naming her Rhiannon.'

'The war goddess.' He admired their handiwork. 'Oh goody, another one.'

As Tory watched Miles with Rhiannon, she suddenly saw the Maelgwn in him — the calm, accepting side of his nature that he'd kept hidden most of the time.

'I told you we'd meet again.' Miles winked, flashing a brilliant smile.

Yet Tory had the strangest feeling that Maelgwn was lurking behind that confident grin. Or, then again, perhaps it was just her imagination? *That thou did*, she conceded as she obliged him with a kiss. 'That you did.'

As requested, Tory waited until she was settled in her new life to break the seal on the scroll Selwyn had given her in parting.

With a cup of tea in her hand, and husband and baby settled comfortably in her lap, she read . . .

A short life hast mine been,
wondrous and blithe.
I have learnt of many a legend.
But who wast the greatest?
I reply . . .
It was she who tamed the Dragon.
It was she who united this land.
It was she who shaped my future,
the Goddess' right hand.
The head-wind of a storm, wast she,
with more radiance than the sun.
The heart of a warrior, had she,
who fought until she won.
I am proud to say I knew her,
for she wast my truest friend.

The years we had together,
art the happiest I shall spend.
Departed now, for some future age,
and mourned by all who knew her,
I shall recount her deeds until
I draw my final breath,
Her name? . . . Tory Alexander.

THE END
AND THE BEGINNING WERE ALWAYS THERE.
BEFORE THE BEGINNING AND AFTER THE END.
—T.S. ELIOT

REFERENCES

The author gratefully acknowledges the use of the following quotations.

The extract in Part I, page 360, is taken from *Taliesin: Shamanism and the Bardic Mysteries in Britain and Ireland by John Matthews and is reproduced with the kind permission of HarperCollinsPublishers*, London.

The extract in Part III, page 586, is taken from *Practical Celtic Magic by Murry Hope and is reproduced with the kind permission of HarperCollinsPublishers*, London.

The poems on pages 354 and 357 are adapted from *The Song of Taliesin* by John Matthews with his kind permission.

BIBLIOGRAPHY

Alcock, Leslie, *Arthur's Britain*, Penguin, London, 1973.

Ash, David A., *The Vortex*, Golden Path Spiritual Development Association, Devon, 1991

Ashe, Geoffrey, *The Landscape of King Arthur*, Webb & Bower, London, 1987.

Ballard, Robert D., *Explorations*, Weidenfeld & Nicolson, London, 1995

Bede, *Ecclesiastical History of the English People*, Penguin, London, 1990.

Berlitz, Charles, *Doomsday 1999 AD*, Souvenir Press, London, 1981

Berliitz, Charles, *The Dragon's Triangle*, Wynwood Press, 1989.

Berresford Ellis, Peter, *Dictionary of Celtic Mythology*, Constable & Co, London, 1992.

Bletzer, June G, *Encyclopaedic Psychic Dictionary*, Donning Co, Virginia, 1986.

Chadwick, Nora K, *Celtic Britain*, Newcastle Publishing Co, California, 1989.

Coghlam, Ronan, *An Illustrated Encylopaedia of Arthurian Legends*, Element Books, Dorset, 1993.

Davies, Paul, *About Time*, Simon & Schuster, USA, 1995

Davies, Paul, *The Cosmic Blueprint*, Unwin Hyman, London, 1989.

Devereux, Paul, *Earth Lights Revelation*, Blandford Press, London, 1989.

Devereux, Paul, *Places of Power*, Blandford Press, London, 1990.

Devereux, Paul, *Secrets of Ancient and Sacred Places*, Blandford Press, London, 1992.

Frederic, Louis, *Dictionary of the Martial Arts*, Athlone Press, France, 1991.

Hope, Murry, *Ancient Egypt — The Sirius Connection*, Element Books, Shaftesbury, 1994

Hope, Murry, *Practical Atlantean Magic: Atlantis Myth or Reality*, Aquarian, London, 1991.

Hope, Murry, *Practical Celtic Magic, Aquarian, London, 1987. See section on* The Nine Metaphysical Laws.

Hope, Murry. *Time: The Ultimate Energy*, Element Books, Shaftesbury, 1991.

Kerrod, Robin, *The Star Guide*, RD Press, Australia, 1993

Lorie, Peter, *Revelation*, Labyrinth Publishing, UK, 1995

Maclean, Fitzroy, *A Concise History of Scotland*, Thames & Hudson, London, 1970.

Matthews, Caitlin, *Mabon and the Mysteries of Britain*, Penguin Arkana, London, 1987.

Mallove/Matloff, *The Starflight Handbook*, John Wiley & Sons Inc., USA, 1989

Matthews, C and J, *The Little Book of Celtic Wisdom*, Emement Inc., London, 1993.

Matthews, John, *The Song of Taliesin*, Aquarian, London, 1991.

Matthews, John, *Taliesin*, Aquarian, London, 1991.

Matthews, John, *A Celtic Reader*, Aquarian, London, 1991.

Moore, Patrick, *Guinness Book of Astronomy*, Guinness Publishing, UK, 1995

Geoffrey of Monmouth, *The History of the Kings of Britain*, Penguin Classics, London, 1966.

Nennius, *Historia Brittonum*, British American Books, California. [undated]

Plato, *Timaeus & Critias*, [Desmond Lee (trans)], London, Penguin Books, 1977.

Roberts, Anthony, *Atlantean Traditions in Ancient Britain*, Rider & Co, London, 1977.

Sitchin, Zecharia, *The 12th Planet*, Avon Books, N.Y., 1976.

Somerset Fry, P, *Castles of the British Isles*, David & Charles, London, 1990.

Stewart, R J, *The Way of Merlin*, Aquarian, London, 1991.

Sitchin, Zecharia, *Stairway to Heaven*, Avon Books, NY, 1983

Sitchin, Zecharia, *The 12th Planet*, Avon Books, NY, 1976

Sitchin, Zecharia, *The Wars of Gods and Men*, Avon Books, NY, 1985

Compendium

A.

Aberffraw (pronounced A-BER-fro) — City of Gwynedd. Ancestral home to the King's of Gwynedd, located on the Isle of Anglesey.

Abred — The Middle kingdoms of Earth, frequented by humankind. The Physical World.

Absalom, Shu Sar (supreme King) — Ruler of Atlantis, who claimed Tory's as his daughter by the Goddess, Danuih. Absalom means 'father of peace'. Husband of Melcah, Orphelia, Salome, Kila, Mahar. Father of, Alaric, Turan, Xavier, Gaspard, Zadoc, Diccon, Seth, Lazarus, Jerrem and Adelgar. For other incarnations see Myrddin.

Adelgar, Shar — The tenth born son of Absalom. Mother — Nin Mahar. Younger twin of Shar Jerrem. Adelgar means 'noble spear'. Ruler of Portea, the hot, tropical capital of the kingdom to the north in the Atlantean mainland, with its Capital at Keriophis. For other incarnations see Brockwell, Calin.

Aella — Of Mercia. Daughter of Ossa. Sister of Eormenric and Ongen. Wife of Prince Bryce. Other incarnations in the Ancient Future Series include: 21st century — Rhiannon Thurlow, AMIE/Universe Parallel — Qusay Sabah Clariona.

Akhantuih — Atlantean God (Pronounced Ar-knan-too-ee). The Negotiator of Chaos. Sacred stone: Topaz. Colour: Yellow. Symbol: Crystal torch. Totem animal: Black Panther. Orders: Astrology, Astronomy & Chaos Studies. Temples & Universities: Dur-na-ga (Astrology & Astronomy).

Alaric, Shar — First born son of Absalom and heir to the kingdom of Cintrala. Ruler of the capital of Chilidocean. Mother — Nin Melcah, Twin of Turan. Alaric means 'noble ruler'. Other incarnations in the Ancient Future Series include: Atlantis — Shar Alaric, 21st Century — Doc Alexander (Cadwaladr), Falcon Tribe — Crow, AMIE — Swithin Gervaise, Grigori — Bezaliel (Male aspect).

Alban — Kingdom of the Picts Ruled by Cailtram.

Alexander, Brian — Tory's twin brother in the 21st century. Son of Renford and Helen Alexander. The chosen incarnation of Calin Brockwell. Other incarnations in the Ancient Future Series include: Ancient Gwynedd — Calin Brockwell, Atlantis — Shar Adelgar, Fall of Atlantis: Orestes, Delphinus Tribe — Zerrah, Leonine Tribe — Tyrus-Leon, Edin — Samson, AMIE — Zeven (Starman) Gudrun, Ancient Zhou — Ji Song, Grigori — Sammael (male aspect).

Alexander, Tory — Born in twenty-first century Australia and teleported back in time to early Gwynedd by Taliesin Penn Beirdd. The creator and trainer of the Dragon's Circle of Twelve and an original member. Daughter of Myrddin, aka Renford Alexander, student of Taliesin, sister of Brian Alexander, wife of Maelgwn Gwynedd and mother of Rhun & Rhiannon. Her other incarnations in the Ancient Future Series include: Atlantis — Temperance, Fall of Atlantis — Electra, Ancient Gaul — Sorcha, Delphinus Tribe — Aquilla, Falcon Tribe — Swan, Edin — Eve, AMIE — Taren Lennox, Ancient Zhou — Jaing Hudan, Grigori — Azazel (female aspect) — Mahaud.

Alma, Lady — Wife of Sir Angus and mother of Javotte. Was one of the original Dragon's Circle of Twelve. Other incarnations in the Ancient Future Series include: Gathering of Kings — Taylnn, The Fall of Atlantis — Sister seven.

Anglesey (pronounced Angle-see) — Is the Isle on which ancestral stronghold of the Kings of Gwynedd was located. Also known as Mon, or Mon Anglesey. Taliesin's base, Lyn Cerrig Bach is also to be found further north on the Island.

Angus, Sir — Maelgwn's knight and one of the original Dragon's Circle of Twelve. Husband of the Lady Alma, and father of Javotte. Other incarnations in the Ancient Future Series include: Gathering of Kings — Ethan, Edin — Incus.

Annwn — The Otherworld — the realm of Gwyn ap Nudd and the Fey. Not to be confused with the Underworld — the realm of the Dead.

Anthea, Nin. — Head Healer of Danuih (Earth). Anthea means 'lady flower'. For other incarnations see Jenovefa.

Antonia, Nin — Shar Alaric's wife. Antonia means 'precious'. For other incarnations see Vanora.

Anu — King of the Annunnaki Islands. Anu means 'he of heaven'.

Annunnaki Islands — Situated across the A-zu straight from the Atlantean mainland, between Atlantis and Antillia.

Antillia — The land beyond the Annunnaki Islands. Ruled by Chief Zutar.

Arwystli (Pronounced R–whist–lee) — stronghold Powys, located at the head of the river Servern. Was the stronghold of Chiglas, before it was taken by Maelgwn Gwynedd. Kingship of Powys was awarded to Maelgwn's cousin, Calin Brockwell, who was also descended from Cunedda Wledig, as Chiglas and Maelgwn were. Was later ruled by Brockwell's son, Blain, and his son Solomon after him.

Asa, Shu — Chief High Magi of the Healing Orders. Asa means 'healer'.

Atlantis — The most powerful nation of the ancient word. The main land was composed of three states, Portea to the north, Cintrala and Usiqua to the south.

Azores, the — An archipelago in the mid-Atlantic, composed of many islands that are characterised by dramatic landscapes, fishing villages, and rich green pastures. São Miguel, the largest island and has lake-filled calderas. Pico Alto is home to the largest mount.

A-zu Straight — situated between Atlantis and Annunnaki Islands.

B.

Bangor (pronounced Bahn-gor) — A river crossing in northwestern Wales on the Menai Strait, where a ferry barge provided transport to and from the Isle of Anglesey.

Bau, Nin — High Preistess in Atlantis. Bau means 'lady who brings the dead back to life'. Lover of the Lord Marduk. Mother of Mryddin. Grandmother of Tory and Brian Alexander. For other incarnations see Gladys.

Blain, Sir — First legitimate son of Brockwell, King of Powys and Queen Katren. Blain married Javotte, daughter of Sir Angus and the Lady Alma, and succeeded to the throne of Powys after his father's death. Other incarnations in the Ancient Future Series include: Atlantis — Shar Diccon, Kila — Asher.

Bridgit — Daughter of Vortipor the Protector of Dyfed, she became Queen of Gwynedd. Wife of Rhun of Gwynedd and mother of Cadwell. Other incarnations in the Ancient Future Series include: Atlantis — Nin Sybil, 21st century — Sybil, AMIE/Universe Parallel — Princess Salome, Grigori — Penemue (female aspect)

Briton — The early pronunciation of Britain, referring to the land of the Britons — England. First cited by the Greek Pytheas who called the British isles collectively, hai Brittaniai — the Brittanic Isles.

Brockwell, Calin, (pronounced Kay-lyn) — King of Powys. Son of Lady Gladys of Gwynedd & Cyngen Brockwell of Gwent Is Coed. Brockwell struck a deal with a Griffin to aid save Lady Katren and Tory Alexander from imprisonment in Arwystli, a deal that would backfire on him during Mahaud's return. He won Kingship of Powys for his part in the taking of the kingdom's capital. Husband of Katren, Father of Bryce, Blain, Owen and Cai. One of the Dragon's original Circle of Twelve. For other incarnations in the Ancient Future Series see Alexander, Brian.

Bryce, Sir — First born, illegitimate son of Calin Brockwell and one of Old Hetty's whores — mother died in childbirth. He joined to Dragon's Circle of Twelve when some of the original members were killed in an attack on Anglesey. After the demise of Vortipor, Bryce was named Protector of Dyfed, until Vortipor's baby boy was old enough to rule the kingdom in his own right. Other incarnations in the Ancient Future Series include: Atlantis — Shar Zadoc, 21st century — Ray Murdoch, Gathering of Kings — Cadwallon, Leonine Tribe — Adair, AMIE/Universe Parallel — President Jabez Anselm.

Brythonic (Pronounced Brithonic) — The ancient Welsh Language.

C.

Cai, Sir — Third legitimate son of Calin Brockwell and Queen Katren of Powys. Brother of Blain and Owen. Half brother to Bryce. He studied to be a bard under Selwyn. Other incarnations in the Ancient Future Series include: Atlantis — Lazarus, 21st century — Daniel Alexander.

Calisto — Son of Anu and Prince of the Annunnaki Islands Calisto means 'most beautiful.' Who teamed up with Tory to expose Keeldar.

Cato, En — Head Priest of the Orders of Akhantuith in Atlantis. Cato means 'cautious'.

Catulas — King of Dumnonia. A long time ally of the Kingdom of Gwynedd, who aided Sir Tiernan to retake Degannwy when it was besieged by Saxons. He joined Maelgwn's alliance against the Saxons at the request of the triple Goddess.

Chailidocean — The main city of Atlantean central state of Cintrala. The City of the Golden Gates.

Chakra System — The seven energy centres of in the subtle body located within the physical.

> **Root Chakra** — Located — at the base of the spine. Superimposing — the prostrate area in the male, uterus in the female. Perceived clairvoyantly — appears like the sign of the cross. Colour — brown to red. Active when — mind is focused on materialistic matters and body sensualities. Represents — the lowest part of human consciousness — the seat of fear and grounding Will power and action.

> **Spleen Chakra** — Located — at the navel. Superimposing — the navel and extends to the spleen. Perceived clairvoyantly — shaped like a wheel with six spokes. Colour — Red — Orange. Active function — absorbs the vitality from the sun dispersing it throughout the body; it draws in the spirit from the air to disperse it to the etheric double and the physical nervous system. Represents -. the seat of sexuality, creativity.& passion.

> **Solar Plexus Chakra** — Located — Behind the stomach. Superimposing — Stomach and the liver. Perceived clairvoyantly — looks like a whirling flower with ten petals. **Colour** — Orange to Yellow — depending on one's emotional state. Active function

— the psychic organ for diffusing the sense of feeling and touch. Represents — The seat of the soul in the body, where on feels the emotions of the universe. It is gut feeling as it is the perception area for both positive and negative energies.

Heart Chakra — Located — In the heart. Superimposing — the thymus gland between the shoulder blades and the pulse point of the heart. Perceived clairvoyantly — appears alike a flower with twelve petals. Colour — Pink — Gold as one progresses. Active function — it separates high and lower states of consciousness. It is a storage place for the Akashic Record to distribute the Karma throughout the blood stream, forming one's body and lifestyle. Represents — the seat of compassion, intelligence love and hate.

Throat Chakra — Located — in the larynx area. Superimposing — the thyroid gland. Perceived clairvoyantly — has sixteen petals. Colour — Blue to silver ripples. Active function — mediates vocal expression Represents — the seat of communication.

Brow Chakra — Located — Forehead. Superimposing — the third eye area. Perceived clairvoyantly — 96 streams of radiation. Colour — Left side (feminine) violet colour. Right side (masculine) golden hue. Active functions — left — pituitary gland (negative) and right — pineal gland (positive) Represents — the seat of the silver cord and the Third Eye.

Crown Chakra — Located — top of the head. Superimposing — around the head. Perceived clairvoyantly — 960 petals on the outside of a circular round shape, with a subsidiary central whirlpool of twelve gleaming white petals, fused with gold at its heart. Colour — White and gold. When fully developed it radiates a most splendid chromatic effect, forming what is referred to as the Lotus flower. Active when — the soul-mind gradually becomes purified making ready to become glorified to the higher realms. Each of the lower chakras unfolds energy into this chakra, giving it its brilliance, the power and intelligence it needs for mans ascension. Represents — the seat of Divine Force.

Chosen, The — The immortal sons and daughters of the Lord Marduk, scattered throughout history to be reunited at the time of the Gathering of Kings.

Cintrala — Central Landmass of Atlantis weather was temperate and akin to such conditions one would associate with the South Sea Islands. The capital city of Atlantis lay on the eastern side of the central zone some twenty-five miles from the sea. This was built on the great river Chalid and was called Chailidocean. Ruled by the Shu Sar Absalom.

Cumbria — A kingdom of Briton located to the north east of Gwynedd.

Cymru (pronounced Kum-ri) — The name by which the ancient people of Prydyn referred to themselves.

D.

Dalriada (pronounced Dal-ree-duh) — The northern kingdom of the Scots ruled by Fergus MacErc.

Degannwy (pronounced De-awn-oo-ee) — The city of, Gwynedd. The mainland stronghold of the Gwynedd dynasty.

Dinas Emrys, Gwynedd — Where Myrddin's cave was to be found, that contained the thirteen treasures of Britain including the Chariot of Arianrod.

Danuih (Pronounced Da-noo-ee) — The Earth Goddess of Altantis. Sacred stone: Emerald. Colour: Jade or Deep-green. Symbol: Tree and Equidistant cross. Totem animal: Horse. Orders: Healing of Human Beings Earth Healing & Studies. Temples & Universities: Shi-im-ti (Healing), E-lum (Germinating Vegetation).

Darand, En — Head Preist of Ta-Khu, and confidant of Turan. Darand means 'lasting'. For other incarnations see Tiernan.

Darius, En — Chief of the Body Sciences. Darius means 'preserver'. He added Tory to find the cure she sought. For other incarnations see Rhys.

Diccon, Shar — Sixth born son of Absalom. Mother — Nin Salome, Younger twin of Shar. Zadoc. Diccon means 'firm ruler' and he had charge of governing Cintrala. For other incarnations see Blain.

Donna — Waitress at the cafe in Horta on Faial in the Azores, who Teo fell in love with. For her other incarnations see Mahala.

Dragon's Circle of Twelve, the: The Masters of the Goddess, trained in martial arts by Tory Alexander. These fighters in turn trained the armies of Gwynedd and her allied kingdoms. There were only ever twelve members and a member would have to retire or die, before a new position would open. They were considered the most elite fighting force in allied Briton.

Dumnonia (pronounced Dom-noe-nee-ah) — The southern Kingdom of Briton, ruled by King Catulus.

Dur-an-ki Plateau, Mount — Located in the mountain range to the east of the city, reached via an underground passage that ran from the High Temple. This was where the Atlantean council secretly gathered to perform the time-loop to aid Tory with her quest.

Dwyran, Castell — Vortipor's capital in Dyfed.

Dyfed (pronounced DUH-ved) — South-west Kingdom of Prydyn, ruled by Vortipor during the time of Maelgwn's reign in Gwynedd.

E.

Engur — 'Lord of the Rockets'. The Antillian Name for Keeldar. Who trapped Tory in a time warp.

Eormenric — Youngest Son of Ossa of Mercia. Husband of Vanora.

F.

Faial — The Island in the Azores, were the team stayed, whilst recovering the Atlantean antidote Tory was seeking to take back to Dark Age Gwynedd, in the hope of saving Maelgwn's life.

Falmengos — Valley below the Caldeira Crater on Faial, leading down to the town of Horta.

G.

Gareth, Sir — Son of Sir Tiernan and the Lady Ione. who became Lord of Caernarvon during King Rhun's reign in Gwynedd.

Gaspard, Shar — Forth born son of Absalom. Mother — Nin Orphelia. Younger twin of Shar Xavier. Gaspard means 'treasure master'. For other incarnations see Gawain.

Gawain, Sir — Son of Sir Rhys and the Lady Jenovefa. Other incarnations in the Ancient Future Series include: Atlantis — Gaspard, 21st centry — Nicholas Pearce

Gwynedd (pronounced Gwen-th) — The Northern Kingdom of Prydyn, seat of Maelgwn Gwynedd's family line. Capitals: Degannwy and Aberffraw.

H.

Helio — Male aspect of the solar deity — Sacred stone: White diamond. Colour: Gold. Symbol: Winged Disk. Totem Animal: Falcon. Orders: Masculine Orders of Passage, Males in the service of the Shu Sar. Temples & Universities: The Great Temple Of Chalidocean, E-nun (the Royal House), Dur-an-ki (Cylindrical Dome atop of a platform that kept Earth in communication with Sirius).

Heliona — Female aspect of the solar deity — Sacred stone: Blue diamond. Colour: Azure Blue or Silver. Symbol: Uraeus (the Cobra — the Egyptian Style Depiction). Totem animal: Serpent or Dragon. Orders: Feminine Orders of Passage, Females in the service of the Shu Sar. Temples & Universities: the same as Helio.

Horta — The main town on the island on Faial in the Azores, where Miles Thurlow's partner John Pearce was based.

I.

Ione, Lady (pronounced I-O-nee) — The Queen's Champion in Gwynedd. Wife of Sir Tiernan. Mother of Sir Gareth. One of the original Dragon's circle of Twelve. Other incarnations in the Ancient Future Series include: Atlantis — Nin Lilith, 21st Century — Boadicea or Bo, Edin — Kya, AMIE — Kassa Madri. Grigori — Sariel (female aspect).

J.

Javotte — Daughter of Sir Angus and the Lady Alma. A member of the Dragon's Circle of Twelve, who is paired with Blain as a sparring partner.

Jenovefa, Lady — Wife of Sir Rhys. Mother of Sir Gawain. Other incarnations in the Ancient Future Series include: Atlantis — Nin Anthea, 21st Century — Jenny Pearce, Edin — Sister 5.

Jerram, Shar — Ninth born son of Absalom. Mother — Nin Mahar, Older twin of Shar Adelgar. Jerrem means 'war raven'. Ruler of Usiqua, the cooler, mountainous land in the south of the main Atlantean landmass, with its capital city at Kudra. For other incarnations see Taliesin.

K.

Katren — Queen of Powys. Born a lowly farm girl and saved from a brutal arranged marriage by Tory Alexander. Through her own heroic deeds during the siege of Aberffraw, Katren rose to the status of Lady, and was one of the original Dragon's Circle of Twelve. She later married Sir Calin Brockwell and became Queen of Powys. Mother of Princes Blain, Owen and Cai. Step-mother of Bryce. Other incarnations in the Ancient Future Series include: Atlantis — Nin Tabitha, Fall of Atlantis: Pandora, 21st Century — Naomi Pearce, Gathering of Kings — Candace, Leonine Tribe — Samara, Edin — Delilah, AMIE — Aurora DeCadie, Anicent Zhou — Hui Ru, Grigori — Sammael (female aspect).

Keeldar — Banished Head of the Mind Sciences in Chailidocean. Keeldar means 'battle.' Known in Antillia as Engur 'Lord of the Rockets.'

Keturah — Wife of Chief Anu. Keturah means 'incense'.

Khe-Ta (Pronounced Kay-Tar) — Feline divinity of music, art, poetry and dance. Sacred stone: Aquamarine. Colour: Turquoise. Symbol: Sistrum. Totem animal: Cat. Orders: Healing of Domestic Animals. Music, Art, Poetry and Dance. Temples & Universities: E-hulhul (Recreation), The Second Island Ring, Stadium & University.

Khiet-Sin (Pronounced Khee-et Sheen) — Leonine goddess of protection and retribution. Dispenser of Cosmic Justice. Sacred stone: Ruby. Colour: Orange.or Red. Symbol: Flaming orb. Totem animal: Lioness. Orders: Healing of Wild Animals. Training of Wild Animals. Warrior Arts. Legal studies. Temples & Universities: Courts of Justice. The Second Island ring where the Stadium and Animals are housed.

Kila, Nin — Forth wife of Shu Sar Absalom, mother of Seth and Lazarus. Kila means 'earth seer'.

L.

Lamamu — The Atlantean name for Tory. Lamamu means 'divine master of love and war'.

Lamorak, Sir — King Brockwell's advisor in Powys.

Lana — The lover of Rastus, son of Zutar. Lana means ' light'.

Lazarus, Shar — Eight born son of Absalom. Mother — Nin Kila, Younger twin of Shar Seth. Lazarus means 'helper/seer'. For other incarnations see Cai.

Lilith, Nin — Head Healer of Kheit-Sin (Wild Animals). Lilith means 'clever'. Lilith was introduced to Darand by Tory, as she knew them to be twin flames. For other incarnations see Ione in section.

Londinium — The capital of Mercia, ruled by Ossa, where Rhun and Bryce were sent with the message of aid to present to the Saxon's.

Lynn Cerrig Bach (pronounced Thlyn-kerrig-bach) — The location of the last stand of the Celts against the Romans. The location of the temple of the Nine Muses, where access to Taliesin's secret Labyrinth could be found.

M.

Maelgwn (pronounced Myle-goon or Mylegwin) — King of Gwynedd, aka The Dragon. First High King of Briton. Taken by the underworld at the end of his reign. Son of Caswallon Lawhir and Sorcha. Brother of Caradoc. Husband of Tory Alexander. Father of Rhun. Other incarnations in the Ancient Future Series include: Atlantis — Turan, Fall of Atlantis: Prometheus, 21st Century — Miles Thurlow, Delphinus Tribe — Durak, Falcon Tribe — Hawk, Edin — Adama, AMIE — Lucian Gervaise, Ancient Zhou — Ji Dan, Grigori — Azazel (male aspect).

MacErc, Fergus — Ruler of Dalriada. He joined Maelgwn's alliance against the Saxons at the request of the triple Goddess.

Mahala — Prisoner of Zotar, who is rescued by Jerram. Mahala means 'sweet singer'. Other incarnations in the Ancient Future Series include: Ancient Gwynedd — Creirwy (Lady Tegid), 21st century — Donna, Gathering of Kings — Seshut, AMIE — Kalayna Zuri, Grigori — Araqiel (female aspect).

Mahar, Nin — Fifth wife of Shu Sar Absalom, mother of Jerram and Adelgar. Mahar means 'woman in red'.

Mahaud — The dark side of Electra, first banished to the sub-planes during the fall of Atlantis. She was conjured forth by Cadfan during his attempt to take Gwynedd from his brother Caswallon, and again by Vanora, daughter of Chiglas in an attempt to murder Caswallon, and seize Gwynedd. Ossa the Saxon King was tricked into summoning her to his aid, whereby

King Maelgwn was enchanted by her and infected with the Yellow Plague.

Mateus, Thomas — Shaman/Healer, who acted as a guide to Tory, during her time in the Azores, exploring Pico Alto. For other incarnations see Thais.

Melcah, Nin — First wife of Shu Sar Absalom, mother of Alaric and Turan. Melcah means 'queen'. Other incarnations in the Ancient Future Series: Helen Alexander — mother of Brian and Tory.

Menai Strait — The strait in northern Wales that runs between the island of Anglesey and the mainland of Gwynedd, that could be crossed via a barge.

Mercia — The large western kingdom of the Saxons. Ruled by Ossa during Maelgwn's reign. Capital city of Londinium.

Micah, Shu — High Magi of the Orders of Passage. Micah means 'godlike'. A direct descendant of 'the Shining Ones' (the Gods, the ascended Nefilim), he deployed a subtle form most of the time.

Middle Kingdoms, The — The physical realms of existence, as opposed to the subtle etheric realms of the Otherworld. See Abred.

Myrddin (pronounced MUR-thin) — Whose consciousness lay dormant inside Tory's 21st century father Renford Alexander. The spell to remembering his former self was contained in a droplet that was guarded in the cave at Dinas Emrys in Gwynedd, by the Merlin's owl Tobias. Other incarnations in the Ancient Future Series include: Atlantis — Shar Absalom, 20th Century — Renford Alexander.

N.

Narberth — Vortipor's stronghold Dyfed.

Norbert, En — Chief of the Mind Sciences. Norbet means 'bright metaphysician'.

O.

Orichalchum — A pinkish metal — rather like gold only much stronger. It was the most valued metal in the Ancient World.

Ongen — Eldest son and heir of Ossa of Mercia.

Orphelia, Nin — Second wife of Shu Sar Absalom, mother of Xavier and Gaspard. Orphelia means 'clever'.

Ossa — Ruler of Merica during Maelgwn's reign who released Mahaud in order to curse the kingdoms of Prydyn. Father of Ongen, Eormenric and Aella.

Owen, Prince — The second legitimate son of Calin Brockwell and Queen Katren of Powys.

P.

Pearce, John — Partner in several archaeological projects with Miles Thurlow, including the Plato Project. Husband of Jenny, father of Naomi and Nicholas Pearce. For other incarnations see Rhys.

Pearce, Naomi (Naomi Alexander) — Daughter of John Pearce, wife of Brian Alexander and mother of Daniel Alexander. For other incarnations see Katren.

Philaeia (Pronounced Phil-ay-ee-ar) — Goddess of wisdom, philosophy, science and architecture. Sacred stone: Sapphire. Colour: Royal Blue. Symbol: Masonic Compass. Totem animal: Parrot. Orders: Mind Sciences, Architecture. Temples & Universities: E-abzu (Mind Sciences), Ki-ur (Communications Centre).

Pico Alto — Is a mountain 586.84 metres tall, on the island of Santa Maria, in the Portuguese archipelago of the Azores.

Portea — Land to the North in Atlantis was dry but by no means barren, weather being extremely warm. Capital city Keriophis. Capital city in the North-East — Menocea. Ruled by Adelgar, the youngest son of the Shu Sar Absalom.

Powys (pronounced Powiss) — The western Kingdom of Prydyn. Ruled by Chiglas during Maelgen's reign and later ruled by Calin Brockwell and his descendants.

Prydyn (pronounced Pridin like 'Britain') — The name of Wales 519 AD

Q.

Quasi-Crystals — Are crystals with five-fold symmetry. These were used exclusively by the secret orders of the priesthood concerned with the exploration of the nature of the cosmos via mental time-travel, and for communication with extra-terrestrial sources. Those students carrying an E.T. memory gene were singled out for the priesthood of the deity Ta-Khu. This order carried the title 'Pursuants of the Arrow', meaning the arrow of Time.

R.

Rastus — Son of Zutar, Chief of Antillia. Rastus means 'staunch'.

Razu, En — The Atlantean's name for Taliesin. Razu means 'Shinning white lord'.

Rhun (pronounced Hreen or Hree-un) — Son of Maelgwn and Tory Alexander. Other incarnations in the Ancient Future Series include: Atlantis — Xavier, 21st century — Rhun, Alban — Bridei, AMIE — Mythric aka Spyridon Vidor, Ancient Zhou — Ji Fa, Grigori — Penemue (male aspect).

Rhys, Sir — Maelgwn's Advisor and cousin. Husband of Jenovefa, Father of Sir Gawain and one of the original Dragon's Circle of Twelve. Other incarnations in the Ancient Future Series include: Atlantis — En Darius, 21st Century — John Pearce, Gathering of Kings — Robin, Leonine Tribe — Kesla.

S.

Salome, Nin — The third wife of Shu Sar Absalom, mother of Zadoc and Diccon. Salome means 'peaceful'.

Seba, En — Lord High Guardian of the Sciences. Seba means 'eminant'.

Selwyn — Maelgwn's squire and court harpist in Gwynedd, who studied under Taliesin and became Merlin to the court in Powys under King Brockwell's rule. Lover of the Siren, Amabel and later Kaileah — Druidess of Talorg. Other incarnations in the Ancient Future Series include: Atlantis — Seth, Fall of Atlantis: Aegisthus, 21st Century — Noah Purcell, Delphinus Tribe — Uriah, Edin — Adapa, Falcon Tribe — Chook, AMIE — Ringbalin Malachi, Ancient Zhou — Fen Gong, Grigori — Armaros (male aspect).

Seth, Shar — The seventh born son of Absalom. Mother — Nin Kila, Older twin of Shar Lazarus. Seth means 'appointed prophet'. For other incarnations see Selwyn.

Sybil, Nin — Head Truth Seer. Sybil means 'prophetess'. For other incarnations see Bridgit.

T.

Tabitha, Nin — Head Healer of Khe-Ta (Domestic Animals). Tabitha means 'gazelle'. For other incarnations see Katren.

Tadgh (pronounced Tie or Taig) — Maelgwn's squire, following Selwyn's departure to study under Talisein.

Ta-Khu (Pronounced Tar-Koo) — The Lord of Time and Space. Sacred stone: Amethyst. Colour: Purple. Symbol: Caduceus. Totem animal: Dolphin. Orders: Time, Space & E.T. frequency study. Temples & Universities: Ki-ur (Communications Centre), Dur-na-ga (Astrology & Astronomy).

Taliesin (pronounced Tahl-YES-in or Talyeshin) — His name means 'Shinning brow'. Penn Beirdd means 'the Bard'. He was the Chief Bard and poet in Briton in the 6th Century. Born Gwion Bach, the lad stirred the wisdom potion of the Goddess, Keridwen — a potion that was meant for her ugly son. But while stirring some drops landed on Gwion's finger and burned into him, and sticking his finger in his mouth, he garnered all the wisdom from the brew and transformed into Taliesin. High Merlin in Briton, Guardian of the Thirteen Treasures, ascended Master, time-lord and mentor to Sorcha, Maelgwn, Selwyn and Tory Alexander. Other incarnations in the Ancient Future Series include: Atlantis — Shar Jerrem, 21st Century — Teo, AMIE — Telmo Decree, Ancient Zhou — Yi Wu, Grigori — Araqiel (male aspect), Nefilim — Anu, The Tibetan Master — Djwhal Khul (D.K.).

Teirnan, Sir (pronounced TEER-nan) — King Caswallon's Champion. Husband of Ione, father of Sir Gareth and one of the original Dragon's Circle of Twelve. Other incarnations in the Ancient Future Series include: Atlantis — En Durand, 21st century — Floyd, Falcon Tribe — Raven, AMIE — Leal Pulson, Ancient Zhou — Jiang Taigong, Grigori — Sariel (male aspect).

Temperance — High Preistess in Atlantis after Nin Bau. Who fell in the love Turan. For other incarnations see Tory Alexander.

Teo — Was the trainer of Tory and Brian Alexander, Tory's first romantic interest and Brian's best friend. Husband of Donna. For other incarnations see Taliesin.

Thais — Centaur scout of Jerrem and Adelgar. Thais means 'gift from the divine', as he is immortal and a shapeshifter. Thais would later seek out Tory in the Azores, under the guise of Thomas Mateus, to help her find the cure she was seeking. Other incarnations in the Ancient Future Series include: 21st Century — Thomas Mateus, Centaur Tribe — Thais.

Three Arrows off Time, the — 1) The Thermodynamic Arrow — the direction of time in which disorder and entropy increases. 2) The Phycological Arrow — the direction in which we feel time passes. 3) The Cosmological Arrow — the direction of time in which the universe is expanding rather than contracting.

Thurlow, Miles, Professor — Was partner in the Plato Project and the archaeological dig at Llyn Cerrig Bach with John Pearce. Husband of Tory Alexander and father of Rhiannon Thurlow. For other incarnations see Mealgwn.

Time Asymmetric — An irreversible instance/event in the continuum, not as easily perceived or understood psychically.

Time Loop — Journeys that loop from present to future and then backward to the present. Or journeys that start in the present and go back in time before returning to the present. Tory performed several of these loops in Atlantis.

Time Slip — Pertains to certain locations in the universe, and indeed the planet, where the connection between inner time and outer time is tenuous. At these places the veil between worlds is thin, and therefore more easily penetrated — i.e. power centres and ley line crossings.

Time Symmetric — A reversible instance/event in the continuum, more easily perceived and interpreted by a psychic.

Time Warp — Synonymous with Black Holes. A distortion or interruption in the flow of time from past to future.

Turan, Shar — Second born son of Absalom. Mother — Nin Melcah, Younger twin of Shar Alaric. Turan means 'bond of heaven'. Turan maintained an etheric form until he was challenged to return to a physical state of being to aid Toru complete her time loop. Would later find his true love in Temperance, the High Priestess of Chailidocean. For other incarnations see Maelgwn.

U.

Usiqua — The cooler, mountainous land to the south of the Atlantean landmass. Ruled by Jerram, the second youngest son of the Shu Sar Absalom. With the capital city of Kudra.

V.

Vanora — Princess of Powys. Daughter of Chiglas, who was tricked into conjuring forth the witch Mahaud once agin to aid Ossa take revenge on Gwynedd. She was eventually rescued by and married to Eormenric of Mercia. Other incarnations in the Ancient Future Series include: Atlantis — Nin Antonia, 21st Century — Vanora, AMIE — Amie Gervaise, Grigori — Bezaliel (female aspect).

Voritpor — Protector of Dyfed. One of Maelgwn Gwynedd's stanchest allies, who married the Lady Cara and was one of Dragon's original Circle of Twelve. Father of Brigit and Vortimor. Other incarnations in the Ancient Future Series include: The Gathering of Kings — Cadwell, Edin — Adin.

W. X.

Xavier, Shar — Third born son of Absalom. Mother — Nin Orphelia, Older twin of Shar Gaspard. Xavier means 'bright'. For other incarnations see Rhun.

Y. Z.

Zadoc, Shar — Fifth born son of Absalom. Mother — Nin Salome, Older twin of Shar Diccon. Zadoc means 'just'. He was head of the Courts of Justice in Chailidocean. For other incarnations see Bryce.

Zutar — Chief of Antillia. Zutar means 'leader'.

Traditions in Atlantis

The Right of Judgement — The scientist/priests would measure the precise sonic, genetic, particle and wave frequencies of each individual. This allowed each individual to be comfortably slotted into the area for which his or her talents were best suited — their karmic path. This took place when a child was aged three. They were given their true name at this time.

The Three Daily Rites of the Atlantean Solar Religion
— Dance of the Rising Sun.
— Hymn to the High Sun.
— Prayer to the Setting Sun

The Four Solar Festivals — All having an eight-day duration.

The Festival of Fire — Held in the middle of the first quarter of the year. Tutelary goddesses Khiet-Sin & Philaeia. Theme: transformation. Rites held in: temples throughout the land. Colours and Symbols: those appropriate to the Sun.

The Festival of the Air — Held three months following. Tutelary deity was the divine ancestor Ta-Khu. Theme: Communication. Rites held in high places, though on the flats stepped pyramid structures were erected. Colour:Amethyst.

The Festival of Water — Held three months later, Tutelary deity was the divine ancestor Khe-Ta. Theme: Creativity. Rites held on the sea-shore. Colour: Turquoise.

The Festival of the Earth — Held three months later. Tutelary deities Danuih & Akhantuih. Theme: Unity. Rites held out of doors in sacred groves, stone circles, and caves. Colours: green and yellow. This festival was also known as the 'Time of the Children', who would parade in masks and strange costumes not unlike those still worn for Halloween. These were known as the 'faces of Akhantuih' and legend had it that the originals rendered the wearer invisible.

Colours of the Priesthood

Garments

High order — white garments

Middle Orders — pale blue garments

Junior Orders — pale green garments

Sashes

High Priestess — white garment/azure sash.

Senior Priest specialising in exorcism — white garment/orange sash.

Junior Scientist — pale green garment/royal blue sash.

Orders of Passage — sage green sash or rose pink sash

Headbands — worn by all members of the priesthood.

Silver — healer specialising in mental or psychological healing.

Orichalcum — healer specialising in physical medicine or surgery.

Plain headbands — lower orders.

Jewels or specific symbols — higher echelons or advanced qualification.

High Priests — wore a headdress not unlike those worm by the pharaohs in ancient Egypt.

Chief High Priest — ceremonial crown or headdress which featured a raised jewel-encrusted winged disk, set in gold.

Priests and Priestesses of the Orders of Passage — platinum headbands with either pink or pale green stones set in the front.

High Priests or Priestesses of the Orders of Passage — wore bands of pale green or soft pink displaying a bi-coloured tourmaline.

Rings

Each Priest wore a ring that displayed the stone appropriate to the deity in whose Order he or she had been ordained — (see individual gods and goddess' in the Compendium above).

Author's Note

I was never going to write a sequel - famous last words, considering the twelve books that have followed *The Ancient Future* to date. There was a caveat to that statement however, that I would never write a sequel unless it was going to take the reader conceptually further and metaphysically deeper than the previous book did.

When I completed *The Ancient Future* I moved straight onto my next idea, which was to do with a strange time phenomena taking place in a grand old manor house in Oxfordshire England — a tale that would later become *The Alchemist's Key*, my first standalone novel.

I don't believe anyone expected *The Ancient Future* to become a best seller in its first months of release, but even when it had shot to number one on the science/fantasy bestsellers list, I still hadn't considered penning a sequel. It was a physic friend of mine, Michael, who, during one of our regular phone chats, mentioned that I should really consider writing the synopsis for another two books. He claimed my publisher was going to want to contract me to turn *The Ancient Future* into a trilogy. Now, being that Michael was usually pretty damn spot on with his predictions, I began to mull the prospect over.

I cannot say I was entirely opposed to the suggestion. I had just purchased a fascinating book called, *Atlantean Traditions in Celtic Britain*, which further explored the ley-lines, sacred sites and ancient trackways that existed in Britain, long before the Romans had ever arrived. It also traced a lot of the symbology and mysticism back to the Atlantean culture. This volume had sparked an interest in me to explore that ancient civilisation, that apart from a few non-fiction books, I'd read very little about. This was most likely due to the fact that most considered Atlantis to be a fable of Plato's creation; even though Plato was not known for writing fiction. If 'Timaeus and Critias' (his text that described the Atlantean continent in great detail) was only a flight of fancy, it was the ancient historian's only work of fiction.

This controversy only made the idea of exploring Atlantis more attractive to me, as I am particularly drawn to eras where history and myth blur to create legends. That being the case I thought, well why not make Atlantis part of the journey of my time-hopping heroine? Who better than Tory Alexander to embark on such an adventure? Then I considered that if we were going even further back into history in the second book, then why not head into the future in the third book? This seemed to be a perfect symmetry to me. Thus I sat down and wrote up my ideas for these tales. And, I kid you not, I was literally printing out the synopsis to read through, when my publishers called to say that they were so thrilled with the success of *The Ancient Future*, would I consider turning it into a trilogy?

So with a lot of help from Murry Hope's wonderful books, *Atlantis: Myth or Reality* and *Practical Atlantean Magic*, *An Echo in Time* came into being.

Both myself and my readers have so enjoyed the romp through this bygone era over the years, that I have never regretted writing this, or any sequel in this series. I hope that you too will enjoy discovering all the fascinating mysteries, science and traditions, of the long-lost and magnificent City of the Golden Gates, otherwise know as Atlantis.

About the Author

Traci Harding, best selling author of 'The Ancient Future Series', has published 21 books through HarperCollins/Voyager Australia and Bolinda Audio. Her work blends fantasy, fact, esoteric theory, time travel and quantum physics, into adventurous romps through history, alternative dimensions, universes and states of consciousness. Her books have been published in several languages throughout the world. Traci's latest release, *This Present Past*, is the prequel to 'The Ancient Future Series' which is currently under option and being developed as a TV series by Film Brand Management, London. Her first three books, 'The Ancient Future Trilogy' have just been re-released in a 25th Anniversary Edition through Booktopia's publishing wing, Brio Books.

To find out more about Traci and her books visit her website at:
traciharding.com

For autographed copies of Traci's books visit her store at:
allthingstraci.com.au

You can also find Traci on Facebook at:
Traci Harding Fans
All Things Traci Store
Trazling
& Mastering Your Reality with Traci Harding — Group

Traci is also on:
Twitter, Instagram, Redbubble and YouTube.